Dark Truths

An Alexis Parker Novel

G.K. Parks

A Modus Operandi imprint

ISBN:
ISBN-13: 978-1-942710-52-3

For my mom and dad

BOOKS IN THE LIV DEMARCO SERIES:
Dangerous Stakes
Operation Stakeout
Unforeseen Danger
Deadly Dealings
High Risk
Fatal Mistake
Imminent Threat
Mistaken Identity
Malicious Intent
Controlled Burn
Dodging Bullets

BOOKS IN THE ALEXIS PARKER SERIES:
Likely Suspects
The Warhol Incident
Mimicry of Banshees
Suspicion of Murder
Racing Through Darkness
Camels and Corpses
Lack of Jurisdiction
Dying for a Fix
Intended Target
Muffled Echoes
Crisis of Conscience
Misplaced Trust
Whitewashed Lies
On Tilt
Purview of Flashbulbs
The Long Game
Burning Embers
Thick Fog
Warning Signs
Past Crimes
Sinister Secret
Zero Sum
Buried Alive
Trouble Brewing
Balance Due
Hostage Situation
Damage Control
Dark Truths

BOOKS IN THE JULIAN MERCER SERIES:
Condemned
Betrayal
Subversion
Reparation
Retaliation
Hunting Grounds

BOOKS IN THE CROSS SECURITY INVESTIGATIONS SERIES:
Fallen Angel
Calculated Risk
Light Them Up
Champagne Problems

ONE

"You're bleeding." James Martin reached for the gauze pads.

I looked down to see blood dribbling out of the wound I'd reopened during my morning run. "It's fine."

"It's not fine, Alexis." He pressed the gauze against my side and reached for the tape. "Once you're dressed, I'll take you to urgent care so they can reseal it."

"I don't need to go to urgent care. It'll stop on its own."

He glared at me, frustrated. "What kind of workout did you do this morning? Were you lifting weights?"

"I went for a run."

"And you thought that was a good idea?"

"Martin, I'm not in the mood to listen to you tell me what to do. I'm an adult. I can take care of myself."

"Are you sure about that?"

I pushed past him. "You son of a bitch."

"Alex—"

"I know. Okay? I know. That asshole attacked me in our apartment. I shouldn't have let him get the jump on me. He surprised me. I shouldn't have let that happen."

Anger burned in Martin's eyes. "That's not what I meant."

"Then what did you mean? You just said you don't think I'm capable of taking care of myself."

"Stop punishing yourself, sweetheart. The attack wasn't your fault." He pointed at my side. "But reopening the wound is."

"I needed to clear my head. That was a little more important than this." I indicated my side. "I can't have this argument with you right now. I just can't."

"Alex, I know how you get. You're hurting yourself. You're pushing me away."

"We've had this argument a million times before. We said we weren't doing this again. *I'm* not doing this again. I promise. But I need to do something. You of all people should understand that, Mr. Can't Sit Still for Two Seconds Without Working."

Understanding dawned on him. "And Cross won't let you work."

"Not on a real case. If I don't find some way to distract myself, those thoughts, those doubts, will seep into my psyche, and it'll be that much worse. I'm trying to stop the spiral. I need you to back off, or I'm bound to go over the edge."

After careful consideration, he said, "I get it. But someone needs to take a look at that gash. You might need more stitches."

"It's fine."

"Alex, please let me take you to get that looked at. If not, I'll worry all day. I'll be useless. Luc will plan a coup."

"I hate to break it to you, handsome, but Luc doesn't want your job."

"He's vice president. Of course, he does." Martin's green eyes twinkled, a sign our fight was over.

"I can get someone to look at it at work." I pointed to the clock on the wall. "You don't have time to take me to the doctor. You're going to be late. And if you don't show up to your meeting, Luc will definitely make a play for your job."

"Shit." Martin grabbed his suit jacket off the chair and put it on, stopping in front of the mirror to make sure his tie was straight and his pocket square was properly displayed. "New plan. I'll drive myself to the office, and Marcal can take you to urgent care."

"How about we stick with the original plan?"

Martin looked confused. "I take you to urgent care?"

"No. Marcal takes you to work. And when I get to the office, I'll have one of the medics take a look at me. Deal?"

"Y'know, I originally thought having medics on staff at Cross Security was a plus. Now, I'm not so sure."

"I'll be fine." I gave him a quick kiss. "I *am* fine."

"Meet me for lunch."

"I can't."

He grasped my chin, forcing me to look him in the eye. "Video call."

"That's how you compromise?"

"It's the best deal you're going to get."

"You win, this time."

Once he left the bedroom and headed down the stairs, I watched the panel on the wall, waiting for the security system to disengage and reengage. As soon as he was gone, most of the tension left my body.

I loved him more than anything, but right now, I could barely stave off the panic attacks whenever he was near. That wasn't his fault. It was mine. Like our fight this morning.

Returning to the bathroom, I changed the gauze which I'd already bled through, put on a black shirt, which would hide any bloodstains, and ignored the voice in my head telling me to pack my things and hit the road. That wasn't a solution to the age-old dilemma that had been plaguing me since the first case I worked as a private investigator. Running would be a return to my self-destructive ways, and I promised Martin I wouldn't do that again.

I had run away from him once, hoping the distance would keep him safe. But bad things happened even if I wasn't around. However, a lot of people had shown up on our doorstep lately looking for me. It had to stop. If it didn't, someone would end up dead, and I didn't want it to be Martin. I'd prefer if it wasn't me either.

When I got to the office, I parked the company car in the garage and took the elevator up. I had to beg my boss,

Lucien Cross, to give me another company car to use because I refused to take my car to Martin's estate. Since I was a Cross Security employee, my boss couldn't necessarily deny my request, but he wasn't happy about it either. Totaling the last car may have had something to do with that.

After stowing my things in my office, I swung by to see the medic. "It's me, isn't it?"

The medic arched an eyebrow. "What's you?"

"I'm single-handedly responsible for keeping your boredom at bay."

He laughed. "Ms. Parker, you aren't the only investigator I've treated this week."

"Who else has stopped by for a patch job?"

"I can't say. That's privileged."

"I don't believe you, but it's nice of you to lie to make me feel better." I unbuttoned my shirt and held it away from the bloody bandage.

After peeling off the tape, he rubbed antiseptic on the wound, which made me wince. "You ripped your stitches again."

"I know."

"How did you do it this time?"

"Treadmill."

He got the glue and pinched the sides together. "We'll try it this way. Again, I'll remind you not to lift anything heavy or twist. No running. No boxing. No kickboxing. No yoga." He reached for a clean bandage. "Should I make a list?"

"Is swimming out?"

"Yes, Ms. Parker, swimming is out."

"What about *Twister?*"

"What do you think?"

"You've seen me half-naked. You can call me by my first name."

"I will if you stop reopening the wound. At this rate, it'll never heal." He moved his fingers up my ribs, feeling around. "Is there any tenderness?"

"No." I resisted the urge to offer a quip. I'd already upset one man this morning. I didn't need to make it two.

He checked my temperature. “The internal injuries appear to have healed just fine. This is a deep cut, but the damage is mainly superficial. However, you need to be more careful. The more times you open it, the worse it’ll scar.”

“What’s another scar?”

He went to the cabinet and came back with a roll of scar tape. “The directions are on the side. This should help. It may even help with your older scars.”

I read the directions and buttoned my shirt. “Thanks. I’ll see you tomorrow.”

“You better not.”

I took a photo of the tape and sent it to Martin as proof of my visit to the medic. Then I went downstairs and ducked into the morning meeting.

Lucien Cross glared at me as I took a seat at the conference table. Blue folders containing new assignments had already been handed out to my colleagues. I waited, wondering if Lucien would push a folder toward me. But he didn’t. Instead, he concluded the meeting and collected his notes.

“What about me?” I asked.

He tapped the stack of pages against the table to even them out before slipping them into a leather portfolio. “Have you completed the background checks I asked you to run?”

“Yes.”

“What about the security audit I assigned you?”

“I finished that last night.”

He pulled out his phone and checked his dropbox. After frowning at the timestamp, he looked at me. “You’re supposed to be taking it easy. Why were you working so late?”

“Shouldn’t you commend me for going above and beyond?”

“Alex, you need to take it easy. Medical informed me you’ve been by twice this week.”

“Three times, if you count this morning.”

“Do you think this is a game?”

“We could turn it into one.”

"I need a drink."

"That's the spirit."

"Alex," he warned.

"I need to work. I need a case. A real case."

"You'll get assigned a real case as soon as medical clears you. For that to happen, you have to stop bleeding on everything, which means you need to take it easy for at least a week, maybe two." His eyes told me he understood, but he wasn't going to budge. "I offered you sick leave."

"I don't want to be at home. Too much quiet is a bad thing."

"In that case, I'll have Justin send you more background checks and assessments to perform. Check your inbox." He left before I could protest.

Getting up, I detoured to the break room, grabbed several pastries from the box, and knocked on Kellan Dey's open door. "Did you have breakfast yet?"

Kellan looked at the overflowing plate. "Is that an apple fritter?"

"It's the last one. I thought you might like it." I moved deeper into his office and put the plate down.

He grabbed the fritter off the top and took a bite. I picked up a croissant, flaky on the outside with just the right amount of chew on the inside. At least the breakfast pastries were always good.

Kellan pushed the second coffee cup toward me. "It may have gotten cold. I stopped by your office when I got in to give it to you, but you weren't there."

"I was getting glued back together." I indicated my side before popping the lid off the cappuccino.

"You shouldn't be at work."

"That's the consensus, but if I wasn't around, who would have saved you the last apple fritter?"

"Is this what we do now? Breakfast every morning?"

"We can go back to not speaking to one another if you prefer."

He wiped his hands on a napkin. "Lucien gave me specific instructions not to let you assist on my case."

"Dammit."

"Before you take that plate of artery-clogging goodness down the hall, you should know, he gave those instructions to every single investigator at this morning's meeting. He knows you're getting antsy."

"Doesn't he know bad things happen when I get bored? I tried warning him about it, but his solution was to assign me more busy work. That isn't helpful."

"The problem is bad things also happen when you're not bored." Kellan nodded at my side. "Case in point."

"Fair." I wondered if Renner would be more willing to defy our boss. "But I can't sit around for another week or ten days or whatever. I will go insane. There are too many thoughts. Too much everything. I need something to take the focus away from that."

Kellan raised an eyebrow. "You could talk to someone."

"You're right." I nudged the plate toward him, but he didn't want anything else for breakfast, so I picked up the plate with the remaining pastries and my cappuccino. "I guess that's what I'm going to do. Thanks for the coffee."

"Thanks for the fritter."

TWO

Cross Security had mental health professionals on standby, but I didn't want to unravel in front of a stranger, particularly one who would report my instability back to the boss. That would be a surefire way to end up benched for weeks, if not months.

I tried calling Detective O'Connell, but he was out on a call. So I tried my other favorite detective.

"Hey, Parker, what's going on?" Detective Derek Heathcliff asked.

"I haven't heard from you in a while. I thought I should check in."

"Right."

"What can I say? I found myself with free time and thought maybe you could use my help with something. Anything. I'm not picky."

"I've been out for a couple of weeks, so unless you feel like helping me catch up on paperwork, there's not much to do."

I gave my inbox a dirty look. "I have plenty of paperwork of my own. We could swap. That might make things more interesting."

"Somehow, I doubt it." He paused. "Is everything okay?"

"Why? What have you heard?"

That question made Heathcliff suspicious. "What happened?"

"Nothing. Well, almost nothing. It's not important. Suffice it to say, I've found myself benched and in desperate need of something to do."

"That's never good."

"Help a girl out. You know you want to. It's why you're my favorite."

"I would if I could. But my plate's woefully bare right now. I've been doing nothing but reviewing old case files."

"Woefully bare? What have you been reading lately?"

He ignored the question. "If I get a hold of anything interesting, I'll let you know. Just stay out of trouble. I know how you get. In fact, we all know how you get. Has anyone notified Jablonsky? He should issue a notice and get someone in the government to put the National Guard on standby."

"Goodbye, Derek." I disconnected to the sound of his snickers. So much for plan B.

Since I had a few hours until my lunchtime video chat, I decided to tackle the busy work piling up. Justin had flooded my inbox with all the menial tasks Cross Security had been asked to handle by our corporate clients. Most of the work required basic background checks. A few security assessments had been penciled in for the next few weeks, which Justin decided could be moved up since I needed something to do.

However, since none of the assessments were for new clients, I was able to pull up the previous assessments Cross Security had conducted. After checking to see what the recommendations had been, I compared that to what changes were listed now and wrote up new assessments. That took far less time than I thought it would. The physical checks would have to be scheduled and performed in person, but Cross wouldn't let me conduct them myself, so I forwarded those details back to Justin.

When my phone rang, I pushed away from my desk and closed my office door before answering. "Hey, handsome."

"Hey," Martin stared at me from the other side of the screen, "I'm glad you're in one piece."

"The medic made sure of that." I twisted the blinds closed and lifted my shirt. "As you can see, I'm good as new."

"How long do you think that'll hold?"

"It'll hold." Lowering my shirt, I brought the phone in a little closer and took a seat on the couch. "How were your morning meetings?"

"Fine."

"Great."

"What about yours?"

I fought to keep from scowling. "Everything's still on hold."

"You can't blame Lucien for that."

"I'm pretty sure I can."

"Alex—"

"I know. You think he's right."

"If he hadn't—" Martin's lip twitched, deciding we didn't need to go for round two. "Do you want to go to dinner tonight?"

"Whatever you want to do."

He gave me a look. "I thought you were tired of being stuck at home."

"Where do you want to go?"

"I don't know. There's a really good Italian place we could try."

"Not Giovanni's?"

"No, I was thinking of this tiny bistro in Tuscany."

"Are you serious?"

His smile brightened. "We probably couldn't pull it off tonight with the time difference and lengthy flight, but maybe this weekend. What do you think?"

"I think you're crazy."

"We'll talk about it when I get home. I'll pick something up on my way, unless you want to meet somewhere instead. We could go to Giovanni's if you aren't afraid of getting burnt out on Italian."

"You're serious?" I studied him carefully. "Do you have to travel for work? Is that the reason for this impromptu trip?"

"No, it's just for fun. I thought you might like a change

of scenery. I wouldn't want you to go stir crazy."

"I'm pretty sure traveling is out. The medic has a list of things I'm not supposed to do. Most of which include physical activity, and when we travel, there's usually a lot of physical activity."

"We could just go for dinner."

"That's a long flight for just dinner. What happens when we get bored on the plane? I know how you get in the confines of your private jet."

"We won't get bored. I'll bring *Scrabble*."

"And you think trapping me in a metal box high in the sky is a good idea when I'm barely hanging on as it is?"

"Maybe it's time we rip off the band-aid."

"If I rip off another band-aid, you're going to make me see the medic again."

"We'll discuss the finer points tonight. Until then, stay safe, sweetheart. I love you." He blew a kiss at the screen and disconnected before I could get a word in edgewise.

"I love you too." But that was never our problem.

I was in the middle of performing another background check from the list that only seemed to get longer, no matter how many of them I completed, when I heard angry voices coming from down the hall. Janet, the receptionist, was arguing with someone. At first, I thought she was on the phone, but when I heard another woman's voice, I went to see what was going on.

"Ma'am," Janet said, "Mr. Cross already gave you his assessment. There isn't anything we can do to help."

"He missed something." The younger woman thrust the folder at Janet. "Let me speak to him again. I didn't explain enough the first time. He didn't understand what I wanted him to do. He needs to look at this again. He has to find her."

"Mr. Cross provided you with his findings after your consultation. There is nothing more—"

"There has to be," the woman screamed.

"I'm sorry, but you don't have an appointment."

"Then make me one. I can wait. I can wait all fucking day."

"Ma'am," Janet said, her voice growing sharper, "if you

don't vacate, I'll be forced to call security."

"Security?" The younger woman grew even more agitated. "Are you serious? I'm the one with a problem. I'm the one—"

I intervened as Janet reached for the phone. "What's going on?" I asked.

The younger woman turned to me, her face contorted in anger and disbelief. Her cheeks were red, and her eyes were puffy. She chewed on the inside of her cheek, her chin trembling. "I hope you're not one of their clients since they don't do shit. The police told me to come here. They swore Mr. Cross would help me, but that was a lie. No one wants to help me."

Janet gave me a warning look, which I pretended not to notice. "I'm not a client." I nodded at the folder. "Do you want to tell me what's going on?"

"Ms. Parker, this is none of your business," Janet hissed.

I picked up the folder which had been haphazardly thrown on top of the desk and flipped through it. Cross hadn't provided any resolution concerning this woman's issue, other than a form letter stating Cross Security failed to find enough evidence to warrant opening an investigation.

"My sister's missing," the woman burst out.

"Let's talk in my office," I said, ignoring Janet's icy glare. I gestured to the hallway from which I had emerged. Once the woman entered my office, I closed us inside. "Tell me what's going on. Are the police investigating?" That was Cross's primary reason for avoiding cases.

"No."

"No?" That struck me oddly. "How long has your sister been missing?"

"I haven't been able to get in touch with her for two weeks. I know something's wrong. I can feel it. But the police said there wasn't much they could do. They said they performed a check and there were no signs of foul play."

"Did they locate your sister?"

"They checked with her boss who said she hadn't missed work. But he has to be lying. Leslie wouldn't go radio silent unless something happened to her or someone was keeping her from talking to me. The last few times we spoke, she didn't seem like herself. Something happened. I don't know what, but I know she was freaked out. And now I can't get in touch with her."

I was starting to understand why Cross hadn't signed this woman as a client, but that level of fear and desperation couldn't be faked. "Where does your sister work?"

"She doesn't."

"You just said—"

"She's an intern. I guess she gets paid for that, not that you could call the pennies they throw at her a reasonable wage. No one could live on that, but that's not the point." The woman took a deep breath. "She's an intern at the Golden."

"The hotel?"

"It's a luxury resort." The woman rolled her eyes. "I went there to find her. The first time, they told me Leslie had already left for the day, so I went by her place. She wasn't home, and she wouldn't answer her phone. So I went back the next day, but they told me she was busy. So I waited. And waited. She never came down to see me. Eventually, they asked me to leave. But I wouldn't. They did something to Leslie. I know it." She shook her head, her jaw clenched in anger. "Those assholes had the audacity to call the police and have me arrested for trespassing. Can you believe that? It's a hotel. People hang around there all the time."

"It's private property," I said.

"That's what they said." She let out a frustrated grunt.

No wonder Janet wanted to call security. More than likely, Cross was going to chew me out for this. I moved the mouse, closing the windows on my computer and opening a new one. "What's your name?"

"Deanna Stiller."

I ran a background check on her. She was twenty with no criminal record, but if the arrest just happened, it may not have gotten put into the system yet. "Did the hotel press charges?"

"No, they just wanted to scare me. They've banned me from the property for life. If I show up again, they said they wouldn't be so nice the next time. Not that they were nice the last time." She let out a huff. "I just want to find my sister. I have to find her. I need her. She's all I have."

"What's her name?"

"Leslie Stiller." She reached into her bag and handed me a notebook. "That's everything you need to know about her. I even stuck a few recent photos in there and printed copies of our last few texts and e-mails."

I flipped it open before entering Leslie Stiller's name into the database. She was twenty-three. No record. No red flags. Nothing amiss.

"How did you hear about Cross Security?" I asked.

"This nice police sergeant took pity on me when I got arrested. She told me the detectives couldn't do much without evidence, but Cross Security could help. She swore Mr. Cross was a good man, that he'd help me. She gave me his card." She fished it out of her bag, as if it were proof we owed her an investigation. "I don't understand why no one believes me. I'm telling the truth."

"What did Mr. Cross tell you?"

"He said the same thing the police did. Leslie's fine, and I'm jumping to conclusions. But I'm not. Something's not right. I know it." She indicated the notebook she handed me. "Leslie would never cut me off. We spoke all the time. After she took the internship, it became less and less, and then nothing but crickets. I haven't been able to reach her. She isn't at home. As far as I can tell, she isn't at work. She's nowhere. My sister is gone."

I opened my mouth to ask a question, but Deanna cut me off.

"I'm not crazy. This is my sister we're talking about. Wouldn't you do anything to protect yours?"

"Give me a second." I sent a message to Cross and Justin, figuring if the boss couldn't respond quickly enough, his assistant would. *What's the deal with Deanna Stiller?*

Justin replied immediately. *She wanted to hire us, but Lucien declined. She doesn't have a case. She's a little unhinged.*

Aren't we all? I replied.

She's more than most.

I wouldn't count on that. Send me the interview notes. I expected Justin to protest or deny my request. Instead, the file was added to my dropbox. I opened it and scrolled through the pages. Inside was saved correspondence between two people. I skimmed a few of the messages which had been private e-mails between Deanna and Leslie. Underneath the e-mails was a photo of Leslie Stiller, her phone number, address, date of birth, height, weight, eye color, hair color, and every known social media handle we had. None of her accounts had seen any activity in two weeks. *What about phone records?*

We didn't pull them, Justin replied. *Lucien located the woman. There's no case.*

"Lucien found her?" I said out loud, even as I typed the same thing to Justin.

"That's what I was told, but he didn't see her, just like the police didn't see her," Deanna said. "He called the Golden. Some asshole said Leslie is there, but she isn't. I know she isn't. They're lying. If she were there, she would have come to the lobby to see me, or she would have been at home when I went by her place. She's gone. Missing. I don't know. I think someone hurt her or worse."

I held up my hand, reading the message from Justin.

Lucien met with Deanna for a consultation, performed his due diligence, and discovered the woman's sister isn't missing. They had a falling out. Leslie Stiller doesn't want to see her sister. It's as simple as that. They need a counselor, not a private eye.

"Did you and Leslie have a fight?" I asked.

"We disagreed," Deanna said. "I thought taking an internship was stupid, but Leslie was so excited about it."

"But you've spoken since?"

Deanna indicated the notebook she'd given me. "As you can see, we were fine. Those are the last messages we sent to each other. I printed them and taped them into that book. Things were good until they weren't. I don't know what happened. Leslie had to go through training. She enjoyed that and meeting new people. But then things changed. She stopped talking about them. She stopped talking about the Golden altogether. And then she just stopped talking to me."

Cross and the cops were probably right. But I couldn't shake the look on Deanna's face. Maybe it was because I needed something to do, or it was because I'd seen people behave like this in the worst situations, when loved ones were taken or hurt.

"Do you need this back?" I held up the notebook.

"No."

"Okay." I reread the message from Justin and waited another beat for Lucien to give me his two cents, but he didn't reply to my message. Under different circumstances, I may have deferred to my boss's expert opinion, but these weren't normal circumstances. Worst case, those sick days he offered might turn into a suspension, but that wouldn't be much different from performing the mind-numbing background checks. I didn't have anything to lose by asking Deanna a few more questions. "Why don't you start at the beginning?"

THREE

Deanna Stiller sipped her chamomile tea, but it didn't make her any calmer. She stared expectantly at me. "Do you know why Cross Security doesn't want to help me? I know I'm just a lowly college student who doesn't have a lot of money, but I'll find some way to pay. All I want is my sister back. I can get the money somehow."

"Money's not the problem," I said.

"So Mr. Cross is certain my sister is fine. That's what you're telling me?"

This wasn't productive. "Tell me how this all started."

"Leslie graduated college this past May with a degree in hospitality. It's basically a fancy way to say she spent four years learning how to wait on people and work in hotels. It was such a waste, but she wanted to travel. To go places. To see things. She hates Ohio."

"That's where you're from?"

Deanna nodded. "She went to the same local college I'm attending now. Nothing fancy. But our dad insisted we go, that it'd give us a leg up. He wanted us to become nurses. He said the healthcare industry would always need people. But Leslie had other ideas. They never see eye to eye on these things. Most things, really."

"Has your father spoken to Leslie?"

"She won't answer his calls or reply to his messages either. They haven't spoken since her graduation. He wasn't happy when he found out she changed majors."

"He didn't know?"

"She never told him, and I always pretended not to know. I had to act shocked about it too. I hoped Leslie was double-majoring, which is what she had originally said she was going to do, that way everyone would be happy, but the science classes were too hard. She didn't have the time to study for them like she needed and keep up with the rest of the workload, so she dropped them."

"Where is your father?" I wondered if he could have done something to his wayward daughter.

"He's at home. He wants nothing to do with Leslie or her escapades." She gave me a half-shrug. "That's what Daddy calls them."

"He isn't concerned?"

"He's too stubborn to be concerned. He thinks she's doing this on purpose for attention, or that she's as angry as he is and doesn't want to have anything to do with the family."

"Is that possible?"

"Leslie may not talk to Daddy, but she'd talk to me. Our parents raised us to rely on one another. Mama always told us to stick together."

"Where is your mother?"

Deanna stared at the floor. "We haven't seen her in five years. She took off with some guy and moved to Hawaii with him. That's why Daddy was so mad when Leslie wanted to travel and see places."

"Is there any chance Leslie could be with your mother?"

"I don't think so."

I'd have to make a call to find out. But that could wait. Instead, I slid a legal pad across the desk. "Write down your parents' names and dates of birth."

The request puzzled her, but she didn't ask why I wanted that information. I entered the details into the computer. Her father had been arrested for public intoxication nearly twenty-five years ago. He had no history of violence and no other hints as to substance abuse issues. So there was no reason to think he kidnapped his oldest daughter. To be on the safe side, I'd check his financials. But that went into the things-to-do-later pile.

I ran the same check on Deanna's mother, finding she had remarried and was running a bed and breakfast in Maui with her new husband. I'd need phone records and internet histories. I put in my requests and waited.

"Are you sure Leslie hasn't reached out to your mom? Given her newly acquired degree and your mother's current occupation, it would make sense."

"No," Deanna snapped. "Leslie would have told me if she talked to Mama."

"Is there anyone else Leslie's close to, friends, significant others, extended family who she might speak to?"

"I asked everyone I could think of if they'd heard from her, but they haven't."

"Is she seeing anyone?"

"I don't think so. She dated a lot back home, but nothing serious. No one lasted more than a couple of dates. Leslie wasn't interested in becoming someone's wife. She wanted to see the world. That's why she applied for this internship. It's a coveted position, at least according to Leslie. Her classmates were all vying for it. People all over the country were applying. She connected with them online and chatted about it. Everyone wanted this lousy job."

"Did Leslie receive any threats after it was announced she'd been awarded an internship?"

"Not that I know of."

I scanned Leslie's social media accounts again, but I didn't see any comments that sounded like serious threats. "Do you know why this is such an important internship?" I asked.

"The Golden is owned by some big resort chain. They have locations around the world. Supposedly, people who perform well as interns get their choice of position and location. I don't know if any of that is true or some internet craze, but Leslie was excited. After she found out she had been selected, she acted like she'd won the lottery. We even made plans so I could join her later in the summer and we could hang out when she wasn't working."

"When did her internship start?"

"About six weeks ago. The first month was orientation and classroom training." She indicated the notebook she'd given me. "The details are in there. We spoke on the phone every night before she went to sleep and texted all the time."

"Did she mention anyone taking a special interest in her?"

"Like a stalker?"

"Or a friend, instructor, anything like that?"

"She mentioned a few people, but I don't remember their names. It was always the girl from Belgium or the guy with the ring tattoos. Oh wait, she said something about a Gini. I remember because I made a joke, asking if she granted wishes or lived in a lamp."

"Any idea what her last name is?"

"Sorry."

I scribbled that on my notepad, but I didn't spot any Gini's popping up in Leslie's friends lists. "How long is this internship supposed to last?"

"Nine months."

"She has seven and a half to go?"

Deanna nodded.

"You said she spoke to people online about this internship. Did she keep in touch with them? Maybe she was working with one of them. Perhaps they know what's going on." But I didn't see any recent activity on Leslie's pages. Everything she posted was dated from before the internship started. When she made the announcement that she'd gotten accepted, her social media accounts blew up. A bunch of people who'd also been accepted into the program had reached out. I spun the screen around. "Do you know any of these people?"

Deanna leaned over, her brow furrowing as she scanned the page. "I never met any of them, but they arranged some sort of mixer. They hung out when they first got to the city. I don't know if they still hang out. She never talked much about her new friends. But I know she studied with them while they prepped for their exams. Can you believe a resort makes its interns take exams?" Annoyance crept into her voice. "I wanted to be happy for her. I really did, but this never felt right to me. These people had the same goal in mind. They may have been friendly, but they wanted to be the best too. This isn't a rising tide situation. This is a competition. Any one of them could have done something to Leslie."

"We don't know that," I said, hoping to stop the spiral. "Right now, nothing indicates she's been harmed."

"Then why can't I find her? Why won't she call me back? Where is she? She's not at home. She's not at work. She's nowhere."

We'd have to ping her cell phone. I sent another request, wondering if Lucien had already done that. "Are you sure she's not at home? Maybe she stayed over at a friend's house the night you went by her place, or she was late coming home. How long did you wait outside her place?"

"I didn't. Leslie gave me a key to her apartment. It's my key since it was going to be our apartment. Like I said, we made plans. We were supposed to do all the stupid touristy things on her days off. We were going to have fun."

"Was this before or after your fight?"

"Both. We didn't have a big blowout. That was Daddy's thing. I tried to keep quiet, to keep the peace. I don't like it when they argue, but Les knows I'm always on her side. She's my sister. I just didn't want her to waste nine months being a corporate slave only to end up back in Ohio. But we talked it out. She understood my concerns but told me it wouldn't be like that. The whole thing blew over after a few days, and we went back to planning out our summer."

"If she graduated in May and came here to start her internship, why didn't you come with her when she left?"

"I was already signed up for early summer session. It's an eight-week long intensive. I have exams coming up in two weeks, but when Leslie stopped answering my calls and texts, I had to find out what happened to her."

"You said she sounded freaked out the last few times you spoke."

"She sounded...different. Like she was afraid to talk about her job. I don't know what happened, but she went from giving me all these tiny details, like how they were taught to fold the towels to one word answers when I asked how her day was." Deanna made a face. "Fine. That's all she would say, which in Leslie speak never means fine. But she wouldn't tell me what was bothering her. Every time I asked, she'd stop responding or find a reason to get off the phone. And then she stopped talking to me altogether."

"Did you find anything inside her apartment?" I asked, unsure what I thought about any of this.

"The place was kind of empty. Most of Les's stuff was gone. It reminded me of the week before she moved out of the dorms, when she started moving stuff out but was still living there. It was weird."

"And you're sure this isn't about your fight?"

"Oh my god, stop asking me that. Our fight wasn't a big deal. We made up. Things were fine until they weren't." Deanna opened the notebook and flipped to an earmarked page which had been printed and taped inside. "This is how we usually talk to one another. But the last few times she replied," she pointed to the last message dated two weeks ago, "I barely got a one word response. No emojis. No nothing."

I read the set of texts and the last few e-mails. "Did you have any disagreements or arguments before this happened?"

"No."

Arguing wouldn't help matters. "Maybe she's really busy with work," I suggested. "Her boss said she hasn't missed any of her shifts."

"You're telling me she's too busy to reply to her only sister?" Deanna grunted. "Whenever I call, it goes straight to voicemail. Watch." She picked up her phone and dialed. Before the phone even rang, the call was redirected to the voicemail box, which meant it was turned off or dead.

"Have you left her messages?"

"Only a million. She won't call me back. I asked one of her friends to call, but she didn't get a response either."

"What about to texts and e-mails? Have her friends tried contacting her that way?"

"Uh-huh, but again, we get no response. No one's heard

from her."

That was troublesome. Leslie Stiller hadn't posted anything online in weeks, at least nothing available for public consumption. I'd have to get the techs to see if she had made private posts or interacted with anyone online, but it looked like she'd done her best to become a ghost. I had no idea if that had been her idea or someone else's. But prior to her internship, she had posted regularly. Something wasn't adding up.

Deanna drummed her fingers on the side of her cup. "Tell me this doesn't seem troubling to you."

"I'm not sure."

She slammed her palm down, making the tea splash over the rim. "I swear, Les isn't avoiding me. Even if she was, why would she be avoiding everyone else in her life? She wouldn't do that. Something isn't right. I know it."

My gut agreed, but we'd been told Leslie was safe at work. Why would the hotel lie about that?

FOUR

As soon as Deanna left, I pulled up the file Cross had on her. As I suspected, he had already performed a thorough background check. He had everything from her financials to her school records. Her finances didn't look that different from most struggling college students. So I dug a little deeper.

Deanna didn't have a history of causing trouble or crying out for attention. Since the campus police didn't have any reports concerning Deanna, either complaints against her or made by her, I hoped that meant she was on the level when it came to this.

The Stillers' family history wasn't great. There was nothing criminal, but they were dysfunctional in a way a lot of families were dysfunctional. Broken homes, estrangements, unrealistic parental expectations. And I thought I had issues.

If Leslie was missing, either of her parents could be considered suspects. Perhaps Leslie hadn't been taken or harmed, but she could be working for her mother and didn't want her sister or father to know. Or her father could have made the long trek to force Leslie to go home with him.

Since I hadn't found any plane, train, or bus tickets in

his name or any corresponding charges on his accounts, he would have had to drive here, pick up his daughter, and drive back while using cash to pay for gas, food, lodgings, and whatever other necessities he needed. That seemed a little farfetched. Sure, abductions like that happened, but usually, the children in question weren't fully grown adults.

I scribbled my half-formed theories on the pad, my brain moving faster than my fingers. This was what happened when I spent too much time not working.

The techs had already started sending me the information I'd requested. I should have deferred to Cross's conclusion, but I couldn't. Part of it was boredom. Part of it was stubbornness. And a tiny part was the fear he'd messed up.

Lucien Cross was not infallible. Neither was I. The gash against my ribs proved I'd made my own miscalculations. But I didn't want to play this game with a twenty-three year old woman's life on the line.

Leslie's financial statements didn't show much. Her bills were automatically drafted out of her accounts. Besides rent and her utilities, I didn't notice many other charges. She had made two grocery purchases in the last month for less than a hundred dollars a trip. I spent more than that, and all I bought was a selection of cereals, chocolate milk, and junk food that Martin didn't think we needed.

There were no takeout charges or delivery charges. I went back to her previous statement, which looked significantly different from the current one. While Leslie hadn't spent an exorbitant amount of money on luxury items, like fancy coffee shop beverages, she had eaten out a lot more and her grocery bills were triple what they were now. Maybe something had happened to her. No charges showed on her statement for the last two weeks.

Small deposits had been directly paid into her account from Experiential Adventures, the company that owned and operated the Golden Hotel and Resort. I could only assume those deposits were what she'd been paid as an intern, but they barely covered her last two grocery trips. They certainly didn't cover her rent, which was quickly draining her savings.

Prior to her internship, Leslie had scrimped and saved by working while going to school. I could only assume she had taken out student loans, which she hadn't started paying back yet or she had a scholarship that had covered her expenses. Maybe she had a work study on top of that. I couldn't be sure, but she had saved as much as she could, and upon graduating, she had deposited ten thousand dollars into her account. I didn't know the source, but I assumed that was a graduation gift since there were no other suspicious deposits before or since. Her account had a little over twelve thousand in it, which probably wouldn't last the length of her internship unless she found someone to split the expenses, like her sister who was supposed to spend the rest of the summer with her.

The techs sent me the results from Leslie Stiller's social media accounts, telling me there had been no activity in the last two weeks, and only a few log-ins prior to that. But she hadn't made any posts since starting her internship at the Golden.

I sent her friend requests using a fictitious account that had been created for this very purpose when I joined Cross Security, figuring if she logged in, she may add me even if she didn't want to make a post or send a message, but she hadn't accepted yet. And it was unlikely she ever would since she didn't appear to be checking her accounts.

Maybe she was on a social media cleanse. It was possible she had found herself stalked or bullied by some whack job on the internet, but I hadn't found any such person, and the techs hadn't alerted me to any such activity. But that would be reason enough to go radio silent. Even if her silence wasn't due to some weirdo, she could have gone through a bad breakup and wanted to avoid an ex.

Deanna said Leslie dated but had never gotten serious. Maybe her sister didn't know the full extent of Leslie's dating life, not that I had any basis for thinking that either. All I knew was what I saw online, and it didn't paint much of a picture. Leslie had been careful about what she posted, always being respectable and professional enough that none of it could come back to bite her.

"What the hell do you think you're doing?" Lucien stood in my doorway, his hands shoved in his pockets, a disappointed look on his face. "I assigned you background checks and security assessments."

"I finished most of them."

"Not all of them." He grabbed the doorknob and pulled it closed behind him. "Deanna Stiller is not a Cross Security client. I made that clear. Janet was handling it. You did not need to interfere."

"I heard an argument and went to check it out. With the way things have been around here lately, I had to assume the worst."

"The worst?" Cross raised an eyebrow. "What exactly would that be?"

"Use your imagination. Deanna Stiller could have been a suicide bomber. Justin said she was unhinged."

"Which you didn't know until you invited this supposed crazed bomber into your office to have a chat."

"I was containing the situation," I said, "and limiting the blast radius."

Cross dropped into my client chair and plucked the legal pad off my desk. "It looks like Deanna isn't the only woman who's come unhinged."

"That sounded like an HR violation."

"Consult with legal and find out." He skimmed my notes, flipping to the next page and then the next before putting the pad back down. "Leslie Stiller isn't missing. This is a waste of your time and Deanna Stiller's money."

"I'm not charging her."

"That's good because if you had signed her as a client, I would have fired you." He pointed at the pad. "What exactly are you doing with this?"

I gave him a look, unsure if he was serious. There was something about his tone and facial expression which gave me pause. "I'm running a preliminary investigation, like you did when she came to you."

"Nothing more?"

"Not yet."

"I want those background checks and security assessments completed by the end of the day. This," he waved his hand at the mess on my desk, "has already been addressed. There's no reason for you to look into it."

Dropping the pen, I stared at my boss, ignoring the warning look in his eyes. We fought about most of the cases he assigned me, but this time was different. "How can you be so sure of that?"

"Leslie Stiller is in the city. She's interning at the Golden. I verified it."

"Did you ping her phone?"

"I spoke to her boss who put her on the phone to speak to me. She told me she was fine but didn't have the time or capacity to deal with her sister." Cross stared at me. "Why are you having such a hard time believing this?"

"And you're sure you spoke to Leslie?"

"Who else would I have talked to? The Golden is a Cross Security client. I have a relationship with their management. They wanted this issue resolved just as quickly and easily as I did."

I stared at him. "Taking Deanna on as a client poses a conflict of interest for you."

"Us. You work here too."

"Is that why you were so quick to send her away?"

"There is no case."

"You didn't even investigate. You made one phone call and gave up."

"I did too. I performed my due diligence."

"Then how come her radio silence, the changes in her shopping habits, her lack of social media presence, all of it, didn't throw up any red flags for you?"

"The Golden has a strict no social media policy for its employees. As for the changes in her shopping habits, I'd say that's because she's been eating at the hotel's restaurants a lot more lately. That is one of the perks of working there. And she explained to me that she and her sister had a fight and weren't speaking. That satisfied all the questions I had."

"You think that's all there is to it?"

"Jesus." He ran a hand through his hair and cleared his throat. "Alex, I assigned you to a desk for a reason. I don't want you on any case, even the ones that aren't cases, until medical clears you. We went over this earlier. The last thing I want is for you to get a troubled young woman's hopes up."

"Do you think Deanna's dangerous? There's no history."

"I don't know. But she's hurt and desperate. That's a scary combination. Her family life is a mess. She feels abandoned by her sister and can't accept it. She didn't take the news well when I told her the truth, and she wasn't exactly civil when dealing with Janet. I don't want to encourage this. What you're doing could cause the situation to escalate."

"But what if she's right? What if something happened to Leslie?"

He adjusted his jacket and gave my office the quick once-over. "Get back to those security checks. I want everything completed by end of business."

"But—"

"What you do on your time is your business, but this is company time. Get back to work."

FIVE

After completing the background checks and another two assessments, I saved the files. Sending them now would result in another flood to my inbox. So I'd wait until later. I didn't want more busy work.

I checked again, but Leslie had not accepted my friend requests. I dialed her number, but it went straight to voicemail. I didn't like that. It was one thing to screen a call. It was another to never receive it.

Grabbing the keys, I went downstairs and got into the company car. It may have been wiser to take my car, but since I already had it out with Lucien, there was no point in hiding what I was doing. Hopefully, he wouldn't notice I had left, and if he did, I'd have to ask for forgiveness, assuming he was right and I was wrong.

For once, I hoped that was the case. I didn't want Leslie to be in trouble, but I had to admit the lack of communication worried me. Sure, Lucien had provided valid reasons for the discrepancies, but Deanna wasn't convinced. All I needed to do was lay eyes on her sister and see for myself that Leslie Stiller was alive and well. After that, I'd report back that everything was fine and call it a day. This should be easy.

Leaving my car at the valet stand, I entered the main

lobby of the Golden. A fountain that looked like a waterfall stood in the center, but I wasn't here to check out the décor. I had one goal to accomplish.

The front desk had four clerks working at different stations. I got into the shortest line and waited. After the family of three checked in, the clerk waved me forward.

"Welcome to the Golden. Checking in?" She smiled brightly.

"Actually, I had a question for one of your employees. Leslie Stiller. May I speak to her?"

The woman held the smile while she reached for her radio, turned her back, and made a request. When she turned back around, I hoped the smile meant the answer was yes. "I'm sorry. Leslie's not here right now. Is there something I can help you with?"

"Do you know when she'll be back?"

"Try again in an hour."

I stepped away and checked the time. It was a little after two. I wondered if I should wait it out, but Deanna had tried that and hadn't had good results. The security guards lingering near the offices made me think the hotel didn't appreciate non-guests hanging out, so I decided to come back. There were other things I could do in the meantime.

Leslie's apartment would be the next best place to check. Since she didn't live that far from the Golden, she may have gone home on her break.

Once I got back into my car, I tried calling her again, figuring if she wasn't working there was no reason her phone should be turned off, but I got the same result as the last few times I'd tried. That didn't make any sense.

Instead of going straight to her apartment, I detoured to the precinct.

"Hey," I said, coming up beside Heathcliff's desk, "I came to spring you from the tedium of paperwork. I'm on the lam and thought you'd like to join me."

He turned in his chair to face me, his left arm in a cast. "So this is a prison break?"

"Derek, what happened?"

"Oh, this?" He glanced at his arm. "That's old news. I was chasing a suspect. We got into it at the top of the stairs.

Our fight ended at the bottom. Something snapped in the middle."

"Jeez. Are you okay?"

"I'm fine. It's no big deal. Another three weeks and I get this damn thing off and can get back to it."

"Three weeks? Why didn't you say something on the phone? You should have told me."

"Like you told me?" He nodded at my side. "O'Connell said you were stabbed. Do you want to fill me in?"

"Not really."

"Cliff's notes version."

"Someone was waiting for me at my apartment. He got the jump on me. He got knocked out, and I got a knife in the side."

"Is that why you said you were stuck doing paperwork?"

"I'm stuck doing paperwork because Cross is a paranoid lunatic."

"You almost got killed, Parker. You're supposed to tell me these things."

"It wasn't important. If he'd succeeded, you would have heard about it."

Heathcliff sighed. "What are you doing here?"

"Taking precautions. I need a police escort and thought of you."

"Backup?"

"Let's hope not. I was thinking more like a study buddy."

"Study buddy?" He rubbed his brow. "Are you on pain meds?"

I bumped my hip against the side of his desk. "Come on, I'll explain on the way, unless you'd rather stay here and do that." I looked at his screen to find him reviewing old case files. "I don't want to get you in trouble."

"That'd be a first." He closed the files and logged off his computer. "Lucky for you, I broke my left, so I can still shoot with my right."

"This isn't that kind of job. I hope." I looked over at O'Connell's empty desk. "Is Nick out on a call?"

"A home invasion turned violent. There were multiple victims." Once we were inside my car, Heathcliff asked,

"How are you doing?"

"I told you I'm fine."

"This is me, Alex. How are you really?"

"Working will help, but Cross doesn't seem to get that." Though the look on my boss's face told me he did. Maybe it was the sadist in him that was enjoying driving me mad. Maybe he wanted to see how stir crazy I could get before I snapped. Or maybe he truly believed Deanna Stiller could be dangerous and wanted to protect me, which was the same reason he'd stuck me behind a desk for weeks.

"What are we doing?" Heathcliff asked.

"Looking into something which may be nothing." I told him everything Deanna had said. When I was done, he scooped the folder off the dashboard and read the e-mails and texts she'd printed. "Taken separately, it doesn't seem like much, but together, I don't know. There could be something to Deanna's concerns. I told her I'd do a little digging. She said she went to the police, but they dismissed her claims. Maybe you could look into it for me. Cross thinks she's unhinged, possibly dangerous. Her records don't indicate that, but—"

"But you were stabbed, so he's exercising an abundance of caution."

"That would be my guess as to why he won't assign me a case, but it feels more specific when it comes to this case. He said he spoke to Leslie, but Lucien knows better than to take someone's word for anything. He should have checked it out himself. He should have gone to see her. I don't know why he didn't. Well, I do know why. The Golden is a client, but I thought he had more integrity than that."

"Lucien Cross and integrity in the same sentence? Now I know you're on pain meds." Heathcliff rubbed his mouth while he read my notes more carefully. "I take it that's why we're on a mission to find Leslie Stiller."

"Someone has to."

Heathcliff nodded at the apartment building as I pulled to a stop. "What are you hoping to find inside?"

"Leslie."

"Do you think she's home? It's the middle of the day."

"Well, she's not at work, and I have no idea where else

she'd be."

"So we start here." Heathcliff followed me to Leslie's apartment and knocked. "Police," he announced, "open up."

We waited, but no one came to the door.

"Now what do you want to do?" he asked.

"Look around."

"Alex—"

"Deanna gave me the key and permission to enter. She said the place looked like it had been cleared out. I need to see it for myself."

"And if someone took her, we might find signs of a break-in or struggle." Heathcliff mulled it over. "You know, I'm a cop. We aren't allowed to break in or search without permission."

"But I have permission."

He didn't believe me, but I'd said it twice and had a key. If her apartment turned into a crime scene, he could argue our entry had been justified. "Fine."

I turned the key in the lock and slowly pushed the door open. "Leslie?" I called. The security panel didn't beep. It wasn't even turned on. After donning a pair of gloves, I flipped on the light and stepped inside. "The power's not out, so I'm not sure why the security system is inactive." I examined the panel, photographing the serial number and model number.

"Leslie could have been in a rush and didn't activate it on her way out," Heathcliff said.

"But it should be on." I pointed to the blank LED screen. "This is completely off."

"Maybe she didn't want to pay for the service, or the battery needs to be changed." Heathcliff picked up his phone and asked if someone could contact the company and find out if they were currently providing coverage to this apartment. "They'll get back to me in a few minutes." He stepped deeper into her apartment. "Police," he announced, "is anyone here?"

When no response came, he led the way through the twisty, tiny hallway of a foyer and into the living room.

The place looked neat and tidy. A velvet throw was

folded over the couch. The pillows were fluffed and placed on the ends. The coffee table had the faintest layer of dust, but it was evenly distributed. Nothing had been touched or moved in weeks.

While Heathcliff examined the living room, I went into the kitchen. The cabinets contained cookware, but the fridge was empty except for a box of baking soda. Two frozen dinners remained in the freezer beside a lone tray of ice cubes. Everything else had been cleaned out.

There was no food in the pantry. No dishes in the sink. No condiments that would expire. It looked like Leslie knew she'd be gone for an extended period and made sure to do what she could to prepare her apartment for that.

"The thermostat is turned off," Heathcliff said from the other room. "Her TV and other peripherals are unplugged."

"So's the microwave."

I went into her bedroom, finding everything just as neat as the living room. The bed was made. A spread covered her pillows. The same light layer of dust coated her dresser. Her closet was nearly empty. Several party dresses, her gown from graduation, and a few pairs of ripped jeans remained. The rest were empty hangers.

On the wall was a large corkboard covered in photos. Ninety percent of them were of Deanna and Leslie, shopping, eating, wearing goofy 3D glasses at the movies, and looking like the best of friends. The frame of the corkboard had the same light layer of dust, and the glossy photos looked dull enough that I didn't think they'd been recently hung or moved.

If these photos were to be believed, Deanna wasn't lying. She and Leslie were close. A falling out would have resulted in the photos being taken down or ripped up, but they weren't. So if Leslie and Deanna weren't on the outs, why couldn't Deanna get a hold of her big sister?

The other photos were of Leslie with other people. Friends, classmates, her fellow interns. I plucked a photo from the top corner which had been placed on top of a family photo of Deanna, Leslie, and their father. The photo was of Leslie wearing what looked like a bellhop uniform beside twenty other people similarly dressed. I took a photo of that photo and then another of the entire corkboard before putting it back where I found it.

After forwarding the image to the techs and asking if they could get me IDs for the people in the photo, I searched the rest of her room. But there was nothing of interest. No luggage. No boxes. Aside from the furniture, the place was empty.

Heathcliff stepped into the room. "It doesn't look like she was taken. There are no signs of a struggle. I haven't noticed any scuff marks or blood spatter. I even checked the ceiling."

"Have you searched the bathroom?"

"There's not much there. Some basic first aid supplies, an opened bottle of hand soap, a few feminine products, and an extra roll of toilet paper."

I went into the bathroom, but I didn't find a toothbrush, hairbrush, or any makeup. "She took everything she thought she'd need with her."

"Considering she graduated from college not that long ago, I'm guessing she didn't have much to begin with."

"Probably not," I agreed.

"Are her clothes here?"

"Most are gone."

Heathcliff gave the apartment one last look. "I don't think she was forced to flee."

"That doesn't mean she isn't in trouble. No matter where she is, she should have her phone or access to a computer. She should have replied to someone's texts or e-mails in the last two weeks, but she hasn't spoken to anyone."

Heathcliff pointed out security cameras in the hallways as we made our way out of the building and back to my car. "What are you thinking?"

"I'm not sure. Did you see a computer or tablet anywhere?"

"No, but she would have taken them with her."

"She left the TV and microwave."

"You can get a microwave and TV pretty cheap."

"But she's paying rent on this place," I said. "If she decided to live elsewhere, why not give up the apartment?"

"Could she be doing that so Deanna has somewhere to spend the summer?"

"Maybe, but why wouldn't she tell her sister what's going on? Wouldn't that make the most sense?"

Heathcliff considered my words. "Maybe she wanted to avoid another fight."

I dialed Amir and asked if he could check Leslie's phone records and her internet history for anything we might have missed.

"I'll see what I can find." Amir hesitated, not wanting to hang up. "What case is this for?"

"It's preliminary research."

"I should have those records for you in a few hours."

"Great." I hung up.

"How exactly is Cross Security getting this information?" Heathcliff asked.

"It's best if you don't ask questions like that. In fact, it'd be best if you pretended you didn't hear any of my conversation."

"Were you actually given the key to that apartment? Or did you borrow it without permission?"

"I didn't lie to you, Derek. As a rule, I try not to do that, unless absolutely necessary." I stared at the apartment building through the car window. "Leslie Stiller left her apartment willingly. I have no reason to doubt that. The last place her phone pinged was somewhere in the city. The hotel staff insists she hasn't missed any work, but none of that explains why she's unreachable and why her apartment looks the way it does."

"Maybe she had a whirlwind romance and moved in with someone. She may be afraid her family and friends won't approve, so she's avoiding them until she figures out the right way to break the news." Heathcliff gave me a pointed look. "That would be the kind of thing you'd do."

"Are you telling me you don't approve of Martin?"

"Not that, but how you like to avoid telling me things when you know you should."

"I'm fine," I repeated more forcefully than necessary. "It's Leslie who may not be." The hour was up. "I need to go to the hotel and find out what's what."

Heathcliff's phone beeped. He studied the screen before tucking it away. "The security system hasn't been active in over a month. The previous tenant had paid for a year, but when they moved out and Leslie moved in, she didn't take over the contract."

"That doesn't help us." I thought about the security cameras inside the building. Maybe I could get eyes on her that way, but that would require greasing palms or hacking into the system. I couldn't do either with Heathcliff around.

"I should head back to the hotel and try my luck again. Do you want me to drop you off first?" I asked.

"How about you let me take a stab at this? My gold shield should have more sway than whatever trick you have up your sleeve. I can say I'm following up on the complaint they filed against Deanna, and I'll ask to question Leslie. That way, you don't get in any trouble, and we can put this thing to bed if there's a simple explanation for everything."

SIX

While Heathcliff spoke to a member of management, I wandered around the lobby, hoping to spot Leslie on her way to the front desk. There were plenty of guests and staff members, all of whom looked particularly happy for no apparent reason. Maybe it was someone's birthday and they had cake in the back room. I had no way of knowing, but the longer I waited, the faster my hope of seeing Leslie faded.

I checked my messages. Amir hadn't gotten back to me yet. But Lucien hadn't sent any threatening texts, so he must not have known I left the office.

Thoughts of my conversation with Deanna and images of Leslie's apartment played through my mind. There was no reason to assume Leslie was in danger. More than likely, this was some sort of misunderstanding or miscommunication between the siblings. But that nagging voice at the back of my head wasn't buying it.

Heathcliff came up beside me. "Let's go."

"What happened? Did you see Leslie?"

"No."

"Why not?"

"I was told she had concluded her shift for the day. They said she'd be back in the morning."

"They told me to try back in an hour."

"I know."

"Fuck."

We headed back to my car, which I'd parked a few blocks from the hotel.

"I left my card and a request that she calls me as soon as possible." Heathcliff eyed the resort through the rearview. "They mentioned interns get assigned different positions, that they rotate their duties. Maybe she worked this morning."

"Then why did they tell me to come back?"

"I don't know, Alex. I'm just the messenger."

I pulled out my phone and dialed Leslie's number again. Since she was supposedly off the rest of the day, there was no reason for her phone to be off, but the call went straight to voicemail. "Do you have any idea where she could be?"

Heathcliff sucked in a breath, debating with himself. "There's something you should know. I've been reviewing old cases these last few weeks. I have a hit-and-run that I never closed and hoped to gain some insight into it."

"Was Leslie involved?"

"No, but the hit-and-run happened in the Golden's self-serve parking garage. A member of the staff was mowed down. I don't have any leads. The surveillance footage wasn't helpful. But that's not the point."

"What is the point?"

"The Golden has had its share of problems. Accidents, mishaps, weird things. I'm not sure it's anything, but with the way we've been given the runaround concerning Leslie Stiller's current whereabouts, I'm starting to wonder if there could be something to all of this."

"All of what? What kind of accidents and mishaps are we talking about?"

"A lot of things. Drownings. Suicides. Just weird things."

I headed back to the precinct, but Heathcliff had turned into his stoic, contemplative self. He only got this serious when he was formulating a theory. "What's your take on the situation?" I asked.

"It's too soon to say."

"Do you think something happened to Leslie? That the Golden is covering it up?"

"I don't know. Maybe. Everything the manager said felt rehearsed, like she prepared her responses in advance. But I was told Leslie would call me when she reports to work tomorrow. I don't see why the Golden would make that promise if Leslie wasn't around. I'll insist on meeting her in person, and we'll take it from there." He turned to face me. "Promise me something."

"What?"

"Wait until the morning before you do anything else. I want to check on a few things and pull the rest of those case files before you run off half-cocked."

"I brought you in to be my study buddy, to help me go over this stuff, not so you could take it away from me. Why do you want me to wait?" Fear hit me hard, in a way I hadn't expected it to. "Do you think Leslie's dead?"

"Alex, you need to take a breath before you spin out."

"What I need is for Leslie to be okay. What I need is for everyone to be okay."

"We could go to a meeting. My shift's almost over."

"This isn't about grief, Derek. I don't need a support group for what's wrong with me."

"What do you need?"

"Reassurance that no one else is going to show up at my home to hurt Martin or me." I hadn't expected those words to come out. We'd been talking about Leslie, but the conversation got flipped without me noticing.

But Heathcliff couldn't give me that reassurance. No one could. That was the job. Precautions could be taken, but there were no guarantees. Unfortunately, the deck was stacked against me because of who I was and who Martin was.

"Will you wait until tomorrow morning?" Heathcliff asked. "I want to look into the hotel and see if anything like this has happened before. There could be missing persons reports or other things that may prove useful."

"I can help you look through the files."

"I don't want you to get in trouble, and I don't want to get in trouble for helping you." He indicated his arm. "Desk duty, remember? Plus, you said the Golden is a client. Cross Security should have plenty of intel on the hotel. Why don't you see what you can find, and then we can meet up and share notes?"

"Fine." Cross Security had a lot of resources at its disposal. And I had a lot of friends who carried federal agent badges.

After dropping Heathcliff off at the precinct, I returned to the office. Amir had IDed most of the people in the photos, but Leslie hadn't had any contact with them, at least not online or via her phone. In fact, Leslie's phone and internet activity abruptly ended two weeks ago. The last known location we had for her was in the vicinity of the Golden. Maybe she was there. Or she lost her phone on her way to work.

A million possibilities played through my mind as far as what could have happened to her. But the main question was why the Golden had told me to come back in an hour only to tell Heathcliff that Leslie wouldn't be back at work for the rest of the day. That made no sense. Had they lied, or had something happened?

Leslie's financial activity wouldn't be able to help me track her down. The grocery charges and ATM withdrawals indicated she hadn't left the city. But I didn't see any charges in two weeks. She was supposed to be at work tomorrow. Was I really supposed to wait an entire day before doing anything else?

I pulled up the information on the Golden that was saved on Cross Security's servers, but it looked like the basics. I had the specs on their cameras and their security protocols. What I didn't have was any way of knowing if they were responsible for Leslie's silence.

Shifting gears, I took my search online. The Golden's website redirected me to Experiential Adventures' website. I tried searching for a complete list of their locations. Unfortunately, they didn't have that information consolidated for easy consumption. Everything was broken into tiers and partnership properties. Had any of these other properties been under investigation for unsafe work conditions, missing employees, or human trafficking?

After a few internet searches and checking forums, I didn't find much, so I called Kate Hartley, my forensic accountant friend who carried FBI credentials.

"Hey, Kate. I need a favor," I said.

"It'll cost you."

"It always does. What do you have in mind?"

"It depends. What do you want me to do?"

"I need a business profile and a list of property holdings. I want to know what hotels and resorts are owned by Experiential Adventures."

She sounded funny when she said, "I thought you worked at a security firm."

"I do."

"What you're asking for is basic. Shouldn't you be able to get that yourself?"

"I could."

"But you don't want to." She hummed a little. "Why not?"

"I was curious if this company might be the subject of any open investigations, particularly the Golden Hotel and Resort."

"Investigations regarding?"

"Anything and everything. Not just white collar crimes. Maybe trafficking. Murder. I don't know. Use your imagination."

"And you know if I put together a profile I'll notice if any department or agency has them under investigation since it'll be flagged in the system."

"That would be correct."

She laughed softly to herself. "Which is the actual reason you called. It's never to trade gossip or check in."

"I check in. I sent you that text on your birthday a few weeks ago."

"That's it. I've decided. I want to go on a booze cruise across the river. I've always wanted to go on one. I was supposed to go on Valentine's Day, but things didn't work out with that asshole I was seeing, so no cruise for me. Instead, we should go. I hear they do singles' night on Thursdays."

"Kate—"

“Agree or no deal.”

“Not this Thursday. But we’ll go on a Thursday.”

“A Thursday sometime this month.”

I looked at the calendar. “By the end of next month.”

“Fine.”

“When do you think you’ll have the intel for me?”

She made a ticking sound, which meant she was consulting her computer screen. “It looks like Experiential Adventures acquired existing properties. Give me a few days.”

“See if you can put a rush on it. A woman’s gone radio silent. I’m trying to figure out what happened to her.”

“And you think it connects to the hotel?”

“She works there, and according to the manager, she hasn’t missed a single shift.”

“Sounds like someone’s lying,” Kate said.

“My thoughts exactly.”

SEVEN

Since Kate had taken the tedious task of checking the law enforcement databases for open investigations off my plate, I focused my attention on finding Leslie Stiller. The Golden wouldn't give me access to their security cameras, so if I wanted to spot Leslie, I'd have to get creative.

Heathcliff had pointed out the cameras in her apartment building. That would be a good starting place. But the building's owner wasn't interested in providing access, not even after I offered a free consultation and system upgrade. He hung up on me, believing I was trying to sell him something. That may not have been the best way to proceed. I'd have to try a different approach in person.

I searched the Cross Security database again, hoping to find something on the Golden that I had missed. Access codes, a backdoor into their computer system, or a way to hack into their camera feeds would have been great. But it wasn't there. Cross Security didn't spy on its clients, not officially anyway. If Cross had any dirt on the Golden, it was locked away behind a firewall or in the filing cabinets in his office.

I needed to update him on the Leslie situation and

convince him to get on board with my investigation, so I sent the completed busy work to him, showing that I was a team player. Then I went to the reception desk to ply Janet for more details before confronting Lucien.

I leaned against the counter surrounding the reception desk. "The young woman who was here earlier, the case Cross didn't want to take, do you know how he determined Leslie Stiller wasn't missing?"

Janet tore her attention away from the computer screen in front of her, where she appeared to be working on the schedule. "I don't know exactly what Mr. Cross's approach was, but he always vets new clients before signing them. He determined there was no case."

"Yes, but how did he reach that conclusion?" Cross told me he called the Golden and spoke to her. He also said he performed his due diligence. I wanted to know everything that entailed.

"He didn't give me a reason. He doesn't have to. He's the boss."

"And you didn't ask?"

Janet made a face. "I've found it's best not to ask too many questions."

"The difference between us is I get paid to ask questions."

"You get paid to do what you're told," Lucien said from behind me.

I spun. "I told you to stop doing that. Seriously? Do you have every room and hallway in this place bugged? Don't you have anything better to do than sneak up on me?"

"I was coming to get a copy of the updated schedule." He held out his hand, and Janet gave him the spiral-bound appointment book. "Thank you, Janet."

"Not a problem, Mr. Cross." She gave me a pointed look before turning her attention back to the computer screen.

"So, Alex," Cross rested his hips against the counter and folded his arms over his chest, the appointment book dangling from his fingertips, "what question would you like me to answer?"

"You don't know?"

"Do you honestly think I have nothing better to do than

spend my time spying on you?"

"The thought has crossed my mind. There is precedent."

"Let's try this another way. You were told this morning that you're not to work any cases. Is that why you're pestering Janet? Are you hoping she'll find something for you to do now that you finished working on the assignments I gave you?"

Since I didn't see any reason to hide things, I said, "I wanted to know more about the research you did into Leslie Stiller and the Golden Hotel."

"I thought I told you to stay away from that."

"You did."

Cross gestured with the appointment book to the hallway which led to my office. "Let's continue this discussion elsewhere." He followed me into my office and closed the door behind us. "Justin said you just finished the background checks. I figured you would have knocked them out much sooner."

"I took a nap."

He stared at me. "What were you really doing this afternoon?"

So I told him. "Lucien, I don't understand what's going on here. But whatever it is, it doesn't look good. And from what I can tell, the Golden is hiding Leslie or concealing whatever happened to her. We need to do something about this."

Cross put the book down and took a seat on the couch. "You informed Detective Heathcliff about this situation, and he told you to wait until the morning. That Leslie should be at work tomorrow and will be told to contact him. I think it's best if you wait."

"Wait? She could be hurt or worse. We owe it to Deanna to look into this, to open an investigation, to find out what's going on."

"I already told you what's going on."

"Do you actually believe that after everything I said?"

Cross squinted at me. "It's complicated."

"It's not. The only thing complicated is that the Golden is your client. You're protecting them. Are you covering for them?"

"I would never."

But I wasn't sure I believed it. "But you won't investigate because that would be a conflict, especially if the Golden Hotel has something to do with Leslie's disappearance. So what's the plan, boss? Bury your head in the sand and gaslight Deanna into thinking she's crazy?" I fought back the horrible thoughts that played through my head.

"I wouldn't do that."

"Lucien—"

"I wouldn't," he snapped. "When Deanna showed up asking for help, I spoke to the person in charge of the interns and was assured Leslie Stiller is perfectly fine. As part of the program, the Golden provides its interns with company devices and asks that they not use their personal devices for the duration of their hands-on training. That's why her phone is off and why she's gone radio silent."

"It sounds like they have her sequestered."

"Don't be so dramatic. The Golden doesn't want any of its secrets or techniques leaked. But Leslie is free to contact whomever she wishes in her free time. However, she made it clear to me when I spoke to her that she would prefer not to speak to her sister."

"But you didn't see her. She could have been forced to say that, or maybe you spoke to someone pretending to be Leslie. Without laying eyes on her, you have no way of knowing."

"I spoke to her."

"How do you know that?"

"I just do."

"That's not good enough. I need to know how," I said.

"I have my ways. That is all you need to know, Alex." He cleared his throat. "I need you to trust me when I tell you Leslie Stiller is alive and well. She is working at the Golden."

Cross sent me home with instructions to drop the case and any other cases I may decide to investigate. He reminded me of the changes that had befallen my employment contract. Though, at this point, we had renegotiated the terms so many times I wasn't even sure what I was prohibited from doing. Was moonlighting out? I couldn't remember.

Despite my boss's warning, I couldn't shake the look on Deanna's face. She was worried about her sister. Once I was satisfied Leslie was safe, then I'd drop it. Until then, I'd have to fly below Cross's radar. I understood this put him and his company in a bad position, but some things were more important.

On my way home, I went by Leslie's place again. I knocked, but no one answered. I tried her cell phone for the sixth time, but that proved pointless. Since she was banned from using her personal device at work, maybe she only used her work-provided phone so as not to get them confused. But Cross hadn't given me her number. I doubted he had it.

After some finagling, I convinced the building manager to give me copies of the security camera footage from the last sixty days. Maybe this would put my mind at ease, if I ever got through it.

The only good thing about getting home early was Martin was still at the office, which meant I had a quiet place to work. Instead of blinding myself by staring at the footage on my computer screen, I sent it to the big screen in the living room, made myself comfortable on the couch, and found the camera that covered Leslie's floor.

I started with the most recent footage and worked my way backward. Heathcliff and I had been the last people who'd gone inside Leslie's apartment. Two days earlier, Deanna had gone in. She used the key, the same as we had.

I checked the timestamp. She spent three minutes in Leslie's apartment. When she emerged, she was empty-handed. At least I couldn't accuse her of stealing.

I continued rewinding, hoping to spot Leslie on the footage. Her neighbors came and went. But no sign of Leslie until I got to the footage from two weeks and two days ago.

Leslie Stiller had three large duffel bags crisscrossed over her chest and a rolling suitcase she dragged behind her. She wore black dress pants and a white blouse with a bow that tied in the front beneath a matching black suit jacket. She looked like most business professionals.

Switching camera feeds, I followed her out of the building. She had illegally parked her car, a twenty-year old silver hatchback that looked pretty good for its age. Why hadn't I thought to track her car? Mentally kicking myself, I furiously scribbled her plate number at the top of the legal pad while I kept my eyes glued to the screen.

She loaded the bags into the rear, closed the hatch, and got behind the wheel. She never went back to the apartment after that. The luggage indicated she was going on a trip. Maybe for a few weeks. Possibly longer. But if she'd gone somewhere, why didn't the Golden say she was away? Why lie and tell us she hadn't missed any work? Could they have transferred her to another one of their resorts?

My preliminary research indicated that was possible. But the intel on the internship program suggested the opposite. All interns went through training at the Golden before getting placed in permanent positions elsewhere, assuming they were offered a permanent position and/or wanted a career with Experiential Adventures.

Could Leslie have been such an impressive candidate that they placed her early? Even if they had, why wouldn't she tell her sister? And why wouldn't the hotel tell us?

After writing down the date and time of Leslie's last known sighting, I rewound the footage until I found where she had returned before leaving that final time. That had been the previous night just before eleven. She wore a similar outfit to the one she wore when she left her apartment for good, except the blouse was a blush color instead of white.

Leslie didn't have any bags with her, only a tiny purse that appeared to be large enough to hold her credit cards and a lip balm or two. I switched back to the feed of her floor and backed that up until I found her entering her apartment.

The hallways were empty when she got home. She didn't speak to anyone. She unlocked the door and went in. That was it.

I sped through the rest of the footage, finding she

followed a similar pattern every night. She never had any guests. None of her coworkers or friends went to her place.

On a few occasions, she came home with a takeout bag, but for the most part, she returned empty-handed. A month earlier, she had returned in a t-shirt and jeans. Her arms were filled with grocery bags. When she unlocked the door, a package of ramen soup fell out of the top of her bag. As she scooped it up, a few more items fell out, all inexpensive, packaged meals.

That explained her cheap grocery bills, but given the size of those bags, there was no way she had eaten all of that prior to her disappearance. I had seen her take out the trash, but those bags were pretty flimsy. So I didn't think she'd thrown out the food. Her purse was too small to think she had taken it to eat at work for lunch, so what happened to it?

I wasn't sure why my brain latched onto that thought or why it mattered, but it bothered me. Unless she chucked the food out the window, the only way it got out of her apartment would have been in the bags she took with her the last time she'd been to her apartment.

Again, the itch nagged at me from the back of my brain. I'd lived off cups of soup and mac n' cheese for years, especially when money was tight and takeout wasn't readily available. Those meals could last on the shelf indefinitely. Everything was dehydrated. Time couldn't make them much worse. So why didn't she leave them in the pantry before going on her trip? Why would she need to take them with her?

I let that thought percolate while I ran her plate number. The Ohio plate made it an oddity, but it was registered to her. There were no parking tickets or moving violations. Leslie hadn't purchased a toll pass, but the last time she'd been sent a bill was when she arrived. Since then, she hadn't driven over any bridges or gone through any tunnels, at least not in her car.

"Planes, trains, and automobiles," I mumbled. Everything indicated she remained in the city. Sure, this place was home to millions of people, but if she was here, I should be able to find her. I had everything I could possibly need, her address, phone number, place of business, and, yet, I had no idea where the woman had gone.

Her financials didn't indicate she had made travel arrangements. No train, plane, or bus tickets had been purchased, unless she used cash or prepaid. If she had been transferred for work, the tickets could have been provided to her by the Golden.

I was halfway through composing a text message to Heathcliff, asking if he could pull DOT footage and track Leslie's car when I remembered the promise he asked me to make. Surely, he knew I couldn't sit on my hands, but he wouldn't be happy about me snooping either. So I deleted the text and scrolled through my list of police contacts. O'Connell and Thompson would be home by now since they'd been on the same schedule as Heathcliff, unless they got stuck working a double. But they wouldn't have time to help me if that were the case.

I could call Jacobs, but we didn't have the best working relationship. Detective Sparrow would help, but she'd tell Thompson and it'd get back to Heathcliff. There was one police detective I'd forgotten about. Homicide detective Jake Voletek. He was Renner's friend. We'd worked together on an arson case.

"Come on. Come on." My leg jittered up and down as I waited for him to answer. By the time the third ring started, I got up to pace.

I was about to hang up when he answered with a rushed, "Hey. Did you miss me?"

"Detective Voletek?" I forced a friendly smile on my face, even though he couldn't see it, but I'd been told he could hear it. "Jake? This is Alex Parker. I'm not sure if you remember me."

"I remember you. The thing with the chef."

"Yeah," I said.

"Is he good? Did something happen to him?"

"Not as far as I know. You work homicide. Have you heard something different?"

He laughed. "No. So now I'm wondering if this is a social call. I always hoped you'd use my number."

"It's not exactly a social call. I wanted to ask a favor."

"Name it."

That may have been too easy, but I wasn't going to look a gift horse in the mouth. "I'm trying to track down a vehicle. I can give you the last known location and direction it was traveling, but I don't know where it is now. Maybe you could pull DOT footage and see if you can determine its final destination."

"That sounds ominous. Have you seen those movies?"

"A few."

"There's like a million." He paused. "Do you like horror movies? There's a movie scare-a-thon at the cineplex this weekend. It's mostly old slasher films."

"I'm not really into that," I said.

"I kind of figured. Hang on one sec while I bring this up." After a pause, he said, "Okay. What am I looking for?"

I gave him a description of the car, the plate number, and the time, date, and location when Leslie last left her apartment. "She was heading east, but she could have made the next turn or gone straight. I have no way of knowing."

"Let me worry about that." He searched the DOT footage. "I see the car." He gave me the play-by-play as he tracked it from camera to camera, lost it, found it, and tracked it some more. "She loses me here." He gave me the cross streets. "I can issue a BOLO. If patrol spots it, they'll radio in the location, and I can get that to you."

"You can do that?" That was an abuse of power, particularly when this wasn't a police matter, unless Heathcliff had turned it into one and hadn't bothered to tell me.

"Let's just say I can call in a few favors. Are you sure you aren't interested in that movie marathon? They have another one on Wednesday night, featuring classics. No horror. Stuff like *Casablanca* and *Citizen Kane*."

"I have a boyfriend."

"Well, if you know anyone who might be interested, have them give me a call."

"Renner warned me about you," I teased.

"You shouldn't believe everything you hear." He chuckled. "I'll get back to you if someone spots that car."

I checked the cross streets on a map. I couldn't be positive, but I had an idea where Leslie Stiller's car might be.

EIGHT

I left Martin a note. Then I drove to the Golden. The nagging voice in my head reminded me I'd given Heathcliff my word that I would wait until the morning, but I had an obligation not to waste the city's resources. If I found Leslie or her vehicle, Detective Voletek could call off the BOLO, and the city's finest could resume their duties without looking for a silver hatchback with Ohio plates.

Like most hotels, the Golden had valet parking. But I wasn't interested in leaving my car with them. Instead, I asked the man working the valet stand where the employees park.

With nearly two thousand staff members, the Golden didn't allow staff to park at the hotel. He directed me to two nearby garages. However, since most employees lived in the city, they typically didn't drive to work. They took public transportation or walked.

I circled the block a few times, checking the vehicles parked on the street. Then I checked the first garage. By the time I finished circling each level, it had started raining.

I continued to the next garage, finding the entrance gate closed. It had reached capacity. I found a metered spot three blocks away and jogged back to the garage. The light mist had turned into a steady sprinkle, which soaked my collar and seeped across my shoulders.

The garage was wall to wall cars. I fought off the shivers caused by the cold rain while I made my way up and down the rows. On the fourth level, I noticed a lot of out-of-state plates. There were a few from Ohio. I double-checked the numbers, even though the cars were different makes and models, but they didn't belong to Leslie. So I kept going.

Hawaii, Texas, Delaware, Vermont. I moved to the next row. Oklahoma, Florida, Pennsylvania. Could this be an annex to the Golden's garage? That would explain all the foreign plates.

I contemplated that as I made my way to the roof. The rain came down in sheets, more powerful than the waterfall showerhead we had at home. I shielded my eyes, giving up on the notion of not getting drenched. Parked in the middle of this mess was Leslie Stiller's car.

Cupping my hands against the window, I peered inside. Her car was clean, like her apartment. If she left anything inside, I couldn't see it in the rain and dark.

Leaning across the hood, I searched the interior of her dash through the windshield until I found her parking slip. She'd pulled into the garage two weeks and two days ago. This was the last place Leslie Stiller had driven.

She had been here. I could only assume she parked her car here because she'd been on her way to work. Her outfit indicated as much, but what did the duffel bags and suitcase mean? Were they still in her car? Had something happened to her after she got here?

I went around to the rear hatch. She hadn't closed the privacy flap, so I could see directly into the cargo area. Her bags were gone, just like her. I had to assume she had taken them with her, which was a good sign. Given where her car was parked, she was probably staying at the hotel. The only question that remained was why no one had bothered to tell us this.

I dug a cheap tracking chip out of my pocket and stuck it beneath her rear bumper. The tech didn't come from the office, which would make Cross happy. It was something I'd picked up at a big box store. It would let me know if Leslie's car moved, assuming the rain didn't wreak havoc on it.

"Where did you go?" I examined the doors and trunk, but nothing indicated someone had tried to break-in.

Pocketing my flashlight, I headed for the exit. Leslie had packed her things, parked in this garage, and what? If she'd taken up residency at the Golden or moved in with a friend or romantic interest, why didn't she tell her sister? Why was she hiding her whereabouts from her family? And why hadn't she tried to get out of her lease?

Cameras were posted on the same poles as the spotlights. Once I got the parking garage's footage, I'd have a better idea of where Leslie might be.

On my way down the stairs, I paid special attention to the items on the ground. But I didn't spot any weapons. No broken glass or anything that indicated she'd been attacked or abducted.

On the bottom level, a group of four headed to their vehicles dressed in the Golden Hotel's uniform. They chatted quietly to themselves as they strolled through the garage.

"Excuse me," I called.

The group stopped, almost in complete unison, and turned to face me. The man nearest to me with a neatly trimmed grey beard was the first to brandish that practiced customer service smile. But the other three quickly mimicked him.

"How may I help you?" he asked.

"Do you work at the Golden?"

He nodded. "Are you a guest? Is there something we can do for you?"

"I'm looking for Leslie Stiller."

He held the smile, but his eyes looked dead. Turning, he exchanged glances with the other three people, but no words were spoken. When he turned back, he had the same hollow, friendly look. "I'm sorry. I don't know who that is."

The warning bells went off in my brain, but I wasn't sure why. I looked at the other members of the group. Despite the phony smiles, I couldn't help but think they were using those to hide something else. Did they know Leslie? "Thanks anyway."

He gave me a curt nod and waited for me to move past before he turned around. I glanced back, watching the rest of the group follow suit. They didn't resume their previous conversation or exchange looks or whispers. That wasn't normal behavior. Had I gotten transported to the Twilight Zone?

I kept looking over my shoulder as I exited the garage. The group didn't appear threatening. Quite the opposite, but that's what made me nervous. Maybe I shouldn't have mentioned Leslie's name. And now I was freaked out that an alien robot army had been sent to take over the staff of the Golden.

Okay, that was ridiculous. But something wasn't right about those people. The sound of the automatic arm lifting made me turn. A dark SUV pulled out of the lot. The driver was one of the three who hadn't spoken to me. The red two-door behind it was driven by the man with the beard. He had a passenger with him. I squinted, trying to make out his plates as he turned in the opposite direction.

Stepping farther from the building, I leaned over the sidewalk, catching the first four digits before the screech of tires and the blare of a car horn made me jump back.

A yellow sports car zipped past me, drenching me as it hit a puddle. The driver rolled down his window. "You fucking idiot. Stay out of the fucking road."

"Bite me." I accompanied my response with a rude hand gesture. That's how normal people interacted under such circumstances.

Having missed my chance to see the rest of the license plate, I wiped the grit and rain off my face and headed back to my car. A dark green sedan slowed as it drove along beside me. The hairs at the back of my neck prickled.

I tried to write it off as a consequence of traffic or the rain, but the driver was gawking at me. I must have been a sight, but that wasn't it. Reaching into my jacket, I wiped my palm on whatever dry part of my shirt I could find before unsnapping the guard on my shoulder holster and grasping the handle of my nine millimeter.

Turning, I stared the driver right in the eye. He didn't flinch. He just gazed at me with the same dead eyes as the man with the grey beard. He didn't speed up or slow down. He didn't even look away.

I didn't like this. As he approached the intersection, he was forced to slow and stop. I kept walking, hoping he'd turn. But he didn't. Should I get in my car, or should I keep walking?

Being outside left me exposed, not only to the elements but to whatever this lunatic may have planned. But I didn't want him to figure out who I was. I hadn't taken my car on this outing. I had the company car, which was a nondescript silver sedan. A million of them were on the road. That's why Lucien chose this specific make and model. He wanted to make it easier for us to blend in when conducting surveillance.

Reaching into my pocket with my free hand, I removed my keys. The green sedan had fallen behind, being forced to stop as the car in front of him turned. But I could still feel that man watching me.

Wondering how much he'd enjoy being tailed, I got into my car and waited to pull out. When he was directly beside me, he tipped his head in a slight nod and kept going. Flashbacks from my last case and being followed by a man who later tried to kill me came to mind, giving me cold chills on top of the ones I already had on account of the rain.

I gripped the steering wheel, hoping the hammering in my chest would stop. I focused on the license plate as the dark green sedan went past, repeating the letters and numbers over and over as my peripheral vision blacked out and the colors dimmed.

Sucking in several ragged gasps, I squeezed the steering wheel and focused on the textured grip. My vision cleared, and I started the engine.

The rapid jackhammering in my chest had slowed enough that I could control my breathing, so I didn't think I'd pass out. I tried to pull out and follow him, but traffic was as heavy as the rain, and my nerves were too shot to attempt something daring. Instead, I waited for an opening, voice-dialed Voletek, and told him he could call off the search. I found the car. Then I asked him to run the plate on the green sedan, which had been repeating on a loop since my panic attack started.

"It's registered to Louis Grable. Thirty-one. Do you want his address?"

"Text it to me."

"Are you okay?" Voletek asked. "You don't sound right."

"Ask me tomorrow."

"Am I calling you tomorrow?"

"If you play your cards right, I'll stop by and see you," I said, but the flirty teasing wasn't in my tone, no matter how hard I tried. This may have been why Lucien didn't want me working out of the office. I hated when he was right, but I was too damn stubborn to give him the satisfaction of admitting it.

NINE

When I got home, Martin's town car was in the garage. The hood was warm, but I didn't spot Marcal, his driver. Bruiser's car remained in its spot, where it had been since he arrived this morning to pick Martin up for work. Hopefully, my beloved had found my note.

Last chance, Parker. If you're going to run, do it now, the paranoid, frightened voice in my head warned. That odd encounter in the garage and being stalked by the green sedan had triggered things that I'd been fighting to suppress. Now, everything was a little too close to the surface.

Bruiser nodded to me as I emerged onto the second floor of Martin's estate. "Any issues?" he asked.

"The area's secure," I said.

Bruiser believed me, but since the incident, he had a ritual of checking the security system logs for any discrepancies. Excusing himself, he went into Martin's home office to make sure I wasn't followed and the house wasn't under attack. I could have kissed him.

Martin had his back to me while he fiddled with the knobs on the oven. "Hey, gorgeous. I found your note."

"I told you not to wait for me to eat."

"I wasn't waiting. I just got here." He turned, still

dressed in what he'd worn to the office. The only thing he'd taken off was his tie, which he'd pulled off during the car ride home. "What happened to you?"

"I got caught in the rain."

Sympathy shone through his green eyes. "Should I make you a pina colada?"

I shook my head, finding it difficult not to unravel.

He pointed to my note. "You must have gotten home early. Is everything okay? You don't usually leave without a reason."

"I wanted to check something."

He jerked his chin at my laptop, which I'd left on the coffee table. I'd closed the surveillance footage, but I'd left open my earlier searches on hotels and resorts. "Were you researching places for us to stay in Tuscany?"

I shivered. "No. I...just...I...shit."

He approached me, running his hands along my arms and finding portions of my shirt drenched from where the rain had seeped through my jacket. My hair was matted down and knotted, the ends frizzing from where they'd started to dry.

"You must be freezing." He ran his thumb over my cheek. "Dinner can wait while you get out of these wet things."

"I'd say you sound like my mother, but we both know that's not true. So I'm going to guess you sound like your mother."

He pressed his lips gently against mine. "That's not an insult. Go."

"I'm fine." I shivered again.

"Are you?"

"Maybe you should start with an easier question."

Martin didn't like that answer. "If you're starving, I'll get you a towel, and we can eat first. I was going to bring home the crab rolls you like, but I thought something heartier would be better."

"You made the right call."

"I picked up Indian food. We haven't had it in a while. But if you'd prefer something else—"

"Indian's great."

He snaked his arms gently around my waist. "How's the side?"

"Holding together."

He pressed his forehead against mine. "Go get dried off. I don't want you to get sick."

Bruiser emerged from the office. "The house is secure. Do you want me to stick around?"

"Only if you'd like to join us for dinner." Martin gestured to an empty spot at the table while he went to retrieve plates from the cabinet. "I ordered plenty."

"That's okay. You two enjoy." Bruiser nodded to me. "Are you feeling better, Parker?"

"Didn't I use to annoy you with that question?"

"Yes, ma'am." He winked, letting me know it was in fun.

I pointed at him. "No more puzzle books for you. But to answer your question, I'm fine."

"You don't look so fine."

I didn't feel so fine either. "Nothing a hot shower can't fix."

"Glad to hear it." But Martin's bodyguard wasn't buying it. "I heard you ripped a stitch this morning."

I gave Martin's back a dirty look before turning to Bruiser. "Good night, Jones. Thanks for making sure the area's secure."

He grinned at me. "Always."

Martin put plates and silverware on the table before grabbing a few glasses and filling them with water. He'd heard my exchange. "Is there any reason to think the area wouldn't be secure?"

"I don't know." I'd been careful coming home. I ran through every training exercise and protocol I'd been taught, but that wasn't always enough. "A driver in a green sedan freaked me out. If you see any green sedans, black SUVs, or red two-doors, let me know."

"Alex?"

I trembled, more from nerves than the cold.

Martin went past me, grabbed the throw off the couch, and wrapped it around me. "Sit down."

"Martin, I'm all wet."

"Sit," he insisted before going into the bathroom. He

came back a moment later with the hairdryer, which he plugged in before crawling onto the couch beside me.

"I should shower first." On autopilot, I climbed off the couch and went into the second floor bathroom, too frazzled to go upstairs.

Martin followed, accustomed to my odd behavior, and watched as I stripped. He took my wet clothes and hung them on the hooks behind the door. I left my holstered weapon on the bathroom counter, turned on the water, and stepped into the shower. I wondered if he'd join me, but he kept his distance on account of my stitched side.

After scrubbing the street grime off, I wrapped myself in an oversized, fluffy towel. Martin had brought me a change of clothes and waited with the hairdryer at the ready. I was still a little shaky, so he led me back into the living room, plugged the hairdryer into the nearest outlet, and let me curl up against his chest while he dried my hair.

"Do you want to tell me what happened?" He brushed my hair behind my ear. "What triggered it this time?" He knew. He always knew.

"The way the driver of the car stared at me."

"Where were you?"

"It doesn't matter."

"You're working a case." It wasn't a question. "I thought Cross had you behind a desk."

"He does." I told him about Deanna Stiller and what Heathcliff had said. "Don't be mad."

"I'm not mad, sweetheart." He sighed. "We should eat. It'll make you feel better. I can open a bottle of something. White wine, maybe? Or sparkling? If you're in the mood for champagne, we can do that, but—"

"I don't feel like drinking. I'm afraid if we start now we'll end up at the bottom of the bottle, which will result in opening another bottle, and another, and things will get messy, and I want to get back to work, which means I have to stop reopening the wound. So we can't do messy right now."

A playful, teasing quality made Martin's green eyes twinkle. "Wow, that's a very mature way of looking at things."

"That's because in the last few hours I've aged decades."

"For what it's worth, you look fantastic for your advanced years."

I kicked him, fighting off a grin. "Jerk."

And just like that, the tension broke.

While we ate, he spoke about his day, his meetings, and ideas for where we could go with the O'Connells on our next double date night. Dinner felt normal, lighter than it had in weeks. It was a reminder of how things were supposed to be.

After dessert, which was a mango rice pudding that I could never remember the name of, Martin cleared the table. I tried to help, but after I put the leftovers in the fridge, there was nothing for me to do. I sat on the counter beside the sink and watched as he loaded the dishwasher.

"I can't go to Tuscany now," I said, "not until I find Leslie Stiller."

"She'll be at work tomorrow."

"You really think so?"

"It would make the most sense. That's what everyone, including Lucien, has said. You saw her leave her apartment in her work clothes with her suitcases. Her car is parked in the employee garage near the hotel. She must be staying there."

"That would explain why she wasn't answering her phone or getting online since the Golden has a policy against personal devices. But why didn't she tell her sister? Why couldn't they have called up to her room when Heathcliff asked to speak to her?"

"Privacy issues," Martin suggested, "or the right hand doesn't know what the left is doing. Maybe whoever you spoke to doesn't know Leslie's living there."

"I hope you're right."

He ran his fingertips up my arm, tickling me. "I usually am."

"Are you okay?" I asked as he put the last dish inside and closed the door.

"Why wouldn't I be?" He opened the buttons on his vest, which reminded me he hadn't changed before dinner.

I pressed my lips together, my gaze traveling to the

police report on the counter. "I saw the photos from that night. I knew intellectually what it must have been like, but I didn't realize the extent." My cheek twitched, and I turned to find him staring at me with an intensity that made me uncomfortable outside the bedroom. "This is why you've been watching me sleep."

"How would you know I've been watching you sleep? You've barely slept in weeks."

"That's how I know."

He brushed my hair behind my shoulder and moved in front of me. Toying with the platinum band on his finger, he slipped it off and held it between us, spinning it as he read the inscription. "You promised you'd always come home. It never occurred to me that it may not be safe for you to come home."

"Martin—"

"I know. That's why this house makes you uncomfortable. I almost bled out upstairs. Then I came up with the brilliant idea that we share an apartment, something closer to work, something that would be neutral territory, a safe space, ours. And this happens." He gently stroked my side.

"No matter where we go, it isn't safe. Here. Los Angeles. It doesn't matter." Anger hit me hard out of nowhere. "It doesn't fucking matter. I can't outrun it or hide from it. I...I don't know what to do."

"You want to walk away."

"I won't." I blinked a few times, making sure I wouldn't cry. I wasn't sad. I was furious and overwhelmed. Luckily, my anxiety remained at the periphery.

"But that was your first instinct." Martin ran his thumb across my cheek before trailing his fingers down to my chin and forcing me to look up at him. "I know you, Alex. I know how you think. That's why you've been so restless. We need to come up with a solution."

"Is that why you've been watching me at night? Are you afraid I'll sneak out while you're asleep? I love you, Martin. But you can't make me your prisoner."

"I would never." He shook his head and stepped back, running a hand through his hair. "Don't you get it, sweetheart? I'm just as scared as you are."

"James—"

"No, Alex. Listen. The only thing I've heard out of your mouth is how grateful you were that I didn't get home first. That it wasn't me. But you don't get it. I wish I had gotten home first. I had Bruiser. I don't know if things would have ended differently, but the odds would have been in our favor. Bruiser's trained. Hell, I trained for things like this. You wouldn't have been alone. You wouldn't have been there." He worked his jaw. "If we'd gotten there a few minutes later—"

"The police would have been there by then."

"You don't know that."

I couldn't argue, not when I'd been on the other side of this for years. "That explains why you didn't fight to keep the apartment."

"I don't give a shit about the apartment. The only reason I ever wanted it was because it tied us together legally. Without it—"

"I won't run. I made you a promise."

He spun the ring on his finger with his thumb, his eyes drawn to it. "I'm starting to wish you hadn't."

That felt like a sucker punch to the gut, a sting that hurt worse than ripping a stitch. "Do you want me to leave?"

His eyes shot up, finding mine. "That isn't what I want."

"What do you want?"

"This isn't just about me. What do you want? You've been distancing yourself, going for runs," he nodded at my side, "and finding things to keep you busy, this investigation for example, which your boss told you isn't a case."

"Leslie may not be missing, but something is going on." Thoughts of the men I encountered came to mind. I needed to run a check on Louis Grable. That man had scared me, and even if that had nothing to do with him and everything to do with me, ignoring my gut had proved harmful in the past. I moved toward my computer, but Martin closed the lid before I could start typing.

"You came home freaked out. Talk to me, Alex. Stop hiding behind distractions."

"I need to stay busy and focus on things I can solve. Our problem doesn't have a solution. We live here. You almost die. We stay at the apartment. I almost die. We go to L.A."

"And Bruiser almost died," Martin said.

"I was going to say a psycho came to our house there too." I saw the sadness in his eyes. "Stop blaming yourself for Bruiser. That's on me."

"It's not. Neither was what happened at the apartment."

"Both attacks linked directly to Cross Security cases. My cases. You can't deny the connection. I'm the commonality. I'm the reason."

"You didn't ask for this to happen."

"But it will happen again," I said. "No matter what we do, I can't stop it. I'm not okay with that, and I'm not sure I ever will be which is why I need to focus on the things I can fix."

Gently, he ran his hands up and down my sides before pressing his forehead against mine. "I'm not okay with this either, which is why I've decided it'll never happen again."

"How do you plan on stopping it?"

"Sheer willpower."

TEN

We didn't come up with a solution. There was no solution. I was no genius, but Martin was brilliant, or so he reminded me whenever the mood struck him, so if there was a solution, he should have said something. However, my brilliant, handsome man was smart enough not to say the one thing he thought would fix this because he knew better.

Quitting my job wasn't an option. Sure, I could walk away from Cross Security, but I couldn't walk away from investigating. For better or worse, that's all I was. I wasn't capable of doing anything else without it sucking the life out of me. I'd tried, but it wouldn't take. This was my calling, my cross to bear. I snickered at the pun. Lucien would love that.

Before going to bed, I had a tech pull the footage from the parking garage near the Golden. Since it wasn't owned by the hotel, I hoped Lucien wouldn't care that I asked our hackers, a.k.a. computer techs, to get it for me. Finding the garage owner and asking or paying for the footage would have required going out again, and I didn't have that in me tonight.

As I suspected, Leslie had parked her car, taken her bags, and left the garage. She hadn't gone back to her car since. Over the last two weeks, a few people had approached her vehicle, but every time, they'd been parked on either side of her. According to the parking garage information, the lot provided short and long-term parking options, meaning Leslie could leave her car there indefinitely without anyone getting annoyed or having it towed.

She has to be staying at the Golden, I told myself. But she just as easily could have left that parking garage, tossed her things into the back of a waiting car, and driven off into the sunset with the person of her dreams. Except she allegedly hadn't missed any work and hadn't used any of her personal devices. In all likelihood, that meant she was living at the hotel where she worked. How could she afford that?

Leslie wasn't making much as an intern, according to Deanna. And I hadn't seen any financial activity indicating she had paid for a room, but if the charges were adding up, they may not appear on her statement until she checked out.

"Martin, when we stay at a hotel, when do the charges show up on your credit card?"

He looked up from where he was reviewing the specs on the latest project from his R&D department. "Reconsidering Tuscany?"

"We'll go, if you want, just not yet." I sighed, resisting the urge to stretch. Stupid stab wound. "I'm not seeing any charges on Leslie's accounts. Wouldn't there be a pre-authorization charge to make sure the card was working?"

"There usually is. But it may have cleared by now."

I still couldn't figure out how she could afford to stay at the luxury resort for two weeks. "Do you think employees get a discount?"

"I'd say so."

I mulled that over while I entered Louis Grable's information into my search box. I'd run so many background checks lately, I could do this in my sleep. Grable's ID photo showed a younger, hairier version of the man I'd seen driving the green sedan.

He'd been arrested once for organizing a protest rally without a permit. That had been when he was a college sophomore. I tried to determine what he'd been protesting, but I couldn't find those details. Since then, he hadn't had so much as a parking ticket.

That seemed strange. Politically or socially minded individuals usually remained motivated to support their ideology, unless whatever issue he'd been protesting had been resolved. Maybe it was something simple, like keeping the dining hall open twenty-four hours. Or he'd done it to impress a romantic interest or mentor. I didn't really care. All I knew was that he'd given me the creeps, but that may have had more to do with my current hang-up than being menaced by Grable.

He never graduated college. Instead, he'd left soon after he'd been arrested, went to trade school to become a mechanic, and somehow ended up working at the Golden for the last seven years.

After checking to see if he had any contact with Leslie and coming up short, I decided to call it a night. Hopefully, everything would make sense in the morning.

But no matter how hard I tried, I couldn't sleep. Martin pulled me closer, but he didn't open his eyes. At least my racing thoughts didn't wake him.

I stared through the dark room, illuminated by the nightlight in the attached ensuite. The floor plan was wrong. The room dimensions didn't match up, but it didn't matter. This was my bed, the one I had from before we met, and in the attached sitting area of the second floor suite was my couch and love seat. I could see the silhouette of the oversized teddy bear Martin had bought seated on the couch, his back to us.

My desk was in the corner, along with my chair. My bookcase and TV stand were beside it. Martin thought sleeping here would make me more comfortable and help ease my mind. It was a nice gesture, but the only thing that would help was distance and time.

I took an unsteady breath, the anxiety pressing against my chest, but I did what I could to redirect my thoughts. I stared at the darkened TV and imagined a show playing on it.

My eyelids started to droop, and my breathing slowed. I

was safe. Martin was safe. Maybe we should think about hiring full-time security guards. Would that help? My thoughts drifted, turning to gibberish as I finally fell asleep.

Martin's alarm woke me the next morning. I turned my head to look at him, my neck sore from sleeping on my back. Our foreheads bumped, and he kissed me before reaching for his phone.

"Go back to sleep, sweetheart."

"What time is it?" I asked.

"Six."

I gave him a lopsided smile. "Who said you could sleep in?"

He graced me with a million-watt smile, the kind that would make supermodels drop their drawers. "I'll wake you up at seven."

"Lucien likes to start the morning meetings by eight, sometimes earlier. It depends on the day. Seven is too late. I should get up now."

"But you're not planning on attending the morning meeting. That gives you at least an extra hour." Martin got out of bed and stretched, his gaze on the nightstand.

"Are you reconsidering that no-sex moratorium? To be clear, the medic didn't say I couldn't have sex. Just no *Twister*."

Martin glanced at me, shaking his head. "You have a message."

"If it's Lucien—"

He held my phone out to me. "It's Heathcliff."

Let's meet for breakfast. 7AM. The diner on King St.

"That sounds cryptic," Martin said. "Should I be concerned?"

I sent a reply saying I'd be there and got out of bed, resisting the urge to stretch. That's how I reopened the wound the first time. "That depends? Are you worried Derek and I are having a torrid affair? If you are concerned, you should start putting out. I'm not into this 'we'll just cuddle' crap."

Martin came around the bed and met me on the other side. He pulled me to him and kissed my neck, which made my heart skip a beat and my stomach do a little flip. He nibbled on my earlobe before whispering, "Stop getting hurt so I can blow your mind all weekend long."

This time, it was the good kind of shiver that went through me. He pulled back and gave me a quick peck, looking self-satisfied and a little smug.

"I'll let Derek know he can skip the foreplay."

Martin's eyes grew dark, but he wasn't going to take the bait. "Promise me you'll be careful."

"Condoms, right."

"Alex, I'm serious."

"I know, and I will."

* * *

Detective Derek Heathcliff was dressed for work in a grey suit and black tie. His usually spit-shined shoes looked rough. The extra large coffee cup beside him and the stack of files clued me in that I shouldn't inquire as to why there were teeth marks covering the toes of his shoes.

I took a seat across from him and looked around. The diner was at half-capacity. For this place, that was considered the morning rush.

"I wasn't expecting you to call so early," I said.

"Something told me I'd better, or you were liable to take matters into your own hands." Dark circles ringed his eyes. "Tell me I'm wrong about that."

I wondered if he knew about my outing last night or if Voletek had ratted me out. I didn't think they were friends. "I told you I wouldn't go inside the Golden, and I didn't. I may have followed up on what we discovered at Leslie's apartment, though."

"Which is why a BOLO was issued for her car last night."

"I thought that got canceled."

"Where did you find it?"

"Parked in a lot near the Golden. According to the valet, that's where the employees park."

"Anything else I should know?"

I filled him in on everything he missed. "Martin thinks

Leslie's staying at the Golden. That would explain a few things, but it makes me question others. I don't know what to think."

Heathcliff rubbed his chin with one hand, scratching at the stubble. He hadn't bothered to shave this morning.

"Did you get any sleep last night?" I asked.

"Some." He gave me the once-over. "You're one to talk." He slid the stack of files toward me before picking up his cup and leaning back in his chair. "The research took longer than I thought since there have been several issues at the Golden in the last fourteen months."

"Besides that hit-and-run?"

"See for yourself."

I sifted through the files, finding reports that ran the gamut, most of which had been written off as accidents or natural causes.

"The hit-and-run happened eleven months ago. A member of the Golden's custodial staff was killed behind the hotel. Initially, I thought it may have been a carjacking gone wrong. The scene didn't make a lot of sense. Surveillance footage was spotty. We never saw exactly what happened. Accounts from other members of the staff said Hugh Pellers, the vic, had gotten out of his car for some unknown reason, when he was mowed down. The driver never stopped. The lack of skid marks suggests the driver didn't even hit the brakes. The door to Pellers' car was still open when police arrived at the scene."

"Which is why you thought carjacking."

"Yeah, but witness accounts and surveillance footage ruled that out. Vehicular homicide had to be the driver's intention."

"Because he didn't brake. Distracted or intoxicated drivers, even if they don't see the person, always try to stop after the fact." I flipped through the pages. Heathcliff took meticulous notes. He'd conducted a thorough investigation, but he never was able to ID a suspect. "Did you like anyone for it?"

"Not really. I could never come up with a reason why someone wanted Pellers dead. A carjacking gone wrong would have explained things, but witnesses said he wasn't carjacked. The surveillance footage showed a silver sedan whizzing past. The windows were illegally tinted, so there was no way to ID the driver. The plates were shielded. We issued a BOLO for the car. Patrol kept an eye out for silver sedans with illegal tinting, and they found dozens. However, none of them had the dents or damage indicative of a hit-and-run." Heathcliff took another sip of coffee before putting the cup down. "But that's not the only death which occurred on or near the Golden. A lot of people have died there. Fourteen to be exact."

"Murdered?"

"That's not what the reports say."

I picked up another folder, which had been ruled a suicide. "Did you investigate any of these?"

"None of them fell under major crimes' purview. Officers responded. If a sergeant couldn't address the issue, the investigation fell to homicide. I spoke to Jacobs since he floats between both units, but he only remembered one case. The accidental drowning."

I sifted through the files again until I found that one.

"Sue Shade, a maid, was restocking the pool towels when she slipped and fell into the pool. Blunt force trauma to her head and blood on the edge of the pool indicated she must have hit her head on her way down. She was unconscious when she landed in the water and drowned. Security camera footage and the coroner confirmed those events," he said.

I put the folder down. "I would say it's hard to argue with the evidence, but you have a lot of files here." I checked the dates. "That's one a month. Do they happen like that? Like clockwork?"

"Not to the day, not necessarily even to the week, but it's like the Golden is cursed. I compared these numbers to incident reports at other resorts of a similar size, and this is double the average." Heathcliff stared at the files. "That doesn't necessarily mean anything, but Leslie Stiller may be missing. And I'm not liking that."

"I don't like that either."

"Most of these incidents were nonviolent. The hit-and-run and a fatal mugging don't fit with the others." He pointed to the file at the bottom. "You didn't get to that one yet, but a bellhop was shot three times. Twice in the stomach, once in the head."

"This happened at the Golden?"

"Half a block away. He was on his way home, got jumped, and dragged into an alley. Reports of gunfire alerted us to the murder. No one saw anything. The only footage we found was of the guy getting grabbed by two men dressed entirely in black."

I studied the crime scene photos, glad that I hadn't ordered breakfast yet. "Were the killers caught?"

"Two arrests were made. The cops who collared them are positive they got the right guys, but the evidence is flimsy. We didn't recover the murder weapon. There's no physical evidence or DNA that ties either suspect to the crime scene, and, of course, they are insisting they're innocent."

"So why were they arrested?"

"They had the vic's belongings. One of them was wearing his watch and sneakers. The other was using his credit cards."

"But you're starting to think they're telling the truth, that they didn't do it."

Heathcliff rubbed his eyes. "I'm not saying that. But I'm tired. I haven't slept well in three weeks. I've been cataloging old cases and looking into our cold case files to see if any new tips or evidence have surfaced. That's involved making a lot of calls, following up with victims, loved ones, etc. So I'm not in the best frame of mind to assess this objectively."

"Are we talking a *Rear Window* scenario?"

"Who knows?"

"But you think there's something going on at the Golden." I gestured to the files. "You wouldn't have brought me this or mentioned any of it otherwise."

"You're supposed to be working from the office," he said.

"So are you." I waved down the server and ordered three large coffees. Two for me, and one for Heathcliff. "How do you think Leslie connects to this?"

"I don't know. But we need to find her and make sure she's okay."

"Agreed."

"Did you find anything useful on Cross's servers?"

"I found a few things, but not what I wanted."

"All right, let's take a ride to the Golden. I'm tired of getting jerked around. They will produce Leslie, or there will be hell to pay."

ELEVEN

Since Lucien prohibited me from taking this case, I left the company car at the diner and rode with Heathcliff to the hotel. Before stepping inside, I adjusted the baseball cap I'd grabbed on my way out, making sure the brim shielded my face.

"Why are you incognito?" Heathcliff asked.

"In case Lucien's right and Leslie's safe, I don't need someone from the Golden calling to ask why one of his investigators is at the hotel. It's best not to piss him off for no reason."

"Do you want to wait in the car?"

"No. This is my case. I have to see Leslie with my own eyes and find out what's going on. I owe Deanna that much."

"I thought she wasn't a client."

"She's not."

Heathcliff gave me a knowing look. "Uh-huh."

"Clients pay. Thus, she's not a client."

Heathcliff made his way to the front desk. Since it was early, there wasn't a line of people waiting to check-in. He sidled up to the counter and flashed his badge. "I need to speak to one of your interns, Leslie Stiller. This is official police business."

The same smile from yesterday returned to her face. "One moment please, Detective." She entered something into the computer. "I'm sorry. Leslie called in sick today."

"Where is she? My colleague and I tried to speak to her yesterday and were given the runaround. I'm not putting up with it again today." He narrowed his eyes at her name tag. "Call your supervisor or the hotel owner or whoever can tell me where Leslie is."

The smile remained on her face. "One more moment." She pressed a button beneath the desk, and a bellhop appeared. I recognized him from the photo on Leslie's corkboard. Brando Tascioni. "Please escort these police detectives to Leslie's room," she said.

Brando greeted us with the same smile. "Right this way." He gestured with a flourish toward the doorway which led to a wide corridor. "How is your day going so far? It looks like we should be having beautiful weather. Hopefully, it won't be too hot."

Heathcliff and I exchanged looks. Was this guy for real?

"Do you know Leslie Stiller?" I asked.

"We were in the same courtesy training sessions." Brando glanced back at us as we followed him to the elevator. He pressed the button. "Has Leslie done something wrong?"

"No." Heathcliff sized up the bellhop as he swiped the attached keycard which hung from a retractable lanyard on his chest through the slot at the bottom of the number panel before pressing twenty-eight. "Are you and Leslie friends?"

"Everyone at the Golden is like family."

I resisted the urge to gag. "Has Leslie ever mentioned her sister?"

"We only had that class together. We were focused on becoming the best versions of ourselves to better serve the guests here at the Golden. We didn't discuss anything outside of work."

"So you're not friends?" I asked. The photo on Leslie's wall indicated otherwise.

Brando kept smiling, but he didn't know how to respond. "I do my best to get along with all my coworkers."

“Do you live at the Golden?”

The doors opened, and Brando stepped out, gesturing to the left. “Leslie does. Room 2804 is on your left. Right this way, please.”

“We can take it from here,” Heathcliff said.

Brando kept smiling, but he looked unsure. “It’s no trouble.”

Heathcliff pushed his jacket aside, making sure his shield was on full display. “We’ve inconvenienced you enough.”

Brando stepped back into the elevator. “Have a wonderful day.” The doors closed.

“He knows her,” I said as we made our way to Leslie’s room. “He was in a group photo I found on her corkboard.”

“That doesn’t mean they’re close. It could be like he said. They took the same class, and everyone from that class was in the photo.”

I wondered if Brando had ring tattoos. Deanna had mentioned Leslie talking about a guy with ring tattoos, but I didn’t see any ink on him, not that I could see very much when the bellhop outfit covered most of his skin. “It must be miserable to wear that all day at work, especially now that it’s summertime.”

Heathcliff knocked on Leslie’s door. “Police,” he said, “open up.” He gave me a look. “What’s your point? Are you contemplating getting a job here?”

“I’m trying to figure out why he was so damn chipper.”

“The lady at the desk was just as friendly. There must be something in the air.”

The door opened with a groan. A pale, sickly looking Leslie Stiller stood on the other side wearing yoga pants and a lightweight hoodie. Her eyes were sunken in. She gave Heathcliff a confused, uneasy look. “How can I help you?”

“I’m Detective Heathcliff. This is my associate, Alex. I was hoping to follow up with you on a matter concerning your sister.”

Leslie’s pale skin turned a shade greener as panic spread across her face. “Is Deanna okay?”

“She’s fine. May we come inside?”

Leslie's gaze went to the security camera in the hallway before she said, "I'm sorry my sister dragged you into this. As you can see, I'm perfectly fine."

"You don't look fine. We were told you were sick," Heathcliff said.

"I got food poisoning from something I ate yesterday. Once it passes, I'll be right as rain."

"Where did you eat lunch yesterday?" I asked.

"At a hot dog cart near here. I guess I got what I deserved."

"May we speak inside?" Heathcliff asked.

Leslie looked uneasy. "I guess that would be okay. My roommates had to relocate until I'm back to normal. The doctor was afraid I might be contagious."

"I didn't know food poisoning was contagious," I said.

"In case it's the stomach flu." Leslie pulled the door open wider. "Deanna knows not to bother me at work. We aren't on speaking terms. I don't know why she behaved the way she did. I'm sorry she bothered you and for the inconvenience it caused." She sounded like a broken record, like she'd been rehearsing that speech nonstop.

"It's no trouble," I said. "We just have to take your statement, and then we'll get out of your hair."

Heathcliff played along. We'd worked together enough to back each other up without question or comment.

Leslie waited for us to enter before closing the door. Once we were inside, she flipped the security bar and melted against the door.

"Is everything okay?" Heathcliff asked. "We went by your apartment, but according to building security, you haven't been there in weeks."

"The Golden tries to be as accommodating as possible. As interns, especially these first few months, our duties rotate. We aren't assigned to do one thing. We're assigned to every position imaginable so the Golden can see where we excel and what would be an ideal fit for each of us. They base it on our aptitude and personality." She tried to muster the same smile we'd been given by every other person who worked at the hotel, but she couldn't quite manage to make it look convincing. "Because of that, we work long hours and a lot of split shifts. Sometimes, we'll only get three or four hours off before reporting to work again, so saving on travel time is ideal."

I looked around. Two sets of bunk beds stood on either side of the room. A rollaway bed was flush against the back wall, beside the dresser, which had five drawers. Each drawer was labeled with a woman's name. Leslie's was at the bottom. Free-standing wardrobes stood on either side of the bunk beds.

"How many roommates do you have?" I asked.

"Four." Leslie looked increasingly uncomfortable. "May we get on with it? I'm not feeling particularly well. What do you need to know about Deanna? She isn't in any trouble, is she?"

"No, but she's afraid you may be," I said.

Leslie arched an eyebrow. "I don't know what you mean."

"No one's been able to get a hold of you. You haven't answered your phone. When we tried to speak to you yesterday, we were given contradicting stories, and now we find you sick and forced into isolation. Are you even allowed to leave this room?"

"The Golden wants to make sure none of the guests end up sick in case this turns out to be the stomach flu instead of a bad hot dog. It's precautionary." Leslie swallowed uncomfortably. "I'm sorry for the misunderstanding."

"We can call an ambulance for you," Heathcliff said. "Food poisoning can be serious."

"The Golden has a doctor on staff. He already looked at me. Rest and fluids." She looked even queasier.

"Do you want to file a restraining order against your sister?" I asked.

"What?" The shock on Leslie's face was obvious. "No. Why would I want to do that?"

"She's harassing you, isn't she? You had a fight. You're not speaking, and she won't leave you alone."

"No. I don't want Deanna to get in trouble."

"Did you know the Golden had her arrested?" Heathcliff asked. "They didn't press charges, but she's banned for life." He glanced at me, unsure what I was doing. "That's why I had to speak to you, to see if you wanted to press charges."

"No, absolutely not."

"Okay, great." Heathcliff pulled out his notepad. "How can we contact you if we have any other questions? The number we have for you doesn't seem to be working."

"I don't have that phone anymore."

"You don't?" Heathcliff asked.

"It's dead. I haven't bothered to charge it."

"Why not?"

"The Golden provides us with everything we need." She pointed to the slim handset on the dresser. "That's my primary number now. You can call the Golden directly and ask to be connected to room 2804." She took the notepad and pen from his hand. "Here. I'll give you the main number." She wrote something quickly on the paper, tore it out of his book, folded it, and handed it to me. Then she clutched her stomach. "Excuse me."

She ducked into the bathroom, leaving the door cracked open in her haste. Heathcliff kept an eye on the bathroom door while I unfolded the paper. Leslie hadn't written down her number. Instead, she'd written, *Follow me*.

I waited a beat before saying, "Leslie, are you okay in there?" She didn't reply. "I'm going to check on her." I handed Heathcliff the slip of paper. "Hang on to that. We don't want to lose the number."

He glanced down at it and then at me. "Careful," he whispered.

"Leslie?" I knocked before slowly pushing the door open. She was sitting on the closed toilet seat lid, her knees pulled to her chest. She fought to keep the tears from falling as she bit her lip.

"Close the door," she whispered.

I gave Heathcliff a nod, letting him know I was okay, before pulling the door closed. "What's going on?" I asked.

"I think they're watching me. I can't leave. I can't talk. I can't do anything."

Automatically, I turned on the faucet, letting it run full blast before reaching in and turning on the shower. Then I pulled out my phone and used every trick and technique I'd learned and read about to check for hidden surveillance devices. It wasn't as foolproof as the scanners and other specialized equipment I usually used, but it'd do for now.

"The room's clean," I said, but I didn't turn off the running water. "What's going on?"

"Who are you?" Leslie asked. "You're not a cop. You don't have a badge."

"I'm a private investigator. Deanna asked me to find you. She was convinced something happened to you. I'm thinking she was right."

"Don't tell her that. I need you to tell her to go home. She has to go back to Ohio where it's safe. She can't be here. I...I don't know what will happen. But I need her far away from here." Leslie's words and timbre made the hairs at the back of my neck stand on end.

"Tell me what's going on."

Leslie stared at the floor.

"Are you safe here?" I asked.

"I don't know."

"The first thing we need to do is get you out of here. Heathcliff and I can walk you out the front door. No one will stop us. It'll be fine."

"No, it won't."

"Leslie—"

"They're on to me. I think they know I saw what they did. I'm not sure, though. But they've been keeping tabs on me ever since. They convinced me to live at the Golden, that it would give me a step up. They made it sound like a bonus, but I don't know. I don't know what to do anymore. And now that Deanna came here and got arrested, the Golden could press charges against her. Any crime, even a misdemeanor, could ruin her life. They could make her look mentally unstable. No one would want someone unbalanced taking care of them. And even if they don't go after Deanna, they can ruin me. This room is paid for out of my wages. It was part of the contract I signed. If I get fired or leave before the internship ends, they'll expect payment in full, and I don't have that kind of money. I can't—" She gasped a few times before jumping off the toilet seat lid, lifting it up, and vomiting into the porcelain bowl.

I knelt beside her, grabbing the few strands of hair that had fallen free from her ponytail and rubbing her back.

"Derek," I called.

He opened the door. "Is everything okay?"

"Call an ambulance. She's sick."

"No," Leslie said.

"It's how we're going to get you out of here so we can speak freely. They won't know why you're leaving. You won't be going with us. It'll be fine. I promise," I said.

She wiped her mouth. "You don't understand. I can't leave. I saw what they did to Gini, how they surrounded her in the laundry room, threatened her, and burned her. They don't know how much I saw. If I leave or go to the police, they'll think I ratted on them. Then they'll hurt me too. I have to stay here. I have to prove I'm with them, that I'm one of them, that I am part of the team. I have to get them to trust me again. It's the only way."

"Take a breath and tell me what happened. What did you see?" Heathcliff asked.

Leslie looked even more frightened. "Please, don't make me say anything. Promise me you'll protect Deanna, that you'll keep her safe."

I sat on the floor beside her, my back against the vanity. "I will, but I promised her I'd do the same for you. So I need to know what's going on."

"You can't do anything about this. You can't ask questions or investigate or flash that badge around."

That piqued Heathcliff's interest. "There's already an open investigation at the Golden regarding a hit-and-run that took place eleven months ago that I'm supposed to be investigating. Anything you say could be looked into under the guise of that. No one will know anything connects to you."

Leslie stared at me. "Did Deanna really come to you?"

"She did." I opened my bag and pulled out the notebook. "She brought me this as proof something was wrong. Your sister knows you better than anyone else."

Leslie flipped through the pages of the book with Deanna's notes written in the margins. "Promise me you will protect her no matter what."

"Okay," I said, knowing promises like that should never be made, "but only if you let us get you out of here."

TWELVE

Pounding on the door made Leslie tense. "Leslie, this is Karen Shaw. I came to check on you."

"They know," Leslie hissed, clutching her stomach.

Heathcliff gave me a look. He'd handle it.

I pulled the cap lower on my head and stood up as Heathcliff opened the door.

"Ms. Stiller's sick." Heathcliff gestured to the bathroom door. "I believe it'd be best to have an ambulance take her to the hospital to get checked out. Wouldn't you agree?"

Shaw entered the bathroom, barely noticing me as she made her way to Leslie, who was still kneeling beside the toilet. She rubbed Leslie's back. "The police officer is right. You should go to the hospital. You don't want to get dehydrated. Come on, I'll help you get your things together."

Leslie looked terrified, but she gave a weak nod before heaving again into the toilet.

Shaw turned to us. "You're upsetting her. She's sick. If you have any other questions—"

"We don't," Heathcliff said. "We just had to make sure she didn't want to file a restraining order against her sister." He nodded to Leslie. "I hope you feel better soon. Thanks for your time. I already called an ambulance.

They're on the way." He jerked his chin toward the door, and I followed him out, noticing that he'd tucked the note into his jacket. At least we hadn't left anything incriminating behind.

We took the elevator back to the lobby. We didn't speak again until we were inside his car. He had parked in the arrival section.

"What are we doing, Derek?" I asked, unsure of his play.

He kept his eyes on the hotel. "I only heard bits and pieces. What did she tell you?"

"Not enough." I went over everything she said, trying to make sense of her frantic, rushed statement. "She's terrified to leave the hotel."

The sirens announced the impending arrival of the ambulance. Soon flashing lights joined the party. The ambulance parked behind us, and Heathcliff stepped out. "Stay here."

"But—"

"Stay."

I wondered if he spoke to Spike the same way. No wonder his shoes were chewed up. But I remained in the car while Heathcliff briefed the EMTs. Once they entered the hotel, he got back into the car.

"Do you think Leslie has food poisoning?" I asked.

"You saw her. She's definitely sick."

"Do you think it's poison poisoning and not food poisoning?"

"The doctors should be able to figure that out." Heathcliff set his jaw and stared out the windshield, paying particularly close attention to the traffic patterns around us. "We need her to give us specifics, to spell everything out. What she said upstairs sounded like delirious ramblings."

"They weren't."

"I know, but without actionable intel, there's not much I can do. We need her to tell us more."

"She'll cooperate, just as long as we protect her sister."

"I thought Deanna wanted you to protect Leslie."

"Yep."

Heathcliff rubbed a hand over his face. "How do you

end up in the middle of these things?"

"Hell if I know."

As soon as the EMTs walked Leslie out, leaving the hotel manager in their wake, Heathcliff drove away. He didn't wait for them to load her into the ambulance. He wanted to make sure Mrs. Shaw saw that we'd left, that our business with Leslie Stiller was concluded.

"Do you think Leslie knows why so many people are ending up dead at the hotel?" I asked.

"The thought has crossed my mind. Regardless, she saw something she wasn't supposed to. That can't be good."

"Do you think the management was keeping her there against her will?"

"I don't know. Even if they were, she'd deny it, so I doubt we could do anything about it. But the situation didn't read well to me. Did you see that room? I've seen better conditions in sex trafficking cases."

"Derek–"

"You have a rapport with her. She'll talk to you. We just need to make sure no one is around to interfere or intimidate her."

* * *

Leslie Stiller had been given a private room in a locked ward to prevent anyone from getting to her. If asked, hospital staff would say that room assignment was temporary while they waited for an opening on another floor. But I didn't think anyone would ask. The only reason someone from the Golden would stop by the hospital to see Leslie was if they planned to threaten her or silence her. And since we couldn't afford for officers to be spotted outside her door, this was the best way to keep her safe and ensure our conversation remained private.

Regardless of the precautions, I'd performed a costume change, borrowing a pair of Jen O'Connell's scrubs, a face mask, and a surgeon's cap to keep me unrecognizable. That had been Heathcliff's idea. Usually, I was the paranoid lunatic, but the goings on at the Golden had him on edge.

"Leslie," I said, entering her room, "how are you

feeling?"

She looked like she wanted to bolt. "I have to get back there. Who knows what will happen if I don't?"

I held up my palms as I approached her bed. "Take it easy. No one knows we're here or that you're talking to us. All they know is you're sick and the hospital is treating you."

Heathcliff stepped into the room with a white lab coat, surgeon's cap, and a face mask. He unhooked it from his left ear and gave her an apologetic smile. "You said they were watching you. We needed to get you away from there. You're safe now."

"I have to go back," she screeched. "You don't understand. I can't afford to quit the program. The Golden owns me. I signed my soul over to them. I have to stick this out."

"That contract isn't enforceable if you were coerced or if you're in danger," I said.

"I wasn't coerced. I applied. I wanted this." She sniffed, her skin growing a little paler. "Well, I thought I did. I didn't know it'd be like this." She winced, grasping her stomach. The ache may have been the only thing keeping her from crying.

"What is this?" Heathcliff asked. "What happened? Start at the beginning."

"In the beginning, things were fine." She hiccupped. "Everything was how I thought it'd be. Hard work, long hours. We were learning the ropes. But some people were taking it too far."

"What do you mean?"

"We did a lot of team building, a lot of morale boosting, pep rally kind of things. They wanted us to have pride in the Golden. The better we made the hotel, the better we'd look. It always felt a little too rah-rah for me. Like those life coaches who try to sell miracle cures. Do you know what I mean?"

"Like a cult leader?" I asked.

Leslie turned to face me. "I don't know. It was about building us up, giving us permission to do things, telling us how great we were doing. They kept saying we were the rising tide and the ships. That we could make our own destiny and reach our own goals."

That's why Deanna had used that same language about the tide and the ships. "What went wrong?"

"Gini fell behind. She fell behind a lot. She didn't expect to have to do manual labor. She thought the internship program would allow us to pick our disciplines. She wanted to learn the ins and outs of running a hotel, not parking cars or cleaning rooms. She didn't like most of the tasks she was assigned, and everyone knew it. She complained a lot, and that was something we were never supposed to do. It was all about being happy."

"I'd never make it," I said.

Leslie snorted. "Neither did Gini. I had finished my duties for the day and thought I'd see if she needed help."

"Rising tide, right?" Heathcliff said.

Leslie nodded. "Gini was on laundry duty. She was running the big steam press to make the sheets crisp. When I got there, she was surrounded. I think there were four of them. They were taunting her, bullying her. It reminded me of the kind of nasty shit you'd see on the playground. Y'know, when the big dumb kid and his friends would surround the smart kid and push him and tease him."

"Were they doing that to Gini?" Heathcliff asked.

"Yes, but it got worse." She turned, picking up the bucket from the table beside her and vomiting into it.

I looked away, circling toward the door to keep my own stomach contents from decorating the floor of the hospital room. The place already had an odor. This would make matters worse.

Heathcliff looked just as queasy, but he didn't move from the spot. A nurse entered, let Leslie rinse her mouth, and replaced the bucket with a new one.

"Do you know what's wrong with her?" I asked.

The nurse looked at Leslie, who nodded that it was okay to answer the question. "Salmonella. She should be able to clear the infection on her own, but we're treating her for dehydration. Once she shows signs of improvement, we can discharge her."

Leslie slid down in the bed. “I told you it was a bad hot dog.”

“It was a bad something,” I said.

“What happened to Gini?” Heathcliff asked, hoping to get her story back on track now that the nurse had left.

“They shoved her arm under the steam press and brought it down on top of her.” Leslie’s chin quivered. “Gini screamed. They threatened her not to say anything or next time it’d be worse. And then, they left her there. I was right outside the door. I had seen what happened, but I don’t know if they know that. They told me there had been an accident, and they were getting help. I went in to see Gini, but she didn’t say anything about it. She was too afraid.” Tears fell from Leslie’s eyes.

“She may have been in shock,” I said.

Leslie sniffed. “Later that evening, I was called into Mrs. Shaw’s office and commended for acting so quickly to help a colleague. I tried to tell her what happened, that four other employees had been in the laundry room, that they had hurt Gini, but Shaw wouldn’t listen. Everything I said she twisted, making it sound like they were there to help, that they got the doctor and called the ambulance. Then she started asking me questions like why I wasn’t staying at the Golden with the rest of the interns. She kept complimenting me, saying what an asset I was, how she wished more of the interns were like me, and how she was sure I could have a bright future with the company. But she made that sound like it was dependent on me living there, so I agreed. I’m not sure why. Everything about that day is a jumble, like a big confusing swirl that doesn’t make a lot of sense when I look back on it. I don’t know why I agreed or why I let her convince me what I saw wasn’t what I saw. Or maybe it wasn’t. I don’t even know anymore. But I can’t get it out of my head. I don’t even know if Gini was attacked. Maybe they were helping. I just...I can’t.”

“What happened to Gini?” Heathcliff asked.

“I don’t know. She never came back to work.”

Heathcliff flipped open his notepad. “What’s her last name?”

“Ruffin.”

"Why didn't you report this?"

Leslie looked ashamed. "Honestly, I'm so twisted around I was afraid the police would tell me I was crazy, and then Mrs. Shaw would fire me on the spot. No one else acknowledged what happened or even brought it up. Security was supposed to investigate. There are cameras everywhere, but they didn't see anything on the footage. Maybe I got it wrong. Maybe it wasn't like that. But what if that is what happened? The Golden made the incident with Gini vanish. No one talks about it. No one even noticed Gini's gone. And now that they had Deanna arrested and I'm on the hook for eight months of rent, I can't bail. I don't have a choice but to keep my head down and wait for the internship to end."

"There's an easy way to find out if you're crazy," I said.

Leslie gave the locked door a look. "Does the hospital test for that?"

"Not in my experience, so I think you can relax. The simpler solution would be talking to Gini."

Heathcliff pulled out his phone and dialed the precinct. "Run Gini Ruffin, like muffin but with an r. I need to know if she filed a report. I'll wait." He paused. "Uh-huh. You're sure?" He paused again. "Okay. Send me her details."

"Okay, what?" I asked.

He shook his head. "She didn't make a report."

"This would be the hospital they took her to for treatment." I looked at Leslie. "When did this happen?"

"A little over two weeks ago. The day before I moved out of my apartment."

"All right. I'll be right back."

THIRTEEN

Getting hospital staff to offer patient information was like asking a Catholic priest to share what a parishioner said in the confessional. It wasn't impossible, but it would require a miracle. Cross had ways of making his own miracles. Those were all highly illegal, the details of which I didn't even want to know, but since I wasn't at the point where I could ask for help, I went a different route.

"Two weeks and three days ago?" Jen O'Connell stood in front of the computer at the nurse's station, scanning the list. "One patient was treated for severe burns to her left arm."

"That would be her," I said. "What else can you tell me?"

"Her bill was paid by Experiential Adventures."

"What about her address, phone number, things like that?"

Jen gave me a look. "Don't you usually ask Nick for these details?"

"Heathcliff already made a call. I'm sure he has all of that by now, but I like to wow him by knowing the answers ahead of time."

Jen chuckled. "I can do you one better."

"Oh yeah?"

"Gini's currently in the burn unit. She was discharged

two days later but was readmitted seven days after that for an infection. She's in room 702."

"Has anyone been by to see her?"

Jen glanced around before tapping a few times on the screen. "Her emergency contact was notified, but her mother lives out of state. I would assume she made the trip, but I can't say for certain."

"All right. Thanks."

Jen gave me a look. "Do I want to know what's going on?"

"Probably not."

I took the elevator to the burn unit. Gini was in a clean room. Getting inside to speak to her wouldn't be easy. Since I wasn't family and didn't have a badge, there wasn't much I could do. So I texted Heathcliff while I made my way back to Leslie's room. He met me in the hallway.

"I'll see what Gini has to say, and I'll meet you back here." He pointed to the chairs near the nurse's station. "I'm thinking it'd be best to discuss this in private before sharing any of it with Leslie."

"Agreed." I glanced at the closed door to Leslie's room. "Text me when you're on your way back." Then I went to see Leslie.

"Detective Heathcliff said Gini's still in the hospital. Is she okay?" Leslie asked.

"She has an infection. That's all I know." I leaned against the wall, wishing we could be having this conversation somewhere a little more pleasant. "Tell me what it's like working at the Golden."

"It's great," she said automatically.

"Really?"

She frowned, thinking about it. "No. It sucks. Even before everything that happened, it still sucked. They work us to the bone. We barely have any time to ourselves. First, we had to go through classes. Then, it was hands-on training. That wasn't too bad. I learned a lot about how things work and how they get done."

"How the sausage is made?"

She scowled, gripping her stomach.

"Sorry," I said.

"Learning that stuff was fun. Sure, a lot of times training would run over or we'd be asked to stay late. But all of that felt beneficial. But once we started performing the work, it stopped being fun. Everyone inside the hotel has a specific job. Those jobs are very important to keep things running smoothly and to keep the guests happy. But they can be miserable. Do you know maids aren't supposed to clean when the guests are in their rooms? Even if the guest doesn't mind or insists, it's company policy. That blows my mind. The food service people, the ones who work in the coffee shops, bars, and restaurants, have to start prepping hours before the places open and stay well past close. There is just so much work that goes into everything that I never even imagined."

"Didn't you major in hospitality?"

"Yes, but seeing real world applications is a lot different from words in a textbook."

"But everyone at the Golden is so happy."

Leslie snorted. "It's because we're all punchy from being sleep-deprived." She shrugged. "I don't know. Before Gini, I would call Deanna every night and she'd ask about my day. And then she'd tell me it sounded horrible. I always got so offended when she said that, and then I'd insist she was wrong. That it was awesome. That I was having fun. I guess I owe her an apology."

"It sounds like you were brainwashed into drinking the Kool-Aid."

Leslie looked around the hospital room. "But even now, I'm itching to get back to it. What is wrong with me?"

"You aren't afraid they could do to you what they did to Gini?"

"I am, but I'm more afraid of what they'll do to me or Deanna if I don't go back. And the voice in the back of my head keeps whispering to me that I'm wrong. That Gini's accident was just that—an accident. That I'm making this shit up in my head and that I'm self-sabotaging myself because I'm afraid to find out I don't have what it takes to make it as a Golden employee, that this whole thing was a mistake, that my dad was right, and that I never should have left Ohio."

"Shit happens. When it does, it makes us question ourselves and our abilities. And sometimes, it makes us think we're losing our minds. Maybe you are." I cracked a smile. "I can see if the hospital can run a test, if you like. But I think you know what really happened and wish more than anything that you're wrong, that the world isn't like this, that it is the way it's supposed to be, the way you want it to be."

"I must sound so stupid. I really owe Deanna an apology."

"Do you want me to tell her where you are?"

"No. I want her on the first flight back to Ohio."

"You could go with her," I said.

"I can't. I have too much to lose."

"So you're going to go back to the Golden?"

"I have no choice."

Maybe Leslie was crazy. Or maybe this was what Martin felt like every time we had a conversation. I should thank him for not locking me in a padded cell. "Do you know of anyone else who was hurt at the Golden?"

Leslie thought carefully. "A guest had a cardiac event. I don't know the details, but we heard whispers about it when we were going through classroom training. In fact, they used that as an excuse to make sure we all had our CPR certifications and were familiar with how to use AEDs, radio for help without alerting other guests, and follow the procedures laid out in the handbook."

"Was that the only instance?"

Leslie studied my expression. "You already know the answer to that question."

"I want your answer."

"A bellhop committed suicide a few weeks ago. The only reason I know that is because everyone's assignments were shifted around for that week to make up for his absence. But management never made an announcement. They never said anything to us. I only heard a few of the full-timers whispering about it, but it was more a rumor than actual news." She stared at me. "Is it true? Is that what happened?"

"That's what the police files say."

"You don't believe that."

"I don't know what I believe." My phone chimed. "I'll be right back. If you need anything, call a nurse."

Heathcliff had his phone in his hand, but he hadn't made a call yet. He stopped pacing when he saw me coming and shook his head. "Gini won't provide a statement. She's too afraid to come forward."

"But someone who works at the Golden hurt her?"

"More than one someone, but she won't name names. She says she doesn't know who was responsible and doesn't want to make waves. She wouldn't go into any details, but I saw the gift basket in her room and a fancy thick envelope from a corporate law office."

"The Golden paid her to keep quiet."

Heathcliff nodded. "Most of the time, I'd be pissed, but this time, I can't help but think it's better than the alternative."

"You think they'd kill her to keep her quiet."

"The files I showed you this morning suggest that's a possibility."

I looked back at Leslie's closed door. "They don't know what Leslie saw. Even she's confused and conflicted about the incident. That's why they wanted her to move into the hotel. They're keeping watch on her to see which way she's going to land."

"She needs to walk away," Heathcliff said. "That's her safest bet."

"Except she refuses." I met his eyes. "You could use her as an informant to build your case. It's not ideal, but at least you could keep tabs on her that way."

"I'm on desk duty. How is that going to work?"

I ran through every scenario, but Leslie was scared and stubborn. Instead of running out of the burning building, she wanted to hide in the closet. No matter what I said or did, I wouldn't be able to coax her out of there. The only thing to do was to find a way to put the fire out before it killed her.

"Alex," Heathcliff eyed me, "whatever you're thinking, you can't do it. You're still on the mend. You're not in the right headspace for this. You know you aren't."

"Headspace for what?"

"Don't give me that. We both know what you're thinking about doing."

"Do you have enough for the police department to open an official investigation, to plant undercovers inside the hotel, and to keep an eye on Leslie?"

He pressed his lips together. "You know I don't."

"Leslie would reject a protection detail or bodyguard, so what choice do I have? Waiting to see what happens isn't a solution. Even if Leslie survives, given what we've seen and heard today, I'm having trouble believing all those deaths were accidents. Someone else is going to end up on that list, and I won't be able to live with myself if I don't do something to stop it."

"What about Cross? Isn't he protecting the Golden?"

"He won't be once I tell him what we found." I reached for my phone, but Heathcliff grabbed my arm.

"Are you sure he won't sell you or Leslie out?"

"I'm betting my life on it."

FOURTEEN

"Lucien, we need to talk," I said, surprised to find him in my office with two members of maintenance mounting a giant whiteboard to the wall. Lucien Cross stood in the doorway, his hands shoved in his pockets, while he supervised. He turned at the sound of my voice.

"I wondered when you'd get here." He glanced at his expensive watch. "You missed the morning meeting."

"Were you going to assign me a real case?"

"No." He jerked his chin toward the blue folder waiting on my desk. "But I have work for you to do."

"More security assessments and background checks?" I didn't have time for this. "They're going to have to wait."

He ran a hand through his hair. "What's going on? Is this about what we discussed yesterday?"

"Oh, you have no idea what's going on."

His sharp look silenced me. "Gentlemen, are you almost finished?"

"Just give us another minute," the guy with the overalls said.

I started to say something, but Lucien gave me the same sharp look. "Wait," he hissed.

Once maintenance was done installing the whiteboard, they collected their tools, nodded to us, and stepped out.

Lucien watched them head down the hall before closing the door and turning to me. "What happened?"

"Where do I even begin?"

"Spit it out, Alex. I have a meeting in twenty minutes."

"Are you aware there have been fourteen suspicious deaths at the Golden in the last fourteen months?"

"Suspicious?" He glanced at his phone.

"That's just the tip of the iceberg." I unloaded everything Heathcliff had told me at breakfast, the things Leslie had said, and what I'd learned since then. "Leslie Stiller is terrified what the Golden may do to her, but she won't leave. She's afraid they'll retaliate against Deanna or try to enforce some kind of charge for the room if she drops out of the program."

"Why did she let them talk her into that if she was afraid someone at the hotel intended to harm her?"

"I don't know. She was scared and confused. She's still scared and confused. She isn't even sure what she thinks happened actually happened."

"Maybe it didn't."

"Maybe you'd like to go to your meeting with a black eye."

Cross snickered, rubbing a hand over his mouth to cover it up. "It's a valid comment. On top of that, why won't Gini Ruffin come forward?"

"They paid her off."

"You're sure?" The look on Cross's face told me he wasn't surprised.

"Pretty sure. I didn't speak to her, but Heathcliff seemed certain."

"Fuck." Lucien cleared his throat and stalked the confines of my office. "Okay."

"Okay what?"

"You said fourteen people have died on the property in fourteen months. Surely, not every case was the result of," he made a vague gesture, "bad actors. The detective told you half that number was typical for a resort that size."

"Seven would be the average," I said.

"All right. I'll look into them and see what can be eliminated. Maybe the hotel had a string of bad luck.

Averages can fluctuate. Things change. Bad luck, bad circumstances."

"That doesn't change any of the things I told you about Leslie. She's sick. The hospital said it's food poisoning, but—"

"You don't believe it."

"I don't want her to become unlucky number fifteen."

"Alex, do you hear yourself?"

"Excuse me?"

"The Golden is a vacation spot. Travelers aren't always in the best health or make the best decisions. Things happen. I don't think someone at the Golden murdered fourteen people and managed to make every death look like an accident or natural causes. No one is that good."

"The hit-and-run, the fatal mugging," I started ticking the incidents off on my fingers, "Gini Ruffin getting attacked. Those three events alone make me wonder about the suicides and accidents that happened to members of the Golden staff. Maybe, and this is a big maybe, the police were correct in ruling out foul play whenever a guest died, but not the staff."

"Like I said, I'll look into it. While I do that, I need you to be sure about this." He pointed to the files he had put on my desk. "You'll want to start there."

"More security assessments. Are you kidding me?"

"For once, do what I say." He headed for the door. "I'll find you after I have time to review everything, and we'll go from there." He stared at me. "Shit. You already have a plan in mind. I told you I'm not letting you work an investigation until your side heals."

"You also told me you can't take Deanna on as a client because you represent the Golden."

"I don't represent—" He stopped, realizing he was yelling. Letting out a resigned huff, he said, "I need time to figure out what's going on. I suggest you do the same. Right now, what you've been told isn't making a lot of sense. There are a lot of moving parts and pieces that don't necessarily fit into this puzzle. Sort them out. Then we'll figure out where we go from here."

I knew where I wanted to go, but I'd need help in the

form of technical support.

"Read the files, Alex." He pointed to the folder on my desk before letting himself out and slamming the door behind him.

If I opened the folder and found more busy work, I'd lose my mind. But the file contained details on the Golden, members of upper management, and our security assessments.

My boss had to protect himself and his company, but he hadn't lied when he said he had no intention of protecting a client who was responsible for heinous acts. He must have found something in this mess, or he deferred to my gut instinct that there could be more to Leslie Stiller's unexplained radio silence than the Golden wanted us to think. Those were the only theories I could come up with as to how he knew I'd need these files, unless he was clairvoyant. That would explain how he amassed enough money to operate Cross Security. Maybe I should ask him for lotto numbers or the point spread on the next big game.

Most of the information contained within the folder looked like run-of-the-mill assessments and background checks. Cross Security had assessed the Golden's digital security, user interface, online bookings, and checkout protocols to ensure they were top of the line. We'd also performed a review of their internal systems, making sure their firewalls and anti-hacking protections were up-to-date.

None of that helped me. Cross Security hadn't created a backdoor into the Golden's systems, at least not according to Cross's notes. Given the hotel's updated protections, rotating passwords, and software upgrades, whatever methods we used to access its systems to conduct these evaluations were no longer viable.

The physical security assessment had to do with proper locking mechanisms throughout the resort, safety features, like fire extinguishers and first aid kits being readily accessible, and enough surveillance cameras strategically placed to minimize blind spots and provide ample monitoring without breaching guest privacy. Diagrams and maps were included, laying out every floor of the hotel.

Those would be useful. I thought about making a copy, but in case Cross and I didn't end up on the same page, which is what our argument indicated, I snapped photos on my phone instead.

Martin and I had spent a lot of time at most of the upscale places in the city, but we'd never gone to the Golden. Given what I now knew about the place, I was glad we hadn't. But a lot of planning and thought had gone into their security. Lucien had made sure the hotel was a fortress, which was why so many of the reported deaths had been ruled accidental or due to natural causes. The place had camera footage of just about everything. Yet, the laundry room, specifically the area near the steam press, had a blind spot. However, cameras covered the doors and half of the room. Whoever attacked Gini would be on the footage, even if the attack wasn't. Management would have names. Why didn't they do anything? Or did they send that mob after Gini because she was holding back the rising tide?

I'd suggested the team building they utilized sounded a bit like a cult. Now, I was starting to think that hadn't been an exaggeration. Could someone be using that to grow a following?

Before going any further down that paranoid rabbit hole, I turned my attention to the background checks. An entire lecture at Quantico had been taught on cult leaders, but that had been a general overview. The more specialized units, like Behavioral Analysis and Violent Crimes, had more in-depth training. But red flags were red flags.

However, the members of the Golden's upper echelon didn't have criminal records. Every member of the team, from operations manager to head of security, was clean. However, Cross had circled one name—Ian Choi.

Choi didn't have a photo attached to his file like the rest of the management team. Choi was the senior executive in charge of public relations. That was a fancy title for a man who didn't have a face. His background check was perfectly tidy and basic. Too basic.

Turning my attention to the computer, I tried running my own check, but the results that popped up were the same as what Cross had found. I tried conducting an internet search. Choi's name was buried on the Golden's website with the legal jargon and the required list of executives. That was it.

I looked at the intel Cross had put together, finding a list of previous positions Choi had held prior to joining the team at the Golden. But the internet had no information on any of that. No photos. No past history. Those were red flags. Yet, Choi still had a job. Surely, Cross had expressed his concerns when submitting his security assessment, but someone at the Golden or Experiential Adventures already knew who Choi really was or didn't care.

While I mulled over what this meant, I examined the new whiteboard which opened in the middle to reveal a giant corkboard with two more magnetic whiteboards on the other side of the doors. This was nice. Maybe nice enough to make me want to try harder not to get fired.

Picking up a marker, I tested it on the interior door, making sure it would wipe off before I started writing. And then it was a flurry of words and thoughts and theories. Somewhere in the midst of the mental diarrhea it hit me. Choi's a fixer.

That meant the Golden knew they had a problem and hired someone to bury it. I went back to the folder. Choi had been hired fourteen months ago, within days of the first suspicious death.

"Knock, knock." Kellan called from the other side of my office door.

I threw the door open, hoping I didn't look as crazed as I felt. "What?"

"Lucien asked me to bring you this." He held up a heavy-duty padlock in one hand while his other maintained a firm grip on a paper coffee cup. "He said it was for your new whiteboard cabinet."

"Thanks."

"It looks like you've been busy. I'm guessing that," he pointed to my insane scribbles, "is why Lucien decided you needed a new toy."

"Jealous?"

"A little bit."

I took the lock and removed the attached keys. "Don't be. I'm sure it was installed to impress my replacement. Lucien's getting cheap. Instead of a signing bonus, the next guy gets this." I gestured like Vanna White revealing a new puzzle.

Kellan held out the cup of coffee which he'd been holding in his other hand.

"Is that for me?" I asked.

"It was, but now I'm afraid to give it to you. It may make your head explode."

"My head may explode anyway. The caffeine will have little bearing on that."

"Well, it's cold, so pretend I got you an iced cappuccino this morning," he said.

"I don't think they make iced, but I don't mind cold."

"That doesn't surprise me." He put the cup on my desk and glanced down at the blue folder. "If you need any help on anything, let me know. I finished that insurance fraud case, so I have a free morning."

"Do you know anything about the security assessment Lucien ran on the Golden Hotel about a year ago?"

Kellan leafed through the folder. "I can't say that I do."

"What about Ian Choi?"

"Choi." Kellan let the name play across his lips. "It sounds vaguely familiar. Not from anything I worked on here, but maybe from my DEA days."

"He was working for the cartels?"

"Not exactly." Kellan shifted his head from side to side like a boxer before a bout. "We never had proof of anything, but he showed up a time or two to keep suspected bigwigs out of trouble. Bodies never turned up. Evidence disappeared. Crime scenes were cleaned. Things like that."

"He's a fixer."

Kellan made a strange noise, a mix of a laugh and a snort. "He called himself a lawyer."

Choi's background check showed he graduated from a top-tier law school and was a card-carrying member of the BAR in several states. "I'd say that doesn't even begin to describe what he is."

FIFTEEN

I put the notebook Deanna had given me on top of my desk and stared at it. A very big part of me was terrified Leslie would end up the fifteenth victim at the Golden. Our short meeting had done nothing to quell my fears. In fact, it only amplified them, so I dove back into Cross's research.

From what I could see, security was sufficient. Surveillance was more than adequate. People shouldn't die at the resort, and they definitely shouldn't be killed.

I leafed through my copies of the police reports, stopping on the drowning. Sue Shade, a member of the Golden staff, drowned in the pool. According to the police report, surveillance cameras had caught the entire thing, but no one ran out to help. Where was security? Where was the Golden's doctor? How come the woman wasn't discovered until the next morning, almost eight hours after she went into the water?

My phone rang, and I jumped. It was Kate. She had called with the list of Experiential Adventures' properties.

"Are they flagged in any of the databases?" I asked.

"No."

"What about the Golden?"

"I've always wondered how you know the things you

do."

My stomach clenched, which made my side hurt. "What's going on?"

"I'm serious, Alex. Your first solo assignment, you stuck your neck out because you had a hunch."

"I wasn't solo. I had Michael."

"He thought you were crazy too."

I wasn't enjoying this painful trip down memory lane. "Would you mind getting to the point, Kate? A woman's life may be in danger."

"Right, sorry. I'm sorry."

"Yeah, me too." I'd never not be sorry about what happened to Michael, even if I'd learned to forgive myself for it.

"The Golden Resort isn't under investigation, but the location has been dinged a few times. I asked around, but it's not currently part of any active ops."

"But it has been in the past?"

"Not exactly, it was the site of passive surveillance. Fact-finding. Data collection. That sort of thing."

I made sure my office door was closed before I said, "Fourteen people have died there in the last fourteen months."

"Shit. You're serious?"

"Unfortunately."

"Are you thinking serial killer? That would—"

"The police ruled most of those deaths accidental or due to natural causes. I don't think anyone is thinking this is a serial crime." Except for Heathcliff and me. "Is OCU investigating the hotel? They're known for their so-called passive surveillance." I looked through the list of Experiential Adventures' holdings, finding properties in Las Vegas, Reno, and Atlantic City. The resorts could be mob-controlled, but if they were, Cross had failed to realize it.

"OCU kept an eye out for a while," she said, "but they didn't find any connection to a crime family. They're all legit businesses."

Okay, so Cross hadn't missed anything major. I'd have to give him brownie points for that.

"The DEA looked into the Golden too," she said, "specifically shipments it was receiving from its resorts south of the border. But they gave up their investigation too."

"Why was everyone convinced the Golden was involved in something shady?"

Kate made a humming noise, which meant she didn't want to answer the question but hadn't figured out how to avoid it. "I'd say it was speculation."

"It's the fourteen bodies in fourteen months."

"Surveillance happened a while ago. We're talking eight and ten months ago. OCU and the DEA stuck with it for two to three months, but never heard or saw anything relevant to their investigations."

"Did they exchange information with the local PD?"

"I'm assuming so. But you'd have to ask Jablonsky."

"Thanks, Kate. This helps."

"Does it?"

I shrugged, forgetting she couldn't see me. "It gives me a few places to start digging. Let's just hope I don't find any buried bodies." The list she gave me included every asset Experiential Adventures owned. In the city, that included the Golden Resort, a warehouse nearby which had been labeled as a storage unit, and a parcel of land they had not built upon yet. "I have to jump off here. Thanks again."

"Don't forget about the booze cruise."

"I won't, no matter how hard I try."

"Alex—"

"Bye, Kate."

I put the phone down and checked to see if Cross Security had any additional information on the Golden or the surrounding area.

Deciding there was nothing else in Cross's files or Kate's that would get me anywhere fast, I reached for the files Heathcliff had given me at breakfast and pulled up everything I could on each of the deceased. The police had reason to believe these weren't murders. But under the circumstances, Heathcliff wasn't convinced they'd made the right call every time, and neither was I.

On the surface, these deaths looked innocent enough.

The victimology, if that's what it was, didn't follow the usual patterns. Age, gender, and race varied. Causes of death ranged from age-related illnesses, accidents, suicides, a hit-and-run, and a violent mugging gone wrong.

None of the deaths followed a pattern. Even if coincidences didn't happen, which was what Mark always told me, these deaths couldn't be attributed to a single source. They were too different, but was there a pattern within this mess?

I only started looking into this to find Leslie Stiller. Now, I had over a dozen deaths to investigate and the growing fear that if I didn't figure it out in time, Leslie would be next. I could already see the report. *Cause of death: Complications due to food poisoning.*

The only way I could stop this from happening again was to get access to the Golden and keep an eye on things. Leslie said four people had surrounded Gini. I'd encountered a group of four in the garage when I'd gone looking for Leslie's car, but that didn't mean anything. The chances that I encountered the same four who had been responsible for the attack were highly unlikely. Yet, Louis Grable had set my radar buzzing. Maybe that panic attack hadn't been about my past experiences and had been about him.

I printed a copy of his photo ID to show to Leslie when I headed back to the hospital later. The mess of notes and intel on my desk reminded me I was spinning too many plates at the same time. "Focus, Parker."

I needed more intel on Ian Choi. Cross's files and the internet hadn't been much help. Choi was a professional. He knew how to erase his tracks. So I left Mark Jablonsky a voicemail asking if he could look into Choi and let me know if the Bureau or any other government agency had a file on the guy.

According to Kellan, the DEA ran across him a time or two. While I had a few contacts at the agency I could call, I didn't want to open that can of worms. If push came to shove, I'd ask Kellan to make some calls on my behalf, but something told me Mark would get me what I needed.

However, it would be nice to convince Cross to get

behind this investigation. I was prepared to go it alone, but the more resources I had at my disposal, the better it'd be. The safer it'd be, and since Heathcliff had pointed out I wasn't in the right headspace and Cross pointed out I wasn't functioning at a hundred percent, it wouldn't hurt to have support teams on standby if I needed them. So I went back to looking for patterns among the fourteen potential victims.

Predators always followed a process individualized to their needs and rituals, but a few fundamentals remained the same. After selecting a victim, isolating that victim was step number two. That was true for lots of crimes. Most premeditated murders required isolation. But it was also true for a lot of con jobs, Ponzi schemes, and terrorist and cult recruiters. Keeping an individual away from family and friends made convincing them to buy into the bullshit that much easier since they didn't have a trusted outside source to point out how bonkers the scheme or ideology was. And from what Leslie had said, the Golden was doing the same thing with its interns.

Maybe these cases Heathcliff gave me were causing me to lose sight of my main objective, so I turned my focus back to the Golden's internship program. Since it was a coveted position for so many young adults, I hoped to find more details about it online. When I originally looked, I'd only been interested in finding people who had contacted Leslie. Now, I'd take whatever information I could get on the program and the Golden.

The first place I checked was the FAQ section on Experiential Adventures' internship application. The website didn't go into many details about the program. Almost every answer said to check with the recruiter, but I couldn't find any contact information or a form to fill out to reach said recruiter.

I found a few people who had been chatting about their experiences working at the Golden on a message board. Half of the posts were the usual internet bullshit, but one person had asked a very specific question: *I need details on where the interns are housed. Does the Golden have a separate facility or apartment building?*

Someone else responded with: *The interns live at the hotel. They have a dedicated floor.*

How many roommates?

That depends on the size of the room.

Do you get to pick?

No.

I right-clicked each of the users, but these were old messages from four years ago. Both accounts were now inactive. Amir could get me their real names, so I called him with my request. But besides that message board post, graduates of the internship program didn't post online. Had everyone else gotten jobs with Experiential Adventures and been prohibited from posting about it? Or did Ian Choi scrub any negative mention of the Golden and the internship program from existence? My money was on the latter. Unfortunately, I didn't know how to prove it.

SIXTEEN

The only things that popped up were travel reviews, business information, conference planning details, restaurant reviews, and a couple dozen travel influencer posts and videos. I watched a few of the more recent ones, anything that had been uploaded in the last fourteen months, but none of them made any mention of the tragedies that happened on the property. However, the videos only reinforced my plan on how to infiltrate the hotel.

An hour later, Lucien knocked on my door. When I opened it, he handed me a slip of paper. "Amir asked me to bring you these names and phone numbers. Neither are local."

"Thanks."

He gave my desk a wary look before turning his attention to the whiteboard which I'd left open. "Make sure you keep everything locked up tight," he said. "I know you value your privacy."

"Lucien, I need to know whose side you're on. Something is going on at the Golden. People have been hurt. I'd go so far as to say a few have even been killed. Ian Choi was hired to cover everything up. I don't know the extent of his capabilities or who he is exactly, but since I can't find anything on him, I have to assume the worst."

"You wouldn't be far from the mark. Choi provides a service to anyone who can pay. He's in it for the money. Once the job is done, it's done. He moves on, making it as though he was never there in the first place."

"He started at the Golden fourteen months ago, and he hasn't left yet."

Cross cleared his throat. "I'm aware."

"Were you aware of this when you conducted that security assessment?"

"Not to any great extent. When I couldn't find anything on Choi, I asked a former colleague to do some digging."

"Who?"

"Ace Darrow." Cross made a face. "The man isn't good for much, but he is good at research. He had prior experiences with Choi in D.C."

"Politicians and dead hookers?"

"More or less."

"Then why were you so adamantly opposed to helping Deanna find her sister? You must have known something was wrong at the Golden since Choi is on the payroll."

He pressed his lips together, fighting with himself. "Cross Security can't be caught in the middle. It'd be bad for business. More importantly, some of our clients require NDAs."

"NDAs don't apply to illegal activity."

"It's a fine line. I wanted to be certain something was wrong. When I spoke to Leslie, she stuck to the script. I had no reason to believe she was lying."

"You should have realized she was coerced."

"How would I have known that? In fact, you admitted she's conflicted about what happened to Gini. She doesn't even trust her own memory. I'm guessing you had to squeeze those details out of her, so what would I have had to do to get her to confide in me?" He had me there.

"What about Gini and the other Golden employees who weren't as lucky as Leslie?"

"How would I have known about any of that? The Golden doesn't broadcast. In fact, they hired someone to make sure none of that leaked." He looked through my notes and files. "Have you narrowed it down?"

"I'd say these five cases are highly suspicious. But I'm not willing to discount any of the other apparent suicides. Those could have been expertly staged."

"Choi?"

"I wouldn't doubt it."

Cross leafed through the files on the hit-and-run, mugging, drowning, a ladder fall, and Gil Fogarty's suicide. "The drowning and ladder fall occurred in view of security cameras. The footage proves it happened the way it looks."

"Maybe. But why didn't anyone check on Sue Shade, the maid who fell into the pool? She was face down in the water for eight hours before anyone found her. You can't tell me with a hotel that size, with that many staff members and that many guests, that no one noticed."

Cross let out a resounding sigh. "You think the footage was doctored."

"I think if someone can scrub the internet, he should be able to doctor surveillance footage." My thoughts drifted to Bastian Clarke, the former SAS operative had skills to pull those things off. I was pretty sure Amir could do the same, and if our resident tech expert couldn't, Cross had a rolodex of former hackers he could call who could. "I'm guessing Choi made that happen."

"Even if you're wrong about those two, I don't think you're wrong about the others."

"You looked?"

"I told you I would," Cross said.

"Where do we go from here?"

He stared at me. "I assigned you security assessments and gave you strict instructions not to take any cases. But we both see how well that worked out. For the record, I don't want you anywhere near this."

"Too late. I'm doing this with or without your help." I searched his eyes. "I get it. This case puts Cross Security in a tough spot. It's a conflict. That hasn't changed. If you drop the Golden as a client, they may realize we're on to them. It could be worse. They may decide to tie up loose ends and cut their losses. Leslie could easily become a casualty. Gini too. You already inquired as to Leslie's whereabouts once. They may already be suspicious, especially since Heathcliff was poking around."

"So nothing changes. The Golden remains a client."

"But we're building a case against them."

"Are you sure?" He held up a hand before I could protest. "We don't know who is responsible or how deep the Golden's involvement goes. If we can couch this as searching for bad actors among the staff, that would fit within Cross Security's obligation to the Golden."

"You spoke to Almeada."

He nodded. "We went over everything. If this breaks wrong, my hand could be forced. They could sue, issue a cease and desist, and have any work product related to their company seized or destroyed. However, there are ways to mitigate the damage. We keep things off book. We don't do anything official, and we keep the circle tight. Almeada believes we'd have a strong argument to make, especially if we discover a dangerous element is at play at the Golden. But the Golden could go after you personally."

"I'm more concerned someone on staff will murder me."

"You don't need to do this, Alex."

"The hell I don't. You just said you want to keep most of this off the books. Cross Security can't tackle this."

"The company can't, but I can."

"Except they know who you are, what you look like, and what you do. The moment you set foot inside that hotel, this is over."

"You were there yesterday and this morning. Both times you asked about Leslie. You can't go near this either."

"Fortunately for you, I have an idea." I laid out my plan to disguise myself and infiltrate the Golden under the guise of travel influencer. With the right prep, I could sell it. I'd done undercover before under much worse conditions.

"I'm not signing off on this. You're injured. Medical hasn't cleared you. And the same reasons you told me I couldn't do this apply to you, but since you're entitled to sick leave, I can't control what you do with your time off. However, I suggest you speak to Detective Heathcliff about a consulting gig. That would make the most sense, seeing as how he brought this to your attention." He pulled out his phone and sent a text. "Lt. Moretti won't have a problem hiring you. The paperwork will be waiting in his office for you to sign."

"I thought you couldn't be involved."

"I'm not. However, you're going to need gear."

"I need a burner phone to give to Leslie. Since they took her phone, I need some way to stay in contact with her once she's released from the hospital."

He nodded, turning one of the pads to a blank page and starting on a list. "You'll need a fake ID, credit cards, a phone, and a massive online presence."

"I may have the ID handled. The credit cards will be a problem."

"But not the massive online presence?"

"I'm not sure yet. I'll get back to you on that." I checked the time. "But first, I have to meet Deanna, let her know Leslie's okay, and convince her to go home."

"Take Heathcliff with you," Cross suggested. "She may be more convinced if you present a united front."

"I was thinking of dropping that burner phone off with Leslie first, in case Deanna insists on speaking to her. Hearing her sister's voice will go a long way in getting her to listen to reason. All she wanted to do was make sure Leslie was okay. Once she finds out her sister is relatively safe, at least for now, she'll be more likely to listen to reason and go home."

Cross pointed to the ceiling. "Grab one from upstairs. They're untraceable. No one will know it came from us."

"Thanks."

"When are you going to get back to me on the other things? The sooner we can get started, the better your chances will be."

"I'll let you know in a few hours. But I thought you didn't want me doing this."

"I don't. But I know I can't stop you."

SEVENTEEN

I had so much to do and only a few days to get everything set up. It'd be a rush job. There was no doubt about that, so I had to make sure my background was rock solid. Choi had experience evaluating and dealing with difficult situations. So I had to make sure I didn't do anything to make him think I could be a liability. I wasn't sure my cover would hold up to his scrutiny.

After grabbing a burner for Leslie, I returned to the hospital. Leslie remained in the same room. As far as the hospital staff knew, no one had tried to visit her. I didn't think they would. But it never hurt to take extra precautions, especially if that bad hot dog she'd gotten had been intentional.

"Hey," I said, "I brought you a present." I gave her the burner phone and explained why I wanted her to hold on to it. "Also, I was hoping you wouldn't mind taking a look at this photo." I held out a copy of Louis Grable's ID. "Do you know him?"

She studied it closely, the bridge of her nose crinkling. "I've seen him at work. He's always in the lobby. Maybe he's a bellhop or security. I'm not really sure. But he's always watching everyone like a hawk."

"Did he attack Gini?"

"I don't remember seeing him."

"But you saw all four attackers?"

"Yes, but I don't think he was part of it."

"Okay." I tucked his photo into my bag. "I'm on my way to see Deanna. Are you sure you don't want her to visit you?"

"If she finds out I'm in the hospital, she'll never leave. It'll make everything worse."

I held up my hand, hoping to calm her sudden panic. "I get it. But I think it might be best if you spoke to her yourself. Your sister's stubborn. No matter what I say, she'll want proof. She'll want to talk to you."

Leslie looked queasy, but I didn't think that had anything to do with being sick.

"I can call her from my phone, and we can speak to her together. Would that be better?" I asked.

Leslie nodded weakly.

I dialed Deanna, put the call on speaker, and waited for her to answer.

"Did you find Leslie?" Deanna asked. "Is she okay?"

"I can do a little better than that," I said. "She's here with me now."

"Les?" Deanna asked.

"Hey, Dee." Leslie leaned closer to my phone. "I'm really sorry. Work's been crazy. They have all sorts of rules regarding visitors at the hotel. I didn't want to get in trouble. I'm sorry."

"You're sorry?" Deanna squawked. "I thought you were dead."

Leslie laughed a little. "I'm just really busy. You should be too. Finals are coming up, aren't they? You should be studying, not missing class."

"Then you shouldn't have ghosted me. You ghosted everyone."

"The Golden—"

"Oh my god," Deanna cut her off, "you're obsessed."

"Dee—" Leslie looked at me, the queasy look getting worse. "I have to go. But I love you. Talk to Alex." She turned off the speaker and pushed the phone toward me before reaching for the bucket. Thankfully, she didn't get sick.

"Deanna?" I asked, pressing the phone to my ear.

"She's safe, right? She's okay?" Deanna asked.

"Yes," I said, hoping that lie wouldn't bite me in the ass. "The Golden changed some of the rules. They want their interns living on campus, so they can assign them split shifts and early mornings."

"Stupid job."

"Needless to say, Leslie moved into the Golden with a few of her fellow interns. I've seen the room and the names on the drawers. She's just busy right now, and since the Golden doesn't allow them personal devices, getting in contact isn't that easy."

"She could have met me in the lobby." Deanna let out a frustrated grunt. "I'm sorry for wasting your time. Everyone said she was fine. I should have listened, but I didn't think Les was that self-absorbed. Obviously, this internship is more important to her than family."

"Deanna—"

"No, it's okay. Les is right. I shouldn't be wasting my time. I have finals to worry about. Thanks again for doing this. Please apologize to Mr. Cross and his staff for my behavior."

"It's not a problem," I said. "I'm just glad I found Leslie."

"Me too."

"I can meet you at your hotel and bring you back the apartment key and your notebook."

"Don't bother. Give the key to Leslie since I don't think I'll be using it."

"Will do." That call made me feel worse instead of better. Maybe I shouldn't have pushed Leslie to speak to her sister.

"She's mad," Leslie said.

"She's hurt. When this is over, I suggest you explain everything. Trust me when I say people will forgive you for wanting to protect them, even if it takes some time and trying out a few different therapists."

Leslie gave me a look. "You have experience with things like this?"

"More than I should." I held out the key. "Deanna said I should give this back to you."

That time, Leslie did get sick.

After I left the hospital, I detoured to the precinct. Heathcliff wasn't at his desk when I arrived, so I slid into his chair and looked up the two names Cross had given me and reached out to both individuals. One was currently working at a resort in Fiji, not owned by Experiential Adventures. And the other was a restaurant owner in Napa.

I left a message for Meredith Hunter but didn't expect an answer any time soon. I wasn't sure what time it was in Fiji, but it had to be late or early. So I tried my luck with Sasha Drew. Unlike Meredith, she answered but didn't have time to talk. She promised to call me back after clean-up. Since I knew how restaurants worked, I wasn't expecting to hear from her until early in the morning, especially given the three hour time difference.

Heathcliff returned to find me searching the police databases for any mention of federal investigations being conducted at or near the Golden. But I didn't find anything. Maybe Organized Crime and the DEA hadn't bothered to mention their passive surveillance. It wouldn't be the first time such things slipped their minds.

"What are you doing?" he asked.

"Pretending I'm you."

He wiped his mouth and put down the sandwich he'd gotten from the vending machine. "Moretti said since I'm on desk duty, it'd be good to hire a consultant to assist. However, he seems to have overlooked the fact that you are injured and not cleared for field work."

"Telling him such things would be a HIPAA violation. Also, private sector means those kinds of rules don't really apply."

"Is that what you told Cross?" Heathcliff stared at me. "Word is he made this happen."

"Cross Security represents the Golden. Investigating this would be a conflict."

"So he's not on board."

I glanced around.

"Come on," Heathcliff said, "we can set up in the empty

conference room."

Once inside, I filled him in on everything that had happened in the last few hours. "Lucien's on board, but he has to protect Cross Security. He's already spoken to Almeada. By consulting for the PD, I'll be better protected should the Golden try to retaliate."

"Why does it sound like Cross is throwing you to the wolves?"

"He isn't. He offered to set up whatever I need. But I want to talk to Mark first about recycling an old cover. In case Choi digs into me, he'll find an extensive backstory that's existed for years. That's bound to be more solid than anything Cross Security throws together in a day or two."

Heathcliff didn't look convinced. "Where did you land on those fourteen cases I let you review? I picked out a few that may not be connected, but I still have several that I can't dismiss."

I looked at the folders Heathcliff had brought into the conference room with us. "Let's talk through them," I said.

He picked up the nearest file. "Mr. Deere suffered a cardiac event while vacationing." He reached for another folder. "Ms. Chumley died due to complications from pneumonia. Their medical records back those findings. Nothing suggests foul play."

"Certain drugs can mimic heart attacks."

"Mr. Deere had a history of hypertension, high cholesterol, and enough visits to his cardiologist to suggest his heart was a ticking time bomb."

"All right." I put Deere off to the side. "I assume the same's true for Chumley."

"Yeah."

I added that file to the growing pile. "They were both guests. What about Brittany Hodges? She worked at the Golden." I flipped to the coroner's report. "She died from blunt force trauma to the head."

"She fell off a ladder." Heathcliff said. "Hodges was changing lightbulbs. She didn't reattach the fixture properly. It came down on top of her, causing her to fall off the ladder. She cracked her head on the ceramic seating around the fountain. When paramedics arrived, she was unresponsive."

"Cross said the same thing. It was an accident, but several of these cases involve head injuries." I put Hodges to the side and picked up the file concerning Sue Shade, the maid who died near the pool. Cause of death was drowning. "Shade sustained a blow to the head prior to her death too. Does the PD still have the Golden's security footage from these incidents?"

"We have footage from all the incidents that happened at the resort. I'd say that's the reason so many of these cases were closed so quickly. Without that footage, these accidents would have required a more thorough investigation."

"Because bonking people on the head with heavy objects is a common way to off someone."

"Except the footage shows no one was intentionally bonked on the head."

I looked through more of the files. Gil Fogarty's file showed blunt force trauma to the top of his skull even though cause of death was suicide via hanging. Unfortunately, that death occurred inside a private suite, where cameras were prohibited. I wondered if the Golden followed the rules or if it spied on its guests. I had no way of knowing, but there was one way to find out.

I flipped back to the medical report. "Was Gil Fogarty depressed?"

"He had diabetes."

I glanced at Heathcliff. "You already made notes." I should have guessed. Heathcliff was the most meticulous notetaker I'd ever met. I scribbled that down, but I couldn't find the connection between the disease and the suicide. "Did that make him depressed?"

"It must have."

"But he wasn't diagnosed?"

Heathcliff shook his head. "He hid it well. His family and friends didn't know. He had been working more, so they hadn't seen him much in the weeks leading up to it."

"Fogarty was a bellhop at the Golden." I put my pen down. "Doesn't that strike you as odd that he killed himself at work inside a guest's room?" I checked the report again.

Blunt force trauma to the top of the head believed to be caused by the shower rod breaking and crashing down on top of his skull. However, cause of death was asphyxiation, and his broken hyoid bone was indicative of a hanging.

"Everything about this situation strikes me as odd," Heathcliff said.

"Well, those are the five cases I find suspicious. Three have blunt force trauma to the head as a commonality, which is the only commonality in this mix, if we rule out the medical emergencies for being just that."

"The fatal shooting and the hit-and-run are definites. There's no doubt about those being murder. But I'm not sure about the other three you selected. Your theory's thin. We have footage of those two public deaths. The other suicides of hotel staff members would make more sense to investigate than the drowning and ladder fall."

I picked up the two other suicide cases involving members of the Golden staff. "The deaths occurred off property. Assuming the responding officers performed their duties, a canvass should have turned up something if someone else was involved. But no one saw or heard anything strange. It's more of a stretch because the scenes would be harder to contain the farther they were from the Golden."

"The fatal shooting occurred away from the Golden."

"Half a block. That's still close. Staff members walk that stretch every day, multiple times a day. No one would think twice if they were spotted on the footage. They could case the area without drawing any unnecessary attention to themselves. But going to people's homes, in strange neighborhoods, that would be harder to explain. Still, if you're not sure, flash Ian Choi's photo around and see if it gets any hits. If there was something to be cleaned up, he'd be the guy to do it. Though, I'm not sure where you're going to find his photo. Most were scrubbed from the internet. The only one I found was his official ID, and it's not a very clear photo, like the lens was smudged and the photographer didn't notice. I think Choi may have performed some photo editing and replaced the official photo that had been taken."

"All right," Heathcliff finally said, "I'm not going to shut the door on any of these cases, but we'll focus on the five you pointed out for now. At least we're in agreement on three of them."

"Three?"

"Fogarty."

I smiled at him. "Welcome to the dark side."

"Speaking of the dark side, I found some online discussions concerning the deaths at the resort. They never mentioned the Golden by name, which may be why it hadn't been flagged or taken down, but the details match concerning the deaths, even the dates and times matched up. I passed it along to cyber division in case the posters work at the Golden and are willing to cooperate."

"You mean we may have a witness?"

"Possibly, but I don't suggest you get your hopes up. This was more along the lines of tinfoil hat wearing conspiracy nuts. People have all sorts of crazy ideas about what goes on inside hotels. The theories run the gamut. The real crazies have the most creative ideas. Stuff like psychological and physical experimentation for a clandestine government agency, extraterrestrial attacks, and serial killers."

"Kate already floated the serial killer idea by me. But she suggested one killer. Singular. How many are you suggesting?"

"An entire collective. Someone suggested these deaths are indicative of a training ground for serial killers, but the details are murky. I wouldn't consider that a particularly reputable source." Heathcliff held eye contact. "Like I said, these are the theories the crazies came up with."

"Did any of these theories involve a bonk to the head?"

"No. And stop saying bonk. It makes these cases sound like a cartoon."

"What about the less crazy theories?"

"Sabotage, cover-ups, unsafe conditions, poor security, and shitty response times by emergency services."

"Those are plausible, but they don't explain the blunt force trauma." I gave him a look. "I mean no disrespect to the dead, but bonk is faster to say."

He rolled his eyes. “Fine.”

EIGHTEEN

After stacking the files beside me, I pulled out my laptop which contained the files from Cross's server. "The FBI's organized crime unit and the DEA investigated the Golden for possible illegal connections but found nothing. However, three suicides, two freak accidents, and two fatal attacks happened to Golden employees in the last fourteen months. I'd venture to say a sinister force is at play here."

Heathcliff ate another handful of chips before wiping his palm on a napkin. "So you don't think this is a serial killer cabal?"

"No."

"What then?" He knew I didn't have a theory. "We're spit-balling. Spout out some ideas."

"The Golden has a fixer on the payroll, Ian Choi. Let's say the resort goes above and beyond to provide guests with things they shouldn't. The dead employees could have seen something they weren't supposed to, or they were asked to do something they didn't want to. Management freaked out that they'd squeal, so they took care of the problem."

"Evil corporation murders people." Heathcliff thought about it. "What are you thinking? Drugs? Prostitution?"

"Possibly both."

He reached for a pen and circled something on the list he'd made. "It's also possible the hotel was covering for a guest."

"You think a guest killed these people?" I checked the dates. "These deaths happened over the course of several months. If a guest is responsible, he must be a frequent flyer. How do we get access to the guest registry without a warrant?"

"Coloring outside the lines is your schtick."

"Unfortunately, I don't have the resources currently at my disposal. It's possible a guest is to blame. It's also possible someone on staff is responsible. I'm not saying they necessarily murdered anyone, but they could have made conditions unsafe. Removed a screw from the light fixture, or put a slippery substance near the pool. Management could have made Fogarty's life a living hell to the point that he had to find a way out."

"You're saying they drove him to suicide?"

"I don't know. You told me to spit-ball, so I'm spit-balling." I looked over the list of suicides. Three members of the Golden staff allegedly killed themselves, and so had four guests. "If the conditions inside the hotel were that atrocious, why didn't these people just leave?"

"The suicidal guests probably checked in with that in mind," Heathcliff said.

I reread the files, finding two of the suicides had a history of mental illness. The third had been given a terminal diagnosis, and the fourth had recently suffered a divorce after his small business failed. None of their autopsies revealed blunt force trauma. I added them to the circumstantial pile. "I'll agree with that for now."

"Maybe the staff didn't think they could walk away. Maybe they were blackmailed. That's how Leslie made it sound, like the hotel owned her."

"I reached out to two people who are no longer affiliated with the Golden but who allegedly went through the internship program. Maybe they can shed some light on this."

Heathcliff looked at the clock. "If what Leslie said is true, if four Golden employees or interns attacked Gini

Ruffin and the management covered it up, we have no way of knowing how far they'd go to keep other things quiet."

"We know how far they'd go." I indicated the files we hadn't pushed aside. "They'll kill to keep things quiet."

"Unless it isn't the management. A bad element could be operating within the Golden, and that's who is eliminating the troublemakers."

"Like the cult theory I floated to Leslie earlier?"

"I have to admit, it's possible someone is taking the training and ideology too far."

"You think someone is thinning out the herd, getting rid of the weak members."

"A rising tide," Heathcliff said. "It may be why management is willing to look the other way. They may not be sanctioning these actions, but they aren't doing anything to stop them either."

"In Gini's case, we're talking serious injury. And if we're right about these," I tapped the files, "we're looking at murder."

"It could all come down to the bottom line. Settlements and hush money may be cheaper if the staff is that much more efficient."

"I can't imagine paying out six figures in each of these cases would be more cost effective than having a handful of staff members who weren't performing their duties at an optimal level."

"It could be about more than that. It could be about control or loyalty."

"Or fear." But speculating wasn't going to get us anywhere. "Have you spoken to the victims' families?" I asked.

"No one wanted to say much. I asked about their loved ones' states of mind. Every one of these deaths came out of the blue, which isn't that odd, but when I asked about their work life, no one had any details to share."

"Do you think someone got to them?"

"There's no way of knowing, but I don't think anyone who works at the Golden talks about it."

"Like *Fight Club*."

He picked through the files. "The security cam footage

shows Hodges and Shade were victims of freak accidents."

I wasn't convinced the footage hadn't been doctored or other factors had been at play that we couldn't see on the security footage. "Maybe, but they didn't find Shade until the next morning. She remained face-down in the water all night. Where was hotel security? The camera footage showed her falling in. Someone should have been monitoring the feed. Even if they missed it when it happened, her body was visible the entire time. No one ever went to check the pool until the lifeguard arrived the next morning to find her dead in the water. I don't care if her fall was an accident. The rest was criminal. And I don't believe for a second a resort wouldn't have someone check the pool or the security feed periodically in case a guest broke in or a kid snuck away. They wouldn't want the liability or negative publicity."

"It was negligent, I'll give you that, but the DA didn't want to pursue charges. And as far as liability, I'm sure they have a sign that says something about swimming at your own risk."

"Her family should have sued."

Heathcliff stared at me. "They said they couldn't talk about it, but given the shiny new car they had when they were interviewed, I'd say the hotel paid out."

"That's why we don't know what's going on. Everyone got paid off to keep quiet."

"Let's focus on Leslie and less on this." He gestured to the files. "She's our priority. Do you think you can convince her to cooperate. If she comes forward and gives a statement, we'd be able to do more."

"How would that even work, Derek? She isn't a reliable witness, not with the way she flip-flopped on her own recollection. And Gini will deny it. If the victim won't corroborate, what do you think the DA's going to say?"

"Fuck."

"Is that verbatim?"

Heathcliff tried not to laugh. "Here's a stupid question. Assuming everything Leslie told us is true, which has yet to be proven, why did Gini only get hurt and not killed? We're looking at two obvious murders and a few potentials."

"Maybe those victims couldn't be scared off. For all intents and purposes, Gini quit the program. She won't be back. But the rest of these victims weren't interns. They were regular members of the staff, which would have made them harder to get rid of."

"Exit interview," Heathcliff said. "If they'd seen something or if they'd been targeted, they could have gone to their union reps or HR. They could have sought outside counsel, making them bigger obstacles than Gini."

"You think they saw something they shouldn't have?"

Heathcliff shrugged. "We have no idea what's going on, so anything is possible right now."

I checked the time. "You're right, which is why we need eyes inside the Golden."

"But if this is an internal problem, which is what we've concluded, how are you planning to get close enough to the staff to find out about any of this?"

"Two words. Travel influencer."

*   *   *

"You want to do what?" SSA Mark Jablonsky asked. "Have you lost your fucking mind?"

"It's solid."

"It's asinine."

"Do you have a better idea?"

My former boss stared at me. "You have no idea what the situation is. You're guessing as to a future target, but the intel you've gotten is far from sound. Leslie Stiller is not a reliable source. She contradicted herself."

"She's scared."

"And the actual victim doesn't want to have anything to do with this."

"She was paid off. And she's not the only victim."

"Just because Detective Heathcliff is bored and is seeing homicides where there aren't any doesn't mean there are other victims."

"Tell that to Hugh Pellers, Sue Shade, Gil Fogarty—"

"Stop." Mark held up his hand.

"You always taught me there are no such things as

coincidences. You can't tell me that each of these things happened separately and it's just a coincidence that they all worked for the Golden." I wove my hand between the stacks and placed a USB drive in front of him. "Take a look at this."

He gave the drive an uneasy look, like it was a cobra preparing to strike. "I don't want to."

"Are you sure? You don't even know what it is. It could be a crypto wallet with millions."

"Crypto's not real money. I don't want it."

"You could sell it and turn it into real money."

Mark frowned at the drive. "Is it crypto?"

"No."

Sighing, he stopped what he was doing. "Let me guess. This is the intel you've put together." He opened the files, seeing everything I had found. "Y'know, you are banned from the federal building for a reason."

"I'm not banned. I just can't consult, which is fine since I'm assisting the PD. They still think I'm a valuable asset."

"More like a pain in the asset." He glanced at my side. "Have you spoken to Lucca? The two of you can exchange stabbing stories."

My death glare might have worked if Mark wasn't immune to it. He steepled his fingers and tapped them against his lips while he rocked in his chair, making it groan and squeak.

"You need to oil that thing," I said.

"I do this to annoy people so they leave my office. But for some reason, it's not working right now." Finally, he sighed. "You aren't supposed to be working. You're supposed to be recovering."

"I'm fine."

"Really?" He gave me that knowing look. "Marty calls me a lot. Are you sure you don't want to rethink that last statement?"

"Working will keep me from spinning out. It always does. And I promised myself I wouldn't fall back into old patterns. Plus, you didn't see Leslie. Food poisoning or not, she looks like she has one foot in the grave. I don't want to tell her sister I saw it happening and didn't do anything to stop it."

"Are you sure you're not projecting?" Mark rubbed his moustache, his pupils moving from left to right and back again, like an old-fashioned typewriter. "Even Cross is smart enough to insulate his company from this."

"The Golden's a client."

"Which you're hoping will give you a leg up."

"It can't hurt."

Mark considered everything I had said. "Fine. Go speak to Lawson about dusting off an old cover identity. I'll let him know you're stopping by to say hi. If his office is locked when you get there, take that as a sign that you should drop this."

"Thanks."

I took the familiar path down the hallway, relieved when I didn't run into Lucca. Agent Lawson was behind his computer, his back to the door while he focused on whatever analysis he was currently conducting.

"Hey," I said, "I see you're working late."

He turned. "Jablonsky said you wanted to ask for a favor and he'd sign off on it, so tell me what I can do to help."

That was easier than I thought. "I was hoping you could repurpose one of my old cover identities and get me set up as a travel influencer. I need to get a behind-the-scenes look at a resort and how they train their staff without raising any eyebrows."

"Travel influencer it is. But I'll give you reporter credentials and a few bylines at some independent travel and vacation magazines too. I can attach your name to some documentaries for research."

"As long as it stands up, you can make me queen. But I need this to be airtight. The person reviewing this is an expert."

"Who'll bc looking at it?"

"Ian Choi."

The name circled around Lawson's brain. By the time it finished its first lap, he had pulled up Choi's information. "It'll be airtight." He cracked a smile. "Why the change in professions?"

"You don't want to know."

"This can't be for an OIO investigation."

"It's a police matter."

He smiled. "I've worked with a few of their techs, but given what a heavy-hitter Choi is, it's a good thing you came to the best."

"You are and always will be my favorite tech."

Lawson slid in front of another screen. "I can get this set up for you no problem. When do you need it?"

"ASAP. Lives are on the line."

"You'll need a travel blog, newsletters, all the things the modern freelance travel writer has. A staff would help add to your legitimacy."

"Are you volunteering?"

"They'll be digital, but they'll hold up. Everything will hold up." He tapped the keys. "I can repurpose that old art student cover of yours and turn her into a travel enthusiast."

"I can be whoever you want me to be. In fact, I can be anyone except myself. I was inside the hotel earlier today. I can't afford to have them recognize me."

"All right." He pulled up a few old photos from cover identities I'd cultivated over the years. "I'd go blonde, short hair, and glasses. Make sure you dress differently and behave differently. You even need to walk differently."

"I remember how undercover goes."

"Deep cover."

"Yes, sir."

"I'll update that defunct account with the photos we have on file, get you a few hundred thousand followers, and generate enough backdated content to make everything believable. I'll need you to provide a few voice recordings. Then I can repurpose someone else's videos, replace them with you, and Bob's your uncle."

"As long as the original content isn't easily recognizable."

"That won't be a problem. We have the old art content and museum tours already on there, so instead of taking them down, I'll add more stuff that will show a gradual shift away from the museums and art and more towards exploring different cities. We'll start with architecture and shift to things to do, which will turn into places to stay and things to eat. Y'know, the usual rigamarole. It'll look natural that way, and since those details have long been established, it'll make it impossible for anyone to determine the truth from the lies."

"Sounds great."

He stared at the screen before inputting more details. "Give me a few hours to figure this out. I'll text you the details as soon as I have them. In the meantime, do you need credentials to go with it?"

"A license and passport." The federal government wasn't going to cover my expenses. "Cross Security can handle the rest."

"Go get a cup of coffee. I should have them ready soon."

NINETEEN

After taking my newly minted IDs, I called Lucien to tell him I needed a phone and credit card to match. When I arrived back at Cross Security, a prepaid credit card loaded with several thousand dollars and a new cell phone were waiting for me.

"How are you going to explain this?" I asked.

"Explain what?"

"This won't tie back to you?"

"If it did, we'd both be fucked." He had a good point. "You'll need equipment. Cameras, mics, lights, everything content creators use."

"I've got that covered. Lawson gave me a crash course. I picked some stuff up on my way here."

Cross sat up from where he'd been sprawled out on my couch, making sure my office door was closed before he said, "Are you sure about this?"

"No, but I can't let that stop me."

"If you get in any trouble, point a camera at it. The Golden doesn't have any bad publicity online. If they think you're live streaming, they'll be on their best behavior."

"Thanks for the tip. Any other words of wisdom?"

"Be careful."

I did one last review of Cross's files concerning the

Golden. "I'm not seeing any mention that the hotel uses facial recognition software."

"They don't, as far as I know."

"Good. That will make it easier to infiltrate the place in my disguise." After copying the floor by floor schematics showing where every camera and safety measure had been installed, I turned off my computer.

Lucien cleared his throat. "When are you planning on conducting recon?"

"I'm not sure yet. Maybe tomorrow. It'll depend on how quickly the hospital releases Leslie. I want to get to the hotel before that happens. I should make reservations and reach out to their media relations department about featuring the hotel on my channel."

"You've already gotten the lingo down."

"I did some research while looking into the Golden. I plan on doing a lot more before I step foot inside. I want to make sure I'm prepared to pull this off."

"If you're not ready—"

"I will be."

Lucien waited for me to put my things into the gym bag I kept in my closet, and then he offered to carry it for me. "You're not supposed to lift anything heavy. You're also not supposed to be working."

"It's a good thing I'm taking those sick days then."

We parted ways at my car. Thankfully, Lucien resisted the urge to remind me not to take the company car to the Golden.

I got home before Martin, which made things easier. Most of my belongings lived in the second floor suite. After going through a few boxes which had been shoved in the closet, I found the one containing clothes and accessories from my undercover days.

I pulled out a blonde wig and a few different pairs of glasses. Then I pulled out the fancy makeup kit I had. Did makeup expire? I wasn't sure, so I opened a few containers and gave them a sniff. Nothing had turned moldy or smelled fermented, so I took that to mean it was safe to use.

Leaving that for now, I went through the rest of my

closet, looking for trendy and stylish outfits. Most of those were in the back with the rest of my undercover gear since I was neither trendy nor stylish in my everyday life.

Are you sure you want to do this? the voice in my head asked. I wasn't sure, but I had to do something. Right now, I was in hurry up and wait mode. Until Lawson gave me the green light, there wasn't much I could do except prepare.

Muscle memory kicked in, and on autopilot, I packed my things, rehearsed my cover, and reviewed everything I knew about the Golden Hotel. Somewhere along the line, my phone rang. I almost didn't bother with the caller ID, believing it was Lawson, but the country code caught my eye.

"This is Meredith Hunter," the woman said. "I got your message. What exactly did you want to know about the Golden Hotel?"

"You worked as an intern there?"

"Yes."

"What was that experience like?"

"It was great. I learned so much. The Golden really tested us, taught us our limits, showed us we were capable of far more than we ever realized, and it was an absolute blast. I made some really great friends. Lifelong friends."

I cut her off. "Did you live at the hotel?"

"For the first few months, before I was given a permanent assignment. Our schedules were so crazy at the beginning. By the time I'd leave the hotel, it was time to come back."

That sounded like it violated labor laws, but I kept the commentary to myself. "Did you have roommates?"

"There were four others in my room. Instead of the usual double beds, they had bunk beds for the interns. Two sets and a rollaway bed. That's the maximum occupancy according to the hotel. I'm not sure if that was due to fire codes or insurance issues. It could have been both. At the time, I was so green, I wouldn't have known one from the other." She laughed. "They taught us so much."

"Us?"

"All the interns. It was one of the best experiences of my

life and also one of the hardest."

I wasn't expecting to talk to someone this passionate about the Golden. "Why don't you work there now?"

"I did for a while, but I wanted to explore the world. When I got a better offer, I moved to Fiji. It's paradise." She hesitated. "Why are you interested in the Golden? You never really said."

"I review hotels. The Golden's spectacular, but the staff really makes it shine. I was surprised when I learned they trained interns, but I couldn't find much online about the program. So I thought I should go straight to the source."

"The Golden's a great place."

"What about in emergency situations? A place that big must have to deal with injuries, illnesses, and death. What are the protocols?"

"They have an entire book on it. Everyone must know basic first-aid and CPR. After that, it's about memorizing the protocols and knowing how to react or who to contact. Evacuation routes and contingencies were drilled into us."

"How often did you see emergencies?"

"I wish I could say never, but something happened every week. It's a big place with a lot of people."

"Every week?" How long had this been going on? We thought fourteen months, but Meredith had worked there five years ago.

"Yeah. Most of it was minor stuff. Someone twisting an ankle on the steps or a fire in the kitchen. Once, a guest caught the drapes on fire with a cigar. Crazy things happen in the hospitality biz."

"I'm starting to realize that."

"The job is a lot of fun too though. You get to see how all of it comes together. You get to goof off with your coworkers when things slow down. It's just...fun."

"Did anyone ever die?"

She made a noise, like she couldn't believe I'd asked that question. "Aren't you morbid?"

"Answer the question."

"Yeah, I guess. But I don't really remember dealing with that personally. However, those were the first protocols we learned. The first thing we were supposed to do was get help. We'd call the on-site doctors and emergency services. As soon as someone else was available to render aid, we'd divert guest attention away so no one realized what was happening."

"Is that common practice for all hotels?"

"I'd say it's pretty standard, but it depends on the hotel's resources and how many people are available to assist."

"All right, thanks."

"Those are the only questions you had for me? Your message sounded a bit more urgent."

"I got excited when I saw the lack of details online and couldn't wait to find a recruiter to speak to."

"How did you find my name?"

"An internet search. You posted on a message board, and I found your business profile and phone number from there." It would be best to cut this short before she could ask any more questions. "If anything else occurs to me, do you mind if I call you again?"

"Not at all. I'm always happy to assist."

I couldn't see her, but I was positive she was smiling in that annoying way sales associates would when they were hoping to land a nice commission.

Would Sasha Drew have the same rose-tinted view of the Golden? When I had spoken to her, she didn't sound nearly as energetic or enthusiastic. But Meredith had given me a few things to think about.

After scribbling a few notes, I phoned Heathcliff to tell him about my conversation. We were going over the specifics of my half-assed plan to infiltrate the Golden and keep an eye on Leslie while determining who or what was responsible for the bodies turning up when Martin came home.

"You're leaving?" Martin nodded at my packed rolling bag.

I gave him a little shrug. "Yes. But not really."

"I'm gonna need more than that. And a scotch." He put his briefcase down and tossed his jacket and tie onto the couch, rolling up his sleeves as he made his way to the bar cart. "What can I get you?"

"Nothing."

He poured a finger of scotch into the glass, gave it a look, and poured another before capping the bottle. "Are you sure? This seems like the kind of situation where you might want to throw a glass against the wall."

"I don't throw glasses against the wall. That's all you, handsome." Though, I had been known to cause property damage on occasion. Smashing coffee mugs was more Martin's thing, but I doubted he'd waste a glass of Macallan like that.

He sat across from me, nodding at my phone. "Don't stop on my account. Please, continue."

I hated when he got like this. "Derek, I'll talk to you tomorrow." Then I disconnected. "It's for a case."

Martin sipped his scotch. "Isn't it always?"

"Work first."

"That stopped being our slogan a long time ago. I thought you were stuck working behind a desk. Are you going to reside at the office now?"

"This case isn't for Cross Security. It's for the police department."

"Heathcliff, right?" The ugly smile on his face made my heart break a little.

"Y'know, I was only joking around this morning. I would never—"

He waved away what I had to say. "I don't care about that. Well, I do care about that, but you've been phoning other men at all hours since the moment we met. What I told you before remains true. I'm secure enough to know better than to think you'd step out on utter perfection." The ugly smile turned into his smug smile. "What we have can't be replicated. We are lightning in a bottle, Alexis."

"I'm not sure that's a good thing. It sounds kind of dangerous."

His green eyes darkened. "It is." Without another word, he got up, went to his briefcase, and returned to the table with three neatly folded sleeveless t-shirts. He dropped them in front of me and retook his seat. "Lucien stopped by the office to deliver these. He said they were prototypes of the new body armor. Strange thing about that though. They're your size."

"Did he say anything else?"

"They're the equivalent of light armor. They won't stop a bullet, but they should stop a blade."

I unfolded the top one which was an off-white. Natural would be the color designation a designer boutique would give it. I'd call it dingy. Just another sign of my lack of style. "Okay."

Martin took another sip and returned the glass to the table with a resounding thud. "What are you doing this time? Or do I even want to know?"

"I'm going to stay in a hotel for a few days to keep an eye on things. The police have an open investigation into a hit-and-run, and—"

"Cross Security isn't backing this play."

"They can't. The hotel is a client. It's a conflict of interest."

"That's why Lucien brought these to me. He can't have anyone know he's helping you." He finished his scotch.

"It's not that bad."

"You haven't fully healed yet."

"Which is why it's a good thing this is an easy case. I'm playing dress-up as a travel influencer. It's the cushiest assignment I've ever had. I'll walk around the resort all day, taking photos and videos without anyone giving it a second thought. I've been watching travel videos to make sure I can do a convincing job, and it looks like all these people do is eat and drink. The only thing that may be in danger is my cholesterol level."

Martin scooted his chair closer to me. He brushed my hair behind my ear before rubbing his thumb against my cheek. "I know your tricks, beautiful. How serious is this?"

"That depends."

"On what?"

"On why seven Golden employees died in the last fourteen months."

TWENTY

Martin nudged me and pointed to the laptop on the bed between us. "I could ask around and see if someone at Martin Tech is interested in doing some video editing on the side."

"I have a few guys for that."

Martin pulled away, so he could see my expression better. "I thought you said Cross Security wasn't involved."

"They're not. I asked Lawson if he could help a girl out."

"Mark knows you're doing this?"

"If I hadn't told him, you would have."

"He was my friend first."

"I don't care. I called dibs. He's mine. You can't have him." I grabbed Martin's phone. "And you aren't telling him I said that either."

Martin laughed. "I could do some video editing for you. In fact, you owe me a trip to Tuscany, but I'm willing to settle for a staycation instead. I could be your assistant. Out of the two of us, I have more experience with photo and video manipulation, not to mention advertising campaigns, professional—"

"No." I pulled myself off the pillow, snaked my hand up his jaw and into his hair, and pulled him to me for a kiss.

"But thank you anyway."

Martin selected another video from the list of recommended views. "Maybe this will make you reconsider."

A woman had been outside, filming herself getting a hot dog from some iconic stand. She had propped her phone up, so both hands were free for her to hold the hot dog, peel away the bun, and show the massive amounts of toppings it contained. She'd just finished giving the life history of the relish, when four pigeons attacked out of nowhere.

I let out a surprised yelp, which made Martin laugh.

"You need backup for no other reason than to keep an eye out for pigeon attacks. They know you have a vendetta against them. They've been planning a counterstrike. I've heard them on the balcony," he said.

"You speak pigeon?" I shut the laptop lid gently with my foot, so I wouldn't have to sit up and pull at the scar tape that Martin had reapplied to my side before we'd gotten into bed.

"Coo. Coo."

"You're not funny, but you are a little cuckoo."

He picked up the laptop. "It could happen. Anything could. I would prefer if you had someone close by in case of anything."

"Heathcliff will make sure a patrol car isn't too far away."

Martin put the laptop on the dresser and joined me under the covers. "Fourteen people are dead, Alex."

"They weren't murdered." I rethought that statement. "Well, some of them weren't murdered."

He wrapped his arms around me. "I don't want to fight. So do not take what I'm about to say as that. This is me asking a question because I want to know. Why do you have to be the one to figure it out?"

"Because I know about it. Because Deanna came to me, and Leslie has food poisoning. She saw something she shouldn't have, and I'm afraid what they'll do to her because of it."

"You think they intentionally poisoned her?" Martin

asked.

"I'm open to the possibility."

"I love that you feel compelled to do this, but I hate that it's always you. Just once, I'd like it to be someone else who saves the day."

"Martin, most of the time it is someone else. You just don't realize that because you don't hear about that stuff. You aren't sleeping with those investigators."

"Are you saying I should branch out?"

"It couldn't hurt. You should fully expand your horizons. Lucien and Jade are in an open relationship, as far as I can tell. You can take your chances with him."

"What about Kellan?" Martin asked.

"He's seeing the server from the Mexican restaurant, but I'm not sure if they're exclusive. Plus, you might as well go straight to the top. Lucien would be able to give you all the dirt on every investigator. That should prove I'm not the only one who takes on this kind of shit."

"I doubt it."

"There's only one way to find out." I nudged him. "Y'know, gay porn is gaining in popularity. If you and Lucien make a sex tape, Lawson can do the editing and make it go viral. If you monetize, I bet you'd make a killing."

Martin smirked. "Is this payback for the pigeon video?"

I took his face in my hands and stared into his eyes. "Did you really hear them planning an attack?"

He kissed me playfully, his nose crinkling. "Good night, gorgeous." He closed his eyes. "If you're interested in turning me into a porn star, it's going to be our sex tape that goes viral."

"Not possible with that moratorium of yours."

He chuckled, his breath tickling my ear. "I love you."

"I worry about that sometimes," I said, sobering.

"Don't."

"But you hate this. And I am this. I'm not sure how you can separate the two. There was a time you couldn't."

He propped himself up on his arm. "Are we having this conversation now, or are you hoping to goad me into showing you how much I love you?"

"Both."

He ran his thumb across my cheek. "We're okay."

I gave him a wicked grin. "Prove it."

He kissed me gently. "Good night, Alex."

At least he thought I was teasing, that this wasn't due to pre-op jitters, which is why I wasn't sure I'd be able to sleep. Once Lawson called, I could get started setting the foundation. Since Leslie's condition wasn't that severe, the hospital would discharge her in the morning.

When I failed to fall asleep, I grabbed my phone, finding no missed calls or messages. I sent a text to Lawson, asking for an updated ETA. He said everything should be ready by morning. He wanted a few of his colleagues in cybercrimes to examine his work under a microscope to make sure it passed muster before giving me the greenlight.

Since there was nothing else I could do, I put my phone on the nightstand and curled up against Martin's side. Through sheer willpower, I managed to fall asleep and stay asleep until my phone rang a little before seven a.m.

Blindly answering, I said, "Is it ready?"

"Um...hello?" a woman asked.

I blinked, recognizing the voice. "Ms. Drew?"

"You can call me Sasha," she said. "I know it's early, but the kitchen just closed. You said you had questions about my experience interning at the Golden."

"Anything you can tell me would be helpful."

"What is this about? You were vague when we spoke yesterday."

"I've been researching the resort for work. There's a lot of hype and fanfare surrounding their internship program, but I haven't been able to find too many details about the program."

"That's because there are confidentiality agreements in place, but mainly, I'd say it has more to do with the brainwashing that goes on there."

"Brainwashing?" I sat up. "I'd like to hear more about that."

"It isn't actual brainwashing. Well, it might be, I guess. I don't know. It's the culture of the place."

"What do you mean?"

"Everything felt so phony there. We had these classes where we were taught to smile and always be polite. We were to make the guest feel heard and to show concern over whatever their issue, regardless of how insignificant it might be. The basis was sound. The Golden wanted their guests to feel valued. That would make them happy, which would make them less likely to complain, which would make our jobs easier. I get it. I trained my waitstaff with some of those same tactics, but there's a limit, y'know."

I wasn't following, possibly on account of the early hour. "A limit to being nice?"

"Yes."

Flashes from the parking garage came to mind. The smiles. The attempted helpfulness even though the man I'd spoken to hadn't done anything to help me.

"It was weird how pleasant they always wanted us to act. And what made it worse were the cliques and reward system. All of it felt like some pseudo-psychology experiment. That place creeped me out. I nearly quit the program."

"What creeped you out specifically?"

"Everything. The hotel gets eerie at night, and when you're sharing a room with four other girls who practice smiling in the mirror, it gets to you."

"They practice smiling?"

"It was this sick game my roommates played. One would try to maintain that polite smile we were told to keep while the others would say the worst, most disgusting things imaginable. I was never down for any of that. I even reported them to the woman in charge of our room assignments, but she applauded their practice and dedication and made me feel like there was something wrong with me for not participating. There were a lot of weird things like that. Half the time, I thought I was crazy."

Leslie felt the same way. "Like you were in the *Twilight Zone*?"

"Basically."

"Did anyone on staff seem particularly creepy?"

"Everyone."

"Who was in charge of all of that?"

"You mean the classes and creepy smiling and stuff? I'm not entirely sure. We had different instructors, but we were bombarded with these things from everyone who trained us. The regular staff wasn't as bad. The longer they'd been there, the less brainwashed they seemed, which is weird since you'd think it'd be the other way around. Maybe they burnt out or realized how stupid it was."

"Or they were trained differently," I said.

"That's very possible."

Sasha's recollection sounded like a horror film, whereas Meredith had made the Golden sound like the best place in the world. I hadn't expected such vastly different experiences.

"Do you remember if anyone died on property while you were there?" I asked.

"There was a heart attack, I think. Maybe it was a stroke. I'm not sure. I didn't witness it myself, but I remember the ambulance arriving. That was the first time I ever saw someone wheeled out in a body bag. And the most fucked up part about it was everyone pretended it wasn't happening. They just went about their business like seeing that was perfectly normal, and they just kept smiling."

"They didn't provide aid?"

"That's not what I meant. The staff member who found the victim called for help. Management was waiting to show the EMTs how to get to where they needed to go. Everyone did what they were supposed to, but the staff members who weren't involved went on like nothing happened. We were told to behave that way so no one panics. It's like saying you smell smoke in a crowded theater. People can imagine things, and then everyone gets hurt. But to act so oblivious...I just...it's like no one had any emotions whatsoever."

"They were cold?"

"They were robots." Sasha exhaled as if she were smoking or vaping. "Look, I may not be a fan, but that internship program helps a lot of people. It opens lots of doors and provides opportunities that few will ever have. It wasn't for me, which is why I got out of hotels and got into restaurants. But for everyone I know who made it through, they are thriving now. I guess all that brainwashing was good for something." She let out another puff. "Please don't quote me on any of this. You said you wouldn't use my name."

"I won't." My phone let out a beep, telling me I had a waiting text which I had ignored the first time it alerted me. "I have a few more questions."

"Another time, maybe. I've already said more than I should have."

"Thanks," I said, but she'd already hung up.

The waiting text was from Lawson. Everything was a go.

TWENTY-ONE

I checked the photo on the fake ID before examining myself in the mirror one more time. Lawson did impeccable work. Cross had his own paper guy and a team on staff, but this was government official, even if it was a fake.

When I had stood in front of the screen for the photo, I'd been wearing the same wig and glasses, but I had used tactical makeup to alter the contours of my face. So I needed to make sure I used the same techniques when applying my makeup today. Since it had been a few years, it didn't have to be perfect, but I wanted it as close as possible.

The prepaid credit cards and phone were registered under the same phony name. The address matched what Lawson had on file for my old cover identity. Everything linked directly to Alexandra Riley. Although, when I'd originally been introduced to her, she hadn't been blonde and didn't wear glasses.

The years hadn't been kind to her. They'd been even less kind to her fiancé, but I couldn't let myself go there. My mental state was too precarious to risk getting locked into that grief loop over my late partner.

Instead, I scanned the social media profiles Lawson had

updated. The content was nearly identical across platforms with just enough differences to appear realistic. Most influencers had a preferred channel, but they'd cross-post to the other platforms. The same was true of Riley.

After I familiarized myself with the content and my new identity, there was only one thing left to do. Put it to use. But I didn't want to dive right in. I wanted to test the waters.

So I packed my things, left the company car in a lot across town, and called for a ride to the Golden. Since the hotel had a few bars, restaurants, a coffee shop, spa, boutique, and tons of other things to see and do, I'd start with whatever didn't require a reservation or serious commitment. The fewer details I had to provide, the better.

The doorman backed against the door, pushing it open and gesturing me inside. The uniform reminded me of a cross between a theater usher and the royal guard. His gloves were white with gold stitching. I had failed to notice that on my previous visits. But I couldn't help but think they'd keep him from leaving prints at a crime scene.

"Welcome to the Golden," he said. "Checking in?"

"Breakfast date," I said.

"You'll find the steakhouse down the corridor, past the waterfall."

"The steakhouse serves breakfast?"

"Most days."

"And the coffee shop?" I asked.

"Straight ahead. You'll see the newsstand first. It's beyond that."

I pulled out my phone and opened the camera app, holding the device up and to the right as I moved forward, capturing my stroll across the fancy lobby. Near the check-in desk was Louis Grable in a grey uniform. He was helping a guest with a luggage cart. Thankfully, he was too busy to notice me.

At the manmade waterfall, I posed in front of my camera before reciting the spiel I'd heard the dozen travel influencers I'd researched give whenever they arrived at a new destination. With that out of the way, I stopped the recording, took a few selfies, and switched the screen around to capture a few other shots. I tried to make sure they looked artistic enough for a content creator and not like the surveillance photos they were.

Once that was done, I headed down the corridor, repeating the process every time I spotted another Golden employee, suspicious looking guest, or something of particular interest, like the large laundry carts that could be used to move bodies. Most employees paid little attention to me. The bellhops barely glanced in my direction. The four people working the check-in desk didn't even look up. They were used to this by now.

Considering the Golden didn't want their employees to have access to their personal devices while at work, I had to assume whatever they didn't want leaked wasn't viewable from any public areas. Whatever was worth maiming or killing over wasn't going to be easy to spot, especially if these deaths were the result of some radicalized ideology based off the Golden's training program.

If what Sasha told me was true, the situation had escalated. It may have taken years before the hazing or bullying, whatever the mirror thing was that she mentioned, turned into burning a woman with a steam press or running someone over. Still, my gut said there had to be more to it than that. Someone had to be encouraging this type of behavior and pushing for violent solutions.

"It's a damn cult," I muttered under my breath.

Stopping in front of the newsstand, I was surprised to find actual newspapers and magazines. After filming the different shelves and sections, I put the phone down, selected a book, which had been on the rack beside the periodicals, and took it to the counter. Signage in the store touted mobile checkout which would be charged to my room, but I didn't have a room. Yet.

The woman working the register offered a big smile when I approached. It didn't exactly look fake. It looked more like the lights were on, but no one was home. "Did you find everything okay?" she asked.

"I guess so." I thought about asking if she knew Leslie, but something about that smile warned me against it.

She scanned the item and tapped the computer screen.

"Are you a member of our rewards program?"

"No."

She tapped the screen a few more times. "Is there anything else I can help you with?" Her name tag read Britt.

"I have a strange question. When did your shift start? I thought I saw someone else working here earlier."

"You probably did. I only started at eight." She upped the wattage of that vacant smile. "Is there anything else I can help you with?"

Hoping to cover so that wasn't the last thing she remembered about me, I said, "It's weird to see real newspapers. I didn't think people still read those."

"We have them for the guests who enjoy them. They also make great souvenirs for scrapbookers." She stared at me with that same no lights on smile. "That will be $22.75. Would you like to charge it to your room?"

"I'll pay cash, if that's okay."

Maybe it was more like a Stepford smile. "Cash is more than okay."

I handed her twenty-five dollars, and she seamlessly gave me my change. Maybe she was a robot, like Sasha said. They'd been making a lot of freaky advancements lately. "Thanks."

"It was my pleasure. Have a wonderful day." She held the smile, waiting for me to walk away.

That wasn't creepy at all. I resisted giving in to the shudder.

With my shopping bag in hand, I pulled my phone out, stood beneath the newsstand sign, and held up the bag while filming myself. At this angle, I got several good shots of Britt and the doorway to the employee only area which was hidden behind the counter. Were other Golden employees hiding inside? Was someone gagged and tied to a chair in the back room? Okay, that seemed unlikely, but Britt's answer hadn't been particularly helpful either.

"Great find at a great price." I gave a big bright smile and made the peace sign before putting the camera down.

I'd only been at this for ten minutes, and I already hated it. How anyone could keep up this level of pep and enthusiasm was beyond me. Had all influencers been cheerleaders in a past life?

As I walked away from the stand, I kept an eye on Britt. She'd seen me make the recording, but if she planned to react or intervene, she never got the chance because another customer had an armful of snacks and travel cups that needed to be bagged.

I repeated the filming process outside the hotel's coffee shop before stepping inside with my camera leading the way. The shop had a bakery counter, brimming with all manner of deliciousness. The line was twelve deep by the time I entered, so I had plenty of time to capture the baked goods and gush over the selections.

Once I made it to the front of the line, I resisted the urge to order my usual. Instead, I opted for the hotel's specialty latte and four different baked goods. After all, I had to sell my cover. Three people were working. Two had dull, gold-colored name tags, but one had a silver name tag, the same color as Britt's.

The two baristas with the gold name tags moved quickly and efficiently with some smiling but not a lot of questions. They had things under control and were dealing with the influx of customers. Jay, the man with the silver name tag, had the same blank smile as Britt. He stood near the condiment bar, offering lids, wiping up spills, and assisting with whatever anyone needed.

The four items I ordered were placed on individual plates atop a tray. I carried the tray in one hand and the coffee in the other while I made my way to the condiment bar.

"May I help you find a table?" Jay asked. "I'd be happy to take your tray for you."

"That's okay. I can manage." I turned up the wattage on my smile, but it didn't even come close to matching his. "Do you mind if I ask you a question?"

"However I may help."

Again, I wondered if the employees had been replaced by robots. That would explain a lot. "Is this where you usually work?"

"I jump around from assignment to assignment. The

Golden has lots of opportunities."

Yep, Sasha had nailed it. They were robots. "Is that why your name tag is a different color?" I indicated my phone, which wasn't currently recording but had all the added bells and whistles content creators utilized. "Enquiring minds would like to know."

For a millisecond, his smile faltered, as if he'd done something wrong or there was a programming glitch. "I'm an intern. Interns where silver. Veterans, the regular employees, wear gold. Those with the most seniority, ten or more years on the job, get a star. Twenty years is two stars." The smile returned to full brightness. "Enjoy your treats."

Since he had taken the time to answer my question, I wanted to ask him more about the internship program, but he took a step past me to assist a woman with a double-wide stroller who was balancing her coffee cup and plate in the other hand. At least I had learned something.

After taking a seat, I snapped a few clandestine shots of Jay while I went back to the influencer schtick, this time channeling the pretentious judges on the food competition shows. I took several shots of the baked goods before selecting one to try. The sticky bun was the gooiest of the four options, so I waited for a lull between customers before making my way back to the condiment bar.

"Would you happen to have any wet wipes?" I asked.

Jay greeted me with the same smile. "I think I know where there may be some." He winked before crouching down and opening a cabinet beneath the bar. Could robots wink? "How many do you need?"

"I'd say one, but I'm a mess."

"Here." He handed me four.

A couple was fast approaching, so it was now or never. "Do you happen to know a woman named Gini? I think she's an intern too. I ran into her a few weeks ago, and she was really nice. I thought if I spotted her again, I'd say hi." I hoped that would be benign enough to keep from triggering his radar or alerting someone else to my question.

The smile lessened, but it looked like a natural response

to Jay thinking rather than from an actual emotion, like fear. "The name isn't familiar, but a lot of people work here. I'd love to meet her. She sounds like a wonderful person."

What the hell? "Do you know how many interns work here?"

He almost whistled but stopped himself, like he'd been instructed not to do such a thing. "About two hundred. I've only had the privilege of working with a handful of my colleagues so far. This is all new and very exciting for me. The Golden is a great place. I hope you enjoy your stay."

I went back to my table, hoping that disconcerting feeling was due to that strange interaction. But no matter how hard I tried, I couldn't quite shake it. I'd never been particularly claustrophobic, but the crowded coffee shop was making me reconsider that stance.

The walls were starting to close in. I needed air. Since I'd photographed everything, including the staff, I picked up my tray and tossed the treats I'd barely tasted and most of the coffee into the trash. The caffeine and sugar were liable to throw me over the edge.

Jay watched me as he smiled his way through an interaction with a ten-year-old concerning the wooden stirring sticks. Before I could make it around the double-wide stroller blocking my escape, he came up behind me.

"Was something not to your liking?" His voice made me jump. Damn nerves. "I'm sorry. I didn't mean to startle you. Are you okay? Is there something I can do to help?"

"Too much sugar and caffeine for one person," I said.

"Savory options are available. Since you weren't pleased with your treats, I'd be happy to get you something more to your liking."

"Maybe later."

"Are you sure? Breakfast is the most important meal of the day." Jay was determined to keep me inside the coffee shop. I didn't know if that was because he was determined that I have a positive experience or if he'd been instructed by someone else who may have heard my question about Gini. Moving in front of me, he held the creepy smile while he listed every savory breakfast item on the menu.

I tried to listen to what he said while focusing on my breath and the mental exercises that helped stave off panic attacks. What did I hear, smell, taste, and see?

A man in a dark suit caught my attention. He remained outside the coffee shop in the main concourse, leaning against the wall where the hallway curved.

Feeling him watching me, I looked in his direction, wondering if he was the reason the walls were closing in. As soon as I looked at him, he looked down, pretending to check his phone. Since I didn't get a good look at his face, I wasn't sure who he was, but my presence hadn't gone unnoticed. He was keeping tabs on me.

"That mushroom, spinach, and tomato frittata sounds interesting," I said.

"Have a seat. I'll get that right out to you." Jay indicated a newly abandoned table near the door.

TWENTY-TWO

I wandered around the main levels, pausing to take selfies every time I spotted something or someone the least bit interesting. If nothing else, my cover provided the perfect reason to take lots of surveillance photos and videos. Unfortunately, I had no idea what I was surveilling.

I kept my eyes peeled for Leslie, but I hadn't seen her. Food poisoning usually cleared up quickly, but she hadn't called to tell me she was getting released. With any luck, she was safe and sound at the hospital. Those were eight words I never thought would go together.

After asking Jay about Gini and getting stalked for my trouble, I decided that wasn't the right move. Luckily, the man in the suit had grown tired of watching me film, photograph, and dissect every bite of the frittata and had wandered off after twenty minutes.

After that, several members of the Golden's staff started paying special attention to me. I wondered if my photo had been forwarded to everyone to be on the lookout.

The rest of the staff offered me the same too bright smiles and pleasant greetings. Every single one of them asked if they could be of assistance, but I told them I was exploring and taking in the sights. Thus far, they'd been satisfied with that answer, but I wasn't sure how long that would last.

According to the Golden's website, guests weren't prohibited from taking photos or video recordings while on the premises. However, they did have a special clause concerning commercial use. Unsure where travel writers and influencers fell on that spectrum, I wondered if that had anything to do with the special treatment I'd been receiving.

I planned to request a meeting with someone in charge to get permission. I even had a boilerplate contract in my bag, one the DA's office had reviewed to make sure the wording would make any surveillance I set up in a public area or in the room I rented permissible as evidence that could be used in court. But I thought it best to look around first before I started planting bugs.

For all I knew, the Golden could deny my request. And while it was usually better to ask for forgiveness than permission, the Golden could kick me out anytime they wanted. That's what they'd done to Deanna, so I wanted to find out as much as I could about what was going on at the hotel before risking everything.

"Good afternoon," a woman with a gold name tag emerged from a room marked *authorized personnel only*, "are you enjoying your stay?"

"I'm just looking around."

"There are maps in the lobby and near the elevators. If you need any assistance, please don't hesitate." Thankfully, she didn't slow as she went past me.

I gave the room she emerged from another look. The door itself was a solid yellowish-beige which blended into the wall. Even the door handle was nothing but a tiny hook that could be tugged on. The panel to enter the unlock code was small and carved into the molding, also colored to match its surroundings. Guests weren't supposed to notice the door, and I couldn't help but wonder why.

I took a quick photo so fast no one would notice. Why did they bother with the plaque when they didn't want anyone to realize that was a room? More importantly, what was inside?

My trek down that hallway led me past a room with an

ice machine and several vending machines. I examined the vending machine selections while noting the locked cabinets beneath the sink which stood on the other side of the room. A roll of paper towel hung from the dispenser beside the sink.

After taking a few photos, I left that room. A block of forty guest rooms, twenty on each side of the hall, stood between me and the elevators. A few do not disturb signs hung from the door handles. Each door had an electronic lock. This place looked like every other hotel. So why did so many people end up dead?

When I made it to the elevator, I pressed the button and waited. A low table with decorative flowers stood between two of the elevators. On the opposite wall, between two other elevators, was a large round mirror. Something about the setup reminded me of a powder room.

The doors opened to my right. I waited as a family of four exited. The woman held the side of the elevator.

"Thanks," I said.

She nodded but didn't say anything. Maybe there was something in the air. Perhaps that's why everyone was so pleasant around here. The happy factor could be enough to drive anyone mad. Could that be what led to the attacks and suicides?

While examining the panel to select a floor, I realized that anything above twenty-five required keycard access. Without a key, I couldn't get to Leslie's room.

"Dammit." After pressing the button for twenty-five, I rested my hips against the handrail. The elevator opened on the next floor. A few people stepped inside. They pressed a button, and we went up another two floors.

When the elevator opened again, I stepped out. The nearby map showed the resort had a rooftop bar on the twenty-fifth floor, even though the building was thirty-two stories. I checked the website, but I couldn't find any details on those top seven floors. At least one housed the interns. But if there really were only two hundred people in the program, they wouldn't need more than a floor to themselves. So what was the Golden using the other six levels for? Since the resort offered a variety of executive, junior executive, presidential, and penthouse suites, I assumed they were up there.

A gift shop stood directly in front of me. Repeating the same things I'd done at the newsstand and coffee shop, I photographed myself in front of the store before going inside and checking out what they had to offer.

Three staff members were chatting quietly amongst themselves, but as soon as I entered, they stopped and painted on those same phony smiles. Didn't they make a horror movie like this?

"Welcome," the one with the ponytail said.

I browsed the nearest shelf which had a collection of travel cups. Some featured the Golden's logo. Others had iconic symbols representative of the city. "I have a question." I picked up the cup and checked the price, figuring Martin might like it. "What's above us?"

The smile didn't falter. "Our VIP rooms."

"Is there a secret rooftop bar up there?"

"No, the rooftop bar is over there." She pointed out the door. "It's around that corner. There is indoor and outdoor seating and an excellent 180 degree view of the skyline."

"I figured a place like this would have a 360 degree view from the actual roof. Or is that only for VIPs?"

"I can assure you we aren't hiding a secret bar on the roof. However, our VIP guests do have special roof access and a dedicated lounge and concierge. Are you interested in upgrading your room? Someone at the front desk will be able to assist you with that."

"I don't have a room reservation yet." All this smiling was making my face hurt. "I wanted to check out the resort first." I picked up a different travel mug that had cartoon drawings of iconic locations and brought it to the register. "180 degrees. I have to see that for sure."

While the woman rang up my purchase, I noticed the other two Golden employees hadn't stopped staring at me. They hadn't said a word or chimed in on the conversation, but they kept an eye on me. Despite the same creepy smiles on their faces, they stared at me like a mall security guard would a teenager with extra baggy clothes and a juvie record a mile long.

"Have a wonderful time at the rooftop bar," Ponytail said, handing me my bag.

"I will." I tucked that bag into the shopping bag I had from the newsstand and nodded to the two other employees. "Try not to work too hard, ladies."

They watched as I left the store, afraid I'd shove a Golden sweatshirt into my bag on my way out. Resisting the urge to record more footage of the shop since I'd done that before I entered, I paused briefly in front of the entrance, held up the bag, made a peace sign, and took a quick selfie. All that I cared about was getting those three women in the shot. I'd seen their name tags. Sarah, Vanessa, and Kayla.

Being able to put names to faces may prove important later. At this point, I had no idea what would prove important, but it was better to have too much intel than not enough.

I went down the corridor, surprised when the walkway took a sharp turn revealing the outdoor patio through a giant wall of floor to ceiling windows. The entrance to the bar was straight ahead. I took a few more shots before going inside. More smiles. More pleasantries.

After requesting a table for one, I was escorted outside. Even the tables near the doors had great views. Two bars stood on either side. One served nothing but beer, wine, and small plates. The other dealt exclusively with cocktails.

I sat down, took some photos, posed for a few selfies, and ordered a sparkling white wine. It didn't matter that it was barely lunchtime. It didn't stop any of the other guests from ordering alcoholic beverages in the middle of the day.

Once my wine was brought to me, I took several pretentious photos and ordered a tray of sliders. While pretending to review the shots I'd taken, I snapped a few of the staff, paying special attention to the dozen silver name tags slinging drinks, bussing tables, serving, and seating guests.

The moment I finished my wine and sliders, three members of the resort staff appeared in front of me. I hadn't seen them coming, but with the bright sun and reflective windows, I hadn't been able to see inside. That led to a tactical disadvantage, which I'd have to remember.

They wore dark grey and maroon uniforms. Louis Grable stood to the left. Despite the movie theater attendant vibes, my gut said they were hotel security. Had he recognized me?

"Miss," the one in the middle gave me a tight smile, "have you been enjoying your stay?"

"I'm just visiting." I looked around. "Though, I have been thinking about planning a stay. Is something wrong?"

"Not at all." But he and his two friends remained in v-formation, his hands clasped neatly in front of him. A profiler at Quantico had said standing like that was a sign a guy was uncomfortable or afraid, as if he needed to shield his favorite appendage.

"Are you sure," I leaned forward, squinting to read his name off the tag pinned to his chest, "Bart?"

He held the tight smile. "The hotel manager would like to speak to you before you leave."

I gave him the biggest, brightest smile I could muster. "Excellent. I was hoping to have a word with her." I fished a ten dollar bill out of my bag, put it on the table beneath my wine glass as a tip, and stood. "Shall we?"

The tension in Bart's face eased, and he stepped back. Louis and the other guard moved in unison, as if they had choreographed their steps. Bart gestured with his palm up, like the doorman had when I first arrived. "After you."

The trip to the lobby didn't take long. The guards were polite. They didn't smile like the rest of the staff, but they smiled nonetheless. Louis remained behind me, but he could easily see my face reflected in the elevator doors. However, he didn't seem to be paying that much attention. The no-lights-on smile remained on his face, but his eyes weren't focused on me. From what I could tell, he was staring into nothingness.

Bart walked beside me, using his outstretched arm to guide us. He led me past the check-in desk and the decorative couches, which were half-filled with guests who seemed to be enjoying themselves, and to an open doorway.

"Mrs. Shaw," Bart said, "you have a visitor."

The woman behind the desk stood, the wattage of her smile increasing like an energy efficient lightbulb heating up. "Welcome to the Golden, Miss...?"

"Riley." I shook her outstretched hand. "Alexandra Riley."

"Please, Ms. Riley, have a seat." Shaw waited for me to sit before she sat back down. She nodded at the shopping bags I'd placed on the floor at my feet. "I see you've been enjoying yourself."

"Gorging myself is more like it. Have you tried the sticky buns? They're amazing. And the lemon loaf," I blew a chef's kiss, "absolutely spectacular. But way too sweet on an empty stomach. The frittata really saved my day."

My words pleased Shaw. "Did you get a chance to tour the gardens? They're my favorite place. Quiet, serene, and lovely, especially at night with the array of colored bulbs we have to make it look like a tropical oasis."

"Not yet, but I will make that a priority. In fact, I was hoping to speak to someone in media relations." I launched into the speech I'd practiced a few times with Lawson concerning who I was and what I did for a living.

"I knew you looked familiar," she said. "I'm a huge fan of your work. I've been following your YouTube page for years. I never miss a new video."

"Oh really?" Liar. "I love that. It's always nice to meet someone who enjoys my adventures. I wouldn't be able to do what I do without people like you."

"I especially loved the videos you posted from Miami. I lived there for a while and stayed in a few of those resorts. You really made them shine." She glanced at my camera and attached equipment. "I take it you were thinking about covering the Golden."

"I was...am." I shook my head. "I've seen a lot of chatter online about the Golden. Most boutique hotels are overhyped. But I'm not getting that vibe from this place. Everything I've seen and experienced so far has been top-notch. With the online excitement about your internship program, I wanted to check it out myself. The research I did didn't turn up much on that program though. I thought covering the basics on that, along with everything else the hotel has to offer, would make a perfect series of videos, assuming the Golden is amenable to allowing me to film this. I always like to ask for permission before creating any in-depth content. But the preliminary stuff I've shot has been stellar."

"What are you planning on using it for?" Shaw asked.

"That depends on you. I can use it for short-form videos and posts, and that'll be it. Y'know, five stars on the frittata. The rooftop bar is an absolute must. Things like that. Or I can use it as B-roll and to create teasers of what's to come. Nothing like whetting the appetites of the internet masses who are looking for their next great travel destination or for those who want to live vicariously through me and my experiences."

"What exactly did you have in mind?"

"Ideally, I want to cover everything. A real behind-the-scenes into the Golden and how it operates."

"Including the internship program?"

"Yes. I would absolutely love to do that. No one else has done that yet, at least as far as I know. If I could talk to the interns and whoever's in charge of the selection process and day-to-day operations, that would be super insightful. Viewers would get a look into what the program entails and what they need to do to qualify. I could take some photos or videos to show how things work, which would be icing on the cake. It'd be a great tool to entice new applicants while also giving me a giant boost. Maybe it'll even go viral. I'll make the Golden look good, and the Golden will make me look good."

Shaw centered her keyboard and reached for her mouse. After clicking a few things, my voice came through her speakers from whatever videos Lawson had put together. "What about room tours?" she asked. "Will you do those? They are my favorites."

"Oh, absolutely. I'll film as much as you'll allow." Since I hadn't paid with a credit card and hadn't been carded at the bar, I wasn't sure how she connected me to the social media profiles Lawson had put together. With my makeup, reflective lenses, and wig, facial rec shouldn't have gotten any hits, assuming they were running facial recognition software, which according to Cross Security they were not.

Had someone heard me making a recording? Had the security cameras picked that up? The equipment the Golden used was good, but I didn't think it was that good. No. Someone on staff had listened and reported me to the boss. The mystery man in the suit came to mind. But it didn't matter who it was. All that mattered was Shaw had bought my cover, which meant no one knew why I was really here.

"The Golden would love for you to do that. We have a standard agreement we use with the media." She checked the screen one more time, possibly making sure my posts matched what she wanted for the resort.

"I have a contract my lawyers approved. It covers basic stuff. But it saves me the time and trouble of having to ask them to review every hotel and restaurant's agreements which can greatly delay things." I reached into my bag and fished it out.

"I'll have someone from our legal team review it." She skimmed the main sections. "But it looks like this should be suitable. I have one last question."

"Sure."

"Why have I never seen you post any negative reviews? Every place you go can't possibly be five-star worthy."

"They aren't. If I come across something I don't like, I don't report on it. If the hotel doesn't meet my expectations after my initial walkthrough, I abandon it and check out somewhere else. If I come across something subjective, like I think a mattress is too firm or the bathroom only has a tub and not a walk-in shower, I'm not going to make those things sound negative because everyone likes different things."

"Like breakfast being too sweet?"

"Exactly like that. It wasn't too sweet. It was great, just not for my empty stomach. But other people love sweet in the morning. So who am I to say that's not the way to go? Now, if I find a dead rat under a table, I'll bail. But I don't want to post that and add to the online drama. Between cries of fake news and fake videos, I find it's best to focus on the positive. Even the best videos get negative comments from time to time, usually in regards to how I'm dressed or the way my voice sounds." I laughed. "I can't please everyone. I also think most of those comments may be coming from my mother. Well, at least the ones saying I should settle down and find a man." I laughed as if it were a joke I'd shared dozens of times.

"That's refreshing, seeing as how most people focus on the negative instead of the positive." Shaw turned away from the screen and stared directly at me. "The Golden has faced criticism from competitors and naysayers, which is why we've never allowed a third party to share information about our internship program before. However, if you agree to allow us final approval on whatever content you plan to post before posting it, I think we can work something out."

"Fantastic." Now all I had to do was figure out why people who worked here were ending up dead and who was responsible.

TWENTY-THREE

I spent the rest of the day wandering the hotel while the Golden's legal team read every word of the contract. Once that was done, I checked into room 110. Shaw wanted to start me out with a basic room. King bed, street view. Nothing special. Regardless, I couldn't help but think she wanted to keep an eye on me. The contract had been signed, which made me feel better, assuming I found evidence the police would need to build a case.

Fourteen dead. Heathcliff and I ruled half of those out as circumstantial. That left seven, all hotel staff, all within the last few months. Not every death occurred at the hotel. Two of them did not, but they connected. I knew it. And whatever happened to them connected to Leslie and the attack on Gini. The Golden wasn't a safe place. But why hadn't Leslie walked out when we gave her the perfect opportunity?

I'd been banging my head against the wall trying to answer that question since yesterday afternoon. The only person who could answer that was Leslie. Between her confusion over the events and Sasha Drew's comments on brainwashing, I was starting to wonder if that was possible.

Leslie would be released later this afternoon and planned to head straight to the Golden from the hospital.

In her downtime, she'd met with a sketch artist who came up with composites of the four assailants. Heathcliff had forwarded those to me, so I was keeping an eye out but had yet to spot any of them.

After carefully examining my room from all angles, I determined how many cameras I'd need to set up inside for my own peace of mind. I'd pulled out Martin's matching set of luggage the previous night, removed all identifiers, and made sure the pieces were empty. The complete set had everything from rolling bags to carry-ons to cosmetic cases. Why he needed those, I did not know, but I'd outfitted each one with a tiny hidden camera. However, the luggage was in my car, which wasn't here because I hadn't wanted to tip off the staff as to my real identity for more reasons than I wanted to count. I'd have to go get them. If I hurried, I might be able to make it back to the Golden before Leslie returned.

Without warning, the door to my room opened. I reached for my bag which contained my gun hidden under the camera equipment and portable lighting pieces that attached to my phone.

A woman in a maid's outfit pushed her way into the room, backing the cleaning cart into the doorway to hold the door open. When she turned around to find me in the room, she looked embarrassed. "I'm sorry. I didn't know anyone was here. I'll come back."

"Wait," I said. "It's okay." She was the first person I'd encountered who hadn't immediately started smiling. Even the security guards had made a half-assed attempt to smile while appearing business-like. "I just checked in. I can get out of here if I'm in your way."

"No, that's fine. I can come back."

"Please," I said, "I'd rather you do whatever you need to before I accidentally use someone's dirty towels."

She gave the room a curious look. "It's my mistake. This room was already cleaned. But I can change the towels anyway." She took the neat stack which had been decoratively splayed on the counter and beds and replaced it with other towels which she carefully arranged just as artfully. "I hadn't been notified about an early check-in.

Diedre cleaned before you arrived."

"Diedre?" I asked.

"Another maid. She does the odds. I do evens, but for early check-ins, whoever's available cleans that room first."

"I'm sorry to make your job more difficult."

"Not at all. This is why we get paid. Usually, we get notified ahead of time. I must have missed it."

"You didn't. My arrival was a surprise. I'm Alexandra, by the way."

"Jane. Again, I'm sorry for getting in your way."

I shook off her apology. "That's all me." Her name tag was gold with two stars. She looked about fifty. "How long have you worked here?"

"Forever." An unintentional sigh escaped her lips.

"Have things changed a lot?"

"You could say that." She tried to smile but didn't quite succeed.

I lowered my voice. "I can't tell you how relieved I am to meet someone who isn't jumping at me with a creepy clown smile on their face. It's kind of freaking me out."

She laughed, covering her mouth in embarrassment. "They want the guests to know how much we love our jobs."

"Is that why there have been so many suicides lately? Because everyone's so happy?"

"How did you—"

"News stories. I did a lot of research before checking in. They were tiny mentions, but they stuck in my head. It looks like something's happening every few weeks."

"It's nothing for you to worry about. The Golden's turned into quite the destination. With increased popularity comes a few more issues. But like I said, that's nothing for you to worry about."

"What do you think made the Golden become so popular?" I asked.

"The place has a little bit of everything. Lots of new restaurants, the spa, and recent renovations. It's undergone quite the transformation over the years. This used to just be a job. Now it's a way of life."

"What do you mean?"

She shrugged, realizing she shouldn't be saying anything, but she had too many years on the job to necessarily care. For all I knew, she could be retiring tomorrow. "Nothing really."

"I hear the interns live at the hotel. Was that always the case?"

"That's one of the newer things that has taken place over the last five or six years."

"That's not that new."

"Maybe not, but attitudes have dramatically shifted recently. Then again, society has changed a lot in recent years too."

"What do you mean?"

She glanced at the door, making sure the hallway was clear. "For some of the new staff, the rules and regs are like being part of something bigger. The newbies are invested in the Golden and making everything amazing, so I'm sure your stay will be extraordinary. A positive experience is the most important thing here at the Golden. The interns are exceptional at emphasizing that."

"You mean they're brainwashed into smiling and asking to assist me?" I shouldn't have said it, but I wanted to get her take.

She laughed uneasily. "They are held to much higher standards than we were when I started here many moons ago. That's why I can say you'll have a wonderful visit. Everyone is determined to make certain that happens."

"What happens if I don't?"

"Well, I really hope you do." She pointed to the phone on the bedside table. "If you need additional towels or more toiletries, anything like that, let us know. A lot of the system is automated now, so you can press a button for most things you may need. Room service is number three."

"Are there any courtesy phones?"

"You'll find them on the tables near the elevators and in the lobby. There are a few others on the twenty-fifth floor outside the restaurant and the bar."

"Thanks."

After she left, I grabbed my bag and thought about hanging the do not disturb, but I didn't see the point and headed for the elevator. On the table, I found the courtesy phone, which looked like something out of a 1950s film. I had thought it was a decorative piece, not realizing it was functional when I passed it earlier.

While I dug out my camera, I read the instructions taped to the inside of the receiver. *To dial a room, enter # followed by the room number.*

After posing with the phone, I went out the main entrance and turned right. In half a block, I'd be passing the alleyway where a bellhop had been gunned down. But it was the middle of the day. The sun was shining brightly overhead. Still, I kept my head on a swivel.

I hadn't even made it half a block when Louis Grable emerged from the hotel. He was no longer in his security uniform. Instead, he wore a pair of khaki pants which could have used some ironing and a sloppy white t-shirt, which I suspected had been beneath his uniform.

Instead of letting on that I had noticed him, I pulled out my phone and called Heathcliff. "Hey," I said, "I just checked in at the Golden. The place looks amazing. I shot some really great footage and tried out the coffee shop and bar. Now, I'm heading back to get my luggage."

"Is everything okay?"

"I'm not sure."

"Where are you?"

"Half a block from the Golden."

"I can send a patrol car to drive past there," he offered.

"Yeah, okay." I kept walking, wondering if Grable was going to head toward the parking garage, but he stayed with me. At the crosswalk, he moved to the other side of the street.

"Do you think you were made?" Heathcliff asked.

I glanced across the street, noting that Grable was keeping pace with me. I slowed near a bodega, debating if I should go inside. A look behind me didn't reveal anyone else on my tail. "I don't know." My disguise was meant to prevent that from happening, but Grable had gotten a good look at me the other night and again when he joined Bart and the other security guard to escort me to the manager's office.

"What's the plan?"

"I'll take the bus to my car and have a taxi or rideshare pick me up from there," I said.

"All right." But he didn't hang up. "Do you know the bus schedule?"

"Do I look like an MTA board?"

"I'll stay on the line with you until you get on the bus and tell me the coast is clear."

Grable didn't enter the parking garage. Instead, he continued moving parallel to me. He'd glance over every now and again, never bothering to conceal his actions. Was he the world's worst tail? Or did he not care if I spotted him? He didn't care the other night. In fact, he made it blatantly obvious. Were these intimidation tactics?

Once I made it to the bus stop, I found a shady place beneath a tree and checked the posted route times. Grable kept going. I watched him continue down the block. I debated if I should follow my pursuer, but that felt like a trap. Instead, I made a few blatant attempts to look around while dithering on to Heathcliff about the things around me. No one else had followed me.

The bus came a few minutes later. I swiped my metro card and found an empty seat near the back. It was a little too early for rush-hour, but after a few more people got on board, it was standing room only.

"I'm clear," I said.

Heathcliff let out a breath I hadn't expected him to be holding. "Are you sure you can handle this?"

"Don't ask me that. I'm just taking precautions. I've promised a lot of people I'd be careful. And you know I aim to please."

"Well, I'm here all day and night. Whatever you need."

"Thanks, Derek."

I put my phone away and settled into the seat, peering out the window to see if anyone was following the bus, but I didn't think that was the case. We stopped one block later. Four people got off. Ten got on. Among them was Louis Grable.

TWENTY-FOUR

Grable held the hanging strap as the bus lurched forward. Since it was standing room only, he remained near the middle. He hadn't looked back at me once. For someone who had been so obvious earlier, I wasn't sure why he was playing it cool now. Maybe he hoped to avoid a confrontation in an enclosed space.

I remained in my seat, doing my best not to stare while keeping an eye on him. Why was he following me? Even if he recognized me from the other night, I hadn't said much. All I asked was if anyone knew Leslie. Grable would have no way of knowing who I was or why I was interested. Right?

I ran the possibilities through my head, coming up with different scenarios, but even if Grable realized I was working with the police, he had no way of knowing what my interest was with the Golden. Heathcliff had made our visit seem routine. It was just a follow-up. Maybe Grable was told to gather intel. Memories of the man in the suit from this morning came to mind. Shit, maybe the hotel was on to me.

Pulling out my phone, I sent a text to Lawson. We needed to meet. The sooner we could get some of today's footage posted, the easier it would be to convince the hotel staff that I was Alexandra Riley, travel influencer.

Meet at the OIO's usual watering hole? Lawson replied.

Forty-five minutes. It would take that long for me to ditch the tail and get there. Or so I thought.

Three stops later, most of the commuters on board had left, replaced by a new set of commuters heading to a different stop. Grable had been inching his way backward. When the person sitting beside me got up to leave, he slid into the empty seat.

I pretended not to notice while I stared at my phone, reviewing the photos I'd taken. He didn't appear armed. His shirt didn't snag in any of the usual places, so I didn't think he had a gun. His pants legs had ridden up high enough that I could tell he didn't have an ankle holster. He could have a knife in his pocket, though.

Putting Cross Security's new body armor to the test wasn't on my list of things to do, so I hoped it wouldn't come down to that. I scrolled through more photos while I ran through my options if he were to pull a weapon. Screaming and then knocking his head into the bar beside the seat was probably my best bet.

"Hey," Grable leaned closer to me, "you were at the Golden earlier today." He gave me that creepy smile. "I thought I recognized you."

I turned to look at him. "Um...yeah. I just have to grab my bags from another hotel so I can transition over." I cocked my head to the side. "Were you at the bar?"

"Sort of." He held the smile. "I work at the Golden."

"We rode the elevator together," I said.

"That's right." He held out his hand. "I'm Lou."

"Alexandra."

"Are you enjoying everything the Golden has to offer?"

"So far."

The smile fell. "You look so familiar. How do I know you?"

"The elevator, remember?"

"Besides that."

I tucked a strand of the blonde wig behind my ear. "Um...my YouTube channel, maybe?"

"Are you internet famous?"

"Not even close. But I try."

Grable kept smiling, but the look in his eyes told me he was considering my words. He pointed to my phone. "Would you mind showing me?"

I brought up the page Lawson had put together. "Here's that video Mrs. Shaw was talking about." I hit play, still surprised when this version of me appeared briefly on the screen to give the introduction before jumping into the resort tour. Since the video was pretty long, I only showed Grable a few seconds. "Do you want to see some of the rough footage I took today at the Golden?" I didn't wait for his response before opening the first saved video. "I'm hoping to get it uploaded later tonight or tomorrow. It needs to be edited, but it'll be a nice little teaser."

He watched the footage until the bus came to another jerky stop. Grable looked up. "This is me." He stood. "I'll be keeping my eye on you." Again, he gave me the same nod that he'd done in his car and disappeared into the throng of disembarking passengers.

Shit. He was on to me. Was that supposed to scare me off or intimidate me?

I stared out the window, watching as the white shirt and khakis disappeared down the street, heading back toward the Golden. I paid attention to everyone else on the bus. But no one was interested in me, and by the time I got off the bus, none of the original passengers remained. Sure, Grable and his buddies could have been leapfrogging, but in my hyper-aware state, I would have noticed if someone was watching me.

Leslie hadn't identified Louis Grable as one of the men who attacked Gini, but Grable had something to do with whatever was going on inside the Golden. He'd have no reason to follow me otherwise.

On my way to the bar, I called Heathcliff back and asked if he could get someone to sit on Louis Grable's place. When Grable got off the bus, he hadn't been heading home. He was heading back to work. Did he have to report on me to the man in the suit? And if so, why couldn't he call with the information? Was he still on the clock when he was sent to follow me?

"Alex," Heathcliff said, "it sounds like you're blown. We should hit this another way."

"I just got checked-in. Let's see where this takes us."

"What happened to being careful?"

"I'm reconsidering my stance on the matter. But if it makes you feel any better, I'm about to walk into a room of exhausted, overworked federal agents who've been drinking too much. If Grable or any of his pals try to make a move on me, they'll find a very rude surprise waiting for them."

Lawson waved me over to the booth where he was sitting. "You're late," he said.

"I was made."

"Shit. Are you sure?"

I told him what happened.

"Are you scrapping the mission?"

This wasn't exactly a mission. I had no clear parameters or mission objective. "Not yet. I want to let it play out. If anything, Leslie could be in more danger now than before."

"Or less. If they think you're working with the police to keep an eye on her, they may back off." He took the phone from me and set it to automatically upload to the cloud. Then he opened his laptop and got to work. "You didn't tell me this was going to require so much time," Lawson said as he performed magic to turn the raw footage I'd taken into internet friendly social media junk food. "How can you be so incapable?"

"I ask myself that every day."

Lawson glanced at me from the corner of his eye. "My grandmother knows how to edit and post videos. You have no excuse, Parker."

"I can do it. I just can't do it well. You're the expert." I pointed to the screen. "Where did you even come up with half that stuff? And don't tell me I did the voice recordings for all of these because I know I didn't."

"They were computer-assisted."

"In that case, why can't you make the robot version of me do the work for you?"

"She's not that capable either," he teased.

"Figures."

He set up a dozen fifteen second clips and scheduled them to post over the course of the next few days. Then he frontloaded four to post within the hour. The Golden wanted to see the kinds of things I planned to use before giving me the behind-the-scenes tour of their internship program. I had to show them how well I could play the game before getting to play in the big leagues, assuming Grable's suspicions didn't torpedo my chances.

"I created a preliminary room tour from that footage you shot and combined it with some other room tours I've found online. It's a rough cut, but you can send that to Mrs. Shaw for approval." Lawson shut his computer and picked up his drink. "Thanks for buying dinner."

"It's the least I can do. I bet the robot version of me doesn't buy you dinner."

"No, but I could program her to put out."

"Do I even want to know how that would work?"

"Probably not." He reached for his burger and took a bite. "You wouldn't believe the kinds of shit cybercrimes has had to deal with in the last few months. It's getting scary fast. The number of scams has skyrocketed. Everything's on another level. We barely had a handle on it before, but now..."

"Clean up on aisle four."

"Have you been facing the same things at Cross Security?"

"You'd have to ask Cross. As far as the security reviews and consultations I provide, they're basic. Our techs run the checks. I rubberstamp." I picked up a fry. "There's one thing that's been bothering me. How did they ID Alexandra Riley so quickly? Even if someone heard my name, there are thousands of travel influencers. It should have taken longer for Mrs. Shaw to stumble upon me."

Lawson looked down at his plate, focusing his attention on the remainder of his burger. "I built your following up quickly which tickled the algorithms. That gave you added visibility. Add to that some highly targeted sponsored ad campaigns that I directed to employees at the Golden. If management hadn't IDed you, I would have been worried."

"Too bad Grable isn't falling for it."

"Maybe he is. He didn't really say or do anything suspicious."

"He nodded and said he'd keep an eye on me."

"Okay, but people do that all the time."

Lawson made a fair point. Sure, I was still a little gun shy, but I also knew what happened when I chose to write things off. I couldn't afford to do that again.

"What about the man in the suit?" I asked. "Clearly, there is an element at the Golden who wants to keep tabs on me."

"Well, you are a hotel critic of sorts. The staff should be wary and over-obliging."

I pushed the basket of fries closer to him. "I don't know."

When he looked up, he had worry in his eyes. "For my own peace of mind, tell me how dangerous you think this might be."

"I don't know yet. But there's no reason you should be targeted. In fact, if this turns into an investigation, it will be a police investigation. Your involvement won't come to light. You won't be called to testify." I knew what happened the last time he had to testify in open court against a violent offender I'd arrested. "I didn't ask earlier, but how are you doing?"

"It's not about me. But Jablonsky said you had a close call, and you have a history of—"

"Getting agents killed?"

"Parker, I'm not going to lie and tell you I'm not worried about that. But my exposure is limited. Yours isn't. And it sounds like you're out there alone. I'm worried about you."

"I'm not alone. You were my second call. Heathcliff was my first. I just have to get the ball rolling. Once I find proof that the people at the Golden aren't safe, the PD will step in." I pointed to his computer. "This is how I get the ball rolling."

TWENTY-FIVE

A rideshare took me back to the Golden. The driver helped me unload the bags from the trunk, and the doorman called over a bellhop to assist. Once I was back in my room, I pulled out the RF scanner and searched for any devices that may have been planted in my absence. The room was clean.

It took twenty minutes to strategically place the hidden cameras and make sure the alerts were sent to my phone, not my cover's phone.

"I'm losing my mind," I muttered. Martin's luggage surrounded me, which only made that worse. His worries had been running through my head on a loop since I set foot on the property this morning. That's why I was wearing the thin sleeveless shirt Cross had dropped off beneath my regular clothes. I had no idea how much protection the prototype could provide, but light armor was better than no armor. Still, it wouldn't help if I got bonked on the head. Maybe I should wrap one around my head and say it was a scarf or kerchief.

Twelve hours undercover, and I was already cracking up. That had to be a new record. By now, Leslie was back at the hotel. She had texted when she left the hospital, but she'd been radio silent ever since. She couldn't risk someone on staff spotting her with a cell phone. Surely, she had silenced the device or turned it off, but I was afraid to test that theory.

Instead, I left my room and ventured to the lobby. Louis Grable wasn't at his earlier post. Another security guard was stationed near the check-in counter. I didn't recognize him, but I snapped a photo anyway before pointing my camera at the big *Welcome to the Golden* sign above the front desk.

After that, I made a quick detour to the manager's office, surprised to find Shaw inside. Her handbag was on the desk beside her. She appeared to be getting ready to go home.

"Excuse me," I said. "I have a rough edit of a quick room tour ready for you."

"Already?" she asked.

"It'll need more editing, but I didn't want to spend too much time making it sparkle if the Golden planned to nix it. I just need to know where to send it."

Shaw grabbed a card from the stand on her desk and handed it to me. "You can use the e-mail listed there."

"Great. Thanks."

She walked me to the door and turned the lights off. "I'll make sure that it gets to the right people. You should know the verdict first thing in the morning, but if it's anything like the rest of your work, I don't foresee us encountering any problems."

"Great." I made a show of looking around the lobby. "Do you know if Louis Grable's still here?"

"I'm sure he went home. Why?"

"I ran into him earlier. He said he was going to keep an eye on me."

Shaw's brow scrunched, despite her best efforts to maintain that now-familiar smile. The combination only made her look that much more confused. "I'm not sure why he said that. He must have been teasing you."

"Either that or he's afraid I'm going to shoplift all the cute mugs from the gift shop upstairs."

Shaw laughed. "I'm sure you have nothing to worry about."

"We'll see." I bid her goodbye and headed for the door which led to the gardens.

Shaw spoke to the staff manning the desk, but she watched me through the oversized windows as I walked the paths, taking photos of the beautiful nighttime scenes. When I couldn't handle the exotic plants and their annoying pollen for another second, I returned to the lobby in time to see her leave.

I ducked into a quiet alcove near the elevators and checked the sketches Heathcliff had sent. I didn't spot any of the assailants on the first floor. So I took the elevator up to level twenty-five.

By now, the place was packed. The bar and restaurant had lines out the door. People who didn't have reservations were being turned away.

Ducking into the gift shop, I found a spot near the exit to keep an eye on things in the corridor. A man dressed as a host stepped out of the restaurant to call for a particular party. He had a thin goatee and glasses with square frames which matched one of the four sketches. I snapped several photos of him, wishing the cheap device I was using had a faster response time.

After finding the least blurry of the photos, I moved to another aisle, relieved that the four Golden employees manning the registers were too busy to notice what I was doing. Deciding to risk it, I sent an innocuous text to Leslie.

Hey, girl. I was hoping to run into you tonight. The words would mean nothing to anyone who may intercept the message.

I stared at the screen, hoping she would respond and fearing what a lack of response might mean. Half a minute later, three dots appeared beneath my message.

I'm going to pick up some ginger ale later. Only one place sells it. It'll be after everything dies down, like around 1 a.m. I'm sick, so I'm not supposed to be around any guests. Sorry.

I reread the message a few times before responding with, *Feel better. And make sure you get that ginger ale.*

Assuming Leslie was afraid our messages would be discovered or someone was with her when she received my initial message, I didn't want to send her the photo or ask for further clarification. More than likely, we'd meet up later tonight when I'd accidentally bump into her during her ginger ale run, except I didn't know where they sold ginger ale.

Calling the front desk and asking would be the easiest route, but since Grable was on to me, I didn't want to risk it. I didn't know who else was watching me besides the mystery man in the suit. So I'd have to do things the hard way.

The Golden's website listed every shop, bar, and restaurant on the premises, along with full menus. But the shops didn't list the items available for purchase. And that didn't take into account the vending machines and soda fountains.

Since I was in the gift shop, I started there, checking the cooler cases and shelves. I found all manner of bottled beverage except ginger ale. I asked one of the employees, but she didn't think the Golden sold ginger ale and suggested I try the bodega down the street.

Leaving the shop, I thought about waiting to get into the bar, but Leslie wasn't supposed to be seen around guests. So I didn't think she'd risk going into one of the few places that would still be operating that late at night. The same could be said for the other bars on the first floor and all the restaurants.

So I went back to the ground floor to continue my search. The vending machines didn't have any ginger ale, so I did a quick check at the newsstand. No dice.

After that, I looked around outside but didn't find any vending machines or soda fountains near the pool or garden area. The pool bar closed at ten, which made that location moot. So I went back inside and up a level.

Each floor had its own set of vending machines. It took almost an hour, but I finally found a machine that dispensed ginger ale on level eighteen. I slid my newly acquired credit card through the slot and made my selection. When the machine ejected the can, I picked it up, tapped on the top, and leaned against the counter while I cracked it open and took a sip.

I didn't spot any surveillance cameras covering the area, but I had seen them on either end of the hallway. Before exiting, I pulled up the schematics I'd found on Cross's servers and compared the floor plan to what I witnessed. The Golden hadn't made any changes, which meant if I met Leslie at the soda machine, we'd have our privacy, but the cameras would catch us coming to this location.

Would it be worth it to try to short one out? If one or both of them went on the fritz that would be more suspicious than a guest grabbing a late night snack. So I'd just have to come back. Timing would be important.

As I ran through the logistics, I bought an overpriced bag of gummy worms from the snack machine and walked out with my bounty in hand. Should anyone in security be paying attention, they'd think I had been looking for these specific items, which I hadn't found on any of the other floors I'd searched.

While I waited for the elevator, I grabbed a tiny security camera from my pocket, peeled off the backing using my thumbnail, and surreptitiously placed it on the side of the courtesy phone. Since the base was black, I hoped it wouldn't be discovered. Now all I had to do was wait for Leslie to make her ginger ale run. That would make timing my appearance that much easier.

Since I had five hours to kill, I went in search of the three other men involved in the attack. The sun had set, but the pool lights burned brightly. Pulling out my camera, I forced myself back into influencer mode and started recording as I headed toward the water.

Since I wasn't in a swimsuit, I sprawled out on a lounger. If I had to stay at the Golden for an extended amount of time, I'd have to find a way to cover my more severe scars. The one on my collarbone wasn't that pronounced, but I'd need a suit that covered enough of my back to show only the surgical scars. Having to explain why a travel influencer had bullet wounds would be a tough sell. And one I hoped to avoid.

The main pool was a large bean-shape. Stairs led into it on one side, and a slide was set up on the other side. A few kids raced up and down the stairs, sliding down into the water only to get out and do it again. Their parents were at the poolside bar drinking iced drinks with little pink umbrellas.

A group of older women huddled together in the hot tub, chatting while they held on to their plastic wine glasses and kicked their legs. No one paid attention to the couple playing tonsil hockey in the far corner of the pool. Another group was laying out on the loungers closest to the firepit, exhausted from a fun day in the sun. The smell of fire and burning sugar wafted through the air. They had marshmallows.

Opening the bag of gummy worms, I ate one while I focused on the pool towels which were stored in a large shelf protected from the elements and insects by flaps of plastic. A return bin for wet towels sat a few feet to the left of it.

Getting up, I grabbed two towels from the shelf and checked the return bin. The structure was a good ten feet from the pool's edge, providing an ample walkway. How had Sue Shade slipped, hit her head, and ended up face down in the water?

The kids playing on the slide had caused quite a flood, making the concrete around the towel area wet and possibly slippery. But it didn't seem all that slippery to me. The nearby hedges served to separate different sections of the pool area, isolating the splash pad, which was currently turned off, from the main pool area and the firepit on the other side. Had someone been hiding in the bushes? Could they have caused Sue's accident?

The lighting in this area wasn't the best. The pathway around the pool was illuminated by tiny lights on either side, but the chairs, tables, and bushes had no light. They were cast in shadow from the illuminated pool.

I took a panoramic photo, sweeping slowly to capture all of it. The police should have looked into these things, but with the surveillance footage showing her taking a tumble, I didn't think they had bothered.

The surveillance cameras didn't cover the bushes. They only covered the walkway. And in the dark, someone dressed in blackout gear could have snuck right up to the edge and never been spotted.

The security footage I'd seen showed Sue had replenished the clean towels and took her now empty cart to the towel return to take the dirty towels back to the laundry. After she started to head back, she stumbled and landed in the pool. I'd watched the footage several times, enough that it made me sick, but I knew how everything had played out. However, I couldn't reconcile the images in my head to the area around the pool.

The space was limited. Unless she'd been pushed, she wouldn't have had enough momentum to tumble sideways, crack her head on the edge of the pool, and slide forward with enough force that she ended up in the water.

Returning to the lounger, I took a few more posed shots of me with the pool as my background. Then I pulled out my phone from where it was hidden in my bag and texted Heathcliff what I was thinking. The crime scene unit should be able to run simulations to determine the likelihood of my theory based on the trajectory of her fall and where she landed in the pool.

Feeling eyes on me, I slid my phone back into the hidden compartment of my bag and looked up. At first, I didn't notice what was different. The same people were in the same relative configurations. And then I spotted him. The mystery man from this morning.

Even in the dark, I could feel the intensity of his stare. The same intensity I had felt this morning that threatened to send me spiraling into a panic attack. But unlike this morning, I wasn't trapped. I was in a wide open space.

How long had he been following me? I'd been on half the floors in the last hour. I would have seen him. Maybe he had been watching me on the camera feeds. I thought about the security camera locations, but I was convinced the hotel cameras hadn't caught me planting the device at the base of the courtesy phone.

"Fuck it." Grabbing my things, I made my way toward him.

TWENTY-SIX

His shiny black suit shimmered in the patio lights, making him stick out like a sore thumb. He'd been watching me as he spoke to the bartender. As soon as he saw me coming, he ducked into the kitchen.

"Hey," I said, sliding onto an empty bar stool not far from the opening that led to the bar's kitchen area. "Can I get something sparkling?"

"Give me one sec, sweetie." The bartender's gold name tag said Stephen.

He finished mixing a drink and called to Charlize, the woman working in the kitchen. She placed a tray on the bar beside him and disappeared back into the kitchen. The man in the suit picked up the tray and drink and went out the side exit. Dressed like that, he looked like he was delivering a snack to a vacationing diplomat.

Stephen finished tallying up whatever he was working on at the register and turned to me. "What did you have in mind?"

"Something light that pairs well with gummy worms."

Stephen gave me a genuine smile, which may have been the first one I'd seen from a staff member at the resort. "I'd say a sparkling white. What do you think?"

"How about a cola?" I indicated the tray containing the

tiny umbrellas. "With one of those."

"Sure." He filled a glass, stabbed a maraschino cherry with the end of the toothpick umbrella, and stuck it in my glass. "Is there anything else I can get for you?"

I took that opportunity to turn and see where the man in the suit had gone with the tray. "Um...I'm not sure yet. Something smells really good though. The restaurants inside are packed, so maybe I could get a sandwich or something."

"We have several options." Stephen indicated the menu on the board behind him.

As soon as I turned, the man in the suit approached. Had the bastard finally grown tired of playing hide and seek?

"Ms. Riley?" Mystery Man stopped beside me. It was about time he introduced himself.

I spun on the stool. "Yes?"

"How was your first day at the Golden? I hear you were doing a lot of exploring."

How had he heard that? Or had he been keeping an eye on me? "A little bit. You should have a master list of vending machine selections somewhere. It would have saved me a ton of time." I pulled out the bag of gummy worms. "But it also gave me an excuse to look around. The hotel is beautiful."

Stephen returned from refilling a few glasses. "Have you made a decision yet?"

"Decision?" Mystery Man asked.

"Dinner. I didn't make a reservation ahead of time since I wasn't sure I'd be checking in so soon. And the restaurants are packed," I said, sensing he was fishing for intel. Two could play at this game.

Mystery Man turned to Stephen. "Put together the house specialty. Ms. Riley is a very important guest. And bring her a cocktail." He scowled at my cola. "On the house."

"That's very kind of you, but it's entirely unnecessary."

He smiled. Thankfully, it wasn't the same creepy smile everyone else in the place had. Mystery Man's smile was more reserved, like he didn't trust me. "It's no trouble at all. Maybe you'll want to take a photo or two with it."

"Only if you join me." I crossed my legs, making sure my bag was safe between my ankles. "I'm sorry. I didn't catch your name."

Stephen brought out a hot honey chicken sandwich cut in half with fresh coleslaw and house chips. "Would you like anything else?"

"Just this guy's name." I winked at the man in the suit.

Stephen looked unsure if he should respond, but he said, "This is Mr. Choi." The fixer himself.

"It's a pleasure to meet you. Please." I indicated the empty seat beside me. "This may be a dream job, but it gets lonely from time to time. I haven't had anyone to eat with in days." I picked up half the sandwich before pushing the container with the remainder toward him. If it was poisoned, he was going down with me.

Choi gave me an uncertain look, as if he wasn't sure he should be doing this, and then he sat down, loosened his tie, tucked a napkin into his collar, and picked up the sandwich. "I appreciate it."

"Well, I appreciate having a dining companion. Thanks for paying for dinner."

"I didn't pay. The hotel did. The Golden wants you to be comfortable. And this isn't dinner. It's a snack." He gave me a confused look. "You don't want to photograph it?"

"The lighting isn't optimal. I'll get better shots during the day. But now I'm curious. How long have you been watching me photograph things?"

"I may have seen you at the coffee shop this morning." He didn't lie. That surprised me.

"You shouldn't have waited so long to introduce yourself."

"In that case, it's nice to meet you. I'm Ian." Choi held out his hand, only to look embarrassed and retract it so he could wipe the sauce off his fingers and onto a napkin. It was an act, but one that he had perfected. But I wasn't sure anyone would take him for a bumbling nerd.

"Alexandra," I said. "But I guess you already know that." I waited for him to take a bite of the sandwich before following suit. If I ended up sick or dead, I'd make the afterlife hell for him. "You look like someone very important. I'm sure I'm not special enough for you to waste your time chatting with me."

Choi chewed thoughtfully, buying time to frame his answer in a diplomatic way. "Every guest at the Golden is important to us." He scrunched his nose in a self-deprecating fashion and whispered, "Don't let the suit fool you. I'm no one special. I work in PR."

"Public relations?" I reached for a napkin. "Well, I'd say you're doing an excellent job. I'd love to interview you if you have time."

"I'll see if we can arrange something before you leave." He nodded at my phone. "Do you mind if I take a look?"

"Not at all. In fact, I sent Mrs. Shaw the rough cut of the room tour I filmed this afternoon. I wanted her to get a sense of what I was doing. I don't want there to be any misunderstandings as to why I'm here." Since that device was purchased specifically for this outing, I wasn't concerned about what he would find.

Choi scrolled through the photos and videos. "You captured some great stuff. With an eye like that, we should hire you to take our promo photos. Do you have a degree in photography?"

"Art history, but that was a lifetime ago."

"Have you seen the art we have on display? We commissioned local artists to do the paintings we have hanging in the hallways. Each floor has its own unique style."

"I wasn't paying that much attention. Now I'm intrigued. I'll have to check those out." If the small talk didn't kill me first. "Can I ask you something, off the record?" I was playing with fire, but I wanted to test his reaction. The easiest way to do that would be to ask a damning question, but one that had nothing to do with Leslie, Gini, or Deanna.

He put my phone down. "I'll do my best to answer."

"When I was researching the Golden, I happened across an old news story. I barely skimmed it, but sitting at the pool reminded me of it." I studied his face, but he didn't look nervous. Either he had no idea what I was going to say, or he was exceptional at playing it cool. My money was on the latter. "Did someone on staff drown in this pool?"

He looked appropriately uneasy.

"I'm not going to mention that to anyone or post it. Like I told Mrs. Shaw, I try to spread positivity, not negativity. I just wondered how it happened. I've never been a strong swimmer. When I was a kid, I had a bad experience at the neighborhood pool, so the news of a drowning left me a little freaked out." I peered up at the kids going down the slide and gestured to my outfit. "That's why you won't see me in a bathing suit."

"There's no reason to be afraid. It was an unfortunate accident. The staff member tripped and fell. It was the middle of the night. No one was around. That's why no one found her until it was too late."

"That's horrific. I'm sorry." I looked him in the eye. "Did you know her?"

"Not really, but everyone was shaken."

"I'll bet. Wow." I looked around the pool area. "Did you change anything after that?"

"We were already taking the right precautions. As you can see, we have all the necessary safety measures in place." He indicated the hook, life preserver, life jackets, lifeguards on duty, the sign with the listed pool rules, and the AED in the glass case, along with a first aid kit on the wall behind the bar. "Unfortunately, no resort is without issues. Accidents happen. Sometimes people get hurt or sick. We do everything we can to make sure it doesn't happen and to help if it does. If you have any questions about any of that, I can have a copy of our safety guidelines and emergency preparedness plans sent to your room." He leaned in a little closer. "Just don't post about it. This is off the record."

"Yeah, no problem."

"I'll make sure you have them. In fact, I'd be happy to personally bring them to your room later tonight. Say around ten?"

TWENTY-SEVEN

First, Grable. Now, Choi. It may have been the paranoia talking, but I was sure Choi was on to me. Did he know Leslie and I planned to meet? Was he trying to prevent that from happening without being obvious?

He was a professional fixer or had been at one point. That didn't always mean buying off reporters, trading favors, and hiring people to clean up crime scenes and make evidence disappear. Briefly, I wondered how many bodies he disposed of or hid. *Fourteen bodies.* Again, Martin's voice reverberated in my ears. We knew about fourteen, but with Ian Choi on the payroll, that number could be a gross underestimate.

Stop it. I hoped to silence the voices in my head. But they only grew louder in protest.

After finishing my sandwich and chips, I returned to my room to wait for Choi. Despite the camera footage showing no one had been inside my room, I performed another sweep before calling Heathcliff from the bathroom. I spoke softly while the water ran full blast.

"When are you going to speak to Leslie?" he asked.

"Around one. That's when I'll show her the photo I took. Hopefully, she'll be able to ID the guy as one of Gini's attackers."

"I'm already running him through facial recognition. It'll take time, but he should be in the system. As soon as I get a last name and address, I'll send units to keep tabs on him. Since he had a gold name tag, he must be local. And we have a first name, Al, so that should speed things up."

"Yeah."

"Are you okay? Has Grable made any more threats?"

"I haven't seen him since the bus ride. I mentioned what he said to Karen Shaw, the manager, to gauge her reaction. She found it odd. I'm getting the distinct impression she's out of the loop on whatever's going on at the hotel."

"She could be playing you."

"It's possible, but if she is, she's doing a much better job than Grable and Choi. Grable went straight to intimidation, and Choi," I considered my words, "has been selective in what he shares and how much he shares. He's feeling me out for sure. I'd also say he's testing me. He's answered my questions, almost as if he's sharing a secret and waiting to see if I can be trusted."

"Which means he doesn't trust you," Heathcliff said.

"Not in the least. He's been watching me since the coffee shop. I don't know if he's had other employees keeping tabs on me and reporting back to him or if he's using the cameras to do it."

"Do you think Grable's working for him?"

"I'm not sure yet. Choi is the iron fist in the velvet glove. Grable's more of a hammer." A noise outside my door caught my attention. "I should go. I'll check in after I see Leslie."

Disconnecting, I turned off the water and opened the bathroom door. Cautiously, I glanced around, but no one had entered my room. The security bar would have prevented that without the use of brute force. But I had heard a noise.

Cautiously, I approached the door. The peephole didn't reveal anyone outside my room, so I unlatched the bar, flipped the lock, and opened the door. Dirty dishes on a room service tray sat on the floor outside the room beside mine. That may have explained the noise.

I leaned out, looking up and down the hall and catching

sight of several guests heading back to their rooms or making their way to the bar. A group of men in suits were outside the lobby bar, which made spotting Choi a little more like playing *Where's Waldo?* He maneuvered around them as he crossed the lobby, passed the waterfall fountain, and headed toward me.

"Were you waiting for me?" he asked, handing me the papers.

"No, just good timing." I pointed to the tray on the floor. "I heard someone at the door and thought it was my door."

Choi waved down the nearest employee and told them to have the tray picked up. "Sorry about that." He nodded at the papers. "Those are our emergency plans and procedures. Did you notice the booklet in the welcome packet and the map on the back of the door?" He gave me the creepy clown grin. "Let me show you." And then he barged into my room.

"I saw the evacuation route," I said. "Pretty standard stuff."

"And the information in the welcome packet?"

"I must have overlooked the safety stuff."

He picked up the laminated sheet which contained important details about the resort and the amenities on property. Flipping it over, he pointed to a paragraph near the bottom which indicated the accessible features, where to find them, and extensions to call for help.

"You have a medical team on staff?" I pointed to the number. "That's impressive. I've only seen that in a few hotels."

"The Golden may be a boutique resort, but we want to be a one-stop destination for everything." He looked around the room, taking in my bags and equipment. The bastard was looking for something or hoping to leave a few bugs behind. "Did you see the safe?" He moved toward the closet.

"I did," I said, stopping him before he could pull the door open. I didn't have anything hidden inside, but I didn't want him to search the place. "Should I be concerned about locking up my valuables?"

"You should do whatever makes you comfortable." He

examined the bag I had on the table. Since it was Martin's, it was designer. "This is a nice set."

"Thanks."

He tucked his hands into his pockets and looked around. "Is there anything else I can get for you? Turn down service? More towels? An extra blanket?"

"I'm good." I held up the papers he brought. "This is more than enough. Again, thanks for dinner."

"Perhaps you'll allow me the pleasure of taking you to dinner some other night."

I gave him a flirty smile. "I'd like that."

"Okay." He nodded. "Sleep well."

After he left, I hung the do not disturb and locked and latched the door. I checked everything again using the RF scanner. My own surveillance devices set it off, so I had to disable them, scan, and reenable. But Choi hadn't left any surprises behind. However, his curiosity bled through his professional exterior. He wanted to know what I was hiding, and since I didn't give him the chance to search, he'd be back.

The hotel room was starting to feel like a prison cell, but I had spent a good part of the day wandering the halls. Normal people would want some downtime to catch up on work, chill out, or sleep. So I changed clothes, made sure the blonde wig was securely pinned to my head, and unmade the bed. Then I sat on top of the sheets and turned on the TV. But my mind wasn't on the show playing.

An hour later, my phone rang. It was Martin. I took the call in the bathroom with the shower running full blast.

"Hey, handsome. Is everything okay?"

The request for a video call popped up on my phone. "I want to see you, Alex."

I pressed the button and held the device farther out. "Surprise."

"Are you okay?"

"I'm fine."

Martin knew fine never meant fine, but he didn't push. "You look...different."

"Bad different?"

"You could never look bad. But I prefer normal you."

"What is normal?" I cracked a smile. "We don't do normal."

"You know what I mean." He sighed. "I miss you."

"It's been eighteen hours, most of which you spent at work."

He pointed at me. "Did you remember to use the tape?"

"Shit."

"Twelve on, twelve off, sweetheart."

I propped the phone on the sink while I lifted up the two layers of shirts I had on, since I hadn't taken off the body armor, and pulled the tape out of the cosmetic bag. Then I unrolled a pre-cut section of it and pressed it against my side. "Happy?"

"I'm happy you're wearing that."

I looked down to see the lightweight body armor. "You moved heaven and earth to make this happen. The least I can do is put it to good use."

Martin's green eyes clouded. "I just hope it was worth it."

"Me too." Before I could say anything else, my phone dinged, alerting me to movement on one of the cameras. "Hang on a second." I switched our call back to voice only and opened the app connected to the security camera. It had been alerting me every time movement triggered it, but since we were fast approaching one a.m., those alerts had become less frequent. "False alarm," I said after watching a couple make their way from the elevator to their room.

"I'll let you get back to work," Martin said. "I just wanted to check on you."

"Are we okay?" I asked.

"Now we are." He sounded relieved. "Good night, Alex. We'll talk again tomorrow when I remind you to take off the tape."

"I'll remember."

"We both know that isn't true."

"I love you."

Talking to Martin put me back on an even keel. Usually, I wouldn't want to have any contact during a job, but things were different. I was different. And I wasn't sure that was for the best.

At 12:45, my phone alerted me to movement on the eighteenth floor. This time, it was Leslie. I grabbed my bag and room key and headed for the elevator. By the time the doors opened, I was four minutes behind Leslie.

She jumped when I pulled open the door to the vending machine room. "I wasn't sure you understood," she said.

"I've been known to read between the lines." I glanced around. "We don't have much time. Are you okay?"

She nodded. "I'm feeling better. The worst of it seems to be over."

I wasn't sure of that, but I wasn't thinking about her food poisoning. "Do you recognize this man?" I held my phone out to her.

The color drained from her face. "He attacked Gini. He didn't push the iron down on her, but he was there. He backed her toward it. It was him and the guy with the thicker beard who shoved her toward it and held her down. Where did you see him?"

"He's the host at the Italian restaurant," I said.

"Not an intern?"

"No."

"Shit." She backed against the sink, bracing herself with her hands. "I wasn't sure, but I thought the other interns were responsible. It's dog eat dog. Gini was holding the rest of us back, keeping us from reaching our full potential. But you're telling me this guy isn't an intern." Leslie stared, her eyes pleading. "Who is he?"

"Al. That's all we know so far. We should know more soon." I didn't like the way she was freaking out. "Are you going to be able to keep it together? I can't let you go back to your room like this."

She pulled away from the sink. "I'm okay. Really."

"I'm here. They put me in 110. If you need anything, you know where to find me. Say the word, and I will get you out of here."

She shook her head. "No. I want to stay. It's fine."

"It isn't."

But she didn't listen. "I have tomorrow off. After that, the doctor will check me out and let me know if I'm fit to return to work. It'll be easier for us to meet after that."

"Be careful," I said, "and watch out for Louis Grable and Ian Choi."

"Who?"

I showed her photos of both men, even though I'd shown her Grable before. "If you notice either of them lurking around, let me know."

"I will." She pushed open the door and disappeared down the hallway.

I bought a few more bags of gummy worms, some chocolate cookies, a bag of chips, and a granola bar before grabbing a drink from the machine. This time, I went with lemon-lime. Then I made my way back to the elevator. Since my hands were full, I put everything down on the table near the courtesy phone while I pushed the button. I tossed half of the junk food into my bag, peeled the camera off the side of the phone, tucked that away, and got into the waiting elevator car.

TWENTY-EIGHT

I didn't sleep well that night. Leslie Stiller needed to leave this place. Self-preservation was the name of the game, which meant she should run far and fast. Instead, she was too afraid to leave, stymied by the possibility of owing the hotel thousands, which she couldn't afford, and the chance they would try to press charges against Deanna.

Her crime, if one could even call it that, would be loitering, maybe trespassing. I doubted the district attorney would pursue charges. Even if Deanna had freaked out on the staff the same way she had at Cross Security, I didn't think her tantrum resulted in property damage or physical injury. But without that security cam footage, I had no way of knowing.

This would be easier if I could gain access to the Golden's system, but the only way to do that would be to hack into it. And that wouldn't fly. Not with the PD. Not with the Golden. And not with Cross.

I let my head sink deeper into the pillow. The pins from the wig poked my scalp. If I were smarter, I'd take the infernal thing off, but I'd done enough undercover to know that was a bad idea. It would be too easy to be caught off guard. I couldn't risk botching the op, even though there was a good chance I was already compromised.

Louis Grable had been smart enough to be vague with his threats. He wanted to intimidate me, but his words weren't actionable. I couldn't report him. I couldn't do a damn thing to him. He would be keeping his eye on me. The same could be said of Ian Choi.

I wasn't sure what the fixer hoped to find in my room. Proof that I was a liar? But even if these men were convinced I wasn't a travel influencer, they had no basis for figuring out who I really was. I had never given anyone on staff my full name or flashed around my business card. Their best guess would be that I was a cop. They could have seen me with Heathcliff and assumed we were both detectives. After all, the PD wouldn't send an injured cop into the field alone.

On the bright side, if they thought I was a cop, they'd be less inclined to attack me and deterred from retaliating against Leslie, at least while I remained at the hotel. I contemplated a few other possibilities, talking myself into believing my presence was helping. Convinced I was safe, I gave in and slept until sounds outside my room woke me.

The bedside clock said it was just after seven. Vacationers should not be up this early. Hadn't they realized the point of vacation was to relax and sleep in?

Bleary-eyed, I sat up, wincing when I felt the pins move. I'd forgotten how terrible they could be. After using the in-room coffeemaker to brew a cup of some premeasured gourmet brand that tasted worse than the mud at the precinct, I grabbed the medium suitcase which contained my clothes and went into the bathroom.

Ditching the wig, I ran through my usual morning routine, covered the scar tape with plastic to keep everything dry, and got into the shower. Washing my hair would probably be the highlight of my day. Any excuse to ditch the wig made me happy. Maybe I should sleep with my hair in a towel or scarf. That would alleviate the need for the wig, at least at night.

I was almost finished lathering up when a bang followed by a groan and creak sounded from outside the bathroom door. I froze, holding my breath while I strained to hear over the running water. Resisting the urge to turn off the water, I silently stepped out of the shower, wrapped the nearest towel around me, and picked up my phone from where I'd placed it beside the sink.

Since I'd moved the medium luggage bag, I'd created a blind spot from the bed to the closet. But the three other cameras in the main room remained active. I flipped through the feeds, immediately noticing the lights were out and the room was dark.

Whoever had gained access to my room wore a knit cap and mask. He wasn't in uniform. For all intents and purposes, the man sneaking around inside my room could be anyone. But I recognized his build. Louis Grable.

He searched the closet and unlocked the safe, finding it empty. He checked the bed I'd slept in and searched the dresser drawers. He stopped in front of the hidden camera attached to the large rolling suitcase. I hadn't packed anything inside that bag, which he found odd.

The jerky camera movement told me he was searching every compartment. When the camera steadied, I saw the outline of a gun handle against the side of the dark jacket he wore. That's when I realized I'd left my gun in my bag.

He moved on to another piece of luggage, the smaller duffel which I'd filled with all sorts of recording equipment. Most of it was legit for my cover, but some of the smaller devices I intended to plant. Before he could discover them, something distracted him.

I watched as he moved away from the duffel and picked up my cover's phone which I'd left near the coffeemaker. That's when he spotted the still warm, half-empty mug beside it. He looked up, his eyes zeroing in on the bathroom door.

Shit. How he missed the door being closed and the shower running was beyond me. The only thing I could see were his eyes, but they looked deranged. Unzipping his jacket, he reached for the gun as he slowly approached the door.

As silently as possible, I flipped the lock, relieved the click had barely been audible. Naked wasn't a good way to fight. Ignoring the sudden barrage of thoughts of my last bathroom fight, I grabbed the sleeveless top from my suitcase and shoved it over my head. He was too close to the door to waste time putting on pants. Instead, I desperately searched for a weapon.

Everything was attached or unmovable. The only thing I could find was a solid water glass. I picked it up, took half a step back and to the right of the door, and glanced at the screen on my phone which I'd propped up against the wall, but from where he was standing, I could no longer see him.

The door handle jiggled. I dropped into a fighting stance, bending my knees and crouching while keeping my hands up and in front of me. If he got the door open, I'd slam it back against him. That would give me the element of surprise. With any luck, it'd knock the gun from his hand, and then we'd have to fight it out. Hopefully, if I screamed, it'd freak him out enough that he'd make a break for it. Maybe I should scream now.

The door handle jiggled again. I crouched down further, wishing I had pants instead of a towel. But the door didn't budge. The lock was cheap. It wouldn't be hard to pick it or break it.

The jiggling stopped. Maybe he'd try to break it. But I didn't hear any sounds. I glanced at the phone again, but I still couldn't see him on any of the surveillance feeds. He'd moved two of my bags. I'd moved the third. And there had only been four in the main room. I wasn't sure how big of a blind spot remained.

From what I could see of the room, there were plenty of places he could be or ways he could get out without me noticing. I remained crouched in that position until my hamstrings and glutes cramped. This was ridiculous.

Cautiously, I took another half-step backward and reached into my bag. The zipper slid a few inches. Could he hear that? Not wasting time, I pulled on the first pair of pants I found and waited. Still nothing. Was he waiting for me to get out of the shower and return to the main room?

I exited the surveillance feeds and texted Heathcliff with an S.O.S. *Call the hotel and have them connect you to room 110.* Then I went back to the surveillance feeds.

A minute later, the phone rang. I watched and waited, but I didn't see any movement in the darkened room.

Clutching the water glass, I unlocked the door and slowly pushed it open. When the door let out a creak, I threw it open, glass raised, ready to heave it at him before charging into battle. But the room was empty. He'd left.

The closet was open. There were no other places to hide. I checked the door, finding the main lock had reengaged, but the security bar was off. He would have had no way to reconnect it after leaving.

I shoved the armchair in front of the door and went to find my bag with my gun. It remained on the floor, half under the bed near the wall. The bastard hadn't found it.

A moment later, my phone rang. My heart continued to pound in my chest, but the adrenaline surge was wearing off on account of all that time spent in the bathroom, waiting to act.

"What the hell's going on?" Heathcliff asked when I answered.

I let out a sigh. "I just got out of the shower. Let me call you back." I disconnected before he could voice a protest. Since someone had found a way inside my room, I had to make sure he hadn't left anything behind. Speaking openly was a bad idea. Instead, I sent Heathcliff a text with a quick breakdown, then I dressed properly, pinned my hair up, put the wig back on, and returned to the main room.

The man in black hadn't left any surprises behind, at least none that were transmitting. I dumped out each of my bags and checked everything inside carefully. I didn't think he had found the hidden cameras. Nothing he came across was particularly damning. Assuming it was Grable, which was what my gut insisted, he would have found nothing to reinforce his theories about me. But he had fulfilled that promise. He was keeping an eye on me.

After getting everything set up again, I sat on the edge of the bed, unsure how to proceed. I could report it to the front desk, but that would open my room up to an entire team of hotel security staff. Maybe that's why he did it. However, since nothing had been taken, I couldn't report anything was stolen. And since I'd been in the shower, there was a good chance I may not have noticed. Only two things gave away that I had a visitor. The lights were out, and the security bar was off. But those could be explained by mental lapses or a member of staff entering only to realize the room was occupied and leaving.

The half-empty mug remained on the desk, but I wasn't about to drink it. Grable could have laced it with something.

I examined the security bar. Whoever entered must have had a swing latch tool or some other contraption to disengage the bar. Since Grable worked security, he'd have access to the equipment and the know-how to get inside. That was his job. Unfortunately, I couldn't prove the masked gunman was Grable, and if I did anything, it'd tip my hand and reveal who I was.

Heathcliff knew that, which was why he hadn't pulled the plug or sent ESU to storm the hotel. A gunman inside a crowded hotel posed a great deal of danger, but I was certain the man who'd been inside my room wasn't interested in harming random bystanders. He'd come after me, so I had to make sure he didn't make a move on Leslie.

I sent her a text requesting a status update. Afraid to send her the gritty details in a series of texts which could be seen or intercepted by someone on the staff who was monitoring her too closely, I did my best to warn her to remain vigilant, and then I grabbed my gear and left my room.

TWENTY-NINE

After leaving my room, everything felt off. The hotel. The staff. The stupid décor. I felt exposed. Every staff member who made eye contact or gave me a creepy smile only made matters worse. Maybe this place was the perfect training ground for serial killers.

I doubled down on becoming Alexandra Riley, upping my recordings and searching every hallway more thoroughly. If they planned on coming for me, I intended to beat them to the punch. But the secure areas remained secure. I'd need my equipment to gain access, but with the placement of the security cameras that would be next to impossible without getting spotted. *Damn you, Lucien.* Why did he have to be so good at his job?

With the sun bright overhead, I went out to the pool to take more photos and videos. The pool and hot tub were near capacity, which made for better footage and gave me the perfect excuse to duck out after snapping a few photos of the fancy drinks and sandwiches.

When I returned to the lobby, I spotted Louis Grable in the doorway beside the check-in desk. He was having an intense conversation with Ian Choi. Neither man spotted me, but I snapped a few photos, more out of habit than anything else, and watched Grable gesture in the direction of my room. I couldn't hear what they were saying, but there was a good chance they were talking about me. Had Choi sent Grable into my room this morning?

I found a place to sit on the concrete surrounding the fountain. Thoughts of Brittany Hodges cracking her skull open on this exact spot made me rethink my actions. Queasy, I found myself half-focused on Grable's exchange while I scanned the marble floors for blood.

Maybe some of the tiles were discolored. Maybe they weren't. Sucking in a breath, I fought to keep the walls from closing in. This place should be one of the most haunted places in the world, considering how many people had died on the premises. The dead should haunt the shit out of this place. Someone had to warn the weary travelers to stay away, and I wasn't doing a good job. In fact, my cover was doing the complete opposite.

Halfway through my morbid contemplations, Alexandra received a message. I read the e-mail from Mrs. Shaw, who had CCed it to someone in charge of media relations at Experiential Adventures, giving me permission to post the room tour and to prepare more videos. At least I'd convinced someone at the hotel that I was a wannabe internet sensation. Too bad Choi and Grable weren't buying it.

They concluded their discussion, and Grable went down the corridor toward the lobby bar. He disappeared through another hidden doorway. I glanced back at Choi's office, but he had gone back inside.

Deciding I needed to keep tabs on them, I returned to my room, picked up a few of the tiny surveillance devices, made sure they were activated, and headed back to the lobby. Getting close enough to Choi's door was easy enough. I stuck the device on the underside of the counter's overhang while I waited to ask the woman working the check-in desk if I could get a few more water glasses in my room.

After checking the angle on my phone and readjusting the hidden camera, I slipped the phone back into my pocket. The woman with the creepy smile promised housekeeping would leave them when they cleaned my room.

"Thanks," I said, tapping the counter and stepping away so she could frighten the next guest with her impression of a clown.

Pulling out my phone, I filmed more B-roll while I headed for the lobby bar. Since it was morning, they weren't serving drinks, but additional seating was available for anyone who had picked up a coffee or breakfast item from the coffee shop. Only a few people were inside. Most were working remotely or catching up on whatever they were missing by being on vacation.

The only place I could plant a hidden camera would be along the archway. I placed it against the molding as I leaned into the bar. Once it was secure, I pulled my hand away from the wall, entered, and circled, checking the screen to make sure the camera was properly placed to keep an eye on the hidden doorway and anyone who entered or left. Neither camera provided the best angles, but they'd do.

However, I didn't have time to stare at the live stream. Setting the cameras to motion detect would be useless since these were popular areas. Instead, I sent Heathcliff the password to access the stream and suggested if he were bored, he could keep tabs on it and let me know if Grable or Choi were on the move. But he didn't have that kind of time either.

Amir or Lawson could set up a program to deal with this, but Lawson was busy providing his services to the federal government, and Amir was off-limits. Still, I left the cameras where they were. I could always review the footage if and when it became necessary.

Already exhausted, I took the elevator up to the eighteenth floor and bugged the vending machine room. Leslie could use that to send me a message if she were too afraid to use the phone I gave her. If not, it'd ensure no one on staff planned to ambush us should we rendezvous again. That thought sounded paranoid, even to me. But after this morning, it was more pragmatism than paranoia.

The rest of the day moved at a snail's pace. The next few hours were filled with the same nonsense as the day before.

At 1:03, the cameras in my room alerted me to unauthorized entry. Fearing it was Grable back for another round, I pulled up the feed to see Jane, the maid from yesterday, pulling her cart into the doorway. I watched her work for the next ten minutes.

She didn't touch any of my things as she made the bed and collected the wet towels from the bathroom. She replaced them with fresh towels, checked to see if I had requested laundry service, and began cleaning the coffee pot. She crouched down to pull extra glasses from the stack on her cart when Ian Choi appeared in the doorway.

The devices I planted didn't record sound, but whatever he was saying, she didn't like. When he left, she rolled her eyes and went back to work. I toggled to the camera I'd planted at the front desk. Once Choi went back to his office, I returned to my room.

Jane grumbled when I pushed my way inside. But she hadn't turned to see who was interrupting her work this time. "I told you I haven't seen any prohibited items out in the open."

"I'd hope not," I said. "I try to follow the rules. Getting kicked out would make my job a lot harder."

She spun, surprised to find me inside. "I'm sorry. I thought you were someone else." She graced me with a forced, apologetic smile.

"What are you supposed to be looking for?"

She swallowed, uncomfortable with the question. "It's common practice to make sure guests aren't bringing weapons or drugs on the premises. There's a list of prohibited items on our website. No candles, slow cookers, or hot plates either. But I don't see any potential fire hazards out in the open."

I sat on the edge of the bed. "Do you perform bag checks?"

"No. Never. That would be an invasion of privacy. It'd open the hotel up to all sorts of lawsuits."

"Did he ask you to search my bags?"

Her eyes told me yes, but she shook her head. "That would be wrong. Here at the Golden, we—"

"Someone searched my room this morning."

She stared at me. "Are you sure?"

"I was in the shower when he entered. Every one of my bags had been opened and rifled through. The closet was open. So was the safe."

"You should report that to hotel security. Whoever did that was not a member of staff."

"What if I told you the person responsible was a member of hotel security?" I was playing with fire, but my gut told me to trust Jane. Worst case, she'd report this to the management who would cover it up or question me about it. Either way, it'd put these bastards on notice that I wasn't going to scare that easily. It may also mean I ended up suffocated in my sleep. Cause of death: allergic reaction to down alternative.

"You saw him?" she asked.

I shrugged.

"You're sure?" The way she asked those questions didn't make me think she was surprised. It made me think she'd seen this happen before.

"Do you know why hotel security would be interested in me, or why Mr. Choi wants you to search my things? I'd think this morning's search would have been more than enough."

"Who are you?"

"Alexandra Riley," I said, "travel reporter."

She didn't look like she was buying that either. "Not an investigative journalist?"

"No." I squinted at her. "Is that what you were told?"

"No, but I figured that would make sense."

"Why would that make sense?"

"You know the Golden's had problems. You mentioned it to me yesterday."

"I do my research."

"You should get out of here."

"This room?"

"The hotel," she said. "It'd be in your best interest to leave."

"I can't leave. I'm supposed to get an exclusive on the internship program. It's supposed to put my channel on the map. It'll be great publicity for me and the hotel." I cocked my head to the side. “Maybe that’s why management’s being careful to verify who I am. But I showed them my videos. In fact, Mrs. Shaw recognized me. I don’t see what the problem is.”

Jane finished what she was doing and replaced the cleaning products on her cart. “Staying here isn’t safe.”

“Why not? What do you think will happen?”

“You said you did your research.” She gave me the kind of look a mother would give her adult daughter when she knew the kid was making a terrible mistake but had to be careful not to overstep her boundaries. “You’re an intelligent and capable woman. Figure it out.”

“You think if I stick around I’ll end up in the hospital?” She didn’t say anything. “The morgue?” I chuckled, like I was making a joke. “That seems overly dramatic.”

“Get out while you can.”

“Now I know that’s gotta be a line from a horror movie.” I blocked her path to the exit. “Tell me what’s going on. Tell me why it isn’t safe.”

“I’m sure everything is fine, and you were mistaken about earlier. However, if you believe someone broke into your room, I suggest you report it. Maybe to the police since you think hotel security was involved.” She inched her cart forward, urging me to get out of the way.

“Do you know Gini Ruffin?” I asked.

Jane faltered but recovered quickly. “Travel reporter, my ass.”

“If you know what happened to her, if that’s why you’re warning me off, then you must realize it’s not safe for you either. Why don’t you go to the police or—”

“Have a nice day.” Jane shoved her cart forward, pushing the door open with it and leaving me to contemplate what she had said.

THIRTY

Heathcliff and I exchanged a few texts throughout the day. He was exploring every lead from the outside while I dug up dirt from the inside. Neither of us was making much headway.

Units were sitting on Albert Glass's apartment. He was the host from the restaurant, the one Leslie IDed as being involved in the assault. At least facial recognition had spit out his name, but it didn't give us much.

Albert Glass didn't have a record. He knew a few people who had been in trouble, but he'd never been blamed for anything. The same remained true now, unless Gini or Leslie came forward. Since Gini was the victim, it'd be better if she spoke out, but that wasn't going to happen.

I showed Gini his photo, Heathcliff texted. *I'd say she recognized him. In fact, I'd go so far as to say she's terrified of him, but she won't cooperate.*

Maybe have a public defender or someone from the DA's office pay her a visit, I suggested. *She needs an advocate with knowledge of the law.*

I'll give it a try.

I tucked my phone into the hidden zipper inside my bag. Gini wanted to put this behind her. But no matter how much hush money she received, it wasn't going to make her forget what happened and it wasn't going to stop something worse from happening to someone else.

A maid pushed her cart past the windows of the arcade, which is where I'd been hiding for the last hour, and I wondered if Jane could be swayed. She'd been a loyal Golden employee for two decades. Speaking out could put her pension and retirement benefits at risk. But she warned me to leave, so I had to believe she'd do what was right if push came to shove. Another thought crept its way into my mind. *Unless getting me to leave was Choi's idea.* For all I knew, the head of PR could have told her to scare me off.

I finished the final lap on the racing game and looked around to find the room empty. It was like that when I arrived. At one point, a young boy and his parents came in, spent twenty dollars to win a stuffed bear in the claw machine, and left. No one had stepped foot inside since.

Getting up from behind the wheel of the racing game, I gave the security camera in the corner a friendly wave, pulled out my camera, and filmed the interior. If anyone had any doubts about what I was doing, this would answer that question. Lawson would be able to get the footage edited and pieced together quickly, which I could share with Shaw at the end of the day.

My next stop was the spa. The management had given me a voucher for a free treatment, but I'd seen how deadly spas could be. Instead, I took several photos and short video clips of the menu, the luxurious waiting area, and helped myself to the complimentary infused water station. They had three varieties, cucumber, citrus, and berry.

"Delicious and refreshing." I sipped the berry water while holding the camera up and away. Once I finished filming, I tossed the empty cup into the recycling. "Thanks. Have a lovely day."

"You too," the woman at the counter gushed.

Maybe it was that encounter or the rough start to my day, but a headache was setting in. Deciding I needed to eat, I checked the three restaurants to find they each had long waits. The coffee shop had a selection of sandwiches, but I didn't want to risk running into Jay again. So I went back to the rooftop bar, hoping to spot Albert Glass across the hallway while I snacked on bar food.

"Can I sit inside tonight?" I asked the hostess when she greeted me at the podium near the door.

The wattage of her smile nearly blinded me. "Absolutely. If you prefer to sit at the bar, seat yourself wherever you like."

The bar wasn't crowded, and since it was a circle, there were plenty of seats that faced the hallway. Most people wanted a view of the skyline. I wanted a view into the nearby restaurant.

I slid onto a stool but found the taps obstructed my view, so I moved over two seats. From here, I could see directly across the hallway to the sea of people waiting to get a table at the Italian restaurant. If Albert stepped into the hallway to call the next party, like he'd done last night, I'd see him.

I kept an eye on that while I ordered a portobello mushroom burger and a rum and coke. Drinking wasn't advisable while working, but the rum would take the edge off my headache. After that, I'd switch to straight cola, which meant the sugar and caffeine would keep me focused and alert.

The bartender poured my drink and sent my order into the kitchen. The bar didn't offer much to eat except what they called small plates. I called it bar food. A basket of fries and a flight of sauces arrived for me to sample while I waited for my burger.

When a man in a nice suit entered, his shirt open at the collar, I didn't react. What the hell was Lucien doing here? He didn't look at me, but he'd seen me. He went around the long way, coming up on my left and sliding onto the stool I'd abandoned earlier.

"Order's up." The bartender slid the plate in front of me, examining the half-empty basket of fries and the nearly empty cup of ranch dressing. "Would you like me to top you off?"

"Sure." I picked up the burger and took a bite while he put in an order for more fries and a refill on the dip.

"Another drink?"

"Maybe just a cola this time. If I keep this up, I'm liable to slurp down half a bottle of rum and not even realize it."

The bartender smiled, grabbed another glass from beneath the bar, and filled it with my soft drink. After that, he turned to Lucien. "What'll it be?"

"Top shelf gin and tonic."

The bartender placed it on a napkin in front of him. "Would you like anything else, sir?"

"Not yet. Though, she is making that burger look delicious." Lucien leaned in. "If you don't mind me asking, what is that?"

"Portobello mushroom burger," the bartender said.

I turned to look at Lucien, unsure what was happening, but since this was a bar and we were both alone, flirting seemed like a safe move. "I make everything look delicious."

Lucien laughed, angling toward me and turning up the charm. "I bet. Is that half as good as you make it seem?"

"It is."

"I'll take a burger too," Lucien said.

"Yes, sir. It'll be up in a few minutes. Chips or fries?" the bartender asked.

"Chips," Lucien said.

"That was a mistake," I said.

My boss held the flirty look. "We'll see." He waited for the bartender to walk away before snagging a fry out of my basket. After eating it, he wiped his hand on a napkin and offered it to me. "I'm Lucien."

"Alexandra." We shook.

"Do your friends call you Alex?"

"Sometimes. Mostly, they call me a pain in the ass."

Lucien snorted, nearly choking on the second fry he stole.

I glanced around, but I didn't notice anyone watching us. "What the hell are you doing here?" I whispered. "Did Derek call you?"

"Why would he call me?"

I shook my head, assuming we were supposed to be strangers, and flashed him a flirty smile before twirling the short blond strands around my finger. "I had an interesting morning."

"So did I." He leaned in closer, snagging another fry and dipping it in the horseradish sauce. "You've made quite a splash. Your presence hasn't gone unnoticed."

"Shit."

Lucien traced patterns on the back of my hand with his fingertip. He was spelling something out, but I couldn't figure out what it was. There were too many distractions. Finally, he gave up, sipped his drink, and excused himself to answer a text.

A moment later, my phone buzzed on my lap. I opened my bag, unzipped the inner compartment, and read the waiting text. The Golden reached out to Cross Security, requesting a background check on me.

I had so many questions, but Lucien's eyes told me not to ask them. It wasn't safe to speak openly. Instead, he turned up the charm and asked a million questions about my cover's background, which was the reason he was here in the first place, to find out about the travel influencer scoping out the hotel.

I showed him my social media pages and the videos I had posted concerning the Golden. Unlike the real Lucien I dealt with every day, this version was working a mark, except I wasn't a mark. I was an employee.

Using my phone, I sent him a text. *Do they suspect I work for you?*

Doubtful.

Are you sure this isn't a test? I grabbed a few chips from his basket and did my best to make any onlooker who was watching us think I was interested in the stranger beside me.

"The thought crossed my mind. I can't be sure, but I don't think so." He nudged the chips closer while he ate the rest of his burger. "How do you feel about dessert?"

"I'm very much for it."

He gestured to the bartender to close the tab. "Bring me the lady's bill. I'll take care of that too."

"You will not," I said. "We just met."

"So?" Lucien handed the bartender his credit card, ignoring my protests.

"Do you always move this fast?" I asked.

Lucien ran a hand through his hair, using his anxious tics to sell his act. "Sometimes. If it'll make you feel better, I'll let you treat me to dessert."

"Ice cream?"

"Do you want ice cream?"

"I always want ice cream."

The bartender waited for Lucien to sign the receipt before wishing us a nice night. With a final sip from my drink, I let my boss guide me out of the bar, his hand at the small of my back. We slowly maneuvered through the crowd outside the restaurant, stopping near the front to read the menu. While we pretended to look for ice cream, I searched for Albert, finding him seating a foursome in the corner.

"Two o'clock," I whispered in Lucien's ear. "See the host?"

"Uh-huh." He took out his phone and snapped a shot before tucking the device away. "Sorry about that. I keep getting texts from work," he said for someone's benefit, though I didn't see anyone from the hotel following us.

"Not a problem. What exactly do you do?"

"I'm a day trader." He pushed the button for the elevator, and that's when I spotted the grey and maroon coming down the hallway behind us. "The job gets to be all-consuming, so I try to sneak away for a night out here and there. I'd imagine you must know what that's like since vacationing is your job."

"It's a dream job."

"Do you have a hospitality suite or one of the club level rooms?"

"No, just a regular room. I report for the masses. Well, I like to cover all my bases. The management thought it'd be best if I start with the base level room and work my way up. They may have meant that literally since they put me on the first floor."

The grey and maroon uniform continued past us, not slowing or stopping. Halfway down the next corridor, the security guard tapped his card against the scanner on the wall and let himself into a restricted area. Lucien watched him go.

"Room 110?" he asked.

"Yeah." So the hotel had supplied my boss with lots of information on me. Did they give him a keycard to access my room too?

Once the elevator doors opened, he pressed the button for the lobby and stood a little behind me, sweeping the blonde hair to the side in a seductive fashion. "I know this great ice cream shop not far from here. It's quiet and pretty private. It's a great place to talk so we can get to know one another. What do you say?"

"Do they have milkshakes?"

"I think so."

I hedged. "I'm not sure I should leave the hotel. There are a lot of things for me to keep an eye on here."

Lucien took the hint. "You need more convincing?" He pulled out his phone and tapped on the screen. "Let me pull up the menu. Then you can tell me no."

He moved in closer, making sure his phone was angled away from the surveillance camera while I read what he'd written on the screen. Kellan was here and keeping an eye on Leslie.

"Wow, they even have crushed peanut butter cups and chocolate sprinkles." I gave him a big, bright smile. "I'm in."

THIRTY-ONE

We didn't go for ice cream. Instead, Lucien drove around, keeping his eyes on the mirrors. I did the same, but no one was following us. At the very least, I didn't spot any green sedans.

"Who called you?" I asked.

"Ian Choi."

"That fucker."

Lucien gave me the side-eye. "Do you want to fill me in?"

"You first. What exactly does Choi want you to do?"

"He said an influencer was staying at the hotel. He didn't find anything when he looked into you, but he wanted to make sure he wasn't missing anything. He said the hotel manager agreed to let you interview some employees and post videos. He was afraid that could turn into a PR nightmare."

"Why? Because I might mention the fourteen dead people or the woman currently in the hospital's burn ward battling an infection because her coworkers threw her the Golden's version of a blanket party, only they used a steam press instead."

Lucien's knuckles went white on the steering wheel. "Why didn't you tell me?"

"I just did."

"You should have told me as soon as you found out." He cleared his throat. "Who's the victim?"

"An intern. Well, she was. I'm pretty sure she quit after that. But I'm guessing that was the point. The interns are brainwashed into this whole function as a unit, you're only as strong as the weakest link bullshit. Y'know, like all the obnoxious bumper sticker mottos, which is why I was surprised to learn one of the party throwers isn't an intern. He's a regular employee, which is making this a lot more complicated."

"I need names."

"No."

"Alex," he growled.

"Not yet. Not until I decide if I can trust you with these details."

"I thought we were long past that."

"The Golden's a client. You have an obligation. You said it yourself. That's why I'm contracted to work with the PD. You told me company resources weren't available, at least not officially. Then again, you told me Kellan was keeping tabs on Leslie in my absence, so why don't you tell me exactly what it is you're doing?"

"I have an obligation to protect people. I told you I would not cover up a client's crimes, not assaults, not murders, not anything like that."

"You should have taken Deanna on as a client."

"Rake me over the coals for that later." He checked the time, made a decision, and headed for the office. "We're here now. Let me help."

"Fine, but you better not screw me, Leslie, or the PD in the process." Then I filled him in on everything that had happened since the last time we spoke. "I planted three cameras. But I don't have the resources to monitor those feeds."

"I'll install more cameras and track the movements of anyone we determine could be involved. Right now, that's Louis Grable and Albert Glass. Do I have that correct?"

"As far as I know. But there are others involved. I first ran into Grable when I went looking for Leslie's car. He was with three other Golden employees. They could all be in on it. They seemed rather chummy walking out like that."

"Have you IDed the other three?"

"No."

"What about the PD?"

"Ask Heathcliff, but I haven't heard anything. And I haven't spotted any of the others at the hotel. But that doesn't mean they aren't there."

"Tell me more about Grable."

"I first ran into him inside the parking garage when I was trying to find Leslie. The way he drove along beside me, the way he looked at me, it freaked me out. When he saw me at the Golden, he remembered me, the real me. The wig didn't fool him. He threatened me on the bus and said he'd be keeping an eye on me. The next thing I know, he's searching my room with a gun."

"Did he find anything?"

"No, which may be part of the problem."

Lucien glanced over at me. "You packed light?"

"I always pack light. But I had extra bags with hidden cameras to make sure I could see what was going on inside my room when I was away."

"Did he find the cameras?"

"I don't think so. He didn't act like he did. Once he realized the shower was running, he acted more like he was considering eliminating me from the equation entirely. Afterward, when I finally ventured out, I saw him talking to Choi. I'm guessing that's why Choi called you."

"Choi wouldn't want you dead," Lucien said. "As far as he knows, you're an online influencer. Killing you would result in a great deal of work to scrub the bits and bobs you already posted off the internet, especially when they've been seen by thousands. Plus, a gunshot inside the Golden would be hard to explain."

"Suicide," I said.

"Did he have a silencer?"

"Not that I noticed."

"That wouldn't give them a lot of time to stage the scene."

"Choi's a professional," I reminded him.

"It doesn't fit. Choi wouldn't have sent the maid to search your room after Grable already did. We're missing something."

"That could be due to whatever Grable told Choi. All I know is within the first hour that I was inside the Golden, Choi started spying on me. I have to assume he was watching me from the moment I stepped foot inside. I don't know why he would do that unless Grable alerted him. Choi would have had no reason to be suspicious of me at that point."

"You were filming. That would have been enough to make him wary of you."

"Everyone films."

"The police have been poking around these last few days. Like you said, Choi's a professional. Your op must have triggered his spidey senses."

"Or Grable did."

Lucien thought it over as he parked in his usual space and led us upstairs to the lab. "Amir," he said, "we need footage from the parking garage. Parker will give you the information. She spoke to a group of four. I need IDs on all of them."

"Okay." Amir waited while I showed him my phone, which had a pin on the map from where Leslie's car remained. He entered the address and the relevant date and approximate time.

"I'll set up surveillance to keep tabs on Grable. I'm going to send a security team to monitor Albert Glass. If either bastard so much as steps on a bug, my team will intervene."

"Won't that compromise your position? You are supposed to be protecting the Golden," I said, "not pounding its employees into the pavement."

"I am protecting the Golden from anyone who poses a threat. That's what Choi asked me to do. It's the subtext of our original contract, and it goes along with Cross Security's mission statement."

"I thought the mission statement was give us all your money and don't involve the police."

Cross's expression soured. "It was until I hired you."

"You know, when you make a joke, you're supposed to crack a smile," I said.

"Tell me about Leslie. Who knows you've made contact?"

"If we're lucky, no one."

"Except you asked Grable and his three friends about Leslie." Cross met my eyes. "Anyone else?"

"No, but I mentioned Gini to Jay, the intern at the coffee shop."

"And that was right around the time you first noticed Choi tailing you." Cross let the thought bounce around. "Maybe that's when Choi started to get suspicious. Gini Ruffin's injured. As far as you know, she quit. If she was paid off, like you suspect, there must be a gag order that came with the money. By asking, Choi may think Gini talked and is hoping to find proof of that."

"Do you think that's why he wanted the maid to search my room?" I shook my head. "It still doesn't fit. Grable entered my room armed and spoke to Choi afterward."

"Let's put a pin in this for now. What about Leslie?"

"I set her up with a burner which links to a bogus name. She has my cover's phone number, but that's it. We've only exchanged a few texts. I have no reason to believe her phone's been compromised."

Cross held out his hand, so I gave him the device. "At least you were careful when you met up."

"It was supposed to look like a coincidence. As far as I can tell, the vending machine room didn't have any security cameras, so—"

"No one knows the extent of your interaction. But you were in the same place at the same time for a few minutes. Choi would be the type to err on the side of caution. He must believe you spoke. Do you think Leslie's right in thinking the hotel knows she witnessed the attack?"

"How could they not?"

"That's just another reason Choi would have reached out to me. You asked about Gini, and then you met up with Leslie." Cross stared at me. "And you confronted Jane."

"I don't think she'll talk."

"But you don't know."

"What else am I supposed to do? Asking questions is how we figure things out." But Cross was right. Choi had every reason to be suspicious of me. "Do you think that's why they assigned me a room on the ground floor when Leslie is trapped on an authorized access only level?"

"Possibly."

A thought occurred to me, making my stomach sink. "How is Kellan keeping an eye on her?"

"Choi gave us unlimited access. NDAs are in place, but I'd say Choi's concern that you or someone else is threatening the Golden is his main priority over guest privacy issues."

"That's good. That means you can make sure Leslie's safe and nothing happens to her."

"Kellan's been planting hidden cameras so we can keep an eye on everyone and everything."

"Are you taking over the case? You'd been adamant about me staying away from it and all other cases."

"I'd say that ship has sailed. What I'm doing and what you're doing aren't the same thing. But there is overlap, so we work together. Cross Security was asked to evaluate potential threats to the Golden. You're protecting Leslie. Same end game, different routes to get there."

"You have access to a lot of things I don't. You'll work back of house, and I'll work front of house?"

"That's the plan."

Lucien had access to the hotel's database and security system, but I could interact with the staff and guests more easily. This could work. I just wasn't sure how Heathcliff would feel about it.

"Leslie's supposed to see the doctor and find out if she can go back to work tomorrow," I said.

"We'll see if anyone goes to her room. At the present, she's quarantining. Her roommates have been temporarily reassigned." Cross moved to an empty terminal, entered a few things, and brought up the view from a hidden camera. It showed the hallway outside Leslie's room. "Amir, make sure we keep an eye on the comings and goings. Ideally, we want to get a camera inside Leslie's room, but until that happens, this is the next best thing." Cross turned to me. "If you meet up with her again, make sure you give her a device, tell her where to plant it, and how to activate it."

I wasn't sure Leslie would want to do that. "Do you think they brainwashed her?"

"It sounds more like behavioral modification. They used a reward and punishment system to make her comply. It's why she's so confused. External motivators are telling her she did a good job, that everything is good and that living at the Golden and working as an intern is the ultimate privilege, but that's in conflict with her internal processes, which are screaming warnings at her. It's why she's so confused. I'd say that may make her unpredictable," Amir said. "It could be why they made her sick. To test her and watch her more closely."

That didn't make me feel any better. "You think she was poisoned?"

"It could be a coincidence, but logically, it makes the most sense under the circumstances," Amir said.

"Pull footage from outside the Golden from around the time Leslie supposedly bought the hot dog and look for any funny business. If someone laced the hot dog, we need to find out who." Cross turned to me. "What do you think would have happened this morning if you hadn't locked the bathroom door?"

I didn't want to think about that. "It would have been a rather embarrassing fight, to say the least."

"How many alleged suicides occurred inside hotel bathrooms?" he asked.

"Three," I said.

"I'm beginning to think they weren't suicides."

"Told you."

He pointed a finger at me. "You get one of those per day. Now give Amir any other information we need to take over surveillance." Once that was done, Cross made several requests and loaded a bag with gear. "Leslie won't trust us, but she trusts you. Between the two of us, we should be able to figure out what's going on inside that hotel and who is responsible."

"I'll need better access to the rest of the hotel."

"I'm sure you'll get it once I tell Choi he doesn't need to worry about you."

"But we don't know what Grable told him." Again, I wondered if the Golden was testing Cross Security and their loyalty. "In fact, you expressed an interest in locating Leslie. They could be on to us."

"They aren't," he insisted, but I saw the uncertainty in his eyes. "I'll put some things together and make a nice presentation to reassure Choi that your cover passes muster. In the meantime, try to avoid throwing up any more red flags. They wouldn't have called me if they trusted you. We need to calm the waters before we start making waves."

"If Leslie wants to meet at one a.m. at the drink machine again, I can't say no."

Cross turned to Amir who'd been diligently working on this clusterfuck of a case. "Can you get us inside their system? If we can put their feeds on a delay, we could scrub out anything suspicious."

"We might be able to do that if you can sell them on conducting a massive system analysis and upgrade. That will give us an excuse to get in and tinker with things. Otherwise, there's a good chance someone will notice." Amir gave the boss a look. "And you just said we were to avoid raising more red flags."

"I'll see what I can do." Cross noted the time. "We should head back. If I keep you away too long, they may start to wonder why."

"They won't care." My phone had been vibrating for the last five minutes. "They're too busy searching my room."

"Give me that." Cross took the phone and examined the feed. Then he picked up his phone, sent Kellan to check things out, and handed it to Amir. "Can you get me IDs on these two security guards?"

"This will be faster once I can plug into their employee database."

Cross nodded. "I'll make that happen tonight." He watched as they continued to search, carefully examining everything before making sure to put it back where it belonged. Thus far, they hadn't found the hidden cameras attached to the suitcases. But they were more concerned with the contents or lack thereof inside the bags than they were with checking out what was on the outside. He tapped on Amir's desk. "All right. We're heading back now. I'll do what I can at the hotel tonight. Once I'm done, we can go over things more thoroughly."

"Yes, sir," Amir said.

"In the meantime, run Jane the Maid and dig up everything you can on her. The police will need someone they can leverage," Cross said.

"You make it sound like blackmail," I muttered as we took the elevator back to the garage. "Even if you find something, it may not be enough. The Golden bought off Gini Ruffin's silence. If they could convince her to keep quiet after an attack like that, I'm sure they'll have no problem making sure the rest of their staff falls in line."

"I think I'd know more about that than you would," Cross said, reminding me of the story Jade had told. "Some people can't be bought."

"Then they had to be silenced another way. That would mean the deaths were meant to cover something else up." I'd been thinking about this backward, believing the supposed accidents and natural causes were covering up murders, but the murders were the last resort to cover up something else. "The hit-and-run and fatal shooting victims must have put up the most fight or gotten the closest to getting away. That's why their deaths were more violent and harder to contain."

"Possibly."

"What do you think is going on inside the hotel?"

"You thought it had to do with the interns."

"It has to be bigger than that. Albert Glass isn't an intern. Jane made it sound like everyone on staff has been indoctrinated with these ridiculous ideas, almost like a creepy, smiling, murderous cult."

Cross gave me a look. "Do us both a favor and stop watching horror films."

THIRTY-TWO

The game had changed since the Golden hired Cross Security to look into me. Of course, Cross told them I was Alexandra Riley. My background and ID held up, which was why I'd asked Lawson to help. But despite Cross's insistence that I did not pose a threat, I remained in Choi's crosshairs.

So I played the part. I kept exploring, filming, and taking photos. But this wasn't getting me any closer to figuring out what was going on inside the hotel, why people had died, why Gini was attacked, or how to convince Leslie she should run for the hills and never look back.

Cross Security had been working overtime to determine who posed a threat to the Golden, or rather the employees and guests staying at the hotel. Amir had identified the three men who'd been with Louis Grable inside the garage. Talon Everett had been the man with the grey beard who'd spoken to me. He worked laundry services. The other two, Milo Rubie and Karl Strader, provided valet parking services. None of the men had criminal records or matched the descriptions Leslie had provided. But Cross was keeping a watchful eye on them at work, and Heathcliff had assigned units to sit on their apartments. So far, those appeared to be dead ends. The only suspicious man from that group was Louis Grable.

Grable's two security guard colleagues, Stan Lauper and Jose Ortiz, had searched my room while I'd been out of the hotel. Amir had enhanced the camera footage I provided, but neither man was armed. They didn't steal anything or cause any damage. As far as we could tell, they hadn't found the hidden surveillance devices and hadn't swept the room for bugs. Cross was convinced Choi put them up to it, but he couldn't prove it.

No internal documents or memos existed on the Golden's servers that indicated management was responsible for any of the horrible things that had befallen the hotel. But that didn't mean the orders hadn't been relayed in person. Again, I wished I'd been able to hear what Choi and Grable had been discussing.

Surveillance cameras were keeping an eye on Leslie. I'd filled her in on a few safe locations where she could leave me a message if she was afraid to use the phone. Since Cross Security was monitoring most of the hotel and watching in real time, I'd get notified if she wanted to be pulled out.

"I think they laced your hot dog," I told her. "Exterior cameras caught sight of Albert Glass on his way to work. He bumped into the cart on his way to the Golden. Though it isn't clear from the footage, he paused long enough that he could have poured or sprinkled something onto your food."

"The hospital said it was salmonella. How can that be weaponized?"

"Everything can be weaponized," I said. "Do you know they can test eggs for salmonella? If he found one that tested positive, he could have siphoned off enough of the clear liquid to cover your food without being obvious. The mustard and relish would have camouflaged it."

"You sound insane," Leslie said.

"Do I? He attacked Gini. He knew you were close by, and between Cross and the police hoping to speak to you, he may have wanted to stop that from happening."

"Shit."

"You don't have to stay here," I reminded her. "You can

leave anytime you want. If you're afraid, I will escort you out of here."

"No, I'm fine. Medical cleared me to return to work in a limited capacity, so I'm assigned to provide online chat support. I'll be safe."

"You'll be stuck in an office away from guests. That doesn't make you safe."

"I'll be fine," she insisted, but I couldn't help but think she was trying to convince herself of that.

"Don't forget, I'm a phone call or note away." With Leslie locked away, I wouldn't be able to check on her or accidentally bump into her.

The only thing I wanted to do was question the hotel staff, which I'd been doing. But all the bright smiles and blank looks did not get me any closer to the truth. I hadn't seen any of the people I'd run into in the parking garage.

Grable hadn't made any more threats, but his eyes tracked me every time I went through the lobby or passed him in the hallway. The same could be said for Ian Choi.

But maybe things would be different today. I stretched out on a sofa near the fire pit. It was early, so no one was interested in this location. From here, I had a nice view of the pool and slide, the pool bar, and the courtyard. Grable had been watching me from the lobby window for the last half hour, but he had finally stepped away. Maybe he'd given up. And then I spotted Ian Choi heading in my direction.

Tag-teaming wasn't fair when I didn't have a teammate. Or maybe Cross was my teammate, except he was at the office. I could call Heathcliff, but cozying up to the badge wouldn't earn me Choi's trust.

After saying good morning to the lifeguard and staff members who were getting the pool bar ready for its afternoon opening, Choi approached me. He carried a mug with white foam on the top and what looked like a cinnamon stick poking through.

"How are you today, Ms. Riley?"

"Alexandra," I said, "or Alex." I gestured to the opposite couch. "I'm doing just fine. How are you?"

Choi moved the cinnamon stick out of the way before

taking a sip. "I'm well, thanks." He turned to see what had my attention. "No photos today?"

"Not yet."

"Thinking about going for a dip in the pool?" he asked.

"I told you I'm not much for pools. I didn't bring a suit."

"There are plenty of places to pick one up. A few are even inside the hotel. Have you visited any of the shops yet?"

"Did you sneak a peek at today's itinerary?" I teased. "I was planning on visiting a few of them once they open. But that's not until eleven." I checked the time. "I have another forty-five minutes, so I thought I'd hang out here. I've been to a lot of places, and it's always the same. But it surprises me every time. Kids will go to the pool the second it opens. And by the end of the day, the only people left are the adults who want to unwind, the ones without kids."

"Maybe they tucked the kids in and came back for some adult-only time."

"Maybe."

Choi sipped his beverage, eyeing me over the rim. "I take it you don't have children."

"No."

"A partner?"

I gave him a look. "I'm curious why you're asking."

"I was hoping to take you to dinner tonight. Shaw wanted you to experience the steakhouse firsthand. And I remember you mentioning not wanting to eat alone."

"Y'know, ever since I arrived at the Golden, I've had a lot of luck finding dining companions."

"Oh yeah?" Choi asked.

"First, there was you. Then, the other night, I ducked into the rooftop bar and ended up talking to some guy. We went for ice cream afterward."

Choi acted like he knew nothing about it, but his eyes gave him away. The way he looked down, directly into his mug instead of at me, the deliberate pause which lasted half a millisecond too long before he recovered with, "What flavor did you get?" gave me insight into his tells.

"Actually, I got a shake. It was this extra thick cookies and cream with crushed up peanut butter cups. It was amazing."

"What did he get," Choi asked, "if you don't mind me asking?"

"Um...it was green. Mint chip, I think, with chocolate sprinkles because I insisted. Chocolate sprinkles just make everything better." I grinned. "What's your favorite flavor?"

Cross and I had perfected our stories, figuring if Choi inquired, it'd be best to head him off. That question proved he didn't necessarily trust my boss either. Again, I couldn't help but wonder if this was a test. If Grable outed me, Choi could have gotten the garage footage and realized I was the same woman sans wig and glasses.

"Butter pecan."

I made a face. "I don't think chocolate sprinkles would make that better."

Choi laughed. "I'll have to try it one day and let you know."

I nodded at his mug. "That looks interesting."

"Chai latte with a sweet cream foam." He held it out for my inspection. "Would you like one? It used to be a regular menu item at the coffee shop, but it wasn't particularly popular. Anyone can order it, but it's part of the secret menu. You have to be in the know."

"Ooh." I sat up, grabbing my camera. "Do you mind if I photograph it?"

"It's not as pretty as it was originally," he said.

"That's okay. It'll make a nice clip."

He put it on the table, and I adjusted it, as if I knew what I was doing. Then I positioned the camera the way most food photographers and recipe creators did, took a few shots, and recorded a short video, spinning it slowly by the handle.

Once that was done, I pulled the camera away and leaned back in the seat while I reviewed the footage. "Thanks for the tip. I'll have to go back to the coffee shop to learn more about this secret menu and the offerings on it. It could be its own series of clips."

Choi picked up his drink and took another sip, smiling at me the entire time. "It's nice to see someone genuinely excited about work."

You have no idea. “Uh...thanks, I think.”

Choi stood. “I should let you get back to it. But you never answered my question.”

“What question?” I knew damn well what question, but it was always smart to play dumb.

“Dinner at the steakhouse.”

“What time?”

“Nine.” He cocked an eyebrow. “Is that too late?”

“Not at all. I’ll see you then.”

* * *

Ian Choi and I were seated at a four-person table at the hotel’s steakhouse. A famous chef’s name was attached to the restaurant, but said chef wasn’t working from this location. Despite that, reservations were hard to come by. Hotel guests had priority, but half the tables were filled with locals looking for a night out.

The server had brought us an assortment of items to try. I had taken a particular liking to the mac and cheese, which Choi had quietly noted. He had tried to steer the conversation to the other hotels and resorts I’d visited. Thanks to Martin, I was able to sell my cover, but I didn’t like the third degree.

“That’s enough about me.” I reached for the crostini he’d already sampled, which meant it was safe. “I’d like to know how PR works for a hotel like this? Is media relations part of the same department?”

“It is. So is our advertising department. A lot of the bigger campaigns are sourced out to agencies, but we have a few people in-house who coordinate with media relations and PR to make sure that any events or specials we’re having get the proper attention.” He gave me that same self-deprecating smile he’d used before. “I’m nothing but a glorified publicist.”

“Is this what you’ve always done?”

He picked up the communal salad bowl and put some on his plate, diverting eye contact and pausing a little too long. At least now I had him pegged. “You make that sound like it’s a bad thing.”

"So you've always worked here?"

"Not always. Less than two years. I bounced around before that. I'm quite the problem solver."

"How do you like working for the Golden?" I snapped my fingers a few times. "What's the name of the parent company? It's on the tip of my tongue."

"Experiential Adventures. I say this job provides a few interesting challenges, but I always enjoy a challenge."

I wondered what he'd do if I asked how he dealt with the challenge of covering up an intern being attacked and burned. "What would you say has been the most daunting task you've had to perform?"

He quirked an eyebrow. "I didn't realize this was a job interview."

"I'm just trying to get a better idea of how things work behind the scenes."

He gave me a bright smile, though not as bright as the server's when she placed a perfectly crusted filet mignon in front of me, along with another helping of mac and cheese.

"Is there anything else I can get you right now?" she asked.

"I can't think of anything." I pointed at Choi with the end of my fork. "Would you care for anything else?"

"Let's get another bottle of red for the table."

"Right away, sir." She gave him a curt nod, removed the dishes we'd finished, and disappeared into the kitchen.

"You didn't answer my question." I sliced into the steak, finding the oozing red unappetizing. Food shouldn't bleed. This was why people became vegan. But I took the obligatory photos anyway, which I had done with all the dishes when they first arrived. Abandoning the steak, I reached for more of the crostini. "Daunting task. Go."

"Answering podcaster's questions."

"I'm not a podcaster."

"But you have a podcast."

"It's part of sharing the experience and adventure."

He reached into his pocket and pulled out his phone. "Can I steal that?"

"Go for it." When Cross inevitably fired me, maybe I would make up slogans for a living.

Choi made himself a note, which was another attempt to avoid my question. For a fixer, he should have been quicker on his feet. But he wasn't used to having to save his own ass. Was the delay part of his act, like he wanted it to look intentional? Or was I giving this guy too much credit?

"Do you have any advertising or marketing experience?" he asked.

"I run online campaigns to boost my channel's exposure, but I was self-taught. I don't have any formal training."

He pointed to my steak. "Is something wrong with the food?"

"I'm not a fan."

He gestured for the server. "We'll get you something else. They make a fantastic linguine with clams."

"I'm okay. The appetizers and side dishes filled me up. Don't worry. My opinion on rare steak will not reflect badly on the Golden. I know tons of foodies who would swoon over this. It's just not my thing. I like my meat cooked a little more thoroughly. A lot of chefs and food critics disapprove." I shrugged. "It's my personal hang-up."

"Are you—" His phone buzzed, stopping him midsentence. The look on his face told me he wasn't supposed to be disturbed. "Excuse me for a moment."

Ian Choi was a professional. He took the call out of earshot and remained utterly impassive to whatever news he heard. But the interruption didn't bode well.

Surreptitiously, I hit the record button and angled my phone to face him. The likelihood the mic would pick up his conversation was practically zilch, but I had to try. While I waited, I picked at the appetizer, but my stomach was in knots. I guess that's why they called it gut instinct.

A minute later, he returned to the table. "I'm sorry, but I have to cut this short."

"Is everything okay?"

"That was a reminder that I have an appointment I had forgotten about. Thank you for allowing me to join you for dinner."

"The pleasure was mine."

Choi studied me carefully, but whatever he was hoping

to find wasn't there. "I'll see about setting up that behind-the-scenes tour of our internship program for you."

"Really?"

"You'd be the perfect person to share the details with the world." He started to walk away, only to return to the table. "Two things before I forget. The management would like to upgrade you so you can see everything the Golden has to offer. We'd like to move you to one of the penthouse suites tomorrow."

I tried to appear excited even though the warning klaxons blared inside my head. These offers were meant to distract me which meant something horrible had happened. Was Leslie dead?

The sight and smell of the steak nearly made me toss my cookies, but I held the smile, even as I ducked my face so he couldn't see my eyes. "I'd love that. You're the best."

He tapped the table. "If you won't consider getting another entrée, at least get one of the desserts. The crème brulé is to die for."

So that's what was killing everyone.

THIRTY-THREE

When three small dessert plates were brought to my table, I took the appropriate photos, posed with a forkful raised to my lips, and made a few notes on what the items were called. But if I had to take another bite of anything, I'd be sick. So I asked the server if the leftovers could be boxed up, took photos of the packaging, and posed outside the restaurant with the takeout bag.

The only thing I wanted to do was search the hotel until I figured out what that call had been about. Assuming my gut was right, the police would be notified. So I made my way to the nearest window and looked outside. No flashing lights. No sirens.

I got into the elevator, wishing I had access to the twenty-eighth floor. Since I didn't, I dug out my phone and texted Amir. Cross was maintaining eyes on Leslie. If something happened to her, Amir would know about it.

She's fine. Still providing online chat support to guests.

When does her shift end? I replied.

Ten. Do you want to attempt an accidental meet?

Something happened to someone at the hotel, but I didn't know anything more than that. Actually, I didn't even know that. I updated Amir on Choi's phone call, but he didn't have any details readily available. However, he'd look into it.

Is Lucien on-site? I asked.

No.

When the cat's away. Now I couldn't help but wonder if whatever happened had been timed just right to keep the hotel's contracted private eye from poking his nose into it.

My stomach turned, and a feeling of dread settled over me. I wasted so much time today, selling my cover. But that had been a total waste, like most things that I'd done since arriving here. I hadn't figured anything out. All I knew was Grable was trouble, Glass should be arrested, and Choi didn't trust me. I'd have to be more proactive, but it may already be too late.

I couldn't think about this. In fact, I wasn't sure I was thinking at all. Fear was commanding my thoughts, which made me reactive. That was the last thing I needed to be, especially when I lacked intel.

Since I was alone in the elevator car, I pressed myself against the side of the elevator and pulled out my phone. But I already had a waiting text from Heathcliff.

9-1-1 received a call. An ambulance is on the way, he said.

Instead of replying, I waited for the doors to open in the lobby. Grable wasn't at his normal post, but since he'd been at work early this morning, he should be off by now. However, his absence did nothing to alleviate my fears that he'd attacked someone and called Choi to cover it up.

The hidden cameras on my luggage showed no one had entered my room while I'd been away, so it should be safe to speak inside. But the paranoid part of my brain made me go into the bathroom and turn the shower and sink on full blast before I called Heathcliff. "What happened?"

"I was hoping you could tell me. 9-1-1 received reports of an injury. Someone allegedly slipped in the shower. I don't know much more than that. Unless EMTs request officers to the scene, the police have no reason to respond."

"Can you find out where it happened? I need a room number."

"Hang on. Dispatch should be able to tell me." I listened as Heathcliff spoke to someone on the other line. When he came back, he said, “Room 640.”

Nothing was on the sixth floor. No restaurants, no shops, no recreational activities, or outdoor seating. Coming up with a plausible reason to be on that level would take some effort. Luckily, Choi had mentioned each floor displayed different commissioned pieces of art.

“Do you think Leslie is the latest accident victim?” Heathcliff asked.

“She’s fine. The cameras Cross planted have a line of sight into the office where she’s been assigned. She’s working online support.”

“Is it possible this was an accident?”

“I doubt it.” I told him about Choi’s abrupt exit. “Let me see what I can find out. Keep an ear to the ground. If anything changes and dispatch calls for other units, let me know. If not, I’ll call you back once I find out what happened.”

The EMTs would assess the situation. They’d call the cops if the injury proved fatal or if there was any reason to believe it was the result of an attack.

I knew one thing for sure. Ian Choi was on top of it, but I doubted someone with his credentials would be called to handle a slip and fall unless the hotel was egregiously at fault. And I wasn’t sure how that could be possible unless they cleaned the shower with extra slippery oil.

I left Alexandra’s recording gear in the room and headed for the newsstand. Every cell in my body wanted to go straight to the sixth floor, but I needed to collect some intel first.

The small shop had a collection of travel essentials, so I perused the racks for something to settle my upset stomach. After selecting a travel-sized bottle of the pink stuff and a single serve packet of the fizzy stuff, I went to the register to pay.

A different intern was working. Her name tag said Cheryl. I offered her a tight smile and placed my items on the counter.

“Not feeling well?” she asked, but the smile remained like a Halloween mask even as she considered my purchase choices.

"My stomach's a little upset."

"If you're feeling sick, there's a doctor who can take a look at you. Just notify the front desk, and they'll send him to your room."

"How long do you think that will take?"

"Let me check." She reached for the phone beneath the counter and picked it up. "A guest isn't feeling well. She was curious how long the wait for the doctor is." She paused. "I see. Okay. Thank you." She put the phone down. "He's having a busy night. It'll be about an hour."

"Are that many people sick?"

She held the smile. "Someone had an accident. It's nothing major. I think they hurt their shoulder. No reason to worry."

"Thanks for letting me know. I think this should do it. If I'm still feeling lousy in an hour, I'll notify the front desk."

"Would you like to charge it to your room?"

"Sure." I took the bag and made my way to the elevator banks. A shoulder injury sounded too simple. Was that the cover-up? Had Choi already put a nice spin on things?

When the elevator doors opened, I stepped inside and pressed six. Before the doors closed, flashing lights caught my attention. They were faint, reflecting off the polished marble floors in the lobby. Wedging my foot against the door, I watched as a team of EMTs entered the hotel. A staff member was waiting for them. The two stars on her name tag indicated she'd been here a while and was used to dealing with emergencies. *Candace.* I read her name tag as soon as she was close enough for me to see it.

Moving my foot, I reached out to hold the door. "What floor?" I called to the trio as they moved purposefully toward me.

"Six," Candace said.

I pressed the button while keeping one hand on the door.

"Thanks," the lead EMT said as he pulled the gurney into the elevator.

"No problem." I moved to the back corner, hoping to be unobtrusive.

"What are we looking at?" the other EMT asked.

"Someone fell in the shower. I'm not sure the extent of the damage, but she says it's her arm. The doctor took a look. He thinks it's broken." Candace stared at the doors in front of her. "He immobilized her arm, but we thought it was best to have you drive her instead of someone on staff doing it."

"Good call," the lead EMT said.

As soon as the doors opened, Candace led them down the hallway. "She's right down here. Room 640."

It took every ounce of self-restraint not to fall into step beside them. Instead, I inched forward. Since I'd searched every floor looking for that damn ginger ale, I was aware there were no cover positions until I reached the vending machine room which was halfway between here and where the EMTs had gone. Security cameras posted in the halls would absolutely see me. There was no avoiding that.

The EMTs entered room 640. I continued after them, hoping to catch drips and drabs of what was going on, until Ian Choi stepped out of the room.

His back was to me as he spoke in hushed tones to Candace. Did Cross set up any hidden cameras near that room? Ducking inside the vending machine room, I stood behind the open door, straining to hear what was going on.

"Is everything okay?" Candace asked.

"Not yet. We'll have to address the fallout later. Right now, we let the paramedics do their jobs." So Choi had been called to clean up whatever had happened in that room.

Footsteps drew closer, but I remained behind the open door, my back pinned against the wall. Once the footsteps went past, I saw that they belonged to the now-familiar suit. I wanted to corner Choi in the elevator and force him to answer me, but that would put an end to my part in this investigation. And if I was out, there was a good chance Cross would be kicked out next. So I resisted the urge to interrogate the man.

I moved out from behind the door and stepped into the hallway to see what was going on. The EMTs were inside the room. Candace was positioned in front of the open door. She had her hands on her hips and a creepy smile on her face. Like she was prepared to block anyone from entering while wishing them a wonderful stay at the Golden.

There would be no getting past her, so I moved closer to the vending machines, slid my credit card through the reader, and made a selection. This would have to suffice as far as my reason for being on this level. Assuming Candace hadn't been warned about me, she wouldn't think anything of a guest grabbing a canned drink to take back to her room.

Moving to the right, I hoped to see a little farther down the hall. I didn't want to miss seeing the victim. This may be my only chance to identify the person, assuming she was alive and had no intention of pressing charges.

The squeak of a wheel caught my attention. Candace led the procession back to the elevator. I half-turned toward the machine, but I kept an eye on the hallway.

The EMTs wheeled Jane, the maid I'd spoken to earlier, toward the elevator. The way they'd immobilized her arm worried me. The c-collar didn't help matters. As they passed, I heard the lead paramedic say, "...shattered her shoulder. Alert the trauma unit. They'll want to have an orthopedic surgeon standing by."

I remained with the vending machines until the elevator doors closed, then I relayed the latest to Heathcliff via text. Jane had spoken to me and defied Choi by refusing to search my room. Was this my fault?

How did the maid slip in the shower? he asked.

I'm not sure she did, but since she was fully dressed in her uniform, I'd say the official line will be she was cleaning it.

At this time of night?

I knew better than to talk in the open. The Golden had great security. Cross had seen to that, so I couldn't risk having a real conversation. Instead of replying to Heathcliff, I sent a text to Cross, telling him what happened and asked, *Can you get over here? I want someone at the hotel to intervene in case whoever attacked Jane goes after Leslie next.*

I'm on my way, Cross promised. *Amir's already*

reviewing footage from that hallway. We should know who's responsible in a few minutes.

I want the name as soon as you have it, I texted.

Ten minutes later, Cross sent me the intel. Harley Daniels. I didn't recognize the name, but I recognized the man from the descriptions Leslie provided. He'd been the man who brought the steam iron down on Gini's arm.

Not wasting a second, I dialed Heathcliff. "Hey, I'm in town. I think we should get together. Are you free tonight?" I asked as I waited for the elevator.

"Are you coming to the precinct?"

"Yeah, I'll see you soon."

THIRTY-FOUR

I'd been trained to run toward danger, not away from it. A crime scene or what I believed to be a crime scene needed a proper investigation. After returning to my room with the can of soda, I paced in front of the door. Remaining here wouldn't get me answers, but I had to wait for Cross before I ducked out. If Gini's attackers were worried they were close to getting caught, they could be tying up loose ends. Leslie could be next.

While I waited, I double-checked that my recording devices were working, grabbed Alexandra's phone and gear, and went back to the lobby. After an incident, I expected to find employees scurrying about. But that wasn't the case. The ambulance had left. The valets remained at their stands. A handful of guests were checking in. Nothing was different.

Instead of taking the elevator, I took the stairs up. I had no reason to think anyone was monitoring me, but Jane had been the only person willing to talk to me. And she'd been scared. If someone was watching my every move, they may be waiting for me to get back into the elevator, so perhaps they wouldn't spot me on the stairwell.

Unlike the higher levels, getting access to six didn't require a keycard. So I pushed open the door and stepped out. The cameras would see me in the hallway. There was no way to avoid it. But instead of going out of my way to mind my business, I was going to lean into the curiosity that I'd exhibited during dinner. Even though I said Alexandra only posted positivity, the old news adage remained. If it bleeds, it reads.

A specially equipped cleaning cart was parked outside 640. The biohazard bins clued me in that this wasn't for usual maid service. And that's when I realized there hadn't been a cleaning cart outside the room while Jane supposedly cleaned the shower. Someone had lured her here.

I continued at a regular pace, not bothering to conceal my destination. Once I reached the doorway, I paused. The cart blocked entry into the room. A container of oxygenated cleaner was tucked on the lower shelf of the cart. The red biohazard bin had been opened. Pieces of bloody, broken glass had been tossed inside.

The room didn't look disturbed. The beds were made. The welcome packet was beneath the TV, beside the remote, which was where mine had been when I checked in. The carpet near the curtains still had vacuum lines. However, those lines disappeared closer to the door from the recent foot traffic in and out.

I shifted to the side, craning my neck to see into the bathroom. The first thing I noticed was the mirror was broken. A team of two wore blue plastic jumpsuits over their uniforms while they scrubbed the floor. I took a few photos and tucked the device into my bag.

"Excuse me," I said loud enough for them to hear me, "what happened in there?"

The two exchanged whispers before the man nearest to the bathroom door came over to me. At least he had the decency not to smile. "Someone fell."

"A guest?"

"I don't really know. They were taken to the hospital to get checked out, but I'm sure they'll be fine."

They not she. He had made it a point to keep the details vague.

"I need to get back to cleaning up. I wouldn't want

anyone else to fall or hurt themselves." He moved closer to the door. "Was there something you needed?"

"No, I...uh...heard the commotion and thought I'd see what had happened. Hopefully, everyone's okay."

"I wouldn't worry. But for everyone's privacy, would you mind moving along?"

"Sure. No problem." I backed away from the door. I was halfway to the elevator when he grabbed the bleach and shut the door.

While I debated my next course of action, my phone alerted me to movement inside my room. I pulled up the streaming video feed. A man in a corduroy suit looked around my room. He went into the bathroom, returned to the main room, opened a closet, and then headed for the patio.

I took the elevator down and headed straight for my room. By the time I entered, he had returned from outside. I made it a point to let out a surprised yelp and back toward the door.

"Whoa." He held up his palms. "I didn't mean to startle you. I work for the hotel." He pointed to his name tag which hung over his left breast. "I received a report you weren't feeling well. I knocked, but no one came to the door. I was concerned, so I let myself in. It's hotel policy if we believe a guest is in danger."

I let the skepticism play across my face. "Do you have any credentials or some way of verifying who you are?"

He reached into his jacket and pulled out a card. He held it out to me, but when I didn't move closer to take it, he put it on the dresser and slid it toward me.

I picked it up and read his name. "Dr. Johnson."

"If you'd like to call to make sure, please do. I don't want to make you uncomfortable."

"That's okay. I startle easily. But the lady at the newsstand said you were detained, that it'd be an hour. I figured I'd feel better by the time you arrived, so I thought I'd save you a visit."

"Are you feeling better?" he asked.

"I'm getting there. I know better than to be such a glutton. But all those fancy drinks and treats kept calling my name."

Johnson eyed the opened bottle of pink stuff. "It looks like you have it under control, but let me get you some electrolytes just in case. Do you have a flavor preference?"

"Not red," I said.

He picked up the phone and told the front desk to send over a bottle. "I wish all my patients were this easy."

"Did you treat the woman on the sixth floor?" I asked. "I was searching the hotel for ginger ale when the paramedics arrived."

"Rest assured, everyone is safe and sound. That's all I can say."

"Sure, Doc. I get it."

A bellhop arrived with a bottle of lemon-lime electrolytes. He handed it to Johnson and left.

"Seems like you do this a lot." I took the bottle from his outstretched hand. "Should I be concerned the stomach flu is running rampant?"

"Not at all. We haven't had anyone sick like that in weeks." He gave my room another careful look. "Feel better. Call if you need anything."

"Thanks." I waited for him to leave before hanging the do not disturb.

Johnson had only gone a few steps when he pulled out his phone to make a call. I couldn't make out what he was saying, so I closed the door and made a mad dash to my duffel bag. In record time, I changed clothes, lost the wig and glasses, pulled my matted down hair into a ponytail, and tugged on a ball cap. Exiting through the door which led to the tiny enclosed patio outside, I stepped out, maneuvering around the chairs, hopping the fence, and moving horizontally along the rest of the rows of outdoor patios until I made it to the walking path.

If I'd read the layout properly, the patios were not within view of any security cameras. Exiting onto the main path, I jogged around and let myself into the first door, which opened at the rear of the lobby using my room key. Dr. Johnson was making his way down the corridor, his attention on the phone screen in front of him.

Keeping my head down, I followed him past the

newsstand. The coffee shop would be closing in an hour. Two people stood at the counter, debating the merits of the loaf cake versus the shortcake. Johnson moved past them and sat at the table beside the wall which separated the counter from the dining area.

I got in line behind them, aware of Britt, an intern I'd met my first morning here, wiping down the tables and cleaning the seats. It'd be best to avoid running into her. My disguise was good, but it wasn't perfect. Damn, I should have remembered to wipe off the makeup before I ran out.

"Go ahead of us," the guy said, tugging on his boyfriend's hand to get him out of the way. "We may be here all night."

"Are you sure?" I asked, making my voice low and raspy.

"Absolutely." He waved me forward.

The barista gave me an exhausted version of the smile. "What can I get you?"

I pointed to the giant cookies. "Two rainbow chips please."

Grabbing the tongs, she plucked three out of the display case and dropped them into the bag. "Enjoy."

I gave her a confused look.

"We're getting ready to close. It's on the house."

I handed her the twenty from my pocket. "In that case, I'd like to treat these gentlemen, and the rest is for you."

"Thank you. That's so kind."

I nodded, pulled the bill of my cap down further, and moved toward the nearest table. I kept my back to Dr. Johnson, afraid he'd recognize me, but I inched as far to the side as I could. Then I pulled out my phone, keeping it at table level while I scrolled with one thumb.

Flipping the camera, I could see he was in deep conversation with Albert Glass. Glass's goatee made him unmistakable, even looking like a guest in a wrinkled button-up, jeans, and flip-flops. I suspected the button-up had been underneath the vest and apron he wore as host, but the jeans and flip-flops were new. Maybe he didn't want to be recognized either.

I adjusted my mic settings and hid the phone on my lap,

so no one would notice. Then I used my free hand to pull out one of the cookies, place it on a napkin, and tear off a piece to nibble on.

"Did Jane leave it in her room?" Glass asked.

"I didn't find it," Johnson said. "But Ms. Riley returned before I could finish my search. I thought she may have concealed it somewhere no one would think to look."

Glass stared at him. "Where would that be?"

"The patio. The janitorial staff rarely goes out there. It'd be the perfect spot."

"I don't think Jane would be stupid enough to risk that. She would have given it to her directly."

"I don't think so," Johnson said. "Security searched Ms. Riley's bags. No one found anything."

"Jane must have it somewhere else." Glass rubbed his eyes. "We searched her place and her car."

"What about her locker?" Johnson asked.

"That was the first place we looked." Glass sighed, growing frustrated. "All we know is Pellers swore he made a copy. Jane's the only person he would have trusted enough with it."

"Unless he gave it to someone who doesn't work here."

"If that were true, we wouldn't be having this conversation." Glass fought not to sneer, shaking his head. "Maybe it was bullshit. I don't know. But I plan on being there when Jane wakes up to remind her what will happen if she doesn't hand it over." Glass scratched the back of his head while glancing around.

I covered the phone with my hand, flattening it against my thigh while I rested my head on my elbow, ducking toward the cookie I was eating. Britt finished cleaning a nearby booth and stopped beside Johnson and Glass.

"Is there anything I can get you?" she asked in that bubbly tone.

"Go away," Glass said.

Britt didn't react. Instead, she bounded over to my table. "Is there anything I can get you?" she asked.

"Napkin, please," I said in the same low, raspy tone I used before.

She smiled even brighter and went to retrieve it. When

she came back, she placed a stack on the table in front of me. "There you go. Have a nice night."

I nodded, keeping my head down as I picked up the oversized cookie and took a bite, struggling to keep the crumbs from cascading everywhere.

Satisfied that their conversation remained private, Johnson said, "Cleaning up the sixth floor is going to be a mess. Explaining the broken mirror and shower door—"

"That's not our problem. We stick to the story. Jane slipped and fell."

"The room doesn't look like that," Johnson said. "It looks like she was viciously attacked."

"No, it doesn't. The others already took care of it. If there had been anything suspicious about the scene, the paramedics would have called the police. No one thought anything of it."

"What if Jane talks?"

"She knows the score. She has one more chance to cooperate, if not—" Glass didn't finish that statement, but his expression spoke volumes.

"I don't like this," Johnson said.

"You should have thought about that before you got involved, Doc. I didn't hear you complaining when you were receiving your share." Glass gave him a look. "Do I need to worry about you?"

"No." Johnson stood. "But I think you're wrong. I think if Jane had given it to a guest, especially a travel reporter, something would have come of it by now."

"We'll have to wait for Jane to tell us where she put it before I'm convinced of anything."

THIRTY-FIVE

I watched Albert Glass leave the coffee shop. Johnson didn't follow him. Instead, the doctor went to the counter, made polite small talk with the barista, and waited for an herbal tea. Somewhere during all that, Lucien sent me a text to let me know he had arrived. After that, I didn't stick around. I made my way out of the coffee shop and to the front door.

What I heard had left me with plenty to contemplate. Now I was even more convinced whatever was happening inside the Golden involved a lot of staff members. Even the doctor was involved. That had to violate the Hippocratic oath, but it would explain why so many of these accidental deaths and suicides had been ruled that way. Johnson would know how to make things look convincing enough to the coroner, particularly in light of supporting surveillance footage.

Now as I went past the bellhops and valets, I couldn't help but get creeped out. Were they watching me? Did they recognize me?

I kept my head down, grunting responses to them for fear my voice would give me away. I was half a block away, approaching the site of the fatal shooting, when my phone rang.

Stifling the inadvertent scream which had been building on account of my imagination insisting there was a cult of killers following me, I pulled out the device to see the message was from Amir. He'd pulled the security cam footage from the sixth floor. Harley Daniels had gone inside room 640 with a Halligan a few minutes prior to Jane arriving and left as soon as Dr. Johnson arrived, before the 9-1-1 call was placed.

According to Amir, no guests were assigned that room for today or the next day, which meant there would have been no reason for Jane to be there. And there definitely was no reason for a member of hotel staff to be walking around with a Halligan. It was a miracle Jane was still alive.

I called Amir. "I need Harley Daniels' address."

"Ms. Parker—"

"Address," I repeated.

Amir gave it to me. "What are you planning on doing?"

"I'll be careful." I hung up, knowing it'd be in everyone's best interest to keep my plans to myself.

Once I was sure no one was tailing me, I called Heathcliff.

"I was getting worried," he said. "You told me you were coming in."

"I had to wait for Lucien. In the meantime, you're not going to believe what I heard." I filled him in as I made my way to my car.

"I'll need copies of the surveillance footage and whatever else you may have. I'll send units to Glass's place. We'll keep an eye on him."

I pulled my phone away from my face and sent the files. "Someone needs to get to the hospital to keep an eye on Jane. It sounds like an interrogation went wrong, and they're planning on giving it another try as soon as she gets out of surgery."

"Don't worry. We'll have police on her door."

"All right."

"Alex," Heathcliff said, "are you on your way?"

"I have one detour to make."

"What are you doing?"

"I'll be careful." Which was the same thing I'd told Amir.

"That's not what I asked. What are you doing?"

"I'm following up on a lead. If I find something, you'll be the first to know." I paused. "This is the part where you tell me to be careful."

"We already covered that. Tell me where you're going."

"I want to pay Harley Daniels a visit."

"Uniformed officers can do that."

"That won't get us anywhere, Derek. We don't have enough yet, unless you've convinced Gini to come forward." His silence worried me. "What am I missing?"

"She's not doing so well. The hospital had to move her into ICU. The infection's getting worse."

I swore. "That settles it. You need something concrete. It's the only way you'll get a warrant."

"Jane—"

"You can't count on that." Briefly, I wondered what dirt Amir had found on Jane. He had been digging into her background at Cross's insistence. "I'm going to take a look around and see what's what. If something happens, you'll be my first call." I waited, listening as Heathcliff let out an uneasy breath. "You're still not going to tell me to be careful?"

"Did that stab wound heal up yet? It's been a few days."

"It's getting there."

"Good." He paused. "Don't do anything to reopen it."

I smiled. "See, I knew you cared."

He cursed me and hung up.

Now that I didn't have Heathcliff to distract me, the jitters started. I only knew three things about Harley Daniels. One, he burned Gini. Two, he took a Halligan to Jane. And three, he had a stupid name for someone who didn't live in a comic book. Getting to his place didn't take long.

It wasn't much to look at from the outside. His car wasn't parked near his place, which made me think he wasn't home yet. He was probably still at the Golden, working on a master plan to eliminate Leslie and make it look like an accident.

Lucien's got this, I reminded myself. My boss may not

have wanted this case, but he would protect Leslie at all costs. That was how he was wired.

I took my shoulder holster out of the glove box and slipped into it. After sliding my nine millimeter into the holster and grabbing an extra magazine, I slipped into my jacket. Leaving it open, I kept a decent distance while circling his place.

Unlike most of his neighbors' houses, I didn't see a doorbell camera or any security cams. So I moved in closer. A golden glow came from the second floor window. It was faint, which made me think he had left a lamp on. On the side of the house, the kitchen window had a similar glow. But I didn't think he was here.

Still, I had to be sure, so I went to the front door. The porch lights turned on, surprising me, but I didn't see movement in any of the windows. The lights had motion sensors.

I knocked, checking again to make sure I hadn't missed a doorbell camera. "Hello?" I called. "Is anyone home?"

The storm door had a basic lock which didn't take long to pick. The main door was a little more complicated. While I was working to unlock the door, the porch lights went out.

When the knob turned, I entered and pulled the door closed behind me. The hood light above the stove had been left on, which provided a minimal amount of illumination. The rest of the first floor was in darkness.

I waited, wondering if an alarm would sound, but I didn't hear a beep or see a panel on the wall. Harley was too tough to think he needed a security system. He would take his Halligan or steam iron to any unwanted guests.

Once I was sure it was safe to move freely about, I turned on the flashlight keychain and peered around the room. I didn't know what I was looking for, but there had to be something. So I started searching for anything damning or that didn't quite fit.

I'd made my way through most of the first floor when I spotted scratch marks in the shape of a half moon on the tiles in the pantry. The shelving wasn't attached to the wall, which is what I'd originally thought, so I gave it a tug, cringing as the metal scraped against the tile. If anyone else had been in the house, they would have heard that.

After pulling the shelving away, I found a hidden latch. I lifted it up and opened the door. A row of identical shelves stood against the newly revealed wall. Only these were built in. Piles of cash and jewelry filled the space. It was mainly cash. But the jewelry was all high-end stuff, diamonds, designer watches, and necklaces that cost more than my car. Maybe this Harley was a comic book villain after all.

A few prescription bottles were mixed in with the mess. After pulling on a glove, I picked up the nearest one. Carol Meeks. The prescription had been written and filled in Albuquerque, New Mexico. The pills inside were opioids. I put that bottle down and picked up another one. Charles Stanfield. Houston, Texas. Different pain pills.

I took a step back, wondering how much money was hidden behind the wall. There had to be close to two million, most of that in cash alone. The names on the pill bottles would prove my hunch correct, that Harley and his friends were stealing from hotel guests. Given how much they'd acquired, I wondered how long this had been going on and why no one had reported it.

I was copying down the names on the bottles, hoping Amir could run them against the Golden's guest registry, when I heard a rumbling engine outside. The rumbling stopped with a sputter and pop.

I pulled the door closed and shoved the shelving back in place. Hurrying to a window, I knelt on the floor and stuck my fingers between the slats to see what was happening outside. Every cell in my body screamed at me to bolt out the back door, but the back was fenced in. I would be trapped.

Harley stepped out of his car, a classic muscle car which rattled and clanked. He grabbed a bag off the passenger seat, threw it over his shoulder, and went to the rear to unlock the trunk.

I pulled out my phone, figuring getting arrested for breaking and entering would be better than getting killed. But before I could dial, Harley pulled the bloody Halligan out of his trunk.

Switching on my camera, I took a few zoomed in shots. As soon as the porch lights caught him, I dove behind the couch.

The front door opened a moment later. Harley's heavy footsteps made the floor vibrate. He dropped the bag on a chair and turned on the lights.

I didn't move. I didn't even breathe. If he found me, he'd put my lights out for good. The vibrations grew fainter as he moved deeper into the house.

Reaching for my gun, I pulled it from my holster before peering around the side of the sofa. I didn't see him, but I could hear him. The bastard was whistling.

Get out, the voice in my head warned. The front door wasn't far, and he hadn't locked it yet. But it would creak. He'd hear it. So I waited.

The sound of running water from the downstairs bathroom told me it was time to move, so I did. Holding my gun firmly, I slid out from between the couch and wall, crossed the living room, and quietly pulled open the front door. Pushing my back into the storm door, I held the knob on the door so it wouldn't close too loudly and gently pulled it shut. I released the knob slowly. Then I crept off his front porch, the bright lights illuminating me for the entire neighborhood to see.

I didn't run, even though I wanted to get the hell out of there. Instead, I kept a careful pace. Should Harley look outside, he wouldn't think anything of a woman on her way to her car. Only after I was safely locked inside and a block away did I send the photos I'd taken of Harley with the Halligan to Heathcliff.

My phone rang a millisecond later. "That's enough for probable cause. Now get the hell out of there," Heathcliff said. "I'll get a warrant."

"How long will a warrant take?" I asked. "He's washing the evidence away as we speak. Can't you try for exigent circumstances?"

"Parker, get the hell out of there."

"I did. But you can't let him get away with this. We can't keep grasping at straws. This is solid."

"I'll take care of it." Heathcliff hung up.

I stopped at the next intersection, debating what I should do. I had a gun. Harley had a Halligan. But the last time I'd had the better weapon, it hadn't helped. But that didn't matter. I wasn't a coward. I knew what I'd found and what it would mean to our case. Barring Leslie or one of the victims coming forward, the police would need the bloody attack weapon as proof of the assault. It would put everything else I found inside his place into context.

So I turned around and drove back to Harley's. A few lights were on upstairs. I may have already been too late. Bolstering my nerves, I reached for the door handle. Before I could pull it open, flashing lights raced toward me. A second later, the lights went off. Detective Jake Voletek parked at a diagonal behind Harley's muscle car.

"I'm going in. Stay here," he said when I took a step toward him. "I mean it, Parker."

Voletek jogged up the front steps and knocked on the door. A few seconds later, the door opened. Harley stood on the other side. His hair was wet, and he had changed clothes. It looked like he'd been in the shower.

Voletek flashed his badge while he barged into the house. I remained at my car, standing on my tippy toes to try to get a better look. The reassuring weight of my nine millimeter against my side told me I was ready to go in. But I didn't have to because a few seconds later, patrol cars arrived to assist.

THIRTY-SIX

"Voletek showed up fast," I said.

Heathcliff looked up from his notes. "He's a legacy. He thinks he has a different rulebook to follow. Based on the surveillance footage you sent from the hotel prior to Jane's alleged slip and fall and the photos you sent of Harley getting out of his car with the bloody weapon which may have been used in the attack and your insistence that he was destroying evidence, Voletek was convinced we'd satisfied all necessary elements to make the exigent circumstances claim."

"You're not convinced?"

"I've learned if I'm in the field, a call like that is fine. But if I'm in the office, procedure dictates running it by a superior."

"Voletek didn't bother?"

"Nope. But he can fight that one out with ADA Winters, who has been reviewing Harley's statement and keeping an eye on evidence collection."

I stared at the corkboards Heathcliff and I had assembled. "This is a mess." I pointed to a photo of Hugh Pellers, the hit-and-run victim. "Glass mentioned Pellers by name. Without details or context, all we can do is speculate, but I'd say Pellers had proof of whatever criminal activity is happening at the Golden. Glass must have been involved in the attack. He said he questioned Pellers. That Pellers said there was a copy. That may have been a lie, something Pellers said to convince the assailants not to kill him."

"But it didn't work." Heathcliff taped crime scene photos on the board beside me. "That would explain why Pellers got out of his car and why his door was left open."

"They dragged him out of the car," I said.

Heathcliff pointed to the bruises on Pellers' arms. "The ME figured that happened after he was struck by the vehicle, when he hit the ground, but I'm thinking those are from being grabbed and yanked."

"A lot of people inside the hotel are involved. Not everyone, but a lot. Louis Grable works security. I bet others do too. Any of them could have altered the video recordings."

"IT's going over that now, but if that is the case, they did a damn good job of covering their tracks."

A knock sounded on the open conference room door. Amir stepped inside, looking more like a former federal agent and less like Cross's personal hacker. "Cameras only capture what we want them to see. I'm sure you're familiar with how body cam footage can be manipulated based on distance and eyeline to make a dance party look like a rioting mob. These *accidents*, if we call them that, occurred in very precise locations where off-screen factors could have played a contributing role. Couple that with expert video editing, and it would be hard to tell that foul play was involved, even though everything suggests otherwise."

"You know this for a fact?" Heathcliff asked.

Amir shrugged. "I'm postulating a theory. Do with it as you see fit."

"A jury would never believe any of that," Heathcliff said.

Amir chuckled. "That's why expert testimony exists, Detective."

"And you're just the expert we'd need." Heathcliff glanced at me, silently asking if everyone at Cross Security was this pompous.

"I do have several degrees, decades of experience, and

was in charge of training FBI agents at Quantico." Amir held out a folder. "But I am not here for any of that. Mr. Cross asked me to bring you this."

"What is it?" I asked as Heathcliff opened the file.

"The background check we ran on Jane Rossum." Amir eyed me up and down. "Are you still in one piece, Ms. Parker?"

"For now."

"Good. You should also know that the police have concluded their search of room 640. It was professionally cleaned using oxygenated bleach and peroxide. Any blood evidence or DNA that existed is gone now. None of the other rooms were cleaned that thoroughly or with those cleaners. The Golden said that's policy in the event of biohazards. Make of that what you will."

"Do we have any footage of the attack or what went on inside that room?" I asked.

"The hotel camera in the hallway."

"What about our cameras?" I asked.

Amir fixed me with a hard stare that rivaled Cross's. "No."

Heathcliff glanced up from the file. "Jane Rossum was having a sexual relationship with Hugh Pellers?"

"That's what our search turned up."

"I didn't find any indication Pellers was seeing anyone." Heathcliff put the folder down. "That would explain why they think Jane has what they want." Heathcliff crossed his arms over his chest and stared at Amir. "Any idea what sort of evidence Pellers might have had or where he would have stashed it?"

"Assuming you searched his place and didn't find it, I'd suggest you try her place." Amir took a step toward the door.

"Any word on Leslie?" I asked.

"Mr. Cross will make sure she's safe," Amir assured before heading out.

"He could have sent you this." Heathcliff tapped the file. "What is he up to?"

I glanced at the boards behind us. "The same thing we are, except he doesn't have as many rules to follow. He figured if he gets a look at our progress, he may be able to piggyback off it."

"No wonder you like playing for their team." Heathcliff dissected the file, sorting the intel and scribbling notes on the sticky pad before pressing the neon pink square to the corkboard. "I just hope Cross remembers we're on the same side." He turned to grab another sticky note. "From where I'm sitting, it looks like there's a lot going on and plenty of the Golden's staff are involved. Are you sure Cross Security isn't going to turn these details over to the management so they can protect their people or cover up their actions? Even if they aren't participating in the crimes, they may be playing an active role in the cover-up to ensure the hotel doesn't get a bad reputation."

"Choi," I mumbled.

"Precisely."

"Cross won't compromise your case," I said.

Heathcliff gave me one last look before turning his attention back to the files on the table. "I wish I had your level of confidence."

We worked for the rest of the night. In between, Voletek would drop in with details on what was found inside Harley Daniels' home or the things Harley had said during his interrogation.

"I wanted to sit in on that," I said.

Voletek scowled at me. "Do you think that would have been a good idea?"

"No," Heathcliff said before I could answer.

Voletek pointed at him. "See. I didn't think so either. But you didn't miss much. He refuses to cooperate. He said the cash is his, that it's not illegal to have cash. When I asked about the other stuff, he shut up. I don't think he's going to give up his accomplices. I think he's hoping we don't have enough on him."

"Jane," I said.

"Only if she comes forward. If she sticks with the story we were told about this being an accidental slip and fall, it'd be hard to prove otherwise."

"Her blood on his Halligan," I said.

"Yeah," Voletek looked from me to Heathcliff, "still hard

to prove though."

"I'd say we're looking at a massive theft ring." Heathcliff helped himself to one of the two giant rainbow chip cookies that remained while Voletek grabbed the other one. "When a guest is ready to check out, he calls for luggage services. Bellhops arrive, load the packed bags onto their carts, and take the bags to the loading area. Even when the guest accompanies his bags downstairs, he still has to go through the check-out process. While he's doing that, his bags are taken outside."

"The guests don't realize anything is missing because when they pack their bags, they have all their belongings," I said.

Voletek tapped the tip of his nose, which reminded me of something Kate usually did. "Bingo. But it gets more complicated than that. Every victim had to catch a flight out. I'm basing that on the pill bottles we found and the watches and jewelry we were able to trace back to their rightful owners. Right now, that's only a handful of people, but every one of them lives far away. They flew in, stayed at the Golden, and flew out. I made a few calls to the airport. TSA is supposed to get back to me, but no one wants to wait for TSA. So I called the airlines and asked about complaints and reports of stolen or missing items. I've matched three different names with different items we found hidden in Daniels' home."

"That's why no one filed complaints against the hotel or left scathing online reviews. The victims think the airlines and TSA are stealing from them. Nothing bounces back on the hotel." I replayed everything I'd observed. "That would explain why Louis Grable was helping with someone's luggage the other day and why there are always so many bellhops and valets out."

"Have you seen anyone steal anything?" Heathcliff asked.

I gave him a look. "I would have told you if I did."

"If the valets are involved, that would explain why the cameras in the garage didn't catch the hit-and-run. They mapped all of that out to utilize blind spots. They'd have plenty of time and access. It'd be just like Amir suggested,"

Heathcliff said.

Voletek scratched his stubble and yawned. “What are we thinking? The staff members who met an unfortunate fate saw what was going on, threatened to report it, and got axed, literally?”

“They were warned first. That’s what the conversation I overheard between Johnson and Glass suggested. But Jane can tell us more.” I looked at the clock, surprised to find it was morning. In the windowless conference room, I had no way of knowing it was a new day. “Has the hospital notified us if she’s woken up yet?”

“Not yet. The surgery took longer than they realized. She should be awake soon, but with high doses of pain meds, it may be a while before we get anything out of her. Probably this afternoon at the earliest.” Heathcliff looked at the board. “Maybe we should call it a night.”

“You don’t have to tell me twice.” Voletek got out of the chair and stretched. “I should swing by my desk and make sure I didn’t miss anything exciting while I was playing with you guys.” He winked at me. “Don’t forget movie night.”

“I may have an idea about that,” I said, “but we finish this first.”

He grinned. “Okay, princess.”

“Princess?” I asked.

“Sorry, wrong brunette.” He shook his head. “I need sleep. I’ll keep you updated on whatever else shakes loose on my end.”

“I’ll do the same,” Heathcliff promised. Once we were alone, he raised an eyebrow. “Movie night?”

“Long story. But for now, I have to get back to the Golden.”

“Word may have gotten out. If Harley Daniels missed a meet or call, someone may have gone by his place and seen the blue and whites parked outside. You need to be careful. They’re already looking at you. Now that one of theirs has been arrested—”

“I’m always careful.”

“Tell that to your side.”

“Tell that to your arm.”

"We are not talking about me right now," Heathcliff said. "You get in trouble, call. I will have ESU storm the building."

"You don't have that kind of pull."

"If I don't, Voletek does. And he thinks you have a movie date. That's extra incentive to ensure we watch your back."

THIRTY-SEVEN

I slipped inside my hotel room the same way I'd exited the previous night, so no one would have any idea I'd been out, locked the patio door, and made sure nothing had been disturbed. Since I hadn't received an alert, I had no reason to believe anyone had been inside my room, but Amir had made me paranoid with his comments about camera placements and altering footage. Everything remained where I'd left it, so I changed, pinned up my hair, put the wig back on, touched up my makeup, and fought to keep from yawning.

Unfortunately, I needed sleep. Lucien had texted to tell me Leslie wasn't supposed to start work until the afternoon. She'd be in her room until her next shift. He had cameras watching her room. If there was any suspicious activity, he'd let me know. But her roommates worried me, especially now that I had some idea of what was going on at the hotel.

Any or all of the women Leslie was sharing a room with could be part of the theft ring. Another thought came to mind. Gini must have known what was going on. That's why they attacked her and the hotel paid her off. Again, I couldn't help but wonder if management was involved. That was a lot of money I'd seen hidden in Harley Daniels' pantry. If that was only his cut, tens of millions of dollars could have been stolen.

As far as we knew, this had been going on for fourteen months. If guests were being robbed every day, that would add up quickly. No wonder they were willing to commit murder to keep this quiet. The thieves had a lot to lose.

My brain told me to make some extra strong coffee and get back to work. Now wasn't the time to take my foot off the gas. Since the police had searched the room where Jane's accident occurred, hotel management would be even more careful and on edge. But my body refused to get on the same page. Hoping a compromise wouldn't result in something horrific, I got into bed and closed my eyes. I could sleep until Leslie had to report for work, then I'd go to work too. I needed to remain close in case they came for her next.

Tapping at my door woke me. I peered at the clock on the nightstand. 12:04. I'd been asleep for almost four hours. "Hang on," I croaked, my throat dry.

Getting up, I was glad I had the foresight to change back into Alexandra before hitting the pillow with my head. But I stopped in front of the mirror to adjust the wig, comb out a few of the obvious tangles, and shove the glasses back on my face.

I pulled the door open. "Yes?"

Choi stood on the other side, surprised to find me so disheveled. "I was told the doctor was sent to your room last night. I didn't realize it was that serious."

"It's not," I said. "Just too much dessert. I tried three after you left. I should have stopped with one."

"Did I wake you?"

"I needed to get up anyway."

"I'm sorry. I never meant to intrude. I should have paid more attention to the do not disturb. I just thought you'd forgotten to take it in."

"It's fine."

"I wanted to let you know the penthouse suite is ready. Luggage services will be glad to move you from this room to that one."

That would give them another opportunity to search my

belongings for whatever evidence they believed Jane may have given me. They were getting even more desperate, but I was tired of playing along. “Can they come back in a few minutes? I need to freshen up. As you can see, I got up this morning, got dressed, realized my stomach wasn’t particularly happy, and ended up going back to bed. So I need a few minutes.”

“Sure.” Choi stepped away from the door. “Let us know when you’re ready.”

I peered through the peephole, watching him speak to the two men waiting with a luggage cart. But the men didn’t disband. Instead, they remained outside my door. How long would they wait? Would they give up if I didn’t come out in the next ten minutes? Twenty minutes? An hour?

I had half a mind to find out, but we were close. I could feel it. The sooner I got upstairs, the sooner I could explore the restricted levels of the hotel and conduct a few interviews. For all I knew, the internship program could be where the theft ring recruited new blood.

I hadn’t brought much with me on this trip. Very few items remained out in the open. Most of the unpacked items in my room were things I’d bought in the shops as part of my cover. I stuffed those bags into separate pieces of luggage to make it look like I had more than I did, brushed my teeth, emptied out the bathroom, and packed half the hotel-provided complimentary toiletries in my luggage.

After a final check to make sure I had everything, I opened the door. “Morning, gentlemen. I’m sorry to inconvenience you with this.”

“It’s not a problem at all.” Brando Tascioni, the bellhop who’d escorted Heathcliff and me up to Leslie’s room, smiled before coming inside. “Is this it?” He pointed to the stack of bags I’d left near the door.

“Don’t you think it’s too much?”

“I’ve seen worse.” He glanced back at me, and I wondered if he recognized me. “Some guests stay the night and pack for a month. Others end up with dozens of shopping bags.” He hung my duffel from the hook on the cart. "This is nothing."

"You're sweet to say that." On the bright side, having just woken up made me sound extra croaky, so I didn't think he'd recognize my voice.

Brando picked up another bag while the other bellhop, someone with a teardrop tattoo on his cheek and dyed orange hair, which he tried to conceal beneath the uniform cap, pulled the cart forward and flipped it around to make it easier for Brando to load the other side.

I nodded at that guy, spotting the iconic prison tatt but the ink job was too clean and professional. He wasn't an ex-con. He was a guy who thought it looked cool. I wondered if he tried to act tough too.

"Do you get a lot of room transfers?" I asked Orange Hair.

"Every now and again." His voice was higher-pitched than I expected. "It's usually only if there's something wrong with the room." He looked around. "Pretend I didn't say that. I don't think I'm supposed to say things like that."

"Don't worry. I won't tell anyone." I eyed his name tag. Silver. "How do you like this job so far?"

"It's great. The Golden is a wonderful opportunity." Orange Hair beamed. "I'm learning so much."

"Do you usually work for luggage services?"

"Today's my first time." He smiled as he backed the luggage cart out of the room so Brando could exit, staring expectantly like a puppy waiting for a treat after performing a trick.

Brando pointed to the elevator. "Let's head that way."

"Yep. Sure. I got it." Orange Hair whose name was Skylar, struggled to get all four wheels facing the same direction. Once he accomplished that feat, he dragged the cart to the elevator while Brando pushed from behind.

"If you want to grab lunch or pick up a coffee," Brando said to me, "we can get everything set up for you."

"I'm too excited to see the room to wait."

"No problem." When he got into the elevator, I noticed him eyeing me again.

Shit. He must have thought I looked familiar.

Instead of letting him stare at my reflection, I pulled out

Alexandra's phone. "Do you mind if I record you bringing my bags to the room? It'd be a fantastic reveal."

Brando and Skylar exchanged looks. "Mr. Choi said to do whatever you wanted."

"I'll make sure I get your good sides."

Skylar grinned. "I appreciate that."

When the elevator stopped on thirty-two, the top floor, they pushed the luggage cart out. I followed behind, filming them while I peered around the hallways. The rest of the hotel was nice. But this was a step up. The carpet looked newer. The yellowish-beige on the walls sparkled, and the accents and art made everything pop.

"Penthouse three," Brando announced before tapping the keycard against the lock. Once it flashed green and the door emitted the telltale click, letting us know it was open, he pushed down on the handle and opened the door. "Your home away from home."

I moved behind him, recording footage of the entryway as he pushed the cart inside and unloaded my belongings. "Wow," I said, moving around him. "This is such a gorgeous room. It's huge." I went to the window, the camera leading the way, and pulled back the privacy curtains. "Look at the view. You can see everything from up here." I did a panoramic sweep, calling out the names of well-known buildings and landmarks as I went.

"Is there anything else we can do for you?" Skylar asked. "Do you need any extra pillows or towels?"

I stepped away from the window, my camera aimed at them. "I haven't even had a chance to look around yet."

"The upper levels have a dedicated concierge. There's a button on the phone for that. He should be able to get you anything you need. If not, you can always reach out to the front desk." Brando gave the room a quick look and put the keycard down. "Enjoy your stay."

"I will." I waited for Brando to leave. Skylar was trailing behind, but I stopped him with a question. "Did Mr. Choi tell you when or how the interviews will be set up?"

"I'm sure he'll stop by at his earliest convenience." Skylar kept grinning. He looked more excited to be in this room than I was. "I really hope you have a wonderful time here."

"Thanks." I reached into my purse and pulled out some cash. "This is for you and your pal."

Skylar tipped his head and backed out of the room.

Once the door closed, I went into full-on Alexandra mode. "And now for the complete room tour." I unzipped my bag, relieved they didn't have the chance to search my things, pulled out one of Cross's handy-dandy bug detectors, and started at the front door, the way most travel reporters did, checking with one hand while filming with the other so it wouldn't be obvious what I was doing.

I wasn't surprised to find two hidden surveillance devices. Unfortunately, I wasn't sure what to do about them. After concluding in the bathroom which was in view of one of the hidden cameras but didn't have any concealed inside, I closed the door, pulled out my phone, and texted Cross.

Someone's spying on me. Any idea who? I asked.

Not sure. Probably Choi. I'll see if Amir can hack into the feed. In the meantime, leave them be. If you remove them or disable them, they'll know.

No kidding. I tucked my phone away, relieved there was one place in the room where I had some privacy. After flushing the toilet and washing my hands, I emerged, just a normal girl going about her business.

After moving my things around so I'd have strong surveillance of my own established, I sat on the couch. If I'd never been in a penthouse suite before, I would have been impressed. But this was like most of the rooms Martin booked.

The television was on when I entered. I scrolled through the information section before switching to the regular channels. I flipped until I found reruns of a sitcom I liked, then I went to the closet, pulled out the extra blanket and pillow, set them up on the couch so I wouldn't have to put my face on cushions that countless people had done unmentionable things on, and decided to continue with my previously scheduled catnap. Since members of the hotel wanted to spy on me, I'd make their jobs as boring and mundane as possible. That way, they'd be less likely to notice if and when I deviated from the humdrum. And given the givens, that was bound to happen sooner instead of later.

THIRTY-EIGHT

Two hours later, Choi came knocking. He personally gave me a tour of the upper levels, showing me the different amenities only the VIPs had access to. For a premium, anyone could book these nicer rooms, but I didn't think the complimentary snacks and drinks made up for the price difference.

"There's a private pool. I know you're nervous about the water, but you have to give this one a try. It's incredible." He looked at his watch. "However, I'm guessing you'd rather get some work done."

"That is why I'm here. Though, I keep forgetting that every time I find something new to explore." I peered around the empty meeting room. It was part of the hotel's conference center. "Do you use this for weddings too?"

"Receptions usually," he said. "Though, I think we had a ceremony or two take place in the grand ballroom."

"On the first floor?" I asked.

"Uh-huh." Choi kept the professional smile. "Guest relations can provide you with a list of options and pricing."

I opened the notes tab on my phone and made a reminder for myself. "First, you tell me about the secret menu at the coffee shop. Now you're telling me about weddings. What else am I missing?" Want to share details on the theft ring while you're at it?

"Every hotel has lots of little secrets. You can't expect me to give them all up that easily." He waved to a woman dressed in a power suit, who had entered from the other side of the room. "This is Dana Smith. She's in charge of the applicant selection process."

"It's so nice to meet you." I held out my hand, which she met with a firm grip.

"It's my pleasure." She indicated the seats at the table. "The Golden prides itself on its internship program. The candidates are held to the highest standards. We're more selective than Ivy League colleges."

"Wow," I indicated the camera, "would it be okay if I record this?"

Dana looked at Choi, who nodded. "Of course. That's the point of this."

"I'll leave you ladies to it." Choi gave us a curt nod. The smile remained as he backed out of the room and disappeared behind the thick door.

"How about you start with the basics? What qualities are you looking for in a candidate?" I asked.

She dithered on about leadership, commitment, loyalty, and taking pride in one's work. As far as actual qualifications, candidates had to have a degree or be working toward a degree in a related field. They needed high GPAs, prior work experience was preferred, and they couldn't have a criminal record. They'd get that after working here. "Beyond that, we focus on those with positive attitudes. It's about making guests feel welcome. Being nice and polite are the cornerstones of our program."

"That's why everyone I've spoken to at the Golden always starts the encounter with a smile," I said.

"That's right. Our internship program is about more than just gaining valuable work experience. It is our training program. This is where all our employees learn the fundamentals to work at this hotel."

"Is it true those who make it through the program can get a job at any of Experiential Adventures' other properties?"

"Historically, that's pretty accurate. But as is true with most jobs, openings aren't always available immediately or there may be a greater need for a specific type of worker at a specific resort."

"But everyone gets offered a permanent position?"

"Most candidates. That's why we make sure to pick the ones with the greatest chances of success."

"Does anyone ever flunk out?"

"A few people have been terminated. A few others have left."

"Anyone recently?"

"Things happen," she said.

Like being threatened and attacked. "Like what?" I asked.

"I can't really say. It varies." She held the smile. "That's not something applicants should fear. As long as they pay attention during training and start each day with a smile, ready to tackle whatever new challenges the day will bring, they'll be fine."

I had a list of names to contradict that, but I held my tongue. "Who monitors the interns?"

"Each department has a supervisor who handles the hands-on training. Roles are assigned daily, at least for the first few months, so the interns have a chance to see how the entire hotel operates and we can see where they excel the most."

"How long has this program been in place?"

"Almost a decade."

"How did the other employees respond to this? Did they have to undergo updated training?"

"Everyone has to go through updated training sessions a few times a year. Anytime anything at the hotel changes, we all have to be trained again."

"Is that the same kind of training the interns get?"

"Pretty much."

I turned off the camera. "Off the record, are the old-timers held to the same standards as the interns and vice versa?"

"What do you mean?"

"The key things you spoke of earlier, that whole being

polite, smiling, taking pride in one's work, is everyone at the Golden expected to do that?"

"It's the only way. Making sure our guests have a pleasant experience is our only concern."

"Who came up with those tenets?" I asked.

"I'm not sure. They date back to the adage the customer is always right. I think Mr. Glass may have been the first instructor who really knocked it home when he was training interns with the proper etiquette to serve food and beverages. It's expanded since then."

Could Glass have masterminded the theft ring? While I pondered that, Dana finished her interview and went to get the next person on the pre-approved list for me to speak to.

This went on for two hours. I spoke to different staff members and a few interns who had been handpicked to provide their experiences. Everyone delivered the same message with the same blank smiles. Was this Albert Glass's doing? Had he brainwashed everyone? Maybe Dr. Johnson helped him come up with it.

While the interviewees spoke, I gave them encouraging smiles and asked questions from a list I'd found online. There was no deviation. They stuck to the company line. Could they think for themselves? Had they adopted a hive mind mentality? Surely, the newest class of interns didn't have millions in stolen cash and valuables stashed in their rooms to make them buy into this bullshit.

"Can I see your room?" I asked, interrupting the woman who'd been telling me how she'd been trained by a barista.

"My room?" Her smile faltered. "What do you mean?"

"I was told most interns live here."

"Oh," the smile returned to full strength, "I guess." She looked around, but we were alone.

"Great." I grabbed my gear. "Lead the way."

We took the elevator to the twenty-eighth floor. She led me down the corridor, past Leslie's room. I checked the time, wondering if I'd catch her on her way to work. We were almost at the end of the hall when another elevator chimed, announcing the doors had opened.

I spotted Choi stepping out. He had his phone in his hand, like he was busy reading something, but he'd used that act before. My guess was he wanted to know what I was doing.

"Here we are," the intern held her wrist near the door. The app on her smartwatch unlocked the door, and she pushed it open. "Hello? I have a guest."

No one responded. I followed her inside, glancing back in time to see Choi duck his head again, hoping I didn't know he was watching.

"How many roommates do you have?" I asked, pretending I hadn't done this before.

"Five. Well, four. Five of us are assigned to each room."

"Do you mind if I film?" I held up my camera.

"I don't know if you're allowed."

"Is it okay with you?"

"I don't know."

"You don't know?"

"I can find out."

I held up my hand. "That's okay. Tell me about the room setup. Are they like college dorms? Co-ed? Do you have any roommates who are not female?"

"No, but some rooms are a mix. However, romantic entanglements are not allowed on the property. They aren't encouraged. We need to be focused on the Golden."

"What about friends and family outside of work? Do they come to visit you?"

"They aren't allowed." She shook her head. "I mean, they aren't encouraged. Distractions aren't encouraged."

"Who decided that?"

"We've been told that by several members of security."

"Louis Grable?" I asked.

She bit her lip, nodding.

"Are you allowed to leave the hotel?"

"Yes."

"When's the last time you left?"

"Last week," she said.

"A week ago?"

"I wanted to pick up snacks. The shops here don't have the gluten-free cookies I like, so I went to the grocery store."

"When's the last time you saw your family or friends?"

"The Golden is family."

They were all brainwashed.

A knock sounded at the door. Choi.

She opened the door. "Are you looking for Ms. Riley? She asked if she could see my room. I didn't know if it was okay for her to film."

Choi looked at me while I played with the camera. "Have you filmed anything?"

"Not yet. I wanted to wait for permission. We were just chatting in the meantime. It's really great that the Golden provides so much for its staff that leaving campus is unnecessary." I gave him a big grin. "The convenience factor alone is a dream." To be more precise, a nightmare, but I wanted to make sure he thought I was onboard, and I didn't want the intern to get suspicious and report me for asking inappropriate questions.

Choi looked around. "Feel free. The living conditions aren't the best, but a quick walkthrough of the dorms would be a great addition to the exclusive."

"Thanks."

After I finished a very brief scan of the room, Choi ushered us out of the room. "Sherry, Ms. Davenport wanted to see you."

"Oh, cake baking." She lit up. "I've been looking forward to this from the start."

"Go on." Choi jerked his chin toward the elevator. "I'll make sure Ms. Riley gets where she needs to go."

After a few parting words and an unexpected hug, Sherry headed for the elevator. I scrolled through the footage and photos I'd taken.

"Do you have everything you need?" Choi asked.

"It'll be hard to say until I start piecing it together, but there's a lot here. It may take a few days to assemble."

"How are you liking the penthouse?"

"The view is the most amazing part. The room's great. Every part of it screams luxury, including the price tags on the upcharge items."

"Too much?" he asked.

"I'm not the type to spend $8 for a bottle of water I could pick up at the newsstand in the lobby for $5 or down the street at the bodega for $2. But I'm not the target audience for a luxury suite."

"Did you open the drawer beneath the coffeemaker? The selections inside are all complimentary."

"Even the chocolates?"

"Yes, and the candies, and the mints."

"I need to amend my last statement. I'm entirely in your target audience."

He laughed. "I'm glad to see you're feeling better."

"I am. A nap was all I needed."

My phone buzzed, but I ignored it. Choi glanced at his own phone. For a moment, I wondered if he had heard the buzz from my phone, but then I realized he'd gotten a message at the same time. Someone was searching my room and told Choi that's what they were doing. He was the bastard who set up the hidden cameras, as if there had ever been any doubt.

Luckily, my gun was in my camera bag, along with my wallet and everything else that proved I wasn't who I claimed to be. The only thing damning I left behind were the hidden cameras I had set up. But I had to hope they wouldn't be discovered. Whoever was searching wasn't looking for surveillance devices. They were looking for whatever they believed Jane may have given me.

"Is everything okay?" I asked, putting my phone away before Choi realized I had two.

"Where are you heading now?"

"I was hoping to record a few interns while they're working, assuming I can find some who won't mind. It'd be nice to show them performing their duties instead of just talking about them."

"Try the Italian restaurant. The lunch rush ended and we still have time until dinner begins. The lull will be the perfect chance. You'll be able to see them work as busboys, servers, hosts, bartenders, and assist in the kitchen. And it'll give you a chance to sample the cuisine for a restaurant review."

I tapped my forehead. "How did you know exactly what I was thinking?"

He shrugged. "Are you also thinking I should escort you

there?"

I gave him a flirty smile. "That's nice, but I don't want to keep you from whatever you should be doing."

"You're not keeping me from anything."

"Your phone suggests otherwise. I think you may be the most popular guy in this hotel."

Choi laughed. "Little fires everywhere."

While we waited for the elevator, Leslie stepped out of her room in a pale yellow blouse and black blazer. She paused a second too long when she spotted me, but since Choi was facing the elevator, he didn't notice.

She looked like a deer caught in headlights. *Don't blow it,* I thought.

Leslie took a breath to prepare herself, shook her head a few times, like an actor before stepping in front of the camera, and marched down the hallway toward us.

"Going down?" I asked when she was a few feet away.

"Ye-yes." Leslie gave me the Golden smile. "How are you enjoying your stay?"

"It's great," I said. "I'm Alexandra." I held out my hand. "It's nice to meet you."

"Likewise." She shook. "I'm Leslie."

"Are you an intern?" I asked, seeing Choi on the brink of saying something.

"Yes. The Golden has provided me with such a great opportunity."

"Are you on your way to work?" Choi asked.

She faced him. "Yes, sir. I'm working online support today."

"Online support?" I asked.

"For our website," Choi said. "We don't outsource. The live chat option connects guests directly with a member of our staff. That way, if you have an issue while you're here and don't want to call the front desk, you can chat using our website or app. It's also an option for future guests who have questions or problems booking their stays."

"Are computers your passion?" I asked her.

"I enjoy working in whatever capacity best serves the Golden and its guests." Leslie had the company line down pat.

"Do you get a break?"

Leslie looked at Choi, who nodded. "Besides bathroom breaks, we get a fifteen minute break after two hours. Then an hour for dinner at four hours. Another fifteen minute break at six hours. And my shift ends at eight hours."

"The Golden makes sure every employee is treated fairly." Choi held the elevator door as it opened. The three of us got in. When the doors opened again on twenty-five, Choi stepped out.

"It was nice meeting you," I said to Leslie. "I hope we can talk again soon." I turned, facing her directly. Choi couldn't see my expression, but the look on my face made Leslie swallow. Even though I couldn't say anything, I wanted her to know the situation had changed. I had to convince her to get the hell out of here.

THIRTY-NINE

"You have to listen to me," I said. I'd spent the last two hours going through the charade of gathering more footage and suffering through the entire menu at the restaurant while Choi offered suggestions on what he thought I'd like or which wine to pair with it. Finally, he'd been called away to deal with another matter, and I went in search of Leslie who was now on her fifteen minute break. Luckily, Albert Glass hadn't been at the restaurant while I was or I would have been afraid he'd try to kill me, like I suspected he'd done to Hugh Pellers.

Leslie kept looking around, afraid of being seen talking to me. But we were in one of the hotel's blind spots. Sure, anyone could walk up and spot us, but the cameras couldn't. This was as close as we could get to a secure exchange without Choi or someone from hotel security getting suspicious. And since the hallways that led to this spot branched in several different directions, it'd take security a while to figure out that neither of us reappeared on any of the other camera feeds. Hopefully, we'd be gone before that happened.

"Leslie, look at me."

She whipped her gaze back to my face. "I heard someone else was hurt yesterday, that it was another accident. We were sent reminders about what to do in emergencies. But it wasn't an accident, was it?"

"No. Jane Rossum was attacked. We know who did it. The police arrested him. We found evidence in his house of the attack and some of his other crimes."

"Who did it?" she asked.

After spending hours speaking to interns who'd been indoctrinated, I wasn't sure I should tell her. But we needed her to cooperate. I had to trust her. "Harley Daniels."

"I don't know him."

"I have his mug shot right here." I held out my phone for her to see.

Leslie gasped, covering her mouth. "That's the man who burned Gini. The look in his eyes...I thought he wanted to kill her. He just left her there. He—"

"He took a Halligan to Jane. She was called to one of the hotel rooms. He attacked her. Dr. Johnson and Albert Glass helped cover it up, along with two members of the janitorial staff."

"You're sure about this?" She knew I wasn't lying, but she didn't want to believe it. "Why would they do something like that? Why would they attack a maid?"

"Before you started here, several other people were attacked. A few were killed. Each crime was covered up, like Gini's. And like Jane's. Hugh Pellers was one of the earlier victims. Does that name sound familiar?"

"I've heard a few whispers, but—"

"He was killed in an alleged hit-and-run. However, Glass admitted to being involved, to questioning Pellers before he was killed."

"Questioning him about what?"

I pressed my finger to my lips, reminding Leslie to speak softly. "He had proof of what's really going on here. He knew some of the people who're involved. Glass and Daniels wanted to make sure that didn't get out. Pellers wouldn't hand it over, so they killed him. Now they think Jane may have that evidence."

The cloud of disbelief lifted from Leslie's eyes. "Gini knew. She tried to tell me. She kept saying she'd seen it happen. She'd seen valets and bellhops taking things out of the guests' bags. She insisted she saw them. No one believed her. I thought she was making it up so she didn't have to carry bags or park cars, but she tried reporting it."

"Who did she report it to?" I asked.

"I'm not sure. Maybe someone in HR. I don't know."

"Leslie, this place is a powder keg. It's all about to go up. You've spoken to the police. I know you don't want to hear this, but there's a good chance your food poisoning wasn't an accident. The hotel wanted to keep you away from people, to keep you from talking, to make sure you weren't going to narc on them. Now that they nearly killed Jane, it'd be best to get you out of here. Please let me get you to safety."

"What about the contract I signed? What about Deanna?"

"Deanna went home. They can't have her arrested. She didn't commit a felony. At most, maybe a misdemeanor, but even that is up for debate. The Golden wanted to scare her away and scare you into compliance. I spoke to another intern today who admitted to not being allowed to have her friends or family visit. No one in law enforcement will go after Deanna. I promise. And if the Golden sues, you'd have a strong case as to why that contract should be nullified. I don't think you'd be forced to pay for anything beyond the amount of time you stayed here, and given the conditions in the room, with so many roommates sharing such a small space, I don't think the charge could be all that high. In fact, the conditions may be grounds for you to sue them. I'm not sure. You'd need an attorney to sort through all of that. I know a few people who could do the work pro bono if push comes to shove. All I know is if you walk out the front door, you'll be okay. You'll be safe and alive. And that's all that matters."

She looked down, toying with the limp bow at the front of her blouse. "I can't just walk out. They'll stop me. They'll want to know why I'm leaving, where I'm going. It won't be safe."

"Do not go back to work." I pointed to the entrance to the ladies' room. "Stay in there. Lock yourself in a stall. If anyone comes to investigate, tell them you're sick again. I'm calling Detective Heathcliff right now. He will personally escort you out of this building."

"What about my things?"

"He and a few officers will help you collect them. No one will interfere."

"They're going to know," Leslie hissed. "They'll come after me next."

"It'll be harder for them to do that if you aren't here. They can do anything to you while you're inside this building. But out there, in the real world, they do not have control."

She let out a shaky breath. "I'm ready to take back control."

It was about damn time.

After making the call, I made sure to make myself look busy. It was more important now than ever to keep up appearances. We didn't know who was involved. Our list of names was short, but there had to be more than three or four people behind this. As soon as more arrests were made, it'd be easier to convince someone to talk, or so I hoped.

Jane was key to figuring this out, especially if she had evidence we could use. Harley Daniels didn't want to talk. He believed if he refused to cooperate, the evidence we found in his home would magically disappear. That wouldn't happen, not with the bloody Halligan in his entryway and surveillance footage from the Golden, showing him entering and exiting with the weapon.

After scouting out the newsstand, a few of the boutiques, and the gift shop, I found Britt stationed at guest relations. Since this was the third time I'd seen her, even if I hoped she wouldn't connect me to last night, I made my way to her.

"Hi," I said, "I was hoping to record you at work. Do you mind? Mr. Choi said it was okay."

"I have to check with Mrs. Shaw," she said.

"Go ahead."

She picked up the phone and asked. Shaw stepped out of her office, which was ten feet away. "Ah, Ms. Riley, I wanted to touch base. Everything you've done has been amazing. You have an eye for detail and a knack for showing the viewers exactly what they ought to focus on."

How employees at the Golden were committing crimes? But I kept that thought to myself. "I try."

"How did the interviews go today? Did you get the behind-the-scenes look you had hoped for?"

"Mostly. All that's left is to show the interns hard at work. I'd also love to get a look at the materials they are taught in the classroom. So many people spoke about that, but I can't even begin to imagine what exactly the lessons entail."

"It's a lot of Golden specific information. Fire routes. Things like that."

"It's more than that," Britt said. "It encourages pride in ourselves, our work, and the hotel."

Shaw turned to her. "Morale boosting?"

"Sort of," Britt said.

"Do you have any notes or materials from the classes?" I asked. I should have asked Leslie about this, but I hadn't been thinking.

"In my room. I have the binder we were given to study."

"May I see it?" I asked.

Britt looked at Shaw. "Would that be okay?"

"You can go get it."

Britt nodded. With the permanent smile, I couldn't be sure if she wanted me to see it, but since she volunteered, I assumed maybe she did.

"How is your new room?" Shaw asked while we waited for Britt to return.

I stared at the floor, hoping to look ashamed. "To be honest, I've barely had time to look around. I ended up taking a nap."

"At least you're comfortable there."

"Very comfortable. I was also told the chocolates and candies in the drawer beneath the coffee machine are complimentary."

"They are."

I gave her a big, cheesy smile. "I am looking forward to that."

"You'll have to check out the VIP only lounge. There's an assortment of snacks and drinks. And the pool." She looked around and lowered her voice, afraid the non-VIP guests might hear. "You have to try the pool."

"I'm not much of a swimmer."

"Make an exception."

"Yes, ma'am."

When Heathcliff entered with two uniformed officers in tow, he didn't waste time speaking to management. Instead, he went down the hallway, turned, and disappeared in the direction of the ladies' room. A few minutes later, the trio returned with Leslie in the middle. The officer beside her helped carry two of her duffel bags.

Shaw spotted them heading for the door. "Excuse me." She hurried away, stopping in front of the entrance. "What's going on here?"

"Ma'am, step aside," Heathcliff said. "This is official police business."

"I'm Karen Shaw, the manager of this hotel."

Heathcliff held his ground. "This matter does not concern you."

Shaw said something else, but Heathcliff insisted she back off. The officers took Leslie outside and got her into the back of their patrol car. Heathcliff stayed behind, speaking quietly to Shaw. I couldn't hear what he was saying, but he wouldn't burn bridges or endanger Leslie.

"Here it is." Britt bounded up to me, a three-inch binder in her hands. "This is our instruction manual."

"Everyone gets one?" I asked.

"Yes."

I flipped pages, my camera in front of me. Click. Flip. Click. Flip. With any luck, there was something damning in here. Something actionable.

I tried not to go too fast for fear the photos would be blurry or unreadable, but I didn't have time to waste. Heathcliff could only delay Shaw so long, and I wasn't sure if the manager would want me to have this kind of access. "You always seem so cheerful, so happy to be here. Are you?"

Britt turned to me. "The Golden—"

"I know. It's a great place. A wonderful opportunity. But being forced to study books this big and smile all the time, that sounds a little rough."

"It's worth it."

"How so?"

"Job experience. Opportunities for advancement."

"Big paydays?"

"We don't make much as interns."

"Does the hotel offer ways to supplement your earnings?"

"Anything like that is only available to a select few who get handpicked."

"Who does the handpicking?" I asked.

"A committee."

"Who's on the committee?"

"I'm not sure exactly. Our professors, Dr. Johnson, Mr. Daniels, Mr. Glass, Mr. Rubie, and I think the big dogs, y'know Mrs. Shaw and Mr. Choi." She looked at the nameplates outside the offices, reading more of them off as she went. "The top executives."

"What about security? Who supervises that?"

"Mr. Grable."

"And bell services?"

"That's Mr. Strader."

"Who runs valet?"

"Mr. Everett."

I finished with the book. "Thanks for letting me see this." I started to walk away.

"Wait. I thought you wanted to film me."

I slapped my palm to my forehead. "You're right. Silly me. Act natural. I'll take some footage and disappear once I get enough." I found a chair in the lobby on the other side, away from the front door. By now, the police and Leslie were gone. The constant vibrating in my bag told me Heathcliff was sending me a few dozen texts. But I couldn't answer. I had to keep up appearances. Luckily, Shaw had gone back to her office. Someone from legal had joined her.

Maybe Shaw was involved. I hadn't gotten that vibe from her, but Britt named her. Then again, she'd named everyone with an office. That may have been more of a guess than anything else.

After Britt finished assisting a guest, I turned off my camera, waved goodbye, and headed outside. I found a pool chair away from everyone else and checked my messages. Heathcliff assured me Leslie would be safe and she'd agreed to remain in protective custody until we sorted out this mess. He also suggested that since Leslie was no longer at the Golden, I should consider jumping ship. She was safe. Nothing was keeping me here. Well, except for Jane, Gini, and the fourteen case files I'd read.

Before I could tell Heathcliff as much, I received another text. Jane was awake and ready to talk.

FORTY

Jane Rossum winced as she shifted in bed. When she opened her eyes, she was surprised to find me in her room. "I knew you weren't a guest. Who are you? What are you doing here?" She reached for the button to call for help.

"I'm Alexis Parker," I said. "That's Detective Heathcliff."

"I was assigned to investigate Hugh Pellers' hit-and-run," Heathcliff said. "Alex is a police consultant."

Jane nodded a few times. "So you know what happened, what's going on, that's why you were at the hotel?"

"It'd be better if you tell us what you know first," Heathcliff said.

Jane looked uneasy. "I'm not sure I should. They killed Hugh. They could have killed me last night."

"But they didn't."

"No, they didn't. They wanted to remind me to keep my mouth shut. To mind my own business. Next time, they will." She looked from Heathcliff to me. "They thought I gave you something. That I spoke to you."

"They've searched my room and belongings a few times, but you know that. They asked you to be part of it, but you wouldn't. Why not?" I asked.

"I'm not going to compromise my integrity for a bunch of thugs." Jane winced again. "Damn them."

"But you didn't want to help me either," I said. "When I asked—"

"I didn't know who you were. You lied to me. For all I knew, this was one of their loyalty tests. They pull that shit all the time. They're always testing candidates, looking for others to join them. I swear, sometimes, it feels like half the staff is working with them. But I don't think there are that many. Just a handful of bad apples."

"Bad apples that poison the entire barrel," I said.

Heathcliff eyed me, an indication I should stop speaking in metaphors. "Tell me about your relationship with Hugh Pellers."

"We were friends," Jane said. "More than friends. We'd been dating for a few months. Hugh was on the janitorial staff with me. We got to know each other pretty well while making beds and cleaning rooms. He was such a nice guy. Sweet, funny. I loved him." She swallowed.

"I'm sorry for your loss," I said.

Jane nodded. "Before he was killed, he started acting strangely. He didn't joke around or flirt at work. I thought he wanted to call things off. The night before he died, I confronted him. He told me he'd gotten a traffic ticket a few weeks earlier. The police officer who pulled him over alleged he'd made an illegal u-turn, but there was no posted sign. Hugh had a dash cam on his car, so he'd been going over the saved footage and he'd found something disturbing on there."

"What was it?" Heathcliff asked when Jane remained silent for too long.

"Hugh used to sit in his car on his lunch break to nap or listen to music while he ate. He'd turn the car on so the radio would play, which would make the dash cam turn on. No one must have realized he was there, but his dash cam caught a group of our coworkers stealing from guests' bags."

"Who was involved?"

"The valets and bellhops. Hugh wasn't sure what he'd seen, so he started setting up his dash cam to record even when he wasn't in the car. And it only got worse. He didn't tell me much, just that a lot of our colleagues were involved and he didn't know who he could trust. I accused him of not trusting me, and he said that wasn't it. That he wasn't sure what to do, and he didn't want anyone to use me against him." She snorted. "Too late now."

"What happened to the footage from his dash cam?" Heathcliff asked. "Do you have it?"

"That's what Harley Daniels and Albert Glass think. They've been on me ever since they learned Hugh and I had been an item. Until yesterday, I'd been ignoring them or getting security to intervene."

"Security?" I asked.

"Louis Grable," she said. "He's always hanging around. Always looking and watching. Whenever he shows up, they cool it."

"Do you think Grable's involved in the theft ring or Hugh's murder?" Heathcliff asked.

"I never even thought of that. I don't know."

"Did you say anything to Grable about any of this?" Heathcliff asked.

"I reported the harassment to HR. They were supposed to look into it, but when they didn't, I went to security myself. I didn't go into detail, but I told Louis they were harassing me, that they weren't fans of Hugh and had been taking it out on me ever since his death."

"Did you see the recordings from the dash cam?" Heathcliff asked.

"I didn't want to," she said. "It's the same principle as cleaning a room. You don't look through the luggage because you don't want to know what's in there. It's always best not to know."

That didn't make me feel better about traveling. Some people would want to know.

"Did Hugh give you a copy of the evidence to keep safe?" Heathcliff asked. "You deflected the question earlier. I need to know."

Jane stared at the waffle print on the blanket. "He left something at my apartment that night. He asked me to hold on to it for safe keeping. I'm not even sure what it is exactly. It's this little Polynesian ceramic figurine."

"Any idea why he wanted you to hold on to that?"

"I figured it had some kind of sentimental value. The first hotel Hugh worked at was in Hawaii."

"Where is it now?" I asked.

"It's in my apartment on the shelf with my knickknacks. I thought about giving it to his family after his passing, but he wanted me to have it, so I held on to it." Jane turned to me. "Last night, Harley kept asking where it was and if I gave it to you, and that's when I started thinking he wanted Hugh's figurine. But I have no idea why. I don't think it's worth much."

"Maybe there's something hidden inside it," Heathcliff speculated.

"I don't know. I barely looked at the thing. I just liked knowing it was there."

Heathcliff made a few notes. "Are you willing to testify against Harley and the other men who harassed and threatened you?"

"Hell yeah. I want those bastards to pay." She pressed her lips together. "I should have gone to the police sooner, after Hugh...but I didn't think they'd believe me. I didn't have proof. I didn't have anything. I trusted HR to do something, but nothing came of their investigation. Security started intervening, but they didn't do enough."

"Gini," I said.

Jane looked ashamed. "After what happened to that poor girl in the laundry room and what they did to me last night, I don't doubt for one minute that these men are responsible for a lot of ugly things that have happened. A lot of staff members have gotten hurt. Some have died or killed themselves. I think they were threatened or pushed to the edge. This needs to stop. I will do whatever I can to make sure of it."

* * *

"At least she'll testify," I said. "Have you had any luck persuading Leslie to cooperate?"

"She's coming around to the idea. Apparently, someone

insisted she was safer on the outside and told her the hotel can't touch her sister." Heathcliff winked at me. "Nice work."

"It's true," I said.

"But she wouldn't listen the first ten times we told her."

"Jane being attacked scared her. Gini was an isolated incident, a fluke, something she had been lied to about and wanted to believe couldn't have happened. Jane made it real."

Heathcliff pulled the key to Jane's apartment from his pocket, pausing when he noticed the door was cracked open. He put the key away and pulled his weapon. With one arm, he was at a disadvantage. "Stay behind me, Parker."

"Not a chance." I pushed in front of him, my own gun out and aimed. Jane's apartment had been ransacked. We cleared the one-bedroom, but whoever had done this was long gone.

"I'll call it in," Heathcliff said.

I went to the shelf which contained several trinkets and knickknacks. Whoever had been inside didn't waste his time with this. He'd been more interested in the desk, file boxes, and junk drawers. The Polynesian figurine remained. I picked up the ceramic and gave it a shake. A faint rattle sounded from within.

"It looks like whoever did this overlooked what they hoped to find." Turning the figurine upside down, I saw the hole in the bottom, which was common in ceramics to keep them from exploding when placed in the kiln. Printed along the rim were the words *Made in China.* I tossed the ceramic to the floor with a crash. "Oops."

"Parker, what the hell are you doing?"

Reaching down, I sifted through the ceramic pieces and pulled out a microSD card. "Just call me butterfingers."

FORTY-ONE

This didn't feel over, but it was. My part in this was finished. Leslie Stiller was safe. I couldn't speak to what her future would look like or if she'd be blackballed from getting another job in the hospitality world, but after her experience at the Golden, I wasn't sure why she'd want another job at a hotel.

Jane Rossum was going to testify against Harley Daniels and everyone else who'd threatened her. Daniels would be going away for at least one attempted murder but probably more. Heathcliff and Voletek were trying their best to get Gini to give a statement. Jane offered to help convince her, but I didn't think Gini would talk. She needed the money for her treatments and to keep afloat while she recovered. It'd be a hard road ahead. She had to do what was best for her.

The microSD card contained dozens of hours of dash cam footage. I didn't stick around to watch all of it. But it would help the police come up with a list. Right now, there were only three names we could prove were involved. Johnson, Daniels, and Glass.

I'd given copies of the footage I'd taken of my hotel room and belongings being searched to the police. Louis Grable broke into my room with a weapon. He'd go down for that. I didn't want to admit how freaked out I'd been, trapped on the other side of that bathroom door. It gave new meaning to the phrase naked and afraid. But I survived, and somehow, I came out on the other side on much more solid ground. When this started, I'd been a wreck. Now, I was back to feeling like myself.

"You shouldn't go back to the Golden alone," Heathcliff insisted. "We don't know everyone who's involved yet, but we know a lot of people are. Hotel management knows I escorted Leslie out of the building, that a crime scene unit checked the room where Jane had her so-called accident, and we have footage of someone in a Golden security uniform breaking into Jane's house."

"I bet it's Grable."

"With any luck, IT will be able to clean it up and get us an ID. But they are on to you, Parker. They've searched your things a few times. They will go after you next. Going back is giving them that chance. Don't do it."

"I have to go back for my gear and to get hard copies of the footage."

"Tell Cross to do it himself," Heathcliff said.

"I thought you were afraid his loyalty was to the Golden."

"Is that why you're going back? You're afraid he'll turn everything over to them?"

"No."

He knew there was something I wasn't saying. "You're being reckless. You aren't bulletproof."

"I may be." I pulled at the collar of the sleeveless body armor which I wore beneath my top. "There's only one way to find out."

"Parker, I will cuff you to this desk."

"I'm just going to get my things. Maybe take a few more videos. Now that we know who to focus on, I'll see if I can get anything incriminating, something you can use to flip someone."

Lt. Moretti stepped out of his office. Our argument had been loud enough to attract his attention. He entered the conference room and blocked the door. "If you're going back to the hotel, I will send uniformed officers to keep an eye out."

"Sir, I don't think my cover is blown," I said.

"You've been blown since the day you arrived. Grable confronted you," Heathcliff said.

"He's suspicious. But I don't think he's sure of anything. No one there is. That's why they want to keep an eye on me. If they were sure, his pals would have come after me like they did to Jane and Gini."

"Is that why you're going back?" Moretti asked. "You can't wrap your head around a streak of good luck?"

"I've never had good luck, Lieutenant. I don't see why it would start now. But we're missing something." I pointed to the folders. "The only one we've explained is the hit-and-run. We still don't know who's responsible for the fatal shooting or how any of these others died. Amir said surveillance footage doesn't always tell the whole story. I want justice for Sue Shade, Brittany Hodges, and Gil Fogarty. Those are the three that have never sat right with me."

"That's our job," Heathcliff said.

"I'm consulting."

"Go back, get whatever you can, grab your shit, and get the hell out of there," Moretti said. "You have three hours. A minute longer, and I will have officers escort you out in handcuffs." He stared at me. "I'm not playing, Parker. Jablonsky's already expressed his displeasure that I let you sign on to assist while you're injured."

"Don't let him scare you," I said.

Moretti growled at me. "He doesn't scare me. But I respect his opinion. Three hours. Not a minute more."

Heathcliff stared at me. "What would Martin say about this?"

"He'd tell me to do what I have to but to be careful."

"Ditto."

* * *

When I returned to the hotel, nothing had changed. Too many valets and bellhops were serving guests. I wondered how much money they'd steal today. Did they split the pot, or was it every man for himself?

Either scenario could lead to a bloodbath if someone got greedy, but as far as I knew, that hadn't happened yet. What was stopping it?

Taking out the camera, I started recording, hoping to catch someone in the act. None of the devices I'd planted had caught the thieves committing a crime. But I'd been more focused on keeping Leslie safe and maintaining eyes on Louis Grable and Ian Choi to worry about the rest. Now, I wished I'd done more. Maybe Cross's cameras caught something. Or the surveillance cameras in my room could shed some light on matters.

On my way to the penthouse, I called Cross Security. Amir was busy, so I spoke to another tech. Cross had made her aware of the spy cameras in my room. "I need to figure out how to tap into them," I said, hoping that my side of the conversation was cryptic enough that no one would know what I was talking about.

"I can talk you through it. Your phone should have remote capabilities. Once you find the network they're using, we'll be able to access them."

"That's great. Have you figured out who stopped by earlier?"

"Louis Grable."

"Again?"

"Yes, ma'am."

I rolled my eyes, hating that term. "Anyone else?"

"No."

That proved it. Grable was working for Choi. This was the second time Grable searched my room on Choi's order.

I unlocked the door, surprised to find everything had been carefully replaced. If I didn't get the alert, I wouldn't have known anyone had been here.

I went into the bathroom, closed the door, and pulled out my other phone. "Give me the directions." Once Cross Security was able to access the devices, I asked if she could check for any other devices that may be in use.

"I found seven," she said.

"Seven? I only found two."

"They aren't in your room. They are in other parts of the

hotel. I should be able to access each live stream and download copies of whatever was saved to the cloud."

"What about the cameras Cross planted?" I asked.

"Those remain live."

"Have you noticed any illegal activity?"

"We—"

A knock sounded at the door. "Shit. I have to go. Keep an eye on things. If someone tries to kill me, send help."

"Ms. Parker?"

But I hung up before she could ask if I was joking.

Choi stood on the other side of the door, dressed in a white t-shirt, khaki pants, and leather sandals. A shopping bag dangled from his fingertip.

"What's this?" I asked, surprised to see him in anything but a designer suit.

"The proper attire for visiting the rooftop pool."

"I'm not much of a swimmer."

"You don't have to swim. Just go see it. Stick a toe in, and take some videos. I'm off the rest of the day and would enjoy the company." His eyes were hard. "In fact, I insist."

What game was he playing? Was he afraid I was wearing a wire? That I had the microSD card concealed on my person? Did he want Grable to search my pockets when I left my clothes in the room?

"Let me reimburse you for—" I peered into the bag, finding a zippered one-piece, "the swimsuit."

"It's a thank you from the hotel. I wasn't sure about style, but this seemed practical."

He meant appropriate and non-sexual, but I didn't have to school the fixer on maintaining proper appearances and etiquette.

"Are you kicking me out of this suite already?" I asked.

"At checkout tomorrow," he said. "Another guest has requested this room. We can move you to the third floor if you would like to continue your stay."

"I think I've gotten everything I need."

"I'm sorry to hear that." He stepped into the room. "Have you tried the chocolates yet?"

"I'm saving those for later. A sweet end to my night." I also hadn't watched the footage from earlier, but if they'd figured out how to give Leslie salmonella, I wasn't going to eat anything that had been left unattended.

"Go get changed. Robes are provided if you'd like a cover-up." He indicated the closet.

"The pool is that great?" I asked.

"It's that great."

My bag was already in the bathroom with my two phones and gun. So I didn't have to worry he'd find those. But I was curious what he'd do while I changed. After locking the door, I watched the live stream.

Choi circled, opening drawers, checking in closets, and sifting through my bags. He wasn't looking too hard, but he was looking for something. He'd have to look a lot more thoroughly if he hoped to find a microSD card. Maybe he didn't know that's where the evidence was saved. He may have thought it was on a thumb drive or computer. Maybe he thought there were printed hard copies of surveillance footage or a stack of cash with fingerprint smudges on it.

While he continued his search, I changed. The suit covered my entire back and zipped in the front, so I could decide if I wanted the neckline all the way up or if I wanted to show a little cleavage. I left on the black sleeveless body armor beneath the suit. Then I made sure my wig was thoroughly pinned. I didn't think it'd survive a dunk in the pool, but it should make it through a splash or two.

I checked the stream one last time, tossed my phone into the bag, and threw open the door. "Ready." But I didn't catch Choi in a compromising position. That would have been too easy.

FORTY-TWO

"No one's here," I said, stepping onto the roof. Potted plants, pool chairs, outdoor couches, tables with candles, and large tiki-inspired lights made the place look inviting.

"It gets a lot livelier at night." Choi indicated a small, covered stand. "A bartender comes up to make drinks."

"I asked if there was a rooftop bar and was told no."

"These are part of the complimentary offerings available only to VIPs. The selections aren't much."

"I'd still call it a bar." I was acutely aware of being alone with Choi.

"It's more of a serving station."

"Do they bring up snacks too?"

"As a matter of fact, yes, they do." Choi gestured to the other side of the roof, the part that I'd been actively avoiding. "There's the private pool."

"Where does the water go?"

"You've never seen an infinity pool?" His tone sounded accusatory.

Martin had one, though the aesthetics were nothing like this, but I didn't feel the need to share that tidbit. "I've seen them. But they always boggle my mind, especially when they're up so high. It looks like the water runs right off the side of the building."

"Why don't you step to the edge and see for yourself? You're guaranteed a great view." The way he said it sounded more like an order than a suggestion.

"I guess I could take a few photos." I moved closer to the pool, clocking his actions, but he hadn't gotten close to me. I put my bag beside the lounge chair nearest the wall. Then I slipped out of my shoes, grabbed my camera, and went down the steps and into the water.

Choi watched me walk from the shallow end to the four feet depth near the edge of the building. I snapped a few photos of the skyline, took a fifteen second video, and continued to the edge. A few feet below was the basin, which is where the water collected before being pumped back into the pool. The basin between the pool edge and the roof's edge was several feet, allowing ample space for safety. Ceramic planters and plants covered the openings on the outside, so no one could gain access to the basin for safety reasons.

"Who are you?" Choi asked when I turned.

"What?"

He sat down near the edge, rolling up his pants legs before sticking his feet into the water and resting his elbows on his thighs. "You heard me. Now tell me the truth. I know you aren't a travel reporter."

"My hundreds of thousands of followers beg to differ."

"That's bullshit. All of it is bullshit. Who are you? A corporate spy? A cop? What?"

I moved along the side of the pool, closer to where I had left my bag. In case I needed a weapon, I'd be much closer to grab my gun from here. But Choi didn't appear armed. Then again, he could find a way to throw an appliance in the pool.

"Ooh, a spy. I'd like to be a spy. But you have me mistaken for someone else." I stared at him. "How about you tell me why a hotel hired a fixer to work PR?"

"A fixer?"

At this rate, we'd be here all night, and neither of us would leave satisfied. Oh well, I had a hard out in two hours. "Your reputation precedes you, Mr. Choi. You're a legend."

He smiled, self-satisfied and prideful. It wasn't the creepy, practiced smile. He liked that someone knew him by reputation. But he looked down and away, hoping I wouldn't see it. But I did.

"Why are you here?" I asked. "What deep dark secret is the Golden hiding?"

"That's why you came here? You're digging for dirt?"

"I may be digging, but I won't post it on the internet. Call it a personal fascination. Morbid curiosity. All I know is you wouldn't be here if there wasn't a big juicy secret that needed to be covered up."

"Do you really think if I was some kind of legend, like you insist, that I would tell you any of this?" He squinted with one eye. "Especially when you have yet to admit anything to me."

"Why did you want me to get in the pool? To trap me? To see if I was wearing a wire? To have someone search my room again?" He hadn't realized he'd been caught. "I know all about that," I said. "What were you hoping to find?"

"The truth about you." He took off his shirt and walked into the water. He moved closer, but I held my ground. "I researched your online presence. Those pages have existed for years, but most of the content is backdated. From what I gather, it was added within the last week."

"Maybe I moved it over from another page."

"It's bullshit." He reached for my device, but I didn't hold back. I let him see it. He checked the messages, the call log, and everything I'd saved on it. "This is a new phone. You got it specifically for this job."

"I dropped my last one in a pool," I said.

"Sure, you did." He put the device on the ledge. Then he took his phone out of his pocket and put it beside mine. Unlike mine, his was waterproof. There was a good chance he was hoping to copy everything off mine using his, but that wasn't the phone I had to worry about. The other was in my bag, but I didn't think it was close enough to pair with his. "Except you said you don't go swimming."

"Tell me what happened to Jane Rossum."

He smiled again. "Tell me who you are."

"What about Gini Ruffin? Sue Shade? Hugh Pellers?"

He took a step back, as if I'd struck him.

"Did you suggest they pay off Gini to keep quiet?" I asked.

"Gini had an accident. The hotel did its best to make things right."

"An accident? Albert Glass, Harley Daniels, and two of their pals trapped her in the laundry room. Daniels brought the steam iron down on her arm. Burns like that can lead to infections and sepsis. He could have killed her. She'll be scarred for the rest of her life. You call that an accident?" I shoved him. "Why are you protecting these assholes? How much are they paying you?"

"Where did you hear that?"

"I know how to do research."

He lunged for me, grabbing my shoulders. "Who are you? Answer me." I shoved him again, but he held tight. "Did Jane tell you this?"

"Jane Rossum, another of Harley's victims. He attacked her with a Halligan. The paramedics didn't believe that was a slip and fall. For one thing, a broken mirror doesn't lend itself to slipping in the shower. For another, Jane didn't have her cleaning cart with her."

Choi was starting to unravel. "I told Candace that story wouldn't fly. That's why the police were here." He let go of me, circling. "Dammit."

I glanced back at my bag, wondering how quickly I could hoist myself over the side, get to my bag, and pull my weapon. But he'd be able to tackle me before I got out of the pool. Instead, I moved closer to where he'd left my phone. I watched him circle while I tapped to open the voice recorder. He didn't notice.

"For a legend, you've gotten yourself into a fine mess."

He stopped circling, the water swishing around us. "This isn't my mess. I am not responsible for any of this." He slammed his palms down, splashing us.

"Harley Daniels was arrested last night. His place was searched. He's going away. With any luck, he'll take the whole thing down with him."

"How—"

"All good reporters have police contacts," I said.

"Fuck." He snatched his phone from the side, dialing as he made his way to the pool steps. He got out, slipping on his shoes, and grabbing his shirt while he waited for the call to connect.

I kept an eye on him, unsure what he'd do next or who he planned to call. I left the voice recorder running and hoisted myself over the side. Once I was seated on the edge, I swung my legs around and backed toward my bag.

"Daniels has been arrested. Why didn't you call me?" Choi asked. "What is he saying?" He looked back at me. "Yeah. I'm on my way. Don't do anything until I get there. Tell him to keep quiet."

"Why didn't they loop you in?" I asked. "I figured you were in charge."

"In charge? Are you kidding me? I get called to clean up messes. If I had any say in any of this, none of this would have happened. None of it." There was truth in his eyes.

"Are you sure they're worth protecting?"

"It doesn't matter. I get paid to do a very specific job. I don't know who you are, but you need to stay away from this or I will find a way to discredit and destroy you. Do I make myself clear?"

"Oh, I'm done."

Choi didn't say anything else. Instead, he gave me a final look and left me on the roof.

Unsure what had happened, I pulled out my phone and called Heathcliff to warn him Choi was on the move. More than likely, he was heading to the precinct, but I could be wrong. He could be heading somewhere else.

I stopped the recording and uploaded it to the cloud. "You can listen to his side of the conversation yourself."

"Are you done yet?" Heathcliff asked.

"I'm going to dry off, get dressed, and head back," I said. "I'll see you soon."

I'd just put my phone back in my bag when the door creaked open. I looked over my shoulder to find Louis Grable standing in the doorway.

"Hands where I can see them," Grable said.

He wore the hotel uniform, which meant he shouldn't have a gun. But he had one when he searched my room. I put my bag down, moving my nine millimeter closer to the top. Then I slipped my hands out of the bag and held them up.

"Are you here to escort me from the property?" I asked. "Choi sent you, right?"

"He wants to make sure you leave without incident."

"That sounds like a threat to me."

"I told you I'd be watching." Grable moved away from the door and went to the covered bar. He unzipped the cover and pulled the bottom half of the tarp away. "I warned you to stay away. I should have made more of an impact that first night."

"First night?"

"I remember you. The drenched brunette from the parking garage. You were looking for Leslie." He finished removing the cover and unlocked the door, letting himself into the bar, which looked more like a snack stand. "When the police escorted her out of here, I thought you would have gone with them."

"Why would I?"

"She's the reason you came here." He ducked behind the counter to retrieve something. "Between Jane and Gini, it's a good thing she got out when she did. You really should have done the same." Just as he popped back up, a gunshot rang out, lodging in the wall a foot from where I stood.

I dove into the pool and stayed near the bottom as bullets whizzed past. Unlike movies, hitting a target underwater was damn difficult, if not impossible. The water density slowed the bullet down and caused it to break apart, making it non-lethal after a few feet. At the bottom of the deep end, I'd survive even if I got hit, just as long as I didn't run out of air.

Peering up, I couldn't see the shooter, just the shadow of someone standing near the water. When the gunfire stopped, I considered my options. I swam along the bottom until I was near the lower side. The rushing of water told me I was in the right spot.

Surfacing, I threw myself over the edge and landed hard in the concrete basin. My entire left side hurt from where it landed on the raised edge. I remained still for a moment, listening and waiting. But all I could hear was the pounding rush of blood in my ears. The sharp sting made me think I tore open my stitches or broke my ribs, but I'd deal with that later. Right now, I had to move.

Crawling across the basin, I made it to the end, lifted myself up, and climbed through the planter, remaining low to avoid being seen. With any luck, the shooter was still searching the pool for me. Once through, I dashed to my bag, no longer in cover.

I pulled my nine millimeter and aimed, finding Louis Grable with a gun pointed in my direction. Before I could fire, he pulled the trigger. I dove to the ground, only to hear a pained grunt two feet to my right.

Grable moved closer to the downed man, and I shifted my aim from him to the man he shot. On the ground was Albert Glass in his host uniform. A red stain bloomed over the right pec of his white dress shirt.

Grable kicked Glass's gun away. "Are you okay?" Grable asked me. He nodded down at my left leg which was scraped and bleeding.

"Never better." I nodded at his weapon. "Hand that over."

"I just saved your life."

"I thought you were shooting at me."

"I was shooting at him." He pointed to Glass who clutched his shoulder while he tried to creep away from us. "Stay there, Al." Grable reluctantly handed me his gun before pulling out a zip tie, flipping Glass onto his stomach, and cuffing him.

I unloaded his weapon, finding the magazine nearly empty. Choi wouldn't be happy about having another mess to clean up.

While I kept an eye on Grable and Glass, I called 9-1-1, then Heathcliff. Pulling off the saturated wig which was clinging to me by the last two pins, I tossed it onto one of the lounge chairs and noted the bullet holes which had nicked the walls and planters. Maybe Cross had hidden cameras up here, but I wasn't sure. However, it looked like Glass had been shooting at me and Grable had been shooting at him.

“Why did you save me?” I asked Grable.

“It’s my job. I’ve been trying to save everyone, but I keep failing.” He looked at me. “Will Jane make it?”

“Yes.”

“Thank god. I barely made it to Gini in time. I couldn’t save the others. But I wanted to.”

“You know what’s going on here?” I asked.

“Shut up,” Glass snarled. “Don’t you say a fucking word. We will end you too.”

Grable pushed down harder on the bullet wound, making him howl. “Don’t talk. Save your strength, Al.”

Al spit and hissed, like the venomous snake he was.

Grable looked back at me and the discarded wig, which looked like a drowned tribble. “Tell me you’re a cop.”

“Private eye, but I’m working with the police.”

“In that case, put in a good word for me. I’d like to make a deal.”

FORTY-THREE

Heathcliff handed me an antiseptic wipe from the first aid kit. "How many stitches did you pop?"

"I'm hoping none."

"You haven't looked?" he asked while I dabbed at the scrape on my leg.

"I'll look later."

He handed me another wipe while he searched the first aid kit. "I think we're going to have to wrap you in gauze and tape."

"I'll look like a mummy."

He gave me a hard look. "That's what you get for doing something stupid."

"It wasn't stupid." I leaned against the mirror above the sink while Heathcliff wrapped my leg. Since Cross had a rule about me not bleeding on things, I figured I should bandage up now before I went back to the office. "What has Grable said so far?"

"He's willing to name names. He has copies of security cam footage that show the thieves in the act."

"What about the violent crimes? The attacks? The murders?"

"He has that too. He knows everyone who's involved. And he has proof to go along with it."

"Did they know?" I stood from my perch at the sink and reached for my jeans to pull on over the now dry bathing suit. I needed to shower and change, but that could wait until later.

"I don't think so." Heathcliff turned away, even though I wasn't taking anything off, just putting more clothes on. "They would have tortured and killed him if they suspected."

"Like what they tried to do to Jane?"

"Yeah, but unlike Jane, Grable was willing to go along to get along. He amassed quite a bit of cash by helping the thieves."

"Do you think he handed all of it over?"

"I do." Heathcliff eyed me. "The DA's cutting him a deal. This is a massive bust. It'll close a lot of cases, cases some members of the department didn't think were still open, and millions of assets will be recovered. Giving up his share of the stash will be worth it to avoid hard time."

"Is Grable worried about anyone retaliating?"

"Maybe in fifteen to twenty."

"What about Jane and Leslie?"

"The icing on the cake. They're a little more skittish, but even if they waver, the case is still rock solid."

"Congrats on closing that hit-and-run."

"I hate to admit it," Heathcliff said, "but I needed the help."

"We all do sometimes."

He looked at me. "How are you holding up?"

"I'm feeling better."

"Yeah?"

"Yeah. I just needed some perspective and a little distance."

"From Martin?"

"From worrying about him. Worrying about hurting him. It's all this big swirly mess in my head." I gestured with my hand.

"I always knew you were a mess."

"Thanks, Derek."

He smiled. "Anytime."

* * *

When I got back to the office, I found Cross in a meeting, so I grabbed my bag and went to the locker room to shower and change. After peeling off the body armor which was still damp from my dip in the pool, I was surprised and relieved to find my side, which had healed substantially during my undercover assignment, had not sustained any new injuries. The cut had finally sealed itself and remained closed without the help of stitches, staples, or glue. Even my impromptu swim and flop over the side hadn't reinjured it. Though, the dark bruising began at the line where the body armor ended which indicated I was not indestructible. Concrete continued to win in the battle against the flesh.

After showering, changing, and tossing the swimsuit into the trash, I went back upstairs to wait for Cross's meeting to end. Justin joined me in the executive kitchen, which was where Lucien kept the good pastries and coffee.

"Choi's in with Lucien," he said.

"Ian Choi?" I nearly choked on the cinnamon raisin bagel I'd stuffed in my mouth.

"I thought you knew."

Justin was smooth. He was one of the few people who could lie and convince me of it, but the look in his eye told me that was a lie. He wanted me to know Choi was in there, but he was smart enough to cover his ass.

"Has he been in there the entire time?" I asked.

"He showed up ten minutes ago."

I put the bagel down and wiped the cream cheese from the side of my mouth. Then I marched across the hall and barged into Lucien's office. Lucien didn't look surprised to see me, but Ian Choi did.

He did a double-take.

"Is the hair throwing you off?" I asked. "News flash, I'm not blonde."

"She works for you?" Choi stared at Lucien. "You said—"

"I said what was necessary to serve the needs of my client. You are not my client. The Golden is, and you've been covering up what's been going on inside the hotel, which has put my client at risk, not to mention every employee and guest who stepped foot inside that building."

"I was doing what I was paid to do."

"Who hired you?" I asked.

Choi glanced at me before turning back to Cross. "You bastard."

"Answer the lady."

"I was hired by corporate."

"That's not a name," Cross said.

"The head of Experiential Adventures sought me out. He read the incident reports. He didn't want the Golden to gain bad publicity after a second body was found on the property a week after the first. Accident or not, he wanted to make sure these things went away. But they kept happening, so I was paid to stay on to keep handling the situation," Choi said.

"But you weren't fixing it," I said. "You were hiding it."

"I asked you point blank what was going on," Cross said.

"Client privacy is a priority here."

"Bullshit." Choi stood. "You turned everything over to the police. We are not on the same side. I was protecting the hotel's interests. You were," he looked at Cross and then at me, "serving your own interests."

"You mean justice," I said.

"We'll sue you," Choi warned. "You breached our contract. You lied about her. You lied about other things. You were deceptive. Experiential Adventures will not stand for that. I'll personally make sure you're ruined, Mr. Cross."

Lucien gave him a lethal smile. "Mr. Choi, I appreciate the predicament you're facing. You're used to fixing messes. But don't think for one second that I am not capable of digging up the dirt that you've buried. I know who your past clients are. I have ways of finding out what happened and what you covered up. All it would take would be a few phone calls. I wouldn't even have to ruin their lives or reputations or companies. But I can ruin you simply by telling them that you told me what you did for them. You'd be facing worse than lawsuits. I doubt killers would sue you for breaching confidentiality. Instead, they'd bury you, literally." Cross held out a business card. "But if you or Experiential Adventures have any other questions or plan to sue, you can contact my attorney." He handed him Almeada's card. "Now get the fuck out of my office before you have an accident of your own."

Choi pocketed the card, glaring at Cross. I stepped out of the doorway, so he could exit. "For the record, this wasn't personal. This is my job," he said.

"And this is mine," I said.

Choi nodded. "I'm sorry you didn't get to sample the chocolates."

We watched him leave the office. Once he made it to the elevator, Cross said, "Justin, have building security escort him out once he gets to the lobby."

"Yes, sir."

Cross gestured to the chair in front of his desk. "Are you okay?"

"I'm fine. Thanks for the body armor. It saved me a few bruises."

"Well, that's something." He stared at me. "Leslie?"

"She's fine. She's going to testify. Is there any chance Choi or anyone else may retaliate against her?"

"You heard Choi. This isn't personal for him. It's business. It's a job."

"He wasn't working with the thieves."

"No, he was working for the hotel."

"But he had Louis Grable doing his bidding."

"Louis was tipping him off as to what was going on so he could get ahead of it."

"Like with Jane," I said, realizing Grable had alerted him with the phone call. "He told Choi what was happening, but Choi didn't stop it. He covered it up."

"Stopping it would have resulted in a lot of bad publicity. The Golden is going to end up being a national news story. This isn't going to go away in a few hours. It will run for weeks. Choi wasn't guided by any sense of right or wrong. His moral code is decided by his paycheck."

"I used to think the same thing about you," I said.

"I'm glad you don't anymore."

"Me too."

He jerked his chin at my side. “Are you still on the mend?”

“Stab wound has finally healed. But I have some new scrapes and bruises. Do you think you can live with them?”

“Why don’t you take the weekend, and I’ll see about assigning you a regular case on Monday?”

“No more security assessments?”

“No,” he said. “I can’t afford to lose more clients because you got bored.”

I grinned. “I thought your pocketbook didn’t control your actions.”

“Sometimes. Not always. The same’s true of a pesky former federal agent who refuses to follow orders.”

“She sounds amazing.”

“She’s a pain in my ass.” He cleared his throat. “Thanks for pushing to take this one.”

“You should have done more.”

“Are you ever going to let that go?”

“Probably not.”

“In that case, add it to the list. Now get out of my office. And stay out of the executive kitchen. You are not an executive.”

“Can I at least finish my bagel?”

Cross sighed dramatically. “Out.”

“Fine, but I’m getting my bagel to go.”

FORTY-FOUR

"You're back?" Martin asked.

I rolled over to see him standing in the bedroom. Bruiser was behind him.

"Didn't the security system alert you?" I asked, sitting up.

"I thought you might want to keep this a surprise." Bruiser knew I didn't want my movements broadcast, which is why he hadn't shared the news with Martin.

"Thank you," I said.

Bruiser nodded and excused himself.

"I've missed you so much, sweetheart." Martin tossed his jacket and tie on the chair as he made his way to the bed.

I climbed to my knees, my fingers tangling in his hair while he kissed me. He pressed against me, holding me upright as he took my breath away. "We talked every day," I said when I caught my breath. "All those constant reminders about the scar tape."

He brushed my hair back, nuzzling my neck. "Has your side healed?"

"It's perfect."

His hands trailed down to my bare midriff where the cropped tank top ended and before my plush pajama shorts began. He raised the shirt up, finding the bright pink patch of healing flesh beneath it.

"Is it sore?" he asked.

"Not anymore." I tried to divert his gaze, but he noticed the bruise, which I'd already iced and treated with arnica gel. But it'd take more than a few hours for that to go away. It'd be a few days, maybe more.

"What happened here?"

"I fell out of the pool."

"My pool?"

"No."

He gave me a confused look. "The medic told you not to go swimming."

"Don't ask."

He gave me another look. "But you're okay? And you're home?"

"Yeah, I'm home. Cross gave me the weekend. Monday, it'll be back to business as usual."

"Tuscany?" Martin asked.

The thought of being at a hotel, any hotel, made my skin crawl. "I had another thought in mind, if you still want to get away."

Martin pressed his lips together, searching my eyes. "I think it'd be good for us to get out of the city for a couple of days. We could use a reset."

"What about your beach house?" I asked.

Confusion and excitement flickered in his eyes. "Really?"

"It's not Tuscany, but we can get Giovanni's tonight, if you want. Or we can find some Italian place while we're there. Whatever you want, I would just prefer to avoid staying at a hotel for a while."

"The beach house it is. Let me make some calls." He smiled at me. "Then I'll blow your mind all weekend."

"I'm looking forward to it, but first I have to make some calls of my own."

"Who are you calling?"

"Jake Voletek."

"Again with finding another man to keep you occupied?"

"Not me, Kate. I'm hoping he will keep her occupied.

She's insisting I join her on a booze cruise. He's hoping for someone to join him at the movies. I'm thinking two birds, one stone."

Martin shook his head. "Again with the pigeons."

I threw a pillow at him. "Stop saying that. They can hear you."

"I'm not sure I like the sound of this Jake fellow," he said as we both started dialing.

"Hey, are you free Thursday?" I asked Voletek.

"Uh...yeah," he said. "What did you have in mind? Another case? More surveillance?"

"Not exactly. How do you feel about going on a booze cruise? My friend Kate really wants to go, but I will be otherwise occupied." I gave Martin a big smile as he made our travel arrangements.

"Is she anything like you?" Voletek asked.

"She's a lot nicer and way more fun."

"I know the second one isn't possible," Martin whispered in response to my conversation.

"She sounds great," Voletek said.

"Great. I'll have her text you the details. And Jake, thanks for the help."

"Anytime."

I disconnected and exchanged a series of messages with Kate while Martin ordered dinner and finalized our travel arrangements for the morning. Even though she wanted us to get together, she wouldn't turn down a date with a roguishly handsome detective.

You still owe me, she warned.

We'll see. Smiling, I put the phone down.

"Finished?" Martin wrapped his arms around me, kissing down my neck.

"I haven't even gotten started yet."

"Good." Martin nipped my earlobe. "Neither have I."

DON'T MISS THE NEXT ALEXIS PARKER NOVEL SIRENS AT NIGHT

FIND OUT MORE AT GKPARKS.COM

ABOUT THE AUTHOR

G.K. Parks is the author of the Alexis Parker series. The first novel, *Likely Suspects,* tells the story of Alexis' first foray into the private sector.

G.K. Parks received a Bachelor of Arts in Political Science and History. After spending some time in law school, G.K. changed paths and earned a Master of Arts in Criminology/Criminal Justice. Now all that education is being put to use creating a fictional world based upon years of study and research.

You can find additional information on G.K. Parks and the Alexis Parker series by visiting our website at
gkparks.com

com/pod-product-compliance